The Anatomy Lesson

By Marshall Goldberg

THE KARAMANOV EQUATIONS

The Anatomy Lesson

by Marshall Goldberg

G. P. Putnam's Sons, New York

To my wife, Darlis

I am deeply indebted to several people for their advice and assistance in the preparation of this manuscript but three deserve special mention: My sister, Dr. Toby Goldberg, for her constant encouragement and unerring sense of the dramatic, Lieutenant Colonel (ret.) Kenneth Kay, a skilled craftsman in the art of expository writing in his own right and my "literary security blanket," and Marcia Magill, my editor.

I humbly thank them all.

MARSHALL GOLDBERG, M.D.

Behold I have set before you this day life and death,
the blessing and the curse, good and evil . . . Therefore
choose life that you may live.
                                    —Deuteronomy 30:19

September 21, 1954

Boston, Massachusetts

part one

The Working Dead

Chapter One

Emotion is the imprinter of memory.

The remembrance of that first day of medical school was forever after like the unfolding of a bad dream for Daniel Lassiter,
never objective or sequential but always beginning with a stark,
haunting vision: the slow-motion opening of the doors to the
anatomy lab, a faint odor of embalming fluid wafting to his
nostrils, and then his sudden immersion into the macabre world
of cadavers within.

Although the briefing by Gil Youngman had come earlier
and the evening with Nora would follow, it was always the
opening of those hard-wood doors that came shiveringly to
mind first—the realization that behind this barrier lay no mor-
tuary with subdued lighting and soothing music but the dere-
lict bodies of the working dead.

The day should have been triumphal: a culmination of all
the arduous years of war and study that had preceded it. But
something in Dan's psyche had been unprepared, had flooded
his mind and gut with protest, and the day had deteriorated
into one of the worst of his life. The Inchon invasion had been
more frightening for a raw, twenty-two-year-old infantry officer, but none had been more morbid. Ghoulish. Packs of medical students poised with their shining new instruments to pick
apart the dead.

The Anatomy Lesson

His college friend, Gil Youngman, now a sophomore at Massachusetts State Medical College, had warned him what to expect in the anatomy lab—though not within himself.

Relieved and cynical at having survived the rigors of that first year, Gil had offered advice freely: "Oh, anatomy's a ball-breaker, all right," he said, between bites into a knockwurst sandwich and sips of beer at a local tavern, "and a lot hinges on luck: the luck of the draw. The best you can hope for is to draw a body that's fairly presentable. I don't mean one you'd necessarily want to bring home to meet the folks, but the kind of stiff who's not too hard to stomach first thing in the morning. Not one who's a hundred years old or too damned fat, either. And preferably a male." Gil wiped beer foam from his lips. "Believe me, they're a lot easier on your nervous system. The few women cadavers the school manages to turn up each year are nearly always what we call coalbarges—big, hefty nigger gals. Takes you months to hack through all the fat and gristle on them without mutilating some important nerve or blood vessel.

"Now a Negro male, on the other hand, is probably the best cadaver you can hope for. That's 'cause they're usually leaner and have better developed muscles. With some of the old white gents we had handed to us last year you could hardly find any muscles and the ones they did have were flabby as jelly . . . Yeah, you got to be lucky, that's all. Now my bunch made out real well. The cadaver we pulled from the tank was a middle-aged Negro and hard as a rock." Gil grinned. "Know what we called him? 'Gold Coast Charlie'—on account of the gold fillings in his teeth. . . See, that's what I mean about lucking out. But, oh, those miserable fat ones just make for a lot more work and trouble!"

So cautioned Gil Youngman, and though impressed by his irreverence, Dan thought no more about cadavers until after lunch. What preoccupied him more for the moment was the heavy study load of a freshman, the thick tomes of anatomy and

4

histology that were required reading. A bright but erratically diligent student in college, Dan realized that such prodigious reading assignments, night after night, demanded a dedication and self-discipline he was not quite certain he possessed.

But fear drove them all: fear of falling behind and flunking out, fear of Nathan Snider, the autocratic chairman of the anatomy department and deity to all fledgling medical students at *State*. Since Snider, not the dean, was the absolute sovereign over the freshmen for as long as they remained on the fifth floor, it was more sensible than shameful to stand in awe of him, Gil had warned.

After lunch, the class gathered in the large, windowless lecture hall to await Snider's appearance. Dan took a backrow seat next to Roger Hickman, an intense, owlish student who shared his workbench in the classroom. Though Dan had known and been forced to compete for grades with many premedical students like Roger in undergraduate school—studious, unathletic, securely financed by their parents—he harbored no ill will toward them. Nor did he particularly seek out their company. While Roger prattled nervously about college days, he barely listened. His seat at the end put Dan a few feet from the side door that led to the anatomy lab, and his thoughts kept returning to the luck of the draw and what he might find in there.

He remembered the slaughter at Inchon, the dead and near-dead piled face-down on the beaches, their torn, hemorrhaging bodies bled ever paler by the waves lapping over them, and tried to transfer such conditioned callousness to his present experience. Think of it as just another beachhead, he told himself, one that you're better prepared for than most.

At that moment, Dr. Lyle Southwell, an assistant professor of anatomy, mounted the platform to inform the class that Snider's introductory lecture would be postponed until morning because he had been called away for a surgical consultation. Southwell, recently of Wheeling, West Virginia, drawled this announcement pridefully, going on to explain that not every professor of anatomy was so preeminent an authority that surgeons begged his advice in the operating room. Having learned from Gil that Snider customarily delivered more of a sermon than a lecture, Dan didn't care whether it was postponed or not. What Southwell said next, however, commanded his attention. Snider had left instructions for the class to spend the afternoon in the anatomy lab, familiarizing themselves with their cadavers.

Southwell grinned mischievously at the effect of this on his audience, particularly a girl in the front row whose mouth appeared frozen in a perfect *O*.

"Oh, come on now," he chided. "You or your pappy's paid tuition so you might as well get your feet wet. Find out once and for all whether you're cut out for this kind of work."

After stepping down from the platform, Southwell paused for a parting instruction. "Don't you all stampede in there like a bunch of wild horses now. And remember—Dr. Snider doesn't like any foolin' around. We'll have smelling salts handy for any of you who look a little peaked."

Dan sprang to his feet and headed for the side exit, sudden impatience overriding his apprehension as Southwell lingered in the doorway, unperturbed by the long line of students forming behind him, and chatted with Pat Walsh, one of the departmental assistants. Scrutinizing the anatomist from a foot away, Dan regarded Southwell's prematurely white hair, wire-rimmed glasses and thin lips without much liking. In the Army he had learned to mistrust certain officers of Southwell's mien, staff officers who, having never commanded, fawned over their superiors while treating men of lower ranks with contempt. But the hell with Southwell, he thought. It was Snider—rotund, cherub-faced Nathan Snider whose portrait hung prominently in the classroom, and who, it was rumored, flunked at least five freshmen every year—whom he had to please.

When the burnished anatomy lab doors finally parted, Dan was one of the first to enter. He was immediately stricken by the acrid stench of formaldehyde filling his nostrils, churning his gut, making him feel an almost irresistible urge to urinate.

Then, as if witnessing a deathly still panorama—like dawn rising eerily over what had been a night-time battlefield to expose the slain—he saw the cadavers as they lay, sallow and rigid, on each metal slab.

Nine slabs to a room.

Three rooms.

Pressed ahead by students in back of him, Dan walked skittishly down the narrow aisle between dissection tables, conscious of nothing but the awesome display of deathshells before him. Although moving on, he lacked any sense of motion, feeling as if he were suspended above some central point with the scene revolving below him, a nightmarish documentary of death projected upon his senses. He felt compelled to Run—Not Walk to the nearest exit, but an opposing compulsion made him stay: two clashing instincts, one repelled, one fascinated. It was astounding, even a bit irrational, he realized, but never before, not even in the bloodiest combat, had he been so struck—not by the fear of dying but of death itself, that incomprehensible end, and the interminable emptiness which might follow it.

Dan rubbed his tingling brow and fought to regain perspective. Though each of the many battle deaths he had seen had always been tempered by the perverse satisfaction it was not his own, he knew he shouldn't be overreacting to this. But the horror gripping him now was different from any he had ever experienced before—for deep in his mind, at the very threshhold of conscious thought, some trick of his imagination kept transposing his body into the collection of cadavers. Through some bizarre psychic transference, his own corpse now lay on one of the slabs in the anatomy lab, his frozen visage silently screaming for recognition at the students parading by. And once vaguely aware of its nature, it was this sense of kinship, this compelling communion he felt with the still bodies that shook him most. Did the other students feel it, he wondered, or was his reaction unique? Did an undertaker ever feel it before becoming inured to the constant company of the dead?

But even with this budding insight to allay his initial shock,

Dan could still not force himself to step closer than two feet from the tables nor remove his clenched hands from their shelter deep in the pockets of his lab coat. He continued his slow march down the aisles, scanning each new cadaver with abstract interest, neglecting to read the brass numbers on the sides of the tables that would tell him which of the many bodies was his.

Gradually the voices of his classmates intruded on his reverie. At first no one had spoken, but now the room fairly buzzed with succinct whispers, suppressed laughter. Tight-jawed, eyes-smarting, mouth-breathing to minimize the stench, Dan moved with the tidelike drift of the crowd toward the next dissecting room. Even though the windows on the street side stood open to dilute the reek of embalming fluid wafting up from the troughs under each table and he saw the glimmer of dust motes in the shafts of sunlight streaming through, he still felt oppressively confined and an air-hunger quickened his breath.

At some unnoticed point between the first and second dissection rooms Dan's composure returned. Bit by bit, his nose grew tolerant of the bite of embalming fluid, his heaving stomach calmed, his bladder overcame the once urgent need to empty itself. By degrees, his vision narrowed, focusing less on the jarring entity of all that surrounded him and more on what lay on each individual table, moving in on them like a movie camera on a gaff for the close-ups.

Some of the cadavers were covered from the waist down by flimsy cheesecloth; others were wholly naked, hip bones jutting forward, a layer of waxy, lacquered-slick skin stretched taut between their ribcages. At the foot of each table lay two ominous-looking tools: a wooden mallet and a fine-toothed saw. They were for use the following day to remove the cadaver's skullcap, Dan heard someone say.

As if the gaff had moved still closer, faces came into prominence. Dan saw mouths, some stuffed with puffy white cotton, some empty—gaping black holes between parched lips, surrounded by unkempt bristles of beard, even on the women. Some of the corpses looked asleep or bored; others, serene, indignant, cynical, long-suffering, or nonchalant—the fixed looks on their faces a travesty of every human expression. One gluttonous female with triple chins rested on huge, spreading buttocks. In grim contrast, the woman next to her had been wasted to a scant, skeletal sixty pounds by some ravaging disease. Her face was a gaunt mask, all beaked nose and sunken orbits, a twisted smear of a mouth.

From the faces, Dan observed chests or bosoms, whole torsos, finally legs which all bore a common brand: a stitched incision inside the thigh at the groin where red latex rubber had been injected to outline the arterial tree. He saw heavy stomachs folded in sinuous convolutions of fat and lean stomachs sucked in below jutting rib cages, some with scars of past operations or the brownish stretch marks of child bearing. Below them, half hidden by fleshy thighs or thick thatches of pubic hair, were the genitalia, the organs of love, now flaccid and withered, yet impossible for Dan to behold with indifference, to merely glance at without feeling a sense of revulsion at their seemingly obscene exposure.

Turning suddenly, Dan brushed past a knot of students in the aisle to seek a place by the open windows. The light breeze blowing in dried the sweat from his forehead but offered him no relief from the repugnant thoughts in his mind. Yet suddenly and unbelievably, with what he took to be a sign of incipient madness, he felt a stir of sexual arousal—as if his libido were struggling against the psychological castration which had threatened him moments before. Instinctively, he looked around for Carey London, one of five girls in the class and easily the most attractive. They had met earlier that day when assigned the same workbench and, after an amiable chat, agreed to be in the same dissection team. Now, in his sudden ache for a woman, Carey was the obvious choice. A moment's reflection, however, assured him that the pert-faced but studious-looking

9

Wellesley blonde would be an unlikely prospect for such wish fulfillment and reluctantly he dismissed her from his mind.

Spotting Roger Hickman at the sink, he joined him to share the balm of cold water on his sweating, if unsoiled, hands.

"Hello! How'd you make out with your cadaver?" Roger asked airily. "We were lucky with what we got. I mean, compared to some."

"Oh?"

"Yeah. He's pretty old but not in too bad shape. Got some funny-looking blotches on his skin. Might've died of syphilis."

"You think so?"

"Who knows? You can't catch anything from him now. I hear they don't tell you what your cadaver actually died of until later in the year. Should be fun trying to figure it out."

"I suppose."

"What's yours like?"

"What's what like?" Dan said absently.

"You know—your cadaver."

"Oh? Haven't found him yet."

"You haven't! Gosh, whatchu waiting for?"

"I guess he must be in the next room." Dan threw his crumpled paper towel in the refuse can and abruptly walked away.

He met Carey in the doorway to the third dissection room.

"Seen him yet?" she asked.

Dan shook his head.

"Well, follow me. I'll introduce you."

"How is he?"

"Not bad," Carey told him. "Different, I'd say—almost disturbingly so."

Before Dan could ask what she meant, she stopped at a corner table and he understood instantly. Below them, at waist level, lay the body that they would dissect for the next six months. Not fat, black, unshapely, or old. Instead, lean, white, young, and even handsome in a rugged way. His nose had been flattened at the bridge and flared at the nostrils: a boxer's nose.

His purplish lips were even and unsmiling and a gray stubble of beard covered his square chin. His eyes were blue, with clouded corneas, and stared at the ceiling.

He almost looks alive, Dan thought with an involuntary shiver—and immediately tried to wrench the unnerving idea from his mind. Yet there did seem to be a residual vitality to those stern features that the other faces lacked.

"Feel the muscles on this guy," Earl Cole, the short, squat third member of their dissecting team, suggested.

Dan reached down to grip the cadaver's cool, firm bicep, keeping a fixed expression on his face.

"And look at something else this guy's got," Earl added in a whispered aside, beginning to remove the cheesecloth from his groin.

Dan reached out quickly to stop his hand. "You got a funny sense of humor, Cole. What do you do for kicks—rob graves?"

A steady procession of students stopped by their table to comment on their good fortune in drawing such a dandy specimen. Pat Walsh confided that it was not only the best of an inferior lot, but some in this year's collection were poor pickings indeed. Hearing the moans at a nearby table, Dan went over to look. Their cadaver was an elderly, corpulent Negress with pendulous breasts and sagging stomach and he felt sorry for the dissecting team. But by week's end, they were all recovered from their initial dismay and on intimate terms with their *Aunt Jemima.*

Minutes later, Dan and Carey went out for a smoke in the corridor.

"Well, how do you feel about him?" she asked curiously.

"Okay. We made out all right. . . At least, compared to some."

"Oh, I know that. That's not what I meant. What I really want to know is how you feel inside. I guess I must be awfully squeamish—just what you'd expect from a woman, huh? But the truth is, this is the first time I've ever seen a corpse, and seeing twenty-seven at a clip nearly threw me into hysterics. Did it bother you any? I suppose not."

"Tell me something," Dan began haltingly.

"Tell you what?"

"I want a straight answer—understand? No cracks. What does he look like to you?"

"Gosh, I don't know . . . In a vague sort of way he reminds me of that movie actor, John Garfield."

Dan wanted to ask if at first glance she thought their cadaver appeared vital and alive, but he decided against it. Carey looked to him for support; no sense confessing his eccentricities.

"And you?" she asked. "What did he look like to you?"

"Like a boxer."

"Is that all?" she said, pouting. "From the strange look on your face I kind of expected something more profound . . . Oh well, I feel a lot better now that the suspense is over. Don't you?"

"Not much . . . I wish to Christ we hadn't been quite so lucky."

Carey smiled wryly. "I know. I feel that way, too. He'll take some getting used to. . . . By the way, have you bought a dissection kit yet?"

"Uh-huh. Want to share it?"

"Thanks. And thanks for the moral support, too. Some of those clowns in there act so damned nonchalant about all this. Especially that cute little bastard, Earl. Don't be too surprised if I take a scalpel to him one of these days. And don't ask where. I'm a lady. A little bloodthirsty, maybe, but a lady all the same."

By five o'clock most of the students had gone home to parents or wives or girlfriends, to audiences with whom they could share the morbid fascinations of that first day. Lingering on to look at the anatomical models in the library, Dan was one of the last to leave. On his way out, he peeked impulsively into the anatomy lab to watch the janitor finish raising up the coffin-like lids on each side of the dissection tables and snap out the lights. The room turned dusky in the wan afternoon light and

12

Dan felt a strange, almost wistful reluctance to leave, thinking that if his body were lying in there, soon to be dismembered, to lose forever its integrity of face and form, he would not want to be left alone.

Chapter Two

Nora McGuire felt a few, final quivers of pleasure between her legs as Dan separated from her and rolled on his side, resting his head on her left breast and draping his arm across the right: counterweights against the heaving of her chest. She blinked a film of sweat and gritty mascara from her eyes. The hotel room was dark, except for a shaft of light from the bathroom across the foot of the bed, and still, except for the muffled cacophony of traffic noises outside the closed window. Nora looked around at the fake-colonial furniture and the textbooks stacked on Dan's writing desk until her gaze settled on the print of Old Ironsides hanging above it, almost a constant fixture in Boston's better rented rooms.

There was no denying it, she mused—she was not only bedded down in Room 202 of the Hotel Somerset but, with brain benumbed and body atingle, had entered it of her own free will.

Still, as the sensations in her pelvis subsided, the strictures of her strict Catholic upbringing broke through, compelling Nora to wonder what libidinous urges could have made her act so far out of character.

Here she was, twenty-eight and single, plain-faced and freckled, but with hazel eyes, full breasts, and a slim figure; a seasoned newspaperwoman, yet a dutiful daughter who lived at home with her mother; a virgin once removed but hardly sex-starved, still attractive enough to have men make sporadic passes and worldly enough to demur without offending them.

And that, Nora McGuire believed, was a fair assessment of herself and her life. So how could she possibly be in bed with this boy she had met for the first time hardly two hours before?

There had been no college courtship, no tacit engagement, no common interest in journalism—none of those conscience cushioners she'd had four years ago with Mark, her only previous lover—yet she had found Dan Lassiter's abrupt seduction far more satisfying. Even now, she felt no vestige of guilt, only a perverse curiosity as to how their two nude bodies might look together in a mirror.

It was scandalous behavior for a chaperone at a college dance, she thought with a twinge.

Dan lay so quietly against her that for a time Nora thought he might have fallen asleep. But soon he raised his head from her breast, smiled down, and slipped out of bed to the bathroom. The sounds she heard, the brief grunt and uneven trickling, distracted her, made her feel a similar urinary urge. But she stirred only enough to cover herself with the bedsheet, then lay back to spend these few private moments in thought.

She knew no glib words, no promises of Dan's, could have seduced her, only the intense need he had managed to convey at a time when her own peculiar mood had rendered her uniquely receptive and vulnerable. . . . She recaptured the moment: at the end of a long dance set while the band played the theme from *Limelight*. Dan's plaintive, "I want you," soft-spoken with a slight quavering, triggering a momentary disbelief (had he really said it?) together with the realization that his bold words had neither shocked nor surprised her, had seemed almost an extension of her own thoughts, numbing her with the fear that he had uncannily read her mind.

Wisely, Dan had not waited for her answer but led her away. Fleeting images of forlorn-looking youths lounging in the lobby, creaking elevator, tunnellike corridor, key unlocking door, all

15

vaguely registered in her brain at the time, yet not another word had been spoken.

She had let herself be undressed and seduced in pantomime, Nora recalled in chagrin.

She knew that no sane, sensible, city-bred girl is ever seduced on the spur of the moment without the inclination being there. But such moments of weakness, of shorn defenses and humiliating desire, she realized, were bound to occur in unmarried women of twenty-eight.

That afternoon she had walked through Boston Common, aware of the late-blooming marigolds wilting and the trampled grass turning to hay, focusing in fear on her own finite life cycle: afraid of her mother's growing senility and her own set-in-her-ways state of mind; afraid of a husbandless, childless future.

Though such brooding had once been rare for her, Nora found herself increasingly immersed in it of late. She had already learned that a single glance in the bathroom mirror at the crow's feet that grew progressively more prominent around her eyes or the slight sag to her breasts and buttocks might evoke such age-conscious anxieties transiently, but she now knew it took a visit to the doctor to make them last all day.

Middle-aged, paunchy, Ireland-born but Boston-educated, Dr. Michael Morrissey was actually her mother's physician, but Nora had consulted him once or twice for minor ailments and so preferred seeing him now about her more intimate menstrual irregularities rather than start fresh with a new doctor.

"Ah, good afternoon, Miss McGuire. Doctor will see you in a moment," Morrissey's elderly but still spry nurse had said and led her to an unoccupied examining room. She would've preferred to talk with the doctor first, but the nurse instructed her briskly to disrobe. "All off, but your shoes and stockings," she said, and soon Nora lay spread-eagled and uncomfortable on the examining table, her feet in stirrups, a sheet draped like a pup tent over her thighs.

"Move down a bit. Doctor likes you all the way down," the nurse told her, and grasping both Nora's hips, pulled her down so that her buttocks overhung the edge of the table, summoning the doctor only after she was satisfied Nora was in the proper examining position.

Dr. Morrissey, dressed in a starched white coat over pin-striped vest and pants, displayed his buckteeth in an automatic smile, asked a few questions, jotted down the dates of her erratic menstrual periods, and then, none too soon—for her back and legs were aching intolerably—proceeded to examine her.

Nora shut her eyes as she felt the slightly ticklish touch of his gloved fingers spreading her labia. After overcoming a tenacious resistance from dry membranes, Morrissey's finger penetrated deeply and swept down, breaking the air seal in the vault of her vagina with a moist, lip-smacking sound. Finally, he removed his finger and Nora felt a warmth spreading over her bottom as he drew a goose-necked examining light close to the table.

Self-consciously, she wondered what he might be thinking as he inspected the outer folds of her vagina, the remaining tabs of hymenal ring whose rupture had caused her so much embarrassment at age twelve . . . Does he think the same thoughts while examining an older woman as a younger one? My mother or me? she mused whimsically, until a related thought began to perturb her. Why, with her period long overdue, had he not inquired, however tactfully, if she could be pregnant? Because he knew the McGuire family and couldn't bring himself to consider such a sinful possibility? Or because he didn't want to embarrass her in the presence of his nurse? Or, most vexing of all, because he simply couldn't imagine a plain-faced, Irish-Catholic lass like her inviting or allowing or responding to such carnal practices? And though at one time she might have appreciated such affirmation of her virtue, she was now at an age where the smugness behind it affronted her. . . .

At last, Morrissey's instruments and painfully probing fingers were removed and he rendered his verdict: Everything feels fine. . . . But everything wasn't fine, Nora reflected as the nurse helped her down from the examining table, feeling rubbery-legged and manhandled and, even with the sheet clutched tightly, nakedly exposed—as if in submitting to the pelvic exam she had suffered an indignity so sexless and impersonal it demeaned her as a woman.

Dan emerged from the bathroom and returned to bed. Nora came willingly into his embrace but resisted the pressure of his knee, then hand, attempting to part her thighs.

"You keep surprising me," he murmured.

"Do I now?" she said in a mock imitation of a brogue.

"Oh, not sexually. There are no real surprises there, only a few accommodations."

"Is that what you're fishing for—some accommodations?"

Dan withdrew his arms and sat up. Nora stared back defensively.

"All right," he said, "say what's on your mind."

"Say what?"

"That no matter how nice it might've been, it's over now. Never again will there be any intercourse, except social, between us."

"Hmmm," she mused, frowning. "Are you always so sure of your women?"

"No—unsure. Especially with ones I like."

"Then what makes you so damned sure of me?" she accused. ". . . I won't lie to you, Dan. I wanted you earlier—every bit as much as you wanted me—only I never could've admitted it. The smartest thing you ever did was to take me by the arm and lead me off the dance floor. I never could've said yes, if you asked. But you sensed that, didn't you?"

He nodded.

"Perceptive of you. What else did you sense? That I'd be so responsive, so uninhibited? Did you sense that, too?"

"Uh-uh," Dan said, shaking his head. "I'd be a fool to try to

18

answer a question like that. Do you really want to be so analytical?"

She shrugged. "I suppose I'm still so astonished, I just want to talk about it. Don't you?"

"No. You murder to dissect."

"What did you say?"

"It's a quote from Wordsworth. I read it earlier today."

"You read poetry?" she asked, surprised.

"No, bathroom walls . . . Some med school philosopher—or maybe an antivivisectionist—had scribbled it on the wall of one of the johns."

Nora looked dubious, then smiled. "I once thought of going to medical school myself."

"What happened?"

"I didn't want to badly enough, I guess. State wasn't accepting many women in those days, and I let your Professor Snider talk me out of it. Then there was the matter of the six-hundred-dollar tuition. I almost wish I'd been more persistent. I envy you the chance."

"Don't. I'm not so sure I'll make it either."

"Oh?" Nora said. "What makes you say that?"

Haltingly, Dan described his introduction to the anatomy lab earlier that day, emphasizing his visceral reactions and playing down his emotional ones, considering them too amorphous and ambivalent to be explainable in their present state.

"You're a sensitive lad," Nora said, smiling so as not to appear patronizing. "But I already knew that, didn't I? It's what really drew me to you. You weren't at all like the usual brash college types prowling hotel dances to dazzle the working girls with their Pepsodent smiles and phony airs. What else is different about you?"

Dan shrugged. "Not much. Both my parents were killed in a car crash when I was twelve and an uncle of mine in Williamstown took me and my brother with him. Great guy, my uncle—a professor at the college. You might even have heard of him—Woodrow McKinley Brock?"

"The political analyst?"

"Yeah, that's him. Writes books about presidents. He's never met any, but after being named for a couple, he writes about them for revenge. He's also a bachelor who chases after Bennington coeds. Apart from that, he's been a good influence on me, and he's all the family I've got left."

"Didn't you say you have a brother?"

"*Had* . . . Pete got himself killed in Germany in 1945, and I came damn near to doing the same in Korea—only somehow I wasn't. Made me feel that since I lived when so many better men didn't, I ought to do something useful with my life. Sounds right out of *Magnificent Obsession*, doesn't it? . . . Trouble is, I'm still not all that sold on being a doctor. I know it's a little late to be thinking that way, but the uncertainty's there, and someday soon I'm going to have to come to grips with it. Today was merely a preview. . . ."

"Go on," she prompted.

"What bothered me most wasn't the sight, or even the smell, of a roomful of cadavers, but my cadaver, the one assigned to me . . . Not because I get particularly queasy at the prospect of cutting him up, but because the only justification I have for doing it is what I might learn to someday help me help others. But if I don't make the grade, if I flunk out first, then all that anatomy goes to waste and it means he's been cut up for nothing."

"Oh, you'll make it," Nora assured him. "You *made* me, and that's a feat all in itself. But the two are connected somehow, aren't they?"

"Sure. I walked out of that anatomy lab so filled with the taste of death, I looked for sex to wash it away. Like turning on hot and cold faucets in my mind to get the right temperature, the right degree of sanity. That make sense to you?"

"Yes. Maybe too much," she answered ruefully. ". . . My father died a few years ago. Left the house one afternoon to buy some pipe tobacco and never came back. Dropped dead of a heart attack. Later on, I got a call at work from the police to go down to Boston City Hospital and identify his body. I'll never forget it!" she said, grimacing. "That sloppy-fat detective —O'Hallaran was his name—taking me down into the morgue. The chill in that room! I must've shook for thirty minues afterward! And that seedy-looking detective with his belly hanging over his belt, saying: 'Is this your old man, lady? Sign this, lady?' He must've called me 'lady' twenty times in the next five minutes—that Mick bastard! . . . And all the time he was trying to make out. Oh, I could tell. Kept offering to take me to some neighborhood bar for a drink. I'm not just imagining it, either, because I ran into that ghoul once more after that and he repeated the offer! But he knew something, didn't he? He knew how vulnerable women can be at such moments. 'Time's winged chariot' and all that. . . ." Her voice trailed off.

Dan took her in his arms. She lay back, welcoming the warm press of his body, but she tensed as she felt him harden.

"Do you want to?" he asked softly.

Nora gave him a kiss before twisting out from under him. "I *do* want to, if it's any consolation, but then I'll never have the strength to get out of bed and I don't think the Somerset dance committee could ever forgive me for staying all night in their hotel. Besides, it's almost midnight and I have a long subway ride home, and if I get in too late my mother will feel obliged to look disapproving all through breakfast—which is much harder for me to take sometimes than her prattling."

"I'll take you home in a cab."

"All the way out to Dorchester? Cost you at least eight dollars round-trip! Or is the offer contingent on what I might be willing to do in the meantime?"

"It's contingent on nothing," he said, "except your having dinner with me tomorrow night."

"And afterward—what? Back here again? Sure you can sit through a long meal when you've already had dessert?"

Dan sighed. "Okay, it's a waste, but no more sex. Have dinner with me anyway?" He liked Nora, not only because she was easy to talk to but because her job on a major newspaper made her more informed and interesting than most girls he knew.

"All right," she agreed after a moment, "but not right away. I need a cooling-off spell. Enough to give my guilty conscience a chance to recover. . . . Call me in a week."

Chapter Three

One of Daniel Lassiter's earliest memories was of witches. A sickly child, plagued by recurrent sore throats and ear infections, he could remember lying ill in bed one day when he was four years old and imagining that a witch was about to spring out of his bedroom closet. Though his mother was somewhere in the house, he did not cry out. Instead, eyes riveted on the half-open closet door, he lay very still and, believing that witches were like certain vicious dogs in their ability to sniff out fear, tried to quell his skin-bristling sense of alarm. Intuitively knowing the witch in the closet was also in his mind, he felt that, if he could only resist the urge to call out for his mother, thereby persuading her he was not afraid, she might decide he was not ripe for her caldron, after all, and go away. Eventually his fright eased, the closet resumed being a closet again and not a witch's lair, and he fell asleep, confident that by not giving in to his fear he had banished the witch from his bedroom forever.

Such stoicism soon became apparent to his father on those occasions when he felt forced to discipline Dan, and though the number of belt lashes meted out remained the same, he was whipped faster, making it easier for Dan not to cry. As he remembered the same trait in himself as a child, it became another of the unspoken bonds between Calvin Lassiter and his younger son.

Born in Schenectady, New York, of Scottish-German ancestry, Cal Lassiter had been a tall, quietly intense youth, and an outstanding athlete in high school. Charles Steinmetz was his father's friend, and the influence of that hunchbacked genius of General Electric had led Cal to study electrical engineering at Union College, where he also played first base so brilliantly that John McGraw personally scouted him for the New York Giants. But Cal was already a married man with a child on the way and so reluctantly declined the great baseball manager's offer. While still a junior at Union he had met and married Lila Brock of Pittsfield, Massachusetts, and upon graduation went to work for the Sprague Electric Company in nearby North Adams. His energy and inventive mind served him so well that within five years he had become chief engineer at Sprague's and owned two patents on radio condensers.

One spring morning, however, Calvin Lassiter stopped off on his way to work to watch a group of teen-agers playing baseball in the park near his Williamstown home. He had been brooding for days over a price and production problem at the factory, one he could solve only through a technical innovation that would result in the laying-off of twenty workers in dire need of jobs. Though he dreaded having to face such a prospect, the defeated looks of the men, he could see no other way out. But the sight of the hustling teen-agers, the well-loved sounds of crack of bat and thump of ball in leather, gradually distracted Cal from the problems of his employer, making him increasingly aware of the dissatisfaction within himself. That same day he quit his engineering job and joined his wife in the teaching profession. Hired as science teacher and baseball coach at Williamstown High, Calvin Lassiter spent the next twelve years so employed before reluctantly giving up active teaching to become school principal.

In the summer of 1939, leaving their two sons with their

maternal grandmother, Cal and Lila Lassiter sailed for a month's vacation in Europe. Such a trip had originally been planned for their retirement, but with the Nazi occupation of Czechoslovakia making the outbreak of war imminent, they had decided not to delay. Ten days and four postcards after they docked at Le Havre, a French camion recklessly speeding along the winding seacoast road between Nice and Cannes at dusk smashed head-on into their rented Renault, killing them both instantly.

Though only twelve at the time of his parents' death, Dan Lassiter's childhood ended there. From then on, he became more taciturn, more self-reliant, never needing reminders from his ailing, elderly grandmother—who lived another year—to do his homework or keep his room clean, and perhaps as an outlet for the inner confusion and despair he felt becoming a scrappy competitor in school sports.

An even more striking change took place in Dan's relations with his brother, Pete. Three years older, Pete favored their mother in both looks and temperament. Not only did he enjoy reading books and participating in adult conversation more than Dan, he was much more outgoing, highly popular in high school as an athlete and student leader—president of his freshman class, perpetually on the honor roll—the exemplar of everything a school principal's son should be. Though Dan did not begrudge Pete those accomplishments, he remained fiercely competitive with him, particularly insofar as their father's attentions were concerned. Challenging him to their first fistfight when he was ten, Dan was badly bloodied in the encounter, yet would not stop throwing punches until they had been separated by their teachers and the contest declared a draw. Thereafter, Pete lost much of his protective, if superior, feelings toward his younger brother and their relationship grew strained.

The tragic death of their parents ultimately healed this breech—though at first it only worsened it. Hearing his older brother crying in bed at night, Dan would cross through the connecting door of their bedrooms to hush him. "C'mon, Pete. Stop the bawling, will you?" he would complain, "I can't sleep."

Sometimes a shamefaced Pete would lash out at such intrusions, and sometimes he would try to draw Dan out as to his own feelings. "Why don't you ever cry?"

" 'Cause it don't do no good."

"How do you know?" Pete angrily accused. "What's the matter with you, anyways? Don't you feel anything?"

"Yeah, I do. But it's better not to give in. Like Woody once told me, It's all right to feel sorry for other people—you know, for Mom and Dad 'cause they had to die so soon—long as you don't go feeling that way about yourself."

"What makes you think I'm feeling sorry for myself?"

"Well, aren't you?"

"What if I am. What's wrong with it?"

"It's selfish."

"Selfish! What's so selfish about missing your folks—wishing they were still around?"

" 'Cause that's all it is—wishing. And wishing dead people were alive ain't healthy."

"Oh yeah? How would a dumb kid like you know what's healthy or not?"

"By looking at you, I guess. . . . Now quit blubbering and let me sleep."

When Pete was seventeen and a senior in high school, he broke his leg skiing. The fracture, involving all three ankle bones, was a severe one and slow to heal. During the months Pete was an invalid, Dan did all he could for him, pushing him to classes in a wheelchair until the ankle could tolerate weight and then helping him hobble along the slippery winter streets on his crutches. The mishap not only ended whatever rivalry still existed between them but drew them closer as brothers— first in a partnership of equals, then with Pete's physical dependence imperceptibly turning into an emotional one as well, favoring Dan slightly as the more decisive.

26

In 1942 their uncle and guardian, Woodrow Brock, already an amateur pilot, took a direct commission in the Air Force and left them, with a day-time housekeeper, in the large old house that sat in the midst of the expanding Williams College campus. Dan was now a tall fifteen, a Life scout working toward Eagle, and a recent, ever-ambitious discoverer of the joys of girls and sex. The competition for the prettier ones his age was stiff, however. With young naval officers enrolled in the V-12 training program filling Williams to capacity, the local girls found themselves in the enviable position of being able to pick and choose among an abundance of men all nattily attired in their serge uniforms. Dan did not resent having to compete with the V-12 students so much as he did the rowdy behavior of some of them in public—the ones who guzzled beer in the local movie house and rolled the empty bottles down the aisle or the loud-mouths who hung around on street corners and made disparaging cracks whenever a town boy went past with a date. Occasionally provoked into fistfights with them, Dan usually found himself outmatched, but within another year that changed. Adding three inches and twenty pounds to his frame, and with the advantage of all that his Uncle Woody, an expert amateur boxer, had taught him, Dan no longer took pains to avoid such street scuffles—he often started them. Admiring his spunk, some of the college students he fought later befriended him and invited him on their nightly prowls of the area for accommodating beer joints or women. One group even offered to take him along on their next visit to a whorehouse in Troy, New York, and buy his first piece for him. But Dan refused. He had already heard tales of Troy whores from others, and some of the things they allegedly liked to do seemed, if not depraved to him, at least unsanitary. He simply could not imagine himself responding to the frenzied manipulations of some blowsy whore any more than Gulliver, he remembered, had enjoyed copulating with Yahoo women. Besides, by that time his sexual fantasies centered almost exclusively on one woman—and though Marge Downing was no whore, to his naïve and somewhat priggish point of view, she often behaved like one.

Dan's first intimate exposure to her came not as a participant but as an observer. As one of the senior scouts in his troup, he had volunteered to serve one night a week as an air-spotter on top of a hotel in North Adams—not only a lonely vigil, but largely a superfluous one since that particular area of the Berkshires was over one hundred miles inland. Posted on the rooftop of the six-story Richmond Hotel with a powerful pair of binoculars, Dan failed to spot a single aircraft during the many months he faithfully maintained his watch, but he was witness to a great deal of the nocturnal activities of certain incautious guests at the adjacent Hotel Wellington. In his novice state, he found that view educational, indeed. But once learning that most naked humans looked more ludicrous than titillating when engaged in the flesh-jiggling, belly-slapping undulations of sex, Dan's voyeuristic fascination, with one exception, waned.

The exception was Marge Downing, a pretty blonde waitress of twenty-five whom Dan knew, having eaten at the restaurant where she worked. He had a nodding acquaintance not only with Marge but with her husband, a star fullback in high school, now in the Marines, and so he knew that the man with whom she shared a hotel room each Friday night was not he. In fact—and this seemed to offend Dan's sense of propriety even more—her lover was not even a serviceman but the middle-aged owner of the restaurant where she worked. Yet even this incontestable evidence of Marge Downing's easy virtue did not stop Dan from lusting after her. All the immature, underdeveloped teen-age girls he dated paled in comparison to Marge's pretty face and voluptuous figure. So aroused did Dan become over visions of her that he took to eating at the Rosewood Grill four and five times a week, always at one of Marge's tables, always on the verge of asking her for a date. She would laughingly refuse, he reasoned, then not so laughingly reconsider, once he told her all he knew about the way she spent her Friday nights. Much as Dan was tempted to put such a proposal to her, he desisted; Marge was really a very pleasant person, not at all stuck-up over her looks, and at the time his conscience would not allow him to act so ruthlessly.

In mid-1944, Pete, who had switched too late from a major in history to premedical studies to get a deferment on this basis, was drafted into the Army. Woody took a few days' leave to enter Dan as a boarding student at the nearby Berkshire Academy, tell Pete to be a good soldier, then flew back to his B-17 squadron about to leave for England.

The next morning, driving Pete's Chevrolet coupé, now his own, Dan took his brother to the train station. Despite a determined effort to keep his emotions under control, Pete's moist, wistful look made Dan fight back tears of his own.

"Don't go getting yourself killed, for Chrissake," Dan growled at him as the train pulled into the depot.

"Try not to," Pete replied. "You be careful yourself."

"Me! Of what?"

"Joyriding around in my car. Just because you got a driver's license, don't go showing off what a hot-shot driver you are."

"Aw, hell, it's only an 'A' ration. Not enough gas to go around the block. Besides, they won't let me keep a car at Berkshire anyway. Against the rules."

"Rules," Pete said. "I know you and rules. You just take it easy, huh?"

Dan mumbled some assurance and then fell silent, a brooding expression on his face. Finally, he blurted, "You dumb jerk! What took you so goddamn long to decide you wanted to be a doctor. If you'd decided earlier, you'd be out of this."

"Aw, I'll be okay," Pete said bravely. "Anyway, the war'll probably be over before I even finish medic training."

"Yeah, I suppose," Dan said, lifting his brother's bulky suitcase onto the train platform. He wanted to hug Pete good-bye, but people were watching. Awkwardly, he thrust out his hand.

As awkwardly, Pete took it. "Well, take care of yourself," he said in a choked voice.

"Yeah. You, too."

In the months that followed, Dan missed Pete and the freedom they'd enjoyed in their own house, yet otherwise adjusted well to boarding school life. Though several cuts below such preparatory schools as Deerfield and Groton, the Berkshire Academy was located in pleasantly hilly surroundings and Dan found the year he was to spend there, the last before going on to college, passing quickly. He skirted the school's policy against students owning cars by renting barn space for the Chevy from a neighboring farmer. Knowing he had been recently spotted by one of his teachers driving, Dan was not too surprised when, the following Monday, he was told the headmaster wanted to see him. Mr. Beechum was a dour man and a strict disciplinarian. But the look on the headmaster's face was more sorrowful than stern when Dan entered his office, and he soon found out why. Shaking so badly that he had to hold the telegram from the Secretary of War in both hands, Dan was only able to read the opening, *We regret to inform you* . . . and Pete's name before the remaining words were blurred by an onrush of tears.

From the moment Beechum had handed him the telegram everything seemed to dim, slow down, grow mute, as if it were all happening under water. Even the words of condolence Beechum uttered seemed to take on a faint gurgling quality as they issued from his mouth. What, if anything, he had said in return, or how he had gotten from the headmaster's office to the farm where he kept his car, he couldn't recall; along with the print on the telegram, the memory of it had blurred.

By the time he reached Williamstown, however, enough of the amnesiac shock had worn off so Dan was able to remember more of what had transpired in Beechum's office; not words—these were so inconsequential as to be forgotten forever—but emotions. Feelings. One, in particular, he remembered vividly.

Don't cry! he had thought as he held the telegram in his trembling hands. *Not in front of Beechum!* In that agonizing moment he had actually believed that if he could only hold back his tears then, as in that long-ago day when he had triumphed over the witch in his bedroom, he might possibly triumph again and Pete could not be dead. It was, of course, childishly naïve of him to have thought that way, Dan now mused, but at the time . . . at the time each bitter tear he shed seemed a further concession to failure and futility.

Arriving at his Williamstown home, he wandered aimlessly around the downstairs of the house until he could bring himself to mount the stairs to Pete's room. Finding no solace there, he lingered only a moment. Then, picking up the phone, he called the Rosewood Grill and asked to speak to Marge Downing. They talked briefly—long enough for Dan to tell her who he was, where he would pick her up after work, and why she must agree to meet him.

He was sitting behind the wheel of his car smoking a cigarette when Marge Downing came out of the restaurant and climbed in beside him. Though her blue eyes blazed with resentment, there was also a flicker of fear in them.

"How old are you anyhow?" she asked Dan.

"Almost eighteen," he lied.

"Why are you doing this? I've never done anything to you."

"I want to get laid."

"All right, so you want to get laid—so do most kids your age," she said disdainfully. "Why pick on me?"

Dan said nothing.

"What if I won't let you?"

"You will! You'll not only let me, you'll probably end up enjoying it. Don't forget, I've seen you in action. I know what you like."

"But it's not fair," she wailed.

"So what? Not much in life is," he said in a hard, flat voice that made him sound older. "You took a chance with your boss and got caught. Now I'm taking the chance." He started the car and pulled away from the curb.

"All right," she said reluctantly after they had driven in silence for a few minutes. "But just once—one time, hear?"

When Dan didn't reply, she started to cry.

"I knew your father," she said between sniffles. "He was a swell guy. Your brother, Pete, too. Pete would never do anything like this."

"No, Pete wouldn't," he allowed, "but I'm me. I'm doing it. And I've been thinking about it for a long time."

"I'll just bet you have!" she said, trying to sound contemptuous. "What took you so long—no guts?"

Dan glanced at her and shrugged. "Maybe. Or maybe my conscience wouldn't let me."

"Your conscience! That's a laugh. You haven't got one!"

"Yes, I have. I just don't listen to it anymore."

Marge Downing spent that night and the following weekend and several weekends after that with him. At first scornful of his inexperience, his clumsy gropings, she soon relented, finding a unique satisfaction in being the more aggressive sexual partner. Even after her husband was discharged from the Marine Corps, Marge expressed a willingness to continue their affair, but Dan demurred. He had had other women by then, and somehow making love to Marge always brought back to mind the scene in Beechum's office when he had been notified of Pete's death. Only with Marge Downing did that happen, not with any of the others. Then again, despite all the cynicism he professed, he had never been particularly proud of sleeping with another man's wife.

Chapter Four

Dr. Nathan Snider, it was popularly held, was a towering egotist. A champion of egotists. Even in a medical community like Boston's whose institutions drew some of the world's best minds, Snider's ego was said to be unsurpassed. He was seldom joined by any of his former students for meals in the hospital cafeteria and their greetings on passing him in the corridors were curt, their smiles twitchy. Only a thoughtful few ever bothered to analyze such abiding hostility. Snider had been a severe taskmaster, an aloof and autocratic figure to many of them. He was the professor they had most feared in medical school, the one who had tested their mettle earliest and so best knew the weaknesses that they now concealed under their physician's panoply.

Actually the man merely held strong opinions about his chosen field, the teaching of anatomy, and thirty years of instructing fledgling medical students in the subject had given him sound ground upon which to base such opinions. Secretly he delighted in the unusual students who dared challenge him. He had a sly way of leading them into digging a deep grave for their argument before executing them with a few terse statements of fact. On the rare occasion when he was wrong, Snider conceded defeat much too graciously for his opponents to gloat.

What irked his critics most was Snider's failure to conform

to their image of anatomy professors as the morticians of the medical profession—frustrated, diffident men who after graduating as physicians lacked the self-assurance to make vital decisions and practice their art and so retreated to the safety of the classroom. Belying such a stereotype, Snider did not appear frustrated and was hardly self-effacing. If anything, he tended to be even more dogmatic with colleagues than with students, particularly the surgeons among them whose field encroached upon his own. And even his detractors here had to concede that he was a damned fine anatomy teacher to whom they were all in debt. Almost to a man they had faced some crisis in an accident ward or operating room where they had remembered and been saved by a Snider axiom drilled into them during their student days.

In his dealings with the class, Snider chose respect over popularity. The discipline he demanded was rigorous, and for the six months of anatomy he was the common enemy. Only in later years, when many of his former students searched in attic trunks for their lecture notes in order to pass some State licensing exam, did any real admiration for the man take root. But by then the advantages he had offered them during that first year could be appreciated only in retrospect. Even at class reunions, few had the courage to approach and thank him, although they remembered.

For a full generation of doctors graduating from Massachusetts State Medical College, Nathan Snider *was* anatomy.

The morning of Dan's second day started promptly at nine A.M. when Dr. Snider entered the fifth-floor classroom by the side entrance and strode briskly to the front. Under his arm he carried two books, one, a Bible. Four assistants followed, drew chairs along the back row, and, once seated, crossed their legs. The hum of conversation in the room dropped off precipitously at Snider's entrance and the class fidgeted uncomfortably on their padded stools.

It was a special moment for Nathan Snider. Although the text of his little sermon had not changed appreciably over the years, he still felt a deep responsibility for impressing upon his flock the sanctity with which one dealt with a dead human body. If anatomy had a spiritual side, a gospel extending beyond its ponderous texts and tomes, he believed it to be here. Befitting this, he spoke to each fall class with their perpetually changing faces in truly humble tones—never to be heard publicly from him again in quite that same manner. And though some of his former students might choose to believe his use of the Bible was a sham, a stage prop that he opened once a year in their presence and never again—others remembered this morning as Snider's finest hour.

"Today, I want you to know," he began, "that we are to undertake the dissection of the human cadaver.

"I regard this as both a privilege and a psychological step forward. One must think seriously about it. No student should be allowed to enter the anatomy laboratory without a certain mature and humane outlook. Along with his tools and his books, he should bring with him an artistic perception—as best exemplified by Michelangelo and Leonardo da Vinci—and, above all, a deep religious sense. For, in the days to come, you will not just be dealing with a cold corpse, a methodical molding of muscle upon flesh, flesh upon bone, but with the bodies of unfortunate souls whose remains went unclaimed—people who have passed tragically through life leaving nothing of any material value behind and few who might mourn or miss them.

"I'm certain that if one of us had been able to tell them beforehand that, in death, their bodies would make a contribution of the highest order to humanity—through you, the medical student—they would've been exceedingly gratified. Their bodies deserve your respect. We *demand* it and, needless to say, we unfailingly receive it.

"There is never any justification for joking or horseplay in the laboratory. The hours we schedule each day for gross anat-

35

omy are meant for that and that alone. I caution you, not only is cadaver dissection the surest road to the knowledge that you must have as physicians but the opportunity for it is not likely to come your way again.

"In previous years," Snider continued, his voice hardening, "we have had a certain few students remove their cadaver's skullcap from the lab and take it home with them to use as an ashtray. I tell you honestly, I can conceive of nothing more vile, nothing more immature or ungrateful, and I hope I never have to make such remarks about any of you.

"Now then—some of you may ask what happens to the dismembered corpses once your work with them has ended? They are each given a decent Christian burial in a plot of ground provided by the medical school, and many of my former students have seen fit to attend the services we hold for them—fully aware, fully appreciative, of the contribution these unfortunate people have made, through their only means, to their training as future physicians.

"At this time, it has been my practice over the years to read the passage from Ezekiel, Chapter thirty-seven, Verse thirteen, 'the vision of the dry bones.' "

As Snider raised the Bible in both hands and opened it to the paper marker, a student in the second row broke into a fit of harsh coughing and quickly smothered it with his handkerchief. Most of the others looked attentively to the front or off at corners. In the back of the room the anatomy assistants shifted their chairs and recrossed their legs. Pat Walsh, the senior member of the quartet, now knew the intended Biblical passage by heart.

Snider began reading, his voice a half-octave lower:

The hand of the Lord was upon me, and the Lord carried me out in a spirit, and set me down in the midst of the valley, and it was full of bones: and He caused me to pass by them round about, and, behold, there were very many in the open valley; and lo, they were very dry. And, He said unto me: "Son of man, can these bones live?" And I answered: "O Lord God, Thou knowest."

Then he said unto me: "Prophesy over these bones and say unto them: O ye dry bones, hear the word of the Lord: Thus saith the Lord God unto these bones: 'Behold, I will cause breath to enter into you, and ye shall live, and I will lay sinews upon you and will bring up flesh upon you, and cover you with skin, and put breath into you, and ye shall live, and ye shall know that I am the Lord.'"

As Snider closed the book, a tray of bottles was wheeled noisily down the outside corridor. He ignored it. "I repeat . . . *no one* has the right to incise a dead human body without the deepest respect.

"In another light, you must be able to synthesize what is broken down, learn the most you possibly can from the experience, and then apply it to living examples. The myriad facets of anatomy are all written down in the various textbooks. You can find them in *Gray's* or *Morris'* or *Cunningham's* with equal ease. But only by being able to visualize what these books have to say from your own dissection, can you ever hope to retain it an hour past examination time. I caution you in all earnestness, it is the student who digs in and does the full share of the cutting and the cleaning who will remember longest the picture of what is there. Those of you who stand around jabbering or spend half the morning smoking in the stairwells, are wasting both your time and ours. You've got to roll up your sleeves the moment you enter the laboratory and begin working. Furthermore, you've got to know something about the material beforehand—lest not half as much will be gained. Dr. Southwell, my assistants, and myself stand ready to help you all we can, but we also expect a maximum effort on your part. We can't do your learning for you.

"The raw material has all been provided. The models and cut-sections in the library have been put there for your use. From time to time, we will show motion pictures to clarify certain problem areas. I take what I feel is understandable pride," Snider said, indulging in a modest smile, "in telling you that, thanks to the generous contributions of Dr. Gerald Mansfield, the noted neurosurgeon and a lifelong friend of mine, we have here at State what may well be considered the most modern, best-equipped anatomy department in the East. All of it is at your disposal. Admittedly, it serves my pride, but, more important, it serves your purpose."

As Snider paused to clear his throat, Dan felt an incongruous urge to applaud. Dropping his hands in time, he glanced from side to side. Carey sat with her back to him, facing front. The student to his right was cleaning his fountain pen with a piece of tissue paper. Another was picking his teeth. At the end of the table, Roger was busy scribbling notes as if trying to preserve Snider's every word for God-knows-what-purpose.

In the time remaining until noon, Dr. Snider began a lengthy discourse on the history of anatomy, a pet topic for him and one for which he taught an elective seminar in the second year to a sparse group of interested students.

"Anatomy has evolved," he said, "from the time of the Egyptians and their supernatural concepts of disease to the Greek Era of five and six centuries B.C. Hippocrates, in his writings on epilepsy—then believed to be an insanity inflicted by the gods—combined both a naturalistic and supernatural approach; though Hippocrates himself believed no one disease was any more divine in origin than another. . . ."

Dan listened for minutes at a time, jotting down unfamiliar names in his notebook for future reference and filling the rest of the page with doodlings of feather-tailed arrows and curving scimitar blades—all phallic symbols, he reflected, once aware of them.

Although he had slept scarcely five hours the night before, he had waked up fully restored, aware of a faint trace of Nora's perfume in the bedclothes and with the memory of her nude, sensuous body engulfing his mind. But now its vividness had faded, and Dan doubted that he could recapture it—or Nora for that matter—so easily again.

". . . Along about the dawn of the second century A.D.," Snider was saying, "the imposing figure of Galen came upon the scene. His gifted mind and driving curiosity led him to experiment with animals . . . Galen, otherwise known as 'The Great Experimentalist,' whose thinking dominated the teaching of anatomy for thirteen centuries!

"It awaited the coming of Vesalius, however, in the middle sixteen hundreds to add real impetus to this field. It is not without justification"—Snider nodded toward the portrait on the wall—"that Vesalius is called the Father of Anatomy. Here was a truly arresting figure! Willing to do dissection with his own hands rather than instruct some grubby underling in its doing, as had his more genteel predecessors. Here, finally, was the man who dared take issue with the entrenched doctrines of Galen; believing—as I want each one of you to believe—only what he could see and dissect out for himself, while that which his dissection repeatedly failed to reveal ceased to exist for him!"

As noon approached, Dan had filled a full page with notes: *Harvey in 1624, heart and circulation; Malpighi, the kidney; Anton van Leeuwenhoek, the microscope; Schwann, nerves . . .* finally, *Darwin.*

"Some of you might think," Snider concluded, "that I have wasted your time this session by mentioning the great names of the past. Nonetheless, I am firmly convinced that they richly deserve mention. That this historical perspective, along with the maturity of mind it takes to appreciate the necessity of such work, is truly of the utmost importance—otherwise, we might just as well let high school students do cadaver dissection . . ."

Snider pasued for an instant, his face stern and solemn. What he said next came as a surprise, almost a reprieve, to the class.

"Because of some malfunction that has developed in the ventilating system, the anatomy labs will remain closed this afternoon. The repairs should be completed late today, I'm told, and so tomorrow we'll begin the dissection of the scalp. Dr. Southwell plans to tell you all about it in the morning, but until then it wouldn't hurt you to do some reading on your own."

      ✿   ✿   ✿

The Anatomy Lesson

The afternoon seemed to pass interminably for Dan as Dr. Julian Laseur, professor of histology, occupied the podium. Not only did his subject lack the appeal of anatomy, but he himself was far inferior to Snider as both teacher and authority —which was not to say he lacked all distinction. The class would soon discover that his moods were as unpredictable as the state of his duodenal ulcer.

Laseur's introductory remarks concerned the microscope as a laboratory tool and the right and wrong way to use it. The very least they could do, he admonished the class, is learn not to obscure their field of vision with their eyebrows.

The students tittered dutifully and he went on: the histology department at State expected them all to know whatever was on the specially prepared slides they had been given. Since the two hundred dollar microscopes saw precisely the same things that the four hundred dollar microscopes saw, each student would be held responsible for what those things were, Laseur informed them, his teeth gleaming in a sardonic smile—whether he actually ever saw them or not.

This particular session, he said, would be spent on the liver cell—a typical cell in its basic architecture but rather an interesting one as far as cells go . . . And so forth until three o'clock when he wound up his peroration, deciding the class was ready to embark upon its maiden voyage into the microcosmic world of brightly stained cells and tissue sections which he inhabited so often and held so dear.

Heads bowed, spines bent, shoulders hunched forward, eyebrows raised, pupils dilated, a hundred students peered intently through microscope lenses, while below them, stretching far as their eye could see, stood row upon row of little liver cells.

At midnight Dan was in bed, smoking a last cigarette and reviewing that part of the dissection manual that pertained to tomorrow's work.

"Obtain a saw, a chisel and a mallet," it said, *"and proceed*

to remove the skullcap and calvaria. Mark out the line along which the saw is to be used by encircling the skull with a piece of string. Make the cut anteriorly, fully three-quarters of an inch above the margins of the orbit, and posteriorly, about half an inch or less above the external occipital prominence. . . ."

And with that, Dan reflected, the cadaver's destruction would begin. Bit by bit, he would be broken down into his anatomical parts, the first division separating him from his skullcap and brain, leaving a gaping hole at the hairline, an ugly crater atop a truncated head for them to stare at each morning; and in return for doing their first craniotomy, three medical students (the fourth of their group, they'd just learned, had dropped out of medical school the previous day) would be that much wiser about the mysterious makeup of that most marvelous of machines, the human body.

Chapter Five

"On the blackboard, right in front of your noses, I have written down seven important terms. Count 'em—seven!" rasped Southwell in a huckster's voice. "Skin, Fascia, Muscles, Bones, Blood Vessels, Nerves, and Lymphatics. Now they just might look simple to you at first, but they're not. I'm here to tell you they're not! These are the structures you all want to get in the habit of thinking about for each region of the body. Like the arm, for instance. The arm's made up of skin, ain't it? Then underneath the skin, there's fascia, muscles, bones, blood vessels, nerves, and lymphatics," Southwell intoned, hands clasped behind him, rocking back and forth on the balls of his feet.

He subsequently repeated the list, elaborating some on each term, and then, whether intending to be thorough or merely playful, recited it a third and fourth time.

"Okay," he said finally, unlocking his fingers behind his back and pulling down an anatomical chart on the wall. "Now let's talk about today's cuttin'. There are—you guessed it—seven layers to the scalp! . . ."

Forty minutes later, having exhausted the subject of the scalp as well as the students' interest in it, Southwell dismissed them and they drifted sluggishly out of the lecture hall—most toward the coffee-vending machines, a stolid or eager few toward the dissection lab.

Once again an obscure trepidation knotted Dan's stomach on pushing past the anatomy lab doors. As he strode through the first two rooms, inhaling the reek of formaldehyde, reluctant to look other than straight ahead, the sick sensation mounted. But by the time he reached the third and last room, the one containing his cadaver, the sensation began to abate. With only a handful of the metal lids to the coffinlike tables lowered, the scene lacked the blunt impact of his initial visit, though his emotions still ranged from fascination to repulsion.

"We'll take turns doing the cutting—okay?" Earl Cole suggested. He had preceded Dan and Carey to the table, opened the lids, and spread his black leather dissection kit over the cadaver's chest. "Anybody feel like going first?" he taunted—and, for lack of a reply, felt obliged to take the first turn himself.

Earl withdrew the scalpel from his kit, positioned its tip in the middle of the cadaver's brow with a tremulous hand, then made his initial incision, plunging it in until he felt bone. The bayonetlike blade sliced through yellowish subcutaneous fat and brownish-red muscle fibers down to the gristly layer of pearly-white fascia, then swept upward to the crown of the head and laterally behind one ear so as to form a triangular flap of skin. The flap, once completely undermined, was then folded back and fixed in place with a needle.

Repressing further thoughts of death, Dan held the flap of skin taut that Carey was undermining with a pair of forceps and tried to concentrate on what Earl was reading to them from the manual. But after watching Carey's plodding dissection for awhile, his gaze wandered: first to the maze of pipes in dusty plaster jackets in the ceiling, and then out the window at a dreary expanse of dark clouds, until Earl's sudden protest drew him back to the cadaver's head.

Carey, it appeared, while trying to clean a tortuous blood vessel, had accidentally severed a major branch of the facial nerve and Earl was righteously indignant.

"Oh, forget it, Carey," Dan consoled. "Don't look so glum.

What's one little nerve among thousands? We can always glue it back together."

"That's not the way you learn anatomy," Earl snapped. "It's sloppy dissection!"

"Hear that, Carey? Earl says it's sloppy. Better hand me the knife and go stand in the corner until our leader decides to forgive you. There's no room in our group for sloppy nerve-cutters. Right, Earl?"

Dan grinned at Earl's tight-lipped scowl, then took the scalpel from Carey and stepped around to the front of the table. He cut with deliberate calm, feeling the flesh yield with gritty reluctance to his strokes, so that when he was done, the bony top of the skull lay bare and four flaps of skin hung down over forehead and ears, partially hiding the cadaver's grim, frozen expression.

That preliminary step was apparently accomplished at other tables, too, because the room suddenly grew deafening with the grating of sawteeth against bone and the hammering of mallets against chisels—a dissonant chorus that continued at each table until a new and disturbingly different note was struck—the sharp crack of a steel wedge splitting open the skull to lay bare the underlying brain.

The sudden snap of bone yielding to the chisel and the shearing away of membranes as the skullcap was forcibly pulled from the head came as such a strange stimulus, so alien and repugnant to his senses, that it sent an involuntary shiver down Dan's spine and forced him to take a step back from the table.

"Man, oh man, will you look at that!" Earl suddenly cried, and every head around them turned sharply in their direction.

Dan edged Earl firmly aside to stare down at the discovery of a *subdural* hematoma: a wine-red blood clot, the size of a small saucer in circumference and more than an inch thick, which bulged out from between its enveloping membranes of dura and arachnoid to press against the convolution of their cadaver's brain. He called Pat Walsh, the anatomy assistant assigned to their section of the room, to come over.

"Found a hematoma, huh?" Pat confirmed, after a quick look at the misshapen brain exposed in the cranial vault. "Well, that's what it is, all right. Plenty big, too."

"Do you think it might've been what killed him?" Carey asked.

"Might have," Pat speculated, pressing the margins of the clot with his fingertips. "Feels pretty soft, wouldn't you say? Go ahead and feel for yourself." He stepped aside for her.

Carey felt the clot gingerly and nodded. "Being that soft," Pat said, "indicates it was fairly fresh—that it probably formed shortly before he died. Otherwise the clot would've had time to organize and feel more rubbery."

"But could it have killed him?" Carey repeated.

"I guess it might've at that. Surprised to find something like this in here, though. Usually a medico-legal case. What I mean is, when a guy dies after a blow on the head, especially one hard enough to give him a skull fracture or something like this, the law requires an autopsy to determine the exact cause of death, and the corpse never ends up here. We get most of our bodies from prisons or mental institutions, you know, or sometimes old-age homes. Rare to see something like this turn up. Whoever the coroner was who examined this guy sure missed the boat!"

"A blow on the head could do it, huh?" Dan asked, after most of the other students had drifted back to their tables.

"Sure," Pat told him, "provided it was hard enough. Any severe trauma to the head—football injury, auto accident, a bad fall even. They happen to boxers all the time."

"This guy even looks like he might've been a boxer," Dan mused.

"Yeah, maybe he was," Pat agreed. "Had the build for it, all right. I guess you ought to consider yourselves lucky the medico-legal boys missed autopsying this guy; that way you got a real good body to work on. In fact, one of the youngest I've seen. We had this colored girl who looked like she might've been around twenty in here two, three years ago. Died of schizophrenia, I think. . . . Well, no, that's not right. You don't die of that, do you? Must've been something else."

"Well, fun's over. What say we get back to work?" Earl said, losing interest in Pat's banter and not wanting the other tables to get ahead of them. Dipping his hands into the cranial vault to grip the flaccid gel of a brain between his fingers, he proceeded to spout directions, and Pat, evidently dismissed, went back to his post in the corner, recognizing and deferring to the aggressive type of student Earl showed himself to be.

Dan followed after him. "Tell me more about it, Pat?" he said. "I mean, how does a doctor go about diagnosing a hematoma like that? What are the signs and symptoms?"

"Well, fellow, you'd probably be better off asking one of the MD assistants that, since I'm strictly an anatomist by trade. From what I've heard though, they can be pretty tricky. Say the victim's a boxer. Well, after getting knocked out, he can come to and seem perfectly well for hours. Sometimes even days. But if that torn vessel keeps oozing—it's usually one of the cerebral veins that empties into the sagittal sinus, you know—then the clot keeps expanding in that closed compartment between membranes and pressing on the brain. The guy starts having headaches or maybe trouble seeing—getting drowsier and drowsier all the time. Finally, when the brain gets squeezed hard enough, he goes into coma. But the tricky part is, each subdural can behave differently. Sometimes the whole picture takes weeks to develop. On the other hand, if he gets another good whack on the head in the meantime, it happens real fast. Just like this!" Pat snapped his fingers.

"Can't they do anything to treat it?" Dan asked.

"Oh, sure, if it's caught in time. In that case, a surgeon can drill some holes in the skull and suction out the clot. Matter of fact, I once knew a fellow—football player from my hometown—who had an operation like that, and afterward—"

Pat was interrupted by a student calling from a nearby table and his story went unfinished. Dan returned to his own table in time to watch Earl remove the cadaver's quivering brain *en masse* and place it in a jar of fixative solution to preserve it for future study.

Twenty minutes later, work throughout the three rooms came to a halt as word was passed that Dr. Snider awaited them in the lecture hall. Since that day's schedule also allotted the early part of the afternoon to dissection, few groups bothered to tidy up their tables or replace the metal lids before leaving the lab. Most of the cadavers were simply left exposed with their skullcaps missing, their brains visible or removed. That they were permitted to remain this way was not out of disrespect, Dan realized, for that was no longer an issue. The day before had been set aside for meditation and reverence; this one and all that would follow were for quick, clean dissection and hard work. It was doubtless the main reason why no one, except authorized medical school personnel, was ever permitted beyond the locked doors of the anatomy lab.

Chapter Six

At five o'clock, in the waning light of the autumn afternoon, Dan stood on the front steps of the medical school, feeling comfortably released from the trying duties of the day and waiting for Carey to join him. He had invited her to dinner after both of them had rejected Earl's proposal to stay on and study the anatomical models in the library.

Carey appeared within a few minutes wearing a tan cashmere coat buckled at the waist and a hastily applied smear of lipstick.

"God, this fresh air smells good!" she said and sniffed gratefully. "The way that formaldehyde makes my eyes water, I don't dare wear much makeup anymore or it'd be streaked all over my face."

"The lipstick looks good," Dan told her.

"Thanks. So do you." She posed flirtatiously for him, arms akimbo, pelvis tilted forward. "Where're we going? Chinese place?"

"No. Let's find some quiet bar first."

"I know a place on Stuart Street. The Saxony."

"Okay," Dan said and took her arm to cross the street. They looked through the plate-glass window of the sandwich shop on the corner at a group of white-jacketed interns and students eating at the counter, then turned left.

"Where're you rooming?" Carey asked.

"Hotel—The Somerset."

"Hmmm, sounds expensive," she said. "Are you that well-heeled?"

"No. It's just until I can find an apartment and maybe someone to share expenses with me. . . . Interested in being my roommate?"

Carey stopped walking to glance up at him quizzically. "Is that a proposal or a proposition?"

He grinned. "Neither. Just wishful thinking. You'd make a good one, though."

"A good what?"

"Roommate, bedmate, studymate—you name it," he said airily.

"Thanks. But how do you know how good a bedmate I'd be?"

"I don't. Do *you?*"

Her face wavered between a smile and a frown. "I seem to be trapped into making some kind of confession . . . Oh, well, might as well confirm it: I *don't* know. Not that I'm not curious —understand?"

Dan felt a stir of arousal. "How curious?"

"I think about it now and then."

"How about lately? Find you're thinking about it more often?"

"You mean, since I've met you?"

"No. Since you've started med school?"

Carey hesitated, then nodded. "How'd you know?"

"Just a guess. Same with me. Every time I leave that anatomy lab I want to grab the first girl in sight."

Carey slipped her arm from his and turned to face him. "Does that mean you're on the make now?"

"That's a hell of a question! Where's your feminine intuition?"

"It's underdeveloped in these matters—along with certain other parts of my anatomy. No, I mean it. Tell me."

Dan walked beside her in silence for a few paces, intrigued by her candor, undecided about his own feelings. Carey wasn't Nora, he realized, just as appealing but far less secure in her femininity, far less practiced in the giving and sharing of it. "Why do you want to know?" he finally asked, as they approached the neon-lit entrance to The Saxony.

"Oh, 'cause if you are, I'm afraid I might get terribly flustered. And if you're not, I'm going to go on talking about it."

"About what?"

"Life, sex, cadavers. I find myself thinking the damnedest things in that anatomy lab and I want someone I like and trust to talk to about them."

"All right," Dan said after seating her at a booth in the dimly lit interior of the lounge and ordering drinks. "But I still think we ought to room together. We could learn a lot of anatomy that way."

"No doubt," Carey said mockingly. "Yours and mine."

"Platonically then?"

"Afraid not. Wouldn't work out. I might sleepwalk some night and rape you in your bed." She waited until the waitress put their drinks down, then suggested, "It might be fun to study together, though."

"Where? Your place or mine?"

"Not the Somerset—that's for sure! I can just picture the house detective spotting me sneaking into your room with a stack of anatomy books under my arm. Probably think I was some kind of call girl looking for new positions to try on my clients. No, I'm afraid it'll have to be my place on the nights my two roommates are out. At least, until you find yourself an apartment."

"And then?"

"Then, if I can find myself a size ten chastity belt, I might even cook dinner for you once in a while. . . ." Her look turned reflective for a moment, then she frowned. "Oh, that's such goddamn virgin talk. The truth is, I'd probably be scared to come to your place."

"Why?" he said, amused. "You must've had passes made at you before?"

"Sure, but they were pretty one-sided. Boy did. I didn't. With you, it might be mutual." Her face colored.

"What's wrong with that?"

"Nothing, I suppose, except it's almost a cliché situation. Boy med student and girl med student leave their cadaver and go off to lose themselves in mad, passionate lovemaking. I know at least one girl that happened to—slept with three or four guys in her class—and I think I'm better able to understand why now. So, if that's reason enough for you, let's talk about something else. . . . What do you think of Earl?"

Dan grimaced. "Not worth discussing. Reminds me of too many grinds I had to compete with in premed."

She laughed. "All right, scratch Earl and order me another drink."

While he did, Carey studied his face. "How'd you get your nose broken?"

"Boxing. I used to box a little in college, and before that Golden Gloves. My Uncle Woody was an intercollegiate champ, almost made the Olympics, and taught me how. Boxing was quite a respectable sport in those days—before the hoods and gamblers ruined it."

"Were you any good?" she asked.

Dan shrugged. "So, so. Won the light heavyweight title at Williams my sophomore year, then tried out for the regimental boxing team in the Army. That was a mistake. Put me up against some real pros . . . One of them, a guy named Harold Johnson—he's a leading light heavyweight contender now—broke my nose."

"I kind of like it," Carey said. "That little bump on it makes you look more interesting. Do you miss boxing?"

"A little. I used to like hanging around boxers, hearing them talk—some of them, like Archie Moore, are real philosophers—and I liked the training. I'd even toyed with the idea of getting back into shape and fighting in some of those semipro matches out on Cape Cod—only no more. Not after today!"

"What happened today?" she asked, puzzled.

"What happened was we took the top of our cadaver's skull off and I decided I didn't want my brain to look like his: Not all dotted with small hemorrhages and not with a big hematoma pushing it lopsided. After seeing that, I know damned well I'll never climb into another ring. Be too scared my brain might bleed. . . . No, boxing used to be fun back in college, but it's over for me now."

"Did you enjoy college?"

"Oh, the first couple of years were okay. But after being in the Army it was hard settling down to study. How about you?"

"I didn't care much for it either. I was Army too—an Army brat. My dad's retired and living in Florida now, but for twenty-five years of his life he was a career soldier. They boosted him up a notch to colonel before his retirement, but for most of those years he only had captain's pay to support the five of us. It took a year-round waitress job and a scholarship to get me through Wellesley, which didn't leave much time for rolling hoops on the green. In fact, I didn't even date my first two years—which means that along with hoops I didn't roll anything else on the green!"

"Do I detect a bitter note in your voice?"

"Possibly. Not that I had all that many offers. The way I looked in those days: the glasses, the hair braided in a bun, the permanent slouch to my shoulders from carrying all those trays—I guess it put the charm boys off. Made them figure they weren't likely to find much action there."

Carey emptied her drink, then stared disconsolately into her glass. "Just once . . ." she began haltingly, "just once I wish one of them might've used some imagination, pictured what I might look like without glasses and with my hair worn long.

I really had it in for some of those Harvard and Yalie bastards who prowled around the dorms on weekends. I swore that if I ever got through medical school and a psychiatric residency, I'd castrate any ex-Ivy Leaguer who ever came to see me as a patient." Her eyes glittered for a moment, then she laughed. ". . . . See what a vindictive virgin I am, Dan. Maybe I'd better let you make love to me, after all, else I shudder to think what a hazard to the profession I'll be."

Dan smiled at the image of Carey verbally deballing legions of bow-tied, tweed-jacketed, anxiety-ridden Ivy Leaguers as an assembly-line conveyor dropped them one by one onto her office couch.

Although aware that her face was flushed, Carey smiled, too, wondering if it was the drinks or the camaraderie she felt or the cumulative horror of the past three days that was making her unravel emotionally. She realized she had told Dan far more about herself than she intended. Yet in doing so, some kind of psychic barrier within her had been breached and she felt so suffused with anticipatory pleasure that all it might take was a nod, a touch of his hand, for an emotional cashing in: for her to go willingly to his hotel, make love at his direction, even spend the night. But whether Dan ever sensed this was her surrendering moment, he said in a gentle, chiding voice, "All right, Car, I'll hold you to it, only let's see if you can cook first."

Out on the street, Carey turned her coat collar up against the chill night air and waited for Dan to pay the check. He joined her a moment later, his wallet still in his hand.

"Put your money away," she protested. "People will think I'm being bought."

Dan gripped her shoulders to prevent her from walking away and grinned at her. The Saxony's neon sign overhead cast a reddish glow over his face.

"God, you look like Satan himself!"

"You've made me horny enough!" he told her. "But now that we're both pleasantly tipsy, how about the Chinese food?"

Carey mulled the matter over with mock solemnity, then announced, "I'm afraid Chinese food's out!"

"How come?"

"To get to the Chinese district from here means we have to walk past the medical school and it looks too spooky at night."

"What do you mean—spooky?"

"Oh, you know. With all those plate-glass windows it looks like a factory full of dead people where only the ghouls work at night."

"My, my," he murmured, "I never knew you had such a warped imagination."

"Oh, I'm full of revelations tonight. But the farthest east I'm willing to walk is that Greek restaurant up the street."

At the end of dinner, as they sipped Metaxa and picked at the flaky crumbs of Baklava remaining on their plates, Carey said, "Your Uncle Woody sounds fascinating, Dan; all those books he writes! I can understand why the Bennington coeds still line up at his door. Ever try to do any writing yourself?"

"You mean, real writing—not term-paper stuff?"

"Real writing! The kind that if you publish pays you money."

"No. Nothing worth mentioning. But it's funny you should ask because, ever since what happened in the lab this morning— you know, us finding that hematoma—I've thought what a hell of a plot it could be for some author."

"Tell me."

"Well, say, a freshman med student like me finds out his cadaver didn't die a natural death but was murdered. Cleverly, diabolically murdered. Poisoned, maybe, or ice-picked through the base of the brain—anything that might get him past the coroner's scrutiny and an autopsy. Now, say, the med student discovers this, or maybe at first only suspects it, but can't prove anything. Nobody, not even his anatomy professor, takes him seriously. Whoever heard of a cadaver being murdered! So he decides the proof is up to him and tries to find out all he can about his cadaver's former life, hoping something might fit together for a motive. He goes snooping around his old haunts and learns he's been something of a shady character. A small-time crook, say, or a gambler. . . . No, wait, maybe it would be better if he were a boxer. Sure, a boxer who's gotten himself mixed up in some fix. In fact, working it from that angle might make it even more realistic, since I suspect our cadaver *was* a boxer at one time."

"Go on."

"Well, let's say the med student pieces enough together to figure out who might've wanted to kill him, only still can't get his hands on any hard proof. And by now the real murderer has gotten wind of what he's up to and goes after him. What then?"

"What?" she prompted.

He shrugged. "I don't know. Haven't thought it out that far. But what do you think of it as a story? I know it sounds a little farfetched, but—"

"But what if it were true!" she exclaimed, her eyes widening. "My God! The mere thought makes me shudder. Now I'll probably have nightmares."

"Then spend the night with me. You won't have nightmares that way."

"No, nor am I likely to get any sleep."

"I mean it," Dan urged, realizing their evening was almost over and loath to return to his hotel room alone, to face the long night and the desolateness which was sure to descend on him the next morning as he steeled himself against returning to the anatomy lab. "No sex even," he promised. "Just company."

Carey hesitated. "Sorry," she said after a moment, "I don't dare. My poor roommates would be scandalized. But let me know when you want to study together and I'll buy a cookbook."

A rueful look passed briefly across Dan's face. Then he

grinned and raised his glass of brandy to her, recognizing their needs were now reversed and that Carey had made certain he recognized it through her choice of words. Clever girl, he thought and felt a lingering regret that he had not taken her to his hotel when he could have earlier. But maybe it was wise to postpone it: Next time he'd be less likely to confuse who was seducing whom.

Chapter Seven

The days faded from October. The weather turned cold and the last withered leaves of autumn fell from the trees and rustled in gutter marches. It was a season that all through his high school years had meant football for Dan: scrimmaging until dusk, and then, with his muscles aching, walking home with gym bag in hand. But that had been long ago—before college and Korea. Now it meant carrying a microscope and books home to study, when he could study, or sleep, when he could sleep, or brood, when he could do neither. For the first time in his life he felt directionless, drifting, hanging on. Was being a doctor what he really wanted? There were times—when he sat in the observation gallery of the hospital across the street and watched a team of surgeons operate—when he felt sure it was. Then, there were the somber moods which overcame him in class, or late at night, when he was sure of nothing. Still, he plodded on in the vague belief that sooner or later something was bound to occur to either fire his interest in medical school or so discourage him that he would drop out. It was nothing tangible, merely a gut instinct on his part, but it helped sustain him through his doldrums.

More than a week had passed since the first anatomy exam: a comparatively peaceful interval. After dividing the weekend between studying and shopping for second-hand furniture to fill his newly rented apartment, he awoke reluctantly to Monday, a dark and drizzly day, knowing that the entire morning was scheduled for cadaver dissection. Feeling faintly guilty for having missed the previous lab session, he left his apartment earlier than usual and made the fifteen-minute walk to the medical school in a light rain.

As he turned the corner onto Stuart Street, he spotted Carey ahead of him and hurried to catch up with her.

"Hi!" she said, as he drew abreast. "Where were you Friday?"

"Overslept. Did I miss much?"

She shrugged. "Some nasty digs from Earl. Otherwise, not too much."

"Did we finish up on the brain?"

"Uh-huh. From the pons straight down to the medulla ob-longata! Start on the thorax today. Did you—as our quaint friend, Southwell, likes to say—read up on it in the *big book?*"

"Sure. Spent all weekend at it."

"Did you really?" Carey asked. "I somehow have trouble picturing *you* staying home all alone on a Saturday night and studying."

"Then, come on over and join me next time. Just you, me, and *Gray's Anatomy.*"

"All right—providing you've got more furniture than the last time. I might've stayed longer then, except the only thing in that apartment was your bed."

"Oh, it's all fixed up. A little seedy, maybe, but the best the Salvation Army had to offer. See for yourself, why don't you? Next Saturday."

"All right, I will," Carey said, openly pleased at the invitation.

Arriving on the fifth floor, they strode down the corridor, passing the grotesque, if now familiar, cross sections of human brain adorning its walls like a collection of gigantic butterflies, until they reached the anatomy lab. As all students automatically did, they paused to take a last breath of formalin-free air before pushing their way past the swinging doors.

After the week of brain-slicing which had spared them the sight of their cadaver, their first glimpse of him in the shadowy setting before the metal lids were completely lowered was jolting. With his skullcap gone and his face and neck dissected to the bone, he vaguely resembled a headless horseman.

A few minutes later, Earl Cole came bustling through the door, his dissection tools rattling around in the oversized black bag he carried, and joined them at the table.

"Well, greetings!" he exclaimed, chipper as usual in the morning, and stood opposite them rubbing his hands together.

"Shhh, not so loud," Dan replied. "You'll wake the dead."

"And a good morning to you, too, Lassiter," he said, undaunted. "Glad you could make it. We missed you Friday."

"Did you? Did he really miss me?" Dan looked at Carey archly.

"Hmmm. . . ." She pretended to concentrate. "Can't remember, off hand. I do recall he had a few choice comments to make, but I don't think missing you was among them."

"Oh, well." Dan shrugged. "It's the sentiment that counts. . . . Say, Earl—ever hear of an old movie actor named Laird Cregar?"

"Laird Cregar? No, I don't believe I have. Why?" he asked warily.

"Just wondered. His most famous role was as Jack the Ripper in the movie, *The Lodger*. Remember him now? . . . No? Well, one of the creepiest parts was the way old Jack kept lugging his butcher knives around with him in a big black doctor's bag. Just like you, Earl. . . . What else you carry in there?"

"Never mind," Earl said, his cheeks coloring. "Just keep your nose out of it." He removed his dissection manual and tools from the bag, then kicked it under the table. ". . . Well, unless you've got some more little wisecracks, what say we get down to work?"

Dan took the first turn. Mouth-breathing until his nose grew tolerant of the stench of putrid flesh and embalming fluid, he made a deep incision in the cadaver's chest, slicing transversely across the upper part of the breastbone, then following in the groove of soft flesh between the first and second ribs until the cut extended from shoulder to shoulder.

The taut, waxy-pale skin parted bloodlessly under the blade, opening up a gaping wound: yellowish from beads of fat at its edges and a meaty, reddish-brown from the thin layer of muscle overlying the ribs at its base. Dan undermined the skin flap he had created and folded it back, covering the cadaver's chin. He then swapped his scalpel for a pair of bone scissors and cut through the gristly-hard rib cartilages bordering each side of the sternum. Once all six joints were clipped, he pried loose and pulled down the entire breastplate so that it hung like an inverted shield over the stomach.

Beneath this windowlike opening in its carapace lay the thoracic contents. From his vantage point atop a stool, with Carey and Earl crowding so close that their breathing made sucking sounds in his ear, Dan looked down at the lungs: paired masses of spongy, mottled, purplish-gray tissue and, between them, a now pulseless heart. There it was, he mused: the pump of life; next to the brain, the most awesome and acclaimed of human structures. The triangular-shaped muscle, tucked in un-prepossessingly between overlapping ledges of lung, was enveloped in a thick membrane, the pericardial sac, transparent and glistening in life but now a pearly-white with streaks of fat the color of fresh egg yolks clinging to its surface. He cut away the tough, tendinous attachment of the diaphragm still anchoring the sternum to the chest and removed it entirely so as to get a better view.

And thus laid bare, the cadaver's heart gave Dan pause. Though at first it had seemed no more real to him than a calf's heart or the plastic model in the library, its reality grew as he peered down at it. This workhorse structure had once beat over one hundred thousand times a day—the closest thing in nature to perpetual motion. And there must have been times, Dan knew, when it had thundered. He only wished there was some way it could tell him why. But a *telltale* heart existed only in the fiction of Poe.

Working methodically with scalpel and probe, he spent the next several minutes exposing and tracing the course of major nerves, stripping away fat and fascia from the sheaths of latex-injected blood vessels; finally, freeing up the lungs from adhesions and cutting their vascular connections with the heart in preparation for removing them.

Earl's turn with the scalpel came next. He took a tight grip on its handle, twisted his wrist to turn the blade sideways, and lowered it into the chest. What he did next made Dan shudder. Like a butcher in a chicken coop, Earl slashed across the cadaver's windpipe high in the chest and severed it in a single swipe.

Dan had once seen a sentry with his throat slit like that. The company commander had ordered the corpse to be left at its post for all the men to see and learn vigilance before finally burying it. Dan had almost forgotten the incident until now, but Earl's slicing blade brought back all its abject horror.

He watched a while longer as Earl removed the lungs and stored them in a plastic bag, then wandered away from the table. Dry as his mouth was, he wanted a cigarette and debated whether to light one here, in violation of the rules, or to go outside to smoke. Southwell's hawk-eyed presence in a corner of the room decided the issue.

In the corridor, Dan was about to light up when he noticed a group of students clustered around the bulletin board outside Snider's office. As he walked toward them, he saw an excited Roger Hickman break away to spread the word inside the lab that the exam marks had been posted. Dan edged forward, hunting the anonymous numeral that told his exam grade. He finally found it in the lowest of four columns that ranked success or failure and his spirits sank. In the company of twelve others, he had failed to survive Snider's harsh judgment.

*   *   *

The Anatomy Lesson

The student lounge, once invaded by freshmen, was a circus of noise and unrestrained revelry at lunchtime.

Larry Parish, a student from Pittsfield, Massachusetts, whom Dan knew slightly, having competed against him in high school sports, waved him over.

"What'ja get?" he asked, in the suddenly popular idiom, the common greeting.

"Nothing too good," Dan replied.

"Me, either. I barely squeezed by myself. . . . Joe Connelly flunked, you know?"

And many others, Dan was told; names that hovered unspoken in the air and after quick, cautious side glances dipped in and out of luncheon conversations. Larry already knew the names of six who had failed and seemed more than a little curious to learn the rest.

"What about Carey?" Dan asked.

"Oh, she passed. The other girls didn't do so hot though—except, of course, for that bitch, Phyllis. You know, the fullback-type from Radcliffe. She must've had plenty of time to study the way she looks . . . Say, speaking of Carey, there's something I've been meaning to ask you. I know it's none of my business, but, uh, you gettin' any there?"

Dan was more amused than offended by the question. He had heard of Larry's prowess with the ladies: seducer of nurses, secretaries, even female med students. Though having no knowledge of what his sex life was like before, Dan wondered if Larry might have reacted to exposure to the anatomy lab with the same rampant sexuality as he. But while Dan's libido had quickly waned after Nora; had, in fact, inverted, leaving him temporarily uninterested in sex, Larry's must have continued unabated. With his swimmer's build, sandy hair, and boyish good looks, he probably deserved his reputation as class satyr, Dan decided. Still, Larry was highly likable. Another ex-veteran —a former medical corpsman—Larry was a capable, hard-working student who, for all his chronic horniness, displayed an underlying seriousness about medicine.

"Well—" he prompted.

"Why do you want to know?" Dan asked lightly.

"No particular reason. Just my nature, I guess," Larry said with a quick grin. "Hell, you know as well as I do she's the best looker in the class."

"So?"

"So, as one ex-Korean *moose* chaser to another, if there's anything there to get, and you're not interested in gettin' it—well, let me try?"

"Jesus Christ! Is getting laid all you ever think about? Don't you have any other diversions?"

"Sure. I play handball once in a while . . . Do you?"

Dan nodded.

"Then, we'll have to get together for a game at the 'Y'."

"How often do you play?"

"Once or twice a week. Keeps me in shape for sex."

At three that afternoon Dan was called out of histology class and told to report to Snider's office. Though surprised and unnerved by the summons, he managed to calm himself while waiting in Snider's reception room. When the door to the inner office finally opened, Joe Connelly came out, glanced at Dan without expression, and quickly left the room. A moment later, Snider appeared in the doorway and beckoned. He waited for Dan to enter, then slipped by him to speak to his secretary.

Dan looked around the office at the diplomas and inscribed photographs of colleagues framed on the walls and at the personal mementos on Snider's desk. One in particular, a silver loving cup bearing the anatomy professor's name as coach of the championship Tufts College wrestling team of 1938–39, surprised him. He never would have suspected that Snider had the slightest interest in athletics. It only went to show how little he or any of his classmates really knew about their professor. And it *was* little, Dan reflected.

Virtually nothing was known of Snider's private life—where he lived, with whom, or in what style—since no student had ever been invited to his home. It *was* known he was married and that he occasionally attended Boston Symphony concerts, for he mentioned these items in class, but nobody ever saw him in any of the local restaurants or cocktail lounges and he never attended any of the medical school's social functions. Two popular theories purported to explain these absences: one, that Snider was too autocratic (a general never mixes socially with the troops). The other, that he was an ex-alcoholic who avoided such bibulous affairs for fear of slipping off the wagon. Though there was absolutely no evidence of Snider's past drinking habits, the rumor persisted from class to class, abetted in part because Snider was known to employ ex-alcoholics as handymen around the department.

One member of the junior class claimed he had spotted Snider riding the Boston-and-Maine train to Pittsfield once, sporting a toupee on his bald pate and enjoying the cozy company of a bosomy young blonde. The story had circulated widely for a time and speculation about the mystery lady abounded—her presumed identity ranging from office secretary to burlesque queen to oversexed wife of one of his colleagues. But since the tale-spreader had once had a severe run-in with Snider, his credibility was in doubt.

Even so, as he sat on the edge of a straight-backed chair in his office, Dan wondered how much more there might be to Snider's human side. His aloofness, his domineering attitude in class, might be merely a pose, a mechanism to insure that his students took him and their work seriously.

Dan's commanding officer in basic training had been that way. Colonel Gunderson had been a martinet: a dour, humorless man who demanded absolute discipline from his subordinates and drove them almost to the point of collapse. But, as Dan was ultimately astonished to learn, he kept a list, constantly updated, of all his trainees who had been in combat, and the survivors received a brief note from him upon their discharge. In simple language, Gunderson had thanked them for serving their country, hoped they now better appreciated the need for the rigorous training he had put them through, and wished them well for the future. The letter had seemed to Dan to be a belated bid for understanding from a sensitive and melancholic man, and it had touched him deeply. Yet he had been too embarrassed to even attempt to reply. Nor, to his knowledge, had anyone else he had served with. He was sure, however, that none of them took the letter flippantly.

Could Snider possibly feel the same sense of mission? he wondered. But he seemed to be a much more urbane and extroverted sort of man than Colonel Gunderson, and so Dan doubted it—especially now as he observed him sitting behind his desk sorting through a pile of blue-covered examination booklets.

"Well," Snider finally said in his quick, distinctive way, implying that whatever followed would be businesslike and to the point. "I assume you know why I've called you in here."

"I've seen the exam grades, if that's what you mean," Dan said, staring him in the eye.

Snider's eyebrows lifted slightly at the cool reply. "Understand, Lassiter," he went on as if trying out a more paternal approach, "it's not my intention to castigate you for failing that exam. That's not the purpose of this talk at all. I realize as well as anyone what a strain the first few months of medical school can be, and so I'm far more interested in finding out the cause of a student's difficulty than in merely rehashing exam blunders with him. The work we ask of you certainly isn't easy, is it?"

"No, sir."

"Is keeping up with the great volume of reading we assign giving you any trouble?"

"Not really."

"The dissection then?"

Dan hesitated; it *was* the dissection, but did he dare talk to Snider about it? An ingrained reticence, an aversion to self-revelation argued against it, yet at the same time something in

The Anatomy Lesson

Snider's probing look seemed to be drawing him out. "I suppose, in a roundabout way, it is the dissection . . ." he began haltingly.

"In what way?"

"Well, not the mechanical part so much as the realization that you're doing it on a dead human body. Makes you think about more than just anatomy. . . ."

"Indeed, it does," Snider said softly. "For some, it's the most difficult obstacle to overcome. But you mustn't allow yourself to dwell on it too much."

"Why not? With all the time we spend at it, there's not much else to distract you."

"Maybe not. But there's a lot to learn and no better way to learn it than by visualizing it from your own dissection."

"Yes, I've heard you say that before. But it's not exactly the same as cutting up a frog in chordate anatomy, you know. It's not that the bodies make me queasy or anything—I've seen worse sights in Korea. But even that's not quite the same, is it? Dead men on a battlefield don't look like cadavers—not after the first day anyway. . . ."

"Go on." Snider prompted.

Dan drew a deep breath. "What I mean to say is, well, what's the purpose of spending so much time in there? Sure, it makes some students drop out the first day, but after that—what? What does it really test: your aptitude or how much you can stomach? Frankly, Dr. Snider, I find it dehumanizing."

Snider's look momentarily hardened, then relented. "I see . . . and rather than take the least offense, let me say I fully understand your feelings. In fact, I believe they do you credit. But as I've tried to explain before, dissecting a cadaver just happens to be one of those things—no matter how disturbing, even dehumanizing, you may find it—that is quite essential to the study of anatomy. There's simply no adequate substitute, I'm afraid."

He hesitated, thinking to temper his unyielding opinion with a smile, but the wry, forebearing look on Dan's face made him

66

change his mind. "All right, so I'm just reciting the old, traditional arguments and that's not being particularly helpful, is it? Telling you to forget what I said that first day—forget there are dead human bodies in there—and just do your job! In other words, since I still have several more students to see this afternoon—a brush-off!" He sighed deeply, then continued. "But, to tell the truth, Lassiter, you're the first of the half dozen or so students I've already talked to who's ever admitted the dissection is giving you trouble. The rest are either too blasé or don't feel it's the manly thing to do. But evidently you're different—or at least that's what you've led me to believe."

Dan nodded, surprised and relieved by the anatomy professor's candor.

"All right. I grant you are," Snider said snappishly. "Now tell me why?"

"I'm not sure—exactly. I don't even know whether it's the dissection or the damned nonchalance of most of my classmates that bothers me the most. You know, the ones who drink Coke in there and think up funny nicknames to give their cadavers. Me, I want to know much more than I already do about where cadavers come from—where mine, in particular, came from—and who the hell he is."

Snider leaned forward in his swivel chair. "What table do you—does your group—have?"

"What number? Oh, twenty-four."

A deeply preoccupied look passed over Snider's face, then he nodded. "He's the youngest one, isn't he? The best preserved. I can see how that could prove upsetting to you." He glanced at his watch. ". . . And I'd be happy to discuss the way we go about obtaining cadavers, the legalities of it, some other time. It has quite a fascinating history, you know: dating back to the sixteenth century when, as a result of certain royal edicts, most cadavers were purchased from grave-robbers or assorted assassins. Nowadays, of course, our sources are much more respectable." He smiled faintly. "I'm still undecided as to what to do with this fat, old carcass of mine. I suppose by rights I should set an example with it and will it to the school. But I've seen the cavalier way some of my students comport themselves and I don't particularly relish the thought of my calvarium being used as an ashtray."

The next moment the phone buzzed, and as Snider instructed his secretary about some administrative matter, Dan collected his thoughts. Though he enjoyed the anatomy professor's unbending and sharing confidence with him, his mind continued to dwell on an earlier event: the strange, almost unmistakable look of recognition Snider had shown on learning who his cadaver was. How much more, besides name and number, might he know, Dan speculated, and had he possibly known him in life? But if Snider had wanted to tell him anything, he probably would have done so by now, instead of talking about cadavers in broad generalities. Was he purposely being evasive, Dan wondered. And did he dare challenge him on it?

Replacing the phone, Snider eyed his watch again. "Well, I don't know how much help I might've been to you, but I've enjoyed our little chat. And as I mentioned before, I'd be more than happy to discuss with you at some future time how a medical school such as ours goes about obtaining its supply of cadavers."

"Thanks. I'll look forward to it," Dan replied. "But in the meanwhile I wonder if you'd mind telling me one thing more? My cadaver's name."

"His name? I . . . I don't understand?"

"I'm just asking for his name."

"I realize that." The perplexed look on Snider's face turned guarded. "Why do you want to know?"

Dan shrugged. "I suppose I could say it had something to do with the business of nicknames; you know—'Socrates' or 'Smiley' or 'Dead Ernest'—but that's not the reason. Maybe it's nothing more than morbid curiosity on my part, but since I'm expected to know the names of all his anatomical parts, I'd like to know *his* name, too. That's not such an unusual request, is it?"

"No," said Snider, "not unusual at all. Many of my students ask it. But it's the policy of the school not to give out names."

"Why not?"

"Oh, many reasons," Snider answered vaguely. "There's always the remote possibility it might turn out to be a relative. We take great care to prevent something like that from happening, but there are stories. I'm sure you've heard them . . . In your case, Lassiter, I'd venture to say there might even be a more cogent reason. Maybe I'm mistaken—I don't know—but I think you might be overreacting. Allowing your cadaver to prey too heavily on your mind. War veterans tend to do that."

"Why—veterans?"

"You'd think just the opposite might be true, wouldn't you? Yet, it's not. It happens only rarely, of course, but I've seen a reaction similar to yours among veterans of World War II. I don't claim to have the precise explanation, but I have a pet theory about it. Care to indulge me?"

Dan nodded vigorously.

"Well, it has to do with conditioning, the development of tolerance to a given stimulus. Only in this case it's not hay fever pollen you're reacting to—it's death! The average freshman student, unless he happened to have worked summers in a hospital or been in the Army, has seen, maybe, one or two dead bodies—usually that of a parent or relative—prior to starting medical school. So what happens that first day? He is so overwhelmed by the array of cadavers before him that the sensory input to his brain overloads it and a kind of psychic short circuit takes place. In other words, the spectacle becomes unreal. No matter how much time he spends in the lab he never truly accepts the reality of what's there. Soon as anatomy's over, it's blocked out for good. My students usually remember me, for better or worse, but most of them can't remember the slightest detail of what went on, day by day, in the course. Oh, they might recall their initial shock and maybe a few humorous happenings, but all of the rest becomes blurred—simply because they were never able to accept its reality in the first place. Do you follow me so far?"

"I think so," Dan said.

"Good. Now a veteran like yourself who's been in combat has seen enough of death so that some of the initial horror has begun to wear off. He's become inured to it—not completely, of course, but enough so that he isn't frightened out of his wits the first time he comes across a cadaver. For someone like that, someone sufficiently conditioned to death, the spectacle of what he sees that first day cannot be denied. As a result, the dissection bothers him not less, but more. . . . That's what I suspect might've happened to you, Lassiter."

"Maybe," Dan said, impressed if not particularly comforted by Snider's analysis. "Say it did—what do I do about it?"

"For one thing, remain as impersonal toward the task of cadaver dissection as you can. Harden yourself to it—but not all the way. In all my years as an anatomist, I never have. . . . Why, I can still remember the cadaver I had as a freshman—quite vividly, in fact—and that was almost forty years ago. He was a robust man in his sixties, a seafaring man. I knew that from his weather-beaten complexion and the tattoos on his body. He even died of rat-borne typhus: a sailor's disease . . . No, I'll never forget him. I too did a lot of soul-searching my freshman year—and a lot of heavy drinking. But I never did find out his name, and I don't advise you to. From all you've told me thus far, I'm convinced you've allowed such matters to preoccupy you too much. After all, that's one of the reasons we assign so much reading material—to get your mind off it. To make you far more fearful of something else—namely, failing the course!"

"Just how badly did I do on the exam?" Dan asked, purposely changing the subject, suspecting more strongly than ever that Snider did know something about his cadaver, but realizing now was not the time to pursue it. He had already stretched the time allotted to him, and Snider's patience, enough.

"Oh, not so bad that you can't redeem yourself on the next. We don't give out actual grades; there's no need. Seventy-five percent is passing, and if you'd done much worse than that, you can be sure I wouldn't be so lenient with you."

Dan rose from his chair. "Well, I've taken up enough of your time. But thanks for spending so long with me. I realize how busy you must be."

"Not at all," Snider said, rising with him. "It gives me pleasure to occasionally find a student who thinks like you. Makes me feel my little talk at the beginning of the term wasn't entirely a wasted effort."

"It wasn't," Dan said. "It wasn't."

Chapter Eight

The rain had slackened by the time Dan left the medical school that evening, but a damp, cold wind off the bay whipped through the streets. With the coming midterm elections a day off, a loudspeaker perched atop a truck on Tremont Street blared Sousa march music, while between selections the doom-mongering voice of a local politician trumpeted above the din of traffic like some heavenly archangel.

Dan wandered through the downtown movie district for a while, reliving the events of the day until, thoroughly chilled by the wind cutting through his thin raincoat, he stopped at a cafeteria for supper. The first few spoonfuls of the highly seasoned chili tasted savory, but then his appetite waned and he merely picked at it. When the cafeteria grew crowded and the waitress asked him to share his table, he got up and left. He roamed through Boston Common, listening to the harangue of one orator and the cajoling of another, until their rhetoric grew repetitious, their voices croaky, and their posturings absurd. Impulsively, he decided to drop in on Nora McGuire at the Boston *Post*. The one time he had visited her there he'd found it fascinating to sit in her small cubicle of an office and watch the mounting tension and last-minute flurry of activity as the nine o'clock deadline for filing copy approached.

The entrance to the *Post* editorial rooms on Washington

Street was up a shabby staircase which vibrated from the roar and hum of rolling presses beneath it. Dan paused outside the city room to listen to the hubbub of clattering typewriters, ringing telephones, and editors shouting frantically to staffers for copy. A sign on the door read: NO ADMITTANCE EXCEPT FOR AUTHORIZED PERSONNEL. He opened it and strode quickly through the long room, trying to appear as inconspicuous as possible. He had almost made it to Nora's office when a short, burly man bustled out of the editor's office, colliding with him in the aisle. "Who're you?" he asked brusquely, pointing a finger at Dan's chest. "You the advance man Haggerty sent over?"

Dan hesitated a split second then nodded, remembering that President Eisenhower was addressing a Republican rally at Boston Garden that night and his press secretary was named Haggerty. "That's me," he said.

The city editor looked leery. "Jeez," he said, shaking his head, "you guys get younger each year!"

"Yeah, well, excuse me. Got to phone in."

Walking away unhurriedly, Dan reached the corridor leading to Nora's office with considerable relief. He entered quietly, catching her with her back to him, busily cutting a photograph to size before trying to fit it into a mock-up of a fashion page. Suddenly aware of someone behind her, she pivoted. "Why Dan! You frightened me," she exclaimed, smiling. "Am I glad to see you! I'm bored to tears and, worse yet, fresh out of cigarettes."

"You about through for the night?"

"Oh, just about. The rest can wait. Pull up a chair, give me a cigarette, and tell me all about the gruesome work you do."

He grimaced. "Must I? I'd rather talk about something else for a change."

"Things tough, huh?" Nora reached for his hand, giving it a consoling squeeze. "All right, what would you rather talk about?"

"I don't want to talk at all. Not here anyway." He described how he had bluffed his way past her editor moments before. ". . . So maybe we'd better get out of here before he catches on."

Nora chuckled. "Maybe we'd better. Two staffers didn't show up for work tonight and Rudy's fit to be tied. Where would you like to go?"

"How about the lounge next door?"

Nora looked at her watch. The lounge was a hangout for *Post* reporters and usually filled up after press time. "All right, shouldn't be too crowded now."

"Or, if you'd rather, we could go to my place?" He gave her a challenging look. "You still haven't seen it."

"What's there to see?" she asked, feigning innocence.

"Oh, nothing much. A few airline posters, a view of Beacon Street from ground level, and a Murphy bed that falls out of the wall when you slam the front door."

"It just falls? Or do you have it rigged that way?"

"Rigged? Hell, no! It's almost brained me a couple of times. But I've got the doorknobs tied together with a rope so there's no chance of it happening now."

Nora laughed. "Good, I'd hate to have to explain to my priest that we ended up in bed again because one fell on us."

"This all right?" Dan asked, seating Nora at a rear table in the lounge.

"Fine," she said, yawning. "Sorry—it's the hour, not the company."

"Why don't you tell that damned newspaper of yours to hire another woman's page editor and let you go back to doing your column? Stop working you so hard."

"Never mind. Guess who I'm interviewing tomorrow?"

"Some flashy dresser, I suppose."

"Yes, but who? Whose picture did you see in the *Post* today?"

"Sugar Ray Robinson's," he answered straight-faced.

"Right on the nose!"

"Really? Wow!"

"No, not really. It's Ann Sheridan, wise guy. The oomph girl."

"Then, I'm damned disappointed. I bet you don't even know who Sugar Ray is."

"The lightweight champion," she answered pertly.

"Lightweight, hell. He weighs one hundred and fifty pounds!"

"Well, how much do lightweights usually weigh?"

"How much does Ann Sheridan weigh?"

"Let's drop the subject or next you'll be asking how much *I* weigh—and I've been putting on a few pounds lately. . . . Say, speaking of boxers, how is that story of yours coming along. You know—the mystery you were plotting last time. The one about your cadaver?"

Before he could reply, their drinks came. Nora exchanged a few pleasantries with the waitress, then turned back to Dan, only to find him staring moodily into his Scotch.

He looked up sharply as she touched his hand. "Oh, the book!" he said, after she had repeated the question. "The truth is, I haven't been giving it much thought lately. Besides, I can't seem to find out any more about him. Not even his name. I took a chance and asked Snider for it today, but he wouldn't tell me. Against school policy, he claimed, so I didn't push it. But without his name to go on, I'm stuck."

"My dear Dan, if you want to write mystery novels, you've got to be something of a sleuth yourself," Nora pointed out. "Now, let's look at the facts—as they always say. How old do you think your cadaver was when he died?"

He shrugged. "Late twenties, maybe. Why?"

"Well, that means two things. If he *was* a boxer, he must've done his fighting in the last ten years. And if he was in either World War II or Korea, that narrows it even further—late forties or early fifties. Now, what else do you know about him?"

"Not much, except that he died of a subdural hematoma sometime last winter."

"What's a subdural wha'cha'macallit?"

"A blood clot on the brain. It's sort of an occupational hazard of boxers, but anyone can get one—and die from it. All it takes is a good knock on the head."

"But do you think he got it boxing? I mean, actually died in the ring?"

He shook his head. "If he had, there'd have been an autopsy—it's the law—and his body never would've ended up at a medical school."

"How did it then?"

"He must've willed it. From what little I know, that's the only way they could've gotten it legally. . . . Still, there *is* another way—"

"What? Tell me!"

"Well, imagine for a second that he didn't die of a boxing injury, that he was beaten to death—murdered. What better place to dispose of his body than a medical school—if you've got the right connections?"

Nora's hazel eyes widened. "But could it be done?"

"Sure," Dan said solemnly, then broke into a grin. "No, not really—not unless Snider himself is the gangleader. Or the murderer! Besides, I'm sure any stray bodies are carefully checked by the police before they're turned over to a medical school."

"Well, even so," Nora persisted. "Even if he did will his body to a medical school, he had to die first, didn't he?"

"So?"

"So, what say we research it in the *Post* morgue? Dig through all last winter's editions and see if we can't come up with a story covering his death. You know, one with a picture you'd recognize. . . . Come on, finish your drink and we can get started on it right away."

Dan smiled at the look of bright-eyed enthusiasm on her face, but motioned her to sit down. "Do you have any idea how many people die in Boston each year? How long it would take to read through their obituaries? Hell, we'd be there all night!"

"I suppose you're right," Nora conceded, frowning. "But what do we do now?"

"Have another round of drinks?" *Get drunk, get laid, get off the subject,* he thought irascibly, suddenly feeling as if he'd so had his fill of cadavers that any further mention of them would be unbearable. What Dan was experiencing, he knew, was more a spell than a mood, another of the sudden seizures of misgivings, never lasting more than a few seconds or minutes, that overcame him at odd intervals. He had no inkling what triggered it, no insight into it, no clear notion as to its origins, except that while in its throes he seemed attuned to something deep and disturbing in his subconscious and it made him morose and edgy.

Nora regarded him with a mystified expression, sensing his mood shift but not sure how to read it and so said nothing. A *Post* reporter greeted her and then stood long enough at their table to be introduced to Dan, to ask—what's he got that I haven't?—and, before moving on to the bar, to touch her breast on the pretext of rubbing her shoulder. Finally she turned to Dan and said plaintively, "Oh, come on! There must be some way to find out who your cadaver is? Some angle we haven't yet hit on? You're just not trying."

"There *is* one thing . . ." Dan admitted after a pause. "Only it depends on a lot of *if*'s."

"Tell me."

"Well, *if* he really was a boxer, and *if* he was any good, then maybe the *Post* might have a picture of him somewhere in their sports files."

"Of course! Wonderful idea. We might even be able to get Jerry Kerson, the sports editor, to help us look." She glanced at her watch. "Gosh, I hope he's still around. Come on now, drink up."

An hour later, the alcove at the rear of the photography lab where old sports photos were stored was a shambles of open file cabinets and glossy prints heaped in small piles or strewn about. Peering over Jerry Kerson's shoulder as he thumbed through each stack, Dan saw pictures of virtually every local or nationally famous fighter of the past decade.

Three cabinet drawers and countless photos later, Dan suddenly reached out to stay Jerry's hand. Taking the top print from him, he held it to the light. It was an action shot of a knockdown in a ring and in the face of the boxer standing over his fallen opponent Dan again saw the visage of his cadaver as it had appeared six weeks ago, before the dissection and disfigurement of it had begun. "That's it! That's him! I'm sure of it," he said, handing the glossy print back to the sports editor. "What's his name?"

Sharing the picture with Nora, Jerry studied it intently. "Rick . . . Rick who?" He groped for the memory. "Rick Ferrar! Sure, that's who it is. A local middleweight. One of Al Lakeman's protégés. Yeah, that's right—and a damned good one, too. I saw him fight a few times in the Garden before he got drafted. In fact, I even recall writing a couple columns about him. You two wait here while I take a quick look around the office for them.

Jerry handed the photo back to Dan, a look of bemused wonder on his face. "Rick Ferrar! That's him all right—big as life. He never fought much nationally, but he had a pretty big local following. Funny, I never heard about his dying. Must've happened while I was out of town. . . . And now you say he's your, uh, cadaver. Jeez, gives me the creeps. . . . Imagine, an ex-pug donating his body to a medical school! Never heard of one doing that before. But I suppose there're a lot worse things you can do with your body."

part
two

Lem

Chapter Nine

At about the same time that Dan was returning to his apartment that night a battle-crippled black soldier named Lemuel Harper got off the train at South Station after having spent two years of infantry duty in Korea and fourteen months of intensive medical care in an Army general hospital in Denver. He made a striking figure in his Pullman-rumpled Ike jacket with the three stripes on the sleeves: a hulking giant who stood almost a foot taller than most men and whose great breadth of shoulder was further emphasized by erect posture and a lean stomach. His head, too, was oversized and his face triangular, broad and flat across the brow, then tapering to hollowed-out cheeks and a blunt, recessive chin—the skin so smooth and taut that it gleamed with a boot-polish luster in the glare of the station lights.

There were few passengers in the train depot that late at night and no redcaps at all, so the soldier had to carry his own baggage: a forty-pound valpack which held everything he owned —his toilet gear, a few changes of clothing, and dozens of paperback books that he had read almost to tatters in the long, painful hospital months. He limped as he walked and leaned on a cane, favoring a left leg that had once been filled with enemy slugs but was still his own leg, attached to his own body, and therefore dearer to him than an artificial limb. His hip socket, however, was stainless steel, and though each step he took wrenched a silent grunt from him, the pain was not allowed to show on his face—not even in his eyes.

As he plodded along, he stopped periodically to put the bag down and rest his hand—although the thoughts in his mind, the full realization of what this homecoming meant, seemed to him the heavier burden.

Outside the station he waited for a cab with a Negro driver. It wasn't that he felt any safer with them, but he knew he was edgy and preferred to avoid trouble. He didn't want to be called "big boy" or "big man" or be patronized in any way by a white man and he feared that in his present mood even an under-the-breath "nigger" might drive him berserk.

The cabdriver he hailed climbed out to help him with his suitcase, then asked: "Where to, soldier?" And he realized it was the last time anyone would ever call him soldier in the usual sense again. Without any particular profound or nostalgic feelings, he watched the passing streets of Boston through the window of the cab until he saw the elevated train platform overhead and knew he was home.

His mother, whom he had not seen for almost four years, gasped and cried out when she opened the door to him and then fell to her knees in prayer.

She urged him to kneel and pray with her, and despite the pain it cost him, he did; not because he believed in her God, but because with her face misshapen by a stroke she was no longer the tall, proud woman she had once been and he wanted to do whatever he could to comfort her.

He waited for her to mutter a last "hallelujah" and "amen," then helped her to her feet. Had she heard from Rick, he asked, and though it was hard at first to understand her garbled words, he gathered that she had not.

Once it had been Rick who was the brooder, the implacable one, filled since childhood with a savage capacity to hurt and hate, but now that burden had passed to him. Though he had missed death in Korea, he instinctively knew he was destined to die violently and prematurely, like his father and grandfather—only now that death would come in his own way and at his own choosing and he was determined to make it count for something. He had been shaped into such a deft destroyer by white men fighting yellow men that he was not only inured to even the most barbarous acts but could kill without compunction. Such conditioning had come gradually, but he realized it was his when the pleas and moans of the wounded no longer bothered him, except for their utter irrelevancy.

He knew that his strength lay not so much in his size, as in his deceptive intelligence. Big men were seldom credited with having much brains, and big black men, none at all. That would provide his camouflage while he went about preparing himself for his mission. Having once loved life, he now loved power. Not the power that came from bloodshed, but from ideas, insights, strategies; not the power to lead—Lem knew he lacked the attributes, the oratory skill for that—but to change. All he intended would not only take years to plan, pull together, put into operation but, to have any chance of success, would have to be done quietly. Yet it would be done, if not by himself, then by men he had personally trained. He had seen the tactics by which white men were demoralized and defeated in Korea, and he knew that by the use of such psychological storms American white supremacy would suffer as inexorable a process of erosion as anything in nature.

He had seen the stoical way that colored men, black or yellow, fought and died, compared to the snivelings of some whites, and he viewed such stoicism in the face of death as an asset which could be used. He had discovered how much the Chinese and North Koreans knew about the American soldier, and how little the arrogant Americans knew about them; how they had considered Orientals almost subhuman, like an army of advancing ants, and so panicked whenever defeat seemed imminent. He had learned a cardinal rule of war from that: *Know thy enemy,* and its crucial corollary, *profit from the past*. And he vowed to do both. His beginning battle would be fought in libraries where knowledge of his enemy was stored. He would learn the nature of the white man's psyche and how to vitiate it; then, armed with such insights, join forces with his natural allies, the oppressed colored people throughout the world.

He saw himself as no Moses, no seeker of promised lands, but he was determined that before he was through his black brothers would learn what a crafty devil they had in him and the whites would discover what color Lucifer and his hordes from hell really were.

Much later, after his mother had gone to bed, he stood by the window, listening to the rumble of the El while waiting for the sleeping pills he had swallowed against his ceaseless pain to take effect . . . And Lemuel Duvalier Harper, seeing how of all the things he had remembered: the run-down tenement house, the street, the sleazy bars, nothing had changed; that only people change—his mother grown sick and old; his beloved friend, Rick, gone; himself obsessed with hate—perceived the grim truth that much as he had longed to come home again, he was still as far away from the *home* he had left as he would ever likely be.

Chapter Ten

Rick Ferrar, mused Al Lakeman, after Dan Lassiter had talked briefly with him and left. Funny someone like this Lassiter fellow would come up here asking about him. A smooth, well-dressed kid like that. Not the type you'd figure Rick to get friendly with. Asked a hell of a lot of questions too.

Worst of all, he'd crowded Al when Al was working. No one did that when Al was busy with one of his fighters. No one who knew. Certainly not the press—and then only once. After that they were dead around him, might as well try to get copy from a bag full of sawdust.

The bell clanged the end of a round and Al's fighter climbed through the ropes to the ring apron. He took a swig of water from the bottle Al held to his lips, rinsed his mouth with it, then spit into a bucket. Elsewhere in the gym a light bag began its flim-flam rhythm, echoing off the rafters in chattering counterpoint with another bag; a chocolate-colored heavyweight glided forward on muscular legs to pound a heavy bag; and nearer the bleachers a slimmer, lighter-skinned Negro did a fancy jig with a skiprope while his friends nudged each other and gleefully exclaimed: "Man, look at that cat jive!"

"Al Lakeman! Telephone!" a raucous voice yelled, and Al left the floor to enter a small office in the rear where Walt Chat-

85

field, a prominent sports promoter and racetrack owner, stood talking with Nick Demaria, a local trainer.

The caller was a fellow matchmaker from Hartford, and after promising a certain date, weight, and price for his fighter, Al relaxed in the swivel chair behind his desk, propping his feet up on the edge.

"Hey, Al—who was the kid I seen you talkin' with a little while ago?" Demaria asked, rolling a cigar from one side of his ample mouth to the other.

Al shrugged. "Never seen him before. Funny thing—he was askin' about Rick Ferrar."

"Rick, huh? Jeez, haven't seen him around in a while. Not since the Red Bishop fight almost a year ago. . . . You know, Al, Rick was one guy who lost a lot of what he had in the war, don't ya think?"

"No doubt about it. I could tell right away he wasn't the same anymore. Kept making faces when he got hit. Never seen faces before on Rick. He was deadpan all the way. The war changed a lot of guys. He never would talk about it though."

"What's Rick doing now?" Chatfield asked as he folded some legal-looking documents and put them in the pocket of his tweed overcoat. "My daughter, Kim, asks about him every once in a while."

"Haven't heard a thing, Walt. Not a phone call or even a line from him in months. Last time I was in New York I asked a few of the boys up at Stillman's about him and none of them knew either. Best I can figure, he must've hung up his gloves."

"You know, there was one guy I thought would never quit," Demaria opined. "Had the right temp'a'ment for a fighter."

"Yeah, but he changed. Remember his last fight? You could see he was pushin' to get it over with, whether he won or not."

"Too bad," Chatfield said. "He looked like a real good boy at one time. Maybe even a champion. But they all change sooner or later, don't they? They always find some reason to let themselves slide."

"Jeez, Walt, remember those New York hoods you had that run-in with a few years back?" Demaria reminisced. "How 'bout the time they tossed that bomb in here? Blew hell out of the place!" As he talked, Chatfield's jaw muscles tightened. "I heard Rick and that big spade friend of his took care of that for you."

"They did a sweet job, all right," Al said. "Christ, Rick could be rough on a guy when he got mad!"

"Were you around when he blitzed them New York bastards?" Demaria asked.

Al chortled. "Around the corner. But I heard it while it lasted—which wasn't any too long, let me tell ya. First, the yellin' and swearin', then the pukin' and moaning, then the police and ambulance sirens. Rick was an even better street-fighter than in the ring. Knew all the tricks. Nothin' I could teach him there."

"You're telling me! Listen—know what I told Solly Green when he asked me who worked over the Miller brothers? *Boston Blackie,* I told 'im. Ain't that a howler!" Demaria laughed until he began to choke on his cigar.

"Any trouble I might've had with hoodlums is now a thing of the past," Chatfield told them. "I'd just as soon have it forgotten."

"Sure, Walt. Things are solid here now. But Boston Blackie, ain't that a hot one!"

"Hey, Al Lakeman! C'mon out!" Al's fighter yelled from the doorway. "I'm coolin' off!"

"Then, go do a couple rounds on the heavy bag," Al ordered. "I'll be out in a while."

"I did 'em already. . . . C'mon, Al, be a good guy. I want'ta get out of here!"

"What'sa matter—pool room closin' early today?" Demaria taunted.

"Al, will ya come!" the fighter pleaded. "I'm coolin' off!"

"Okay, okay." Al swung his feet to the floor and stretched.

" 'Bout time you showed anythin' resembling ambition around here."

"Al, if you happen to hear anything about Rick, let me know," Walt Chatfield said. "I'm interested."

"I will, Walt. Soon as I hear."

"Ask around, will you?"

"I'll do that, Walt. First chance I get."

Later that day, as an early dusk settled outside the Front Street Gym and the helmet-shaded light bulbs hanging from the ceiling cast moving shadows and a yellowish pall over the floor; when the last of the lunchtime spectators had left—the aspiring kids, the bettors, the old-time fighters who sat in the bleachers with snow melting from their overcoats—Al Lakeman stood before an ice-glazed window overlooking the street. It was the place where he did his thinking. No one disturbed Al when they saw him staring out that window. They all knew his habits and nobody crowded him.

Behind him he heard the grunts of the few fighters still working on the floor, the creak of the heavy bag as it swung on its chain, the three-minute and the four-minute bell. But thirty years in one gym after another had made him so accustomed to such sounds that they blended into his reverie and he hardly heard them at all.

Though Al had a reputation for showing more compassion toward ex-fighters than most of his fellow trainers, there remained only a handful of the countless pugilists he had known whom he considered worthy of a passing thought. Rick Ferrar was one of them, one of the few Al missed not having around Rick had paid him back fully for the early interest he'd shown in him. . . . Still, he never would've guessed it would work out that way the first time they'd met. Not in a million years, Al thought, smiling to himself, as he recalled the day Rick came in, followed by that oversized shadow of his, Lem Harper, and asked Al to train him for a pro bout. . . .

"How many fights you already had?" Al had asked.

"Fourteen," Lem answered, while Rick ignored their talk to watch the sparring in the ring.

"Can't he answer for himself!"

"Fourteen's right," Rick repeated. "I won 'em all."

"Yeah, but amateur crap," Al said disdainfully. "Doesn't amount to a hill of beans. Everybody up here wins bean-bouts!"

"He's good, though, Mr. Lakeman," Lem said. "Real good. I bet he can lick your boy, Marino, right now."

Al snickered but wasn't amused. Hal Marino was his best fighter, a ranking middleweight, and a cocky claim like that rankled him. "Is that a fact?" he drawled. "You like to go a few rounds with Marino, kid?"

Rick nodded.

"Okay. Come back with your gear in a few hours and we'll fix it."

"I got my gear now."

"So just come back with it! Right now I'm busy," Al said and turned his back on them to follow the action in the ring.

"We'll wait," Rick said quietly.

Al emerged briefly from his reverie as the neon sign on the tavern across the street lit up, its blinking red flashes turning the icicles hanging from its frame into flickers of flame. With the clanging of the three-minute bell, however, his reminiscing began anew and he recalled that day, seven years before, when Rick had sparred his two rounds with Marino.

"Oh, the kid had what it took, all right," Al mused aloud. Anyone watching him work in the ring could see that. Some of it came naturally and the rest Al could teach him. He was all hooks, of course, not a jab in a carload, and the veteran, Marino, made him look awkward in the clinches. Still, he moved well and took Marino's best punches without backing off, and what really caught Al's trained eye was his ability to stay in close and punch short. He could forgive most flaws in a novice who knew enough and had guts enough to do that from the start.

Once their sparring had ended, Al paid an uncommon bit of attention to Marino: sponging off his head and unwrapping the protective bandages from his hands—seemingly ignoring Rick's presence in the ring but keeping him within sight.

"Listen," Marino said, panting. "The kid's plenty good! You should take him on, Al."

"I dunno, he's a funny duck. Might be hard to handle. I haven't made my mind up yet."

"Take him on, I tell ya," Marino urged. "He's a natural. Don't miss out on a good thing, Al."

"Hey, kid!" Al yelled across the ring. "Go take a shower and get dressed. We'll talk later."

Without a word or flicker of expression, Rick walked past them, slipped through the ropes, and jumped down from the ring apron to where Lem waited, holding a tattered robe open.

Minutes later, after taking a phone call in his office, Al spotted him still in his trunks punching a heavy bag that Lem braced for him.

Visibly annoyed, Al snapped, "Hey, kid—you deaf? I thought I told you to get dressed!"

"I need work," Rick said. "Made up your mind yet?"

"Look, see that guy over there in the pinstripe? His name's Cassidy, and he handles amateurs. Ask him, why don't you? I'll even put in a good word for you."

"I asked for *you!*" Rick said, revealing the anger he felt by the vicious blow he struck the heavy bag.

"Why me?" Al asked, pleased by this draw of emotion.

"They told me you're the best. If you won't take me, I'll go find somebody in New York."

Al squinted at him appraisingly and shrugged. "Okay, kid, I'll give you a whirl. Come around first of the week and we'll start working on some fundamentals. . . . And for Chrissake, buy yourself a decent-lookin' robe! You want people to think you're tryin' to look like young Dempsey?"

"Thank *you,* Mr. Lakeman," Lem said, grinning. "Thanks a lot! You won't be sorry."

Al remembered that Rick had nodded but not bothered to thank him himself. A real tough kid, Al had judged, which of itself didn't impress him one damn bit. He had known plenty of street toughs who'd wanted to make a quick buck boxing—all a bunch of lazy bums who quit on him before their first fight.

But the following Monday Rick was the first fighter on the gym floor and he wore a new black rayon robe with his name, painstakingly embroidered in yellow thread by Lem's mother, on the back. . . .

"Hey Al, baby! You gonna lock up?" Demaria shouted to him from the street door.

"Yeah! See you tomorrow."

Al moved into the office to get the five o'clock racing results on the radio and wait for a phone call from Chicago. After it came through, he was about to go home when a photograph hanging on the wall caught his eye: a group picture of Rick Ferrar, Walt Chatfield, and himself taken shortly before Rick went into the Army. On the lower margin of the photo Rick's name and fight record were penned in—a total of twenty-two professional bouts, twenty-one wins—and given time to think, Al could have described them all. Rick Ferrar, he thought, shaking his head gloomily; could have gone all the way, that one.

It seemed strange as hell to him that Rick hadn't kept in touch. All these months and not even a postcard! No fight listings in the newspapers or in *Ring* magazine and nobody, until this kid who showed up today, who as much as mentioned his name.

Could Rick be in some kind of trouble with the law, Al fretted. And could this Lassiter fellow possibly be a cop—plainclothes or FBI? What was the line Lassiter had handed him; that he and Rick had met while both were waiting to be discharged from the Army and gone a few rounds in a gym. Somehow it had a phony ring to it. Even when sparring, Rick always meant business: He would've cut a smooth-faced kid like that to pieces. But even if the story had been more convincing, Al still wouldn't have been able to tell him where to find Rick, since he didn't know. He had, however, given him the name and address of Rick's buddy, Lem Harper. Not that it would do him any good. Lem himself had been by to see Al a week ago, wondering if he knew what had become of Rick.

Al decided he was going to ask this Lassiter fellow exactly who he was next time he saw him. Just before leaving, he'd asked Al if he could come up to the gym to work out occasionally and Al had said sure, mainly to get rid of him. But whether he ever saw Lassiter again or not, Al made up his mind that he was going to find out just what *had* happened to Rick Ferrar.

Chapter Eleven

From the back of the Cape Ann boxing arena the ring blazed like an island of blinding light, reflecting off the canvas and obscuring the ringside seats in a whitish haze.

Dan hung back in the shadows until the winner of the last bout was announced and the ring cleared amidst a mixed chorus of boos and applause, then he followed Al Lakeman down the aisle. The din of the crowd subsided slightly as he climbed the stairs to the ring apron. He scuffed his shoes in the resin box and then ducked through the ropes with an agile bounce. The inside of the ring appeared small, smaller than he'd remembered, and as he continued to gaze at it a strange sense of unreality, of dreamlike detachment possessed him—making it seem as if the limbering-up exercises he did, the arm-flapping and deep knee bends, were all in slow motion.

Al Lakeman tugged his robe off over his gloves, exposing his bare torso and black satin trunks, and after an appraising glimpse the crowd began jeering.

"Hey, pretty boy!" a woman shrilled. "This your first fight? You better watch out or you ain't goin' to look pretty for long!"

Dan started to turn in her direction, but Al Lakeman rasped: "Ignore the mouthy bitch!" and, taking Dan's gloves in his hands, began to knead the leather away from his knuckles. "You feelin' okay, kid?"

Dan nodded, even though the protective metal cup he wore was cutting into his crotch and he could barely suppress his bladder spasms.

"Hey, ref!" Al Lakeman shouted at the bow-tied, gum-chewing referee standing nearby. "Where the hell's our opponent? What's the hold-up?"

The referee shrugged, leaned his pot belly over the ropes and yelled down at the timekeeper, "Hey, Rudy! Hit the bell a couple of times. What the hell's that Spic doin' back there so long—jerkin' off?"

The timekeeper struck a few resounding clangs, and a moment later another fighter jogged down the aisle and climbed jauntily into the ring. A hush fell over the veterans in the crowd as they strained for a better look; then, as the fighter's handlers removed his towel and robe, their suspicions were confirmed and they erupted in an indignant chorus of hoots and catcalls:

"Hey, ref! That guy's no amateur, he's a pro! What'chu tryin' to pull!"

"Get that ringer out of there!"

"C'mon, ref—do somethin'. We don't want to see the kid slaughtered!"

Dan's view had been blocked temporarily by Al Lakeman inserting his mouthpiece, but as Al stepped aside he got a clear look at his opponent: a swarthy, muscular man appearing several years older than he. A grizzly stubble of beard showed through the protective coat of vaseline smeared on his chin, and from scarred brow to saddle-flat nose, his face displayed the battered features of the veteran pugilist. He did a little shuffling dance in his corner and then, snorting through his nose, unleased a flurry of vicious shadow punches.

"Sonuvabitch! That guy's a ringer, all right," Al Lakeman muttered. "A seasoned pro! Must be nuts to fight for free like this. Yeah, I remember him now. And he is nuts: a mean, sadistic bastard who no self-respectin' manager will touch 'cause he likes to hurt guys so much he's gonna kill somebody in the

ring someday." He turned to Dan with a concerned look. "The hell with this! I'm gonna stop it right now. Believe me, you're no match for him."

Dan continued to stare at his opponent, hearing Al's admonition only vaguely. The trancelike state that first overcame him on entering the ring had now intensified and he felt benumbed, dimly aware that he was in some physical danger but too preoccupied by his inability to recollect the events that had brought him here to act against it. He recalled—barely—that it somehow involved a sports editor friend of Nora's and his own sense of dissatisfaction with medical school, but beyond that he was unable to think clearly.

"Well, kid, how 'bout it?" Al prompted. "You want me to stop it or not?"

"No," Dan answered dully. "I'm all right."

"You sure?"

"Yeah, fine."

"Well, okay," the trainer said dubiously. "But he'll murder you for sure if you try to slug it out with him, so keep on the move. I'll stop it quick, if it gets too rough for you."

The houselights dimmed; Dan's shoulder muscles suddenly jerked and his detachment lifted as the bell clanged. He bounced forward, touched gloves with his opponent across the referee's arms, then backed off, and squinting in the harsh glare of the ring lights. sought for an opening. His opponent crouched, elbows and gloves drawn in close to his body, yet remained a few feet from his corner. Dan bit down on his mouthpiece and resolutely shuffled in, knowing from previous fights that the tension he felt would only start to ease after he'd traded a few punches, triggering the flow of adrenalin through his veins and the emotional anesthesia it produced.

He darted in, feinted with both hands, and snapped a jab off his opponent's cheek, liking the sharp thwack *of leather hitting bone and the impact transmitted up his arm.*

"That's it! Jab him!" Al Lakeman shouted. But except for a

slight wince, his lead drew no response. Dan circled left, turning but not moving his stationary opponent, jabbing him in the ribs until he lowered his guard, then smashing a hook to the face and a right cross to the heart. The man grunted and tried to clinch, but Dan slipped away, gaining confidence fast as the crowd oohed and aahed over him.

Dan threw a long, loping right to the head and then, as they clinched, took a lancinating blow to his side, which hurt all the way down to his groin. Angrily, he retaliated with kidney punches of his own until the referee separated them.

Dan stepped back with a quick toss of his head to keep strands of hair from falling over his eyes and was hit by a punch he never even saw. The blow landed with jaw-crunching impact, jarring his brain so hard that it set off a shower of scintillating lights on his retina. He reeled back and his opponent was immediately upon him, pummeling him with short hooks and crosses, then, as Dan doubled over, turtlelike, to protect his head, shifting the attack to his body.

Still hunched over, Dan lurched forward, arms flailing until he managed to tackle his opponent around the waist and tie him up. As he tried to straighten, his eyes were painfully raked by glove laces and a swiveling shoulder butted him in the head. That brought the crowd to their feet in a pandemonium of protest. "Foul! Call the fight!" they clamored, but the referee merely grinned and Dan was too dazed to hear them.

Rubbery-legged, he tried to retreat, but found himself trapped in a corner, each sideways movement producing rope-burns across his back. He ducked and bobbed, avoiding a flurry of wild punches until his opponent burrowed in and caught him squarely on the cheek with a right cross. Dan's rubber mouthpiece went flying along with a spray of blood and spittle. He tried desperately to clinch, but his opponent let him lean against him only long enough to snarl—"Keep away from me! Stay the hell away, hear, or I'll kill you!"—before shoving him off.

Again his opponent closed. Dan threw a feeble jab, but he slipped under it and landed a hard uppercut to the stomach. Fall down. Take the count, Dan thought, breathless. But he was too far gone to control his legs, make them buckle, even know which way to fall. Had time simply stopped? He wondered vaguely. The round seemed endless. Where was the referee? Al Lakeman? Why didn't they stop it?

With his arms wrapped protectively around his head and his spine bent double, Dan tried to catch his wind, clear his head, defend himself against his opponent's savage onslaught. He knew that he was being bludgeoned into unconsciousness, his brain battered to a pulp—that if the fight wasn't stopped soon, he would be beaten to death. Was that what this suddenly hushed mob of Gloucesterites out there secretly craved to see—a fatal beating? The thought of such a senseless death infuriated Dan. He waited for the paralyzing spasm in his gut to ease, his lungs fill with a little air, and with a raging, last-ditch fury recoiled off the ropes and sprang forward. His opponent grunted loudly as he butted him in the stomach and then, with a sudden upthrusting of his neck muscles, caught him a glancing blow on the chin.

A searing pain, unbelievable in its capacity to inflict further punishment in his already stuporous state, burst in Dan's skull, then centered like a dentist drilling on an exposed nerve in his jaw. Coughing and choking on blood, he staggered blindly around the ring until the referee caught and held him against his big belly.

Firm fingers pried Dan's eyelids open. Blearily, he perceived only dazzling streaks of light and then, as if through a wavy, watery film, the referee's pudgy face. It was finally over, he thought with boundless relief; the fight would surely be stopped. Instead, the referee stepped back, leaving him on tottery legs, and to his utter disbelief Dan heard him say: "All right, break clean and keep fightin'."

There was no hope, he realized; he was being sacrificed to the crowd's unappeasable blood-lust, and though appalled and angered, Dan dropped his guard and let the punishment come.

His opponent's next punch caught him flush on the mouth, breaking off several teeth and thus fulfilling a nightmarish prophecy, one that had haunted him throughout his boxing career. The following blow smashed the cartilage in his nose and blood gushed from his nostrils like that from a mortally wounded bull.

Still, he made no effort to defend himself.

Finally, his opponent stepped back to measure him, then brought up an uppercut in a short, vicious arc. It landed on Dan's chin with a concussive blaze that lifted him off his feet. He hung suspended in air, waiting for his body to fall and hit the canvas, but the impact never came. Instead, to his bewilderment, the referee was holding his arm up in victory—while his opponent lay at his feet, his face ashen and his features transformed by a death rigor so that they were clearly those of his cadaver.

As the boxing arena imagery faded, Dan tried to struggle up from the dream into the safe, sane reaches of reality, but he couldn't. The final bizarre twist to his nightmare had so stupefied him that he found himself in a cataleptic state. Unable to move, shout, wake himself—he felt as if he were experiencing a small taste of death: not the terminal process that ends in nothingness, but more a suspended animation, a form of living death, and far more frightening.

By a supreme effort of will, he managed to open his eyes, perceiving first a glimmer, then a burst of sallow light coming from the ceiling. Was it day or night? *Look out the window,* he thought. But he felt too torpid to move and a residual panic still reverberated in his brain.

He held his wristwatch up to his eyes: five A.M. He must have dozed off around one, shortly after finally settling down to study—and he didn't have to be up until seven!

Go back to sleep, he told himself, yet knew it was futile. The same pattern of fitful sleep and early waking had plagued him for weeks now. He should have taken a few Seconals, he thought; that would have insured a good night's sleep. But they sometimes left him so groggy he skipped class the next morning. Now, after hardly more than a catnap, he'd be groggy anyway. A vicious cycle.

Dan rose unsteadily from bed and looked out the window of his basement apartment. Above the crescent of snow that had drifted against the glass, he could see the sidewalk, ice slick and glistening in the light from the streetlamp. He started for the shower, then decided to reheat a pot of leftover coffee. Suddenly remembering he had drunk it all and that the sink was full of dirty dishes, he sank into a chair, surrendering to an overwhelming sense of apathy.

What's wrong with me? he thought in despair. *Why can't I study? Or sleep? Or want a woman? Or have pleasant dreams anymore?*

He knew he had been having periodic nightmares since starting medical school three months before, but none as bad as this! *Jesus!* he thought, remembering the brutal beating he had taken. Then he grimaced. *Beating, hell!* That was no beating—with his nose smashed, his teeth broken, he had been mutilated! In the dream his cadaver had reversed roles on him—had mutilated *his* face, *his* brain. Why? he puzzled. Was he really so guilt-ridden over the dissection that some perverse side of him subconsciously longed to be punished for it?

It seemed a masochistic notion, far too Freudian, even absurd, but it made him shudder.

He rubbed his eyes with a knuckle, then ran it down his stubble of beard. *Shave, take a shower, make coffee—do something!* he argued with himself. Yet he just sat.

It wasn't so much the dissection that was bothering him, he reflected. Oh, it had at first. The mere thought of having to face that mound of fetid, rotting, flesh each morning had once triggered such a wave of nausea in his gut that he hadn't eaten

99

breakfast for weeks. But he was over that now. That kind of visceral revulsion had largely been supplanted by a stronger, more threatening concern: fear of flunking out.

Dan knew at the time he handed in his test booklet that he'd done poorly on the first anatomy exam, yet he hadn't expected to flunk it. Maybe he just hadn't thought out his answers clearly enough before writing them down, or maybe Snider had graded the papers too severely. But whatever the cause, the failure weighed heavily on him. He had probably made matters even worse for himself during his little session with Snider afterward. All that vague talk about cadavers, especially his own. . . .

Cadaver. Why did he still persist in thinking of him as that, Dan wondered, when he now knew his name? Why was he so reluctant to call him Rick? Rick Ferrar? Because it kindled a private fear? Made it harder to dissect him?

He thought about his phone conversation the night before with his Uncle Woody. . . .

"What'you doing these days?" Woody had asked.

"Oh, same old thing. Cutting up a cadaver." *Not—cutting up Rick Ferrar—what's left of him.*

"He must be pretty well carved up by now."

"Yuh, he is. In a few days, we're going to transsect him. Make like a magician in a carnival and saw him in half."

"Good Lord!" Woody had gasped. "What for?"

"So he won't decompose too much on us over Christmas vacation. . . . We save all the pieces to bury him with, you know."

"You do?" Woody had replied dubiously. "Glad to hear it. You must tell me more about your . . . uh, cadaver when you get home."

No, not cadaver. Rick Ferrar.

Dan's neck muscles contracted convulsively. As embellished, the dialogue between them sounded so ghoulish he wondered what was worse: a nightmare in which his dream-self had been mutilated or the mutilation which he and two others were inflicting on a real body every day?

Finally getting up, Dan trudged into the kitchen. He rummaged through the pile of dishes in the sink for the parts to his percolator, then made coffee. A calendar showing a nude Marilyn Monroe, head thrown back, breasts out, looking a baby-pink in her bare skin, hung over the stove. Dan glanced at her, then the date: December 15, three days before Christmas vacation began. He really would have a lot to tell his uncle when he got home. Or would he? How could he possibly hope to explain to Woody those things he found so hard to understand himself.

From where in the death-haunted depths of his psyche had come this compulsion to know more about his cadaver? Not just to learn his name, who his friends were, but to find out how he had lived and maybe even (though he always shied away from this notion) how he had died. For what purpose? he wondered. Out of what inner need? Certainly not the feeble pretense of writing a mystery novel? . . . He had abandoned that long ago. Was it to rid himself of vague feelings of guilt over the destruction of his cadaver's body? Perhaps. But why should he bear such an onus when so few of his classmates ever thought of them as real people. And even though recognizing the perversity of it, he couldn't deny the growing sense of kinship he felt for the dead man. Possibly it was nothing more than the sense of universality, the bell-tolling sentiments of a John Donne. Or the penalty for reading too much Kafka. But if that were truly the case, why did he feel so driven? Why were there nightmares?

With the janitor not due to fire up the furnace for another hour, it was too cold in the apartment to take a shower. Instead, Dan filled the basin in his bathroom with cold water and submerged his head in it until his breath gave out.

The momentary sense of suffocation, the lung-burning, pulse-pounding panic it brought, again reminded him of the dream. Seeking a distraction, he stared at his reflection in the mirror: pallid, puffy-eyed, unshaven, haggard-looking. *The mask of depression,* he thought, remembering a phrase from a drug advertisement. *Admit it!* he told himself. *Admit you're depressed as hell. Maybe worse than that: deranged, demented, obsessed by an* idée fixe. Still, the nightmare he'd just suffered might only be a harbinger of what lay ahead for him if he didn't shake off this obsession with his cadaver.

But after having relentlessly pursued matters this far, could he stop now? At the start, he'd only wanted to learn his name, then, after that, to read the boxing stories about him filed in the Boston *Post*'s morgue. But they were so scanty in their portrayal of Rick as a person that it had only piqued his curiosity more. So he had sought out Al Lakeman.

That this might entail any danger had never occurred to Dan until he learned that Lakeman didn't know Rick was dead. Apparently no one knew, and this puzzling revelation impelled him to want to find out more. Al Lakeman had given him the name and address of someone called Lem Harper, Rick's closest friend, and though Dan had not yet visited him, he planned to do so soon. One last inquiry.

The stove hissed as boiling coffee spilled over the percolator spout. Dan took it off the burner, then went to the refrigerator for cream. As he bent to look in the door, he suddenly felt light-headed; the kitchen floor seemed to tilt under his feet and the enamled walls of the freezer, glaring a morguelike white, appeared about to swallow him. Startled, Dan straightened, holding onto the refrigerator door for support.

Though the dizzy spell rapidly subsided, it left him with a lingering sense of unease: a malaise made worse by the bleakness of the hour and the damp chill seeping into the basement apartment and the bitter aftertaste of the coffee he had drunk without cream. He recognized the mood as a shadowy, if all too familiar presence: the same dark spirit that had been implanted in his mind the first day of medical school, then so stubbornly persisted that not even the move from the Somerset Hotel to this Beacon Street apartment nor study dates with Carey nor cheery phone calls from Nora nor the insouciant pose and turgid nipples of a Marilyn Monroe could hope to dispel.

102

Chapter Twelve

If the white man must hate, let him, but keep raising the price! . . .

—From the notebooks of Lemuel Harper

Lem's father, Joshua Harper, died when Lem was fourteen. While many boys his age lost fathers during the Second World War, what embittered Lem was that his had not died fighting a foreign enemy but the domestic kind. That same strange selection that had once chosen his maternal grandfather, Auguste Duvalier, to die on a prison gallows in Martinique in 1902 after leading a bloody uprising against that island's repressive French rule, had also chosen his father to die leading an insurrection, and Lem felt that it was destined someday to choose him, too.

A soft-spoken, intelligent man, Joshua Harper had enlisted in the Army shortly after Pearl Harbor and had been assigned to a tank battalion in Louisiana. He soon found—as did many Northern black soldiers sent into the more rural, set-in-their-ways South—that his war had begun before leaving the country.

Born and raised on his family's isolated and self-sufficient farm in northern Florida, Joshua Harper had not been exposed to much Jim Crow racism until late in his teens and so had not become inured to some of its more flagrant practices. But wartime or not, the racial climate that prevailed around Camp

103

The Anatomy Lesson

Claiborne, Louisiana, was not ready for change. The white soldiers lived in barracks, the Negroes in leaky tents. The white MP's were sent on patrol with guns; the Negro MP's with sticks. Though scorned in the local bars, the black soldiers were sought out in the alleyways: a half-dozen of them, yet not a single white, having been rolled that first week.

Finally, Joshua Harper had had enough. At his instigation a secret meeting of all black tank crews was called and a drastic plan of action drawn. The next morning, as the soldiers of Camp Claiborne mustered for reveille, they were surprised to see the entire administration area ringed with tanks. The white sentries on duty bristled with indignation, but respecting the steel and canon—if not the drivers—of the mechanized monsters that confronted them did nothing.

A high-ranking representative from the Inspector General's office was hastily flown in from Washington to deal with the situation, and by midnight, after he had acceded to virtually all the Negro soldiers' demands for equal treatment, the cordon of tanks was withdrawn. According to the report he later filed with the War Department, the melee had been swiftly and fairly adjudicated with only a single shot—unfortunately, a fatal one—having been fired. A stray bullet, possibly discharged accidentally from an unknown sentry's rifle in the dark, had killed one of the tank drivers. He concluded the report by stating that the investigation into the slaying of Private Joshua Harper was continuing.

> *Just as each man is formed of sperm and egg, each is a union of hard and soft parts. The hardness, the will to endure any adversity, is his masculine side, while the goodness and compassion in him derives from the mother. And though it alone is able to afford him any joy in life, this softness must be shed—for unless all is hard to the core his defenses will crack like an egg and spill his guts out. . . .*
>
> —From the notebooks of Lemuel Harper

Even after the death of his father, Lem's teen-age years were not unhappy ones. His mother, though much of her time was

104

taken up working and caring for his asthmatic younger sister, saw to that. Still, the acceptance, the companionship he yearned for with other youths his age eluded him. Not only was he black, but he was big. He was always the tallest in his class, and while moving with a natural agility and grace, he was forever outgrowing his clothes and appeared awkward and gangling. High-spirited and energetic, he enjoyed athletics and played various playground sports. But his size forced him to compete with much older boys whom his mother would not allow him to pal around with in the evening. Evenings were for home-work and reading and sometimes listening to the radio, she told him, not for prowling the streets with older boys who were only on the lookout for girls and trouble. Some of the teen-age Ne-groes in the neighborhood had a clubhouse in the basement of an abandoned shoe factory where they smoked and played cards and sometimes brought complaisant girls. But Lem's mother forbade him to go there, and he never did. It wasn't so much a longing for girls or sex which made him feel so lonely at times as not having a buddy his own age: a close male com-panion who might counterbalance the strong female influence his mother and sister exerted over him.

Still, Lem was an obedient son. Knowing how hard his mother toiled as a seamstress to support their family and buy the costly medicines for his sister, Susan, he always came directly home after school to help with the housework and do odd jobs. One job he hated above all, however, was cleaning out cellars. It wasn't so much the dirt and musty smell that bothered him as an ever-present fear of spiders—a skin-crawling dread that one might fall on his head or climb up his pants leg. Spiders even more than rats. But there were several old women on the block who were willing to pay a quarter or fifty cents to have their furnaces cleaned and so, overcoming his distaste, Lem would gingerly descend into one of these dark, dank cobweb-curtained places whenever his mother told him to.

It was while carrying out one such chore that he met Rick.

The furnace he was sent to clean that day belonged to their

landlady, Mrs. McFee, an arthritic, elderly woman who lived a block away. Because of her arthritis, Mrs. McFee kept her house so overheated it turned her cellar into a hothouse, an ideal breeding ground for all sorts of household bugs.

Yet it wasn't a spider Lem encountered in Mrs. McFee's sweltering cellar, but a ragged, grimy-faced white boy about his age sleeping on the floor of the coalbin.

"Hey! What'chu doin' here?" Lem exclaimed, nudging the intruder with his foot.

Two things happened in response. The boy awoke and Lem saw the wildest, most hate-filled pair of eyes he had ever seen glaring back at him. And almost simultaneously the boy's hand snaked out to grab the handle of a broom lying near him. Lem jerked his neck sideways in time to avoid a blow on the head but still caught a stinging rap on the shoulder. Then, as his attacker sprang to his feet and, gripping the broom like a baseball bat, began to swing it again, Lem charged forward, pulling him down to the floor. There, on a bed of back-jabbing chunks of coal, in swirls of choking dust, they thrashed about, writhing and twisting and bucking, as first one then the other managed to get on top long enough to throw a few punches before being toppled.

Lem tried but failed to flip his opponent over his head, and then kicked out, sending him stumbling back against the coal pile. Warily, they circled each other, wiping soot and sweat from their eyes, then came together with their arms pumping like pistons in a fresh flurry of blows.

Though almost a foot taller and several pounds heavier than his attacker, Lem soon realized he was in the fight of his life. He had fought many times and many different opponents, but never anyone so feral-eyed and ferocious. Nor so silent. Except for an occasional grunt or snarl, Lem realized he hadn't been sworn at or even called "nigger" once. Was his attacker deaf and dumb? he wondered.

But there was no time to find out. Despite being knocked

106

down many times by Lem's fists, he kept getting back up and wading in. And though many of the punches he threw were wild, enough landed so that Lem's eyes were swollen and his face stung like fire. His opponent, knuckles raw, his face an ugly smear of soot and blood, looked as if he hurt just as badly. . . . Finally, arms growing so heavy he could barely raise them, Lem lunged forward, flinging his full weight against his opponent and shoulder-butting him into a corner, then pummeling him on the head with both fists until he fell forward on the floor.

Blearily, he watched the boy try to struggle back up, making it to his knees but no further. Lem caught his breath and then, confident the fight was over, bent to help his opponent to his feet; there was a lot he meant to ask this white boy. The next instant, a thunderous blow on the side of his head staggered him back. Almost unconscious, he slumped to the floor, cradling his aching head in his hands.

As soon as his hazy vision cleared, Lem realized he had been hit by an iron furnace stoker. He tried to look around, but the sudden movement of his head triggered a twinge of pain, and by now he knew his attacker had fled.

Who was he—a house thief, an escapee from some reform school or mental institution? He had to be something more than a mere runaway, Lem figured, or else he never would have fought so hard. And though wanting to get even for the unfair beating he had taken from a white boy, Lem really never expected to see him again.

Yet he did see him, less than a week later, although at the time, having been waylaid in an alleyway by four neighborhood toughs, Lem found himself in even greater bodily danger and was far too busy defending himself to entertain any thoughts of revenge. One of his attackers was the brother of a white girl Lem had walked home from school that day; the brother now accused him of trying to lure her to the black's clubhouse for sex. Lem hadn't even bothered to deny it, knowing from past experience that the gang surrounding him was intent on "teaching this big nigger a lesson." Rather than waste breath pleading his innocence, he wanted to get the first blow in; it was better tactics.

Once again Lem fought hard, but under attack from several directions, he was finally forced to move out from the wall at his back and was instantly grabbed from behind. Though he struggled frantically to free his arms, a vicious uppercut to the stomach bent him double and a knee to the face sent him sprawling on the ground. As he looked up to guard against a kick to the head, Lem's eyes fell briefly on a familiar face emerging from one of the shacks bordering the alleyway—that of his attacker in Mrs. McFee's cellar. While his sudden appearance surprised Lem, it hardly heartened him; not only didn't he figure on getting any help from the white boy, but he half-expected him to join the others. Still, in the split-second look they'd exchanged, Lem sensed something different about him. Though his eyes gleamed with excitement, they were no longer wild but appraising, almost mischievous. Then he saw his former attacker approach his present attackers and ask the brother: "Who's the nigger and why you beating him up?"

"None of your goddamn business!"

"Yeah, suppose not," Rick said and, moving his right hand no more than a foot, hit him so hard in the gut that he gasped and sank silently to his knees. Because Rick had first positioned himself so that his back was to the other gang members they were slow to react. Stepping aside, Rick let them look down on their fallen leader, then caught the nearest of them squarely on the jaw. Astonished, Lem scrambled to his feet, and fighting side by side, he and Rick made quick work of the remaining two.

Minutes later, as they left the alleyway together, Lem asked, "Why?"

Rick shrugged. "I like to fight, that's all. . . . And I already fought you."

Lem stared dubiously at his adversary-turned-ally for a moment and then, noticing the self-conscious look on his face, the way his feet fidgeted, broke into a smile. It was a lie, he sensed, and though it was no more than a hunch on Lem's part, he felt this runaway white boy had helped because he was ashamed he hadn't been able to beat him fairly the first time.

He might not be much to look at with his straggly hair and ragged clothes, Lem observed, but he sure could fight and he had his own code of honor. It didn't even seem to matter that his skin was white underneath all that grime, he had found himself a buddy, Lem thought happily on the walk home.

Like Lem, Rick Ferrar was fatherless, was, in fact, an orphan. Whether or not he was born legitimately, he never knew. The director of the public orphanage had told him once that his parents had perished in a fire, then later, contradicting himself, in a flood. When he was sixteen and in constant trouble for fighting, a young social worker whose nose he had bloodied told him he was worse than a bastard—that his father had been a rapist and his mother a teen-age Mexican girl. Rick ran away from the orphanage the next day. He hid out that summer on the Boston waterfront, fishing or scrounging in trash barrels for food and sleeping in warehouses. He finally stowed away on a tramp steamer heading for Panama. He was discovered and put to work in the galley, which he enjoyed, until he found out that the consideration shown him by the Greek cook, a vain and muscular Adonis who taught him to weight-lift and wrestle and let him share his cabin with him, was more than fraternal. The man was homosexual. And though Rick—a sexual innocent—was grateful to him, he rebuffed his advances. Still, the cook persisted, offering gifts of clothing and money and wandering around nude in the cabin. Then late one night Rick awoke to find the cook's hands and ouzo-reeking mouth on him and a vicious fight ensued. Finally realizing that the man was not only drunk but so crazed with passion that he meant to rape him,

Rick was seized with a raging anger. Waiting for the cook to lunge at him again, he stepped aside and slammed him against a bulkhead. He then reached out, pivoted him around, and kneed him in the groin. The cook sank to the floor, his eyes wide with accusation and disappointment and pain—an oddly feminine look, Rick thought; one that evoked a strange compassion in him.

When the ship docked in Panama City, Rick found the nearest brothel and paid all the money he had for the youngest, most attractive whore in the house.

Afterward, the petite, olive-skinned girl had asked, "First time, *niño?*"

"First time," he admitted.

"Plenty good for first time. You goin' to make lots of *chicas* happy."

Rick left the whorehouse feeling more consolation in the conviction that he wasn't a homosexual than over his prowess as a lover. Though he might have preferred to go elsewhere in case the orphanage still had the police looking for him, the next steamer he hopped returned him to Boston.

Lem Harper knew about this episode in Rick's life. From the time they had met in Mrs. McFee's cellar until they entered the Army, the two of them were inseparable and there was little they didn't know about each other. Mrs. Harper, grateful to Rick for having saved Lem from one beating, unaware that he had been responsible for the other, began by inviting Rick to supper, and then, learning he had no permanent place to go at night, to live with them.

With regular meals filling out his frame and with a slightly Spanish cast to his features, Rick at eighteen was a lithe, muscular, darkly handsome man. Though his eyes were large and blue, the skin surrounding them always appeared creased at the corners like a nearsighted man straining to see. And except when he and Lem were alone, he seldom smiled. "Smile, boy!"

Mrs. Harper would chide. "Stop looking like you got all the miseries of the world on your shoulders!" And in response Rick would smile, for he liked Mrs. Harper and was eager to please her. But her chiding always made him aware of the strange undercurrent of sadness that ran through his being, a sense of worthlessness and impending doom, as though his life had somehow never been intended in the first place.

Lem sensed this about Rick, knowing how his upbringing and final traumatic experience at the orphange had robbed him of any identification and almost all self-esteem. There was also much about his friend to admire: his muscular body, his courage, his quiet, almost gentle disposition when not provoked. Conscious of his own broad features, Lem not only envied Rick his well-molded face but, at times, even its color.

Occasionally both Rick and Lem found themselves targets for homosexual advances. Yet, rather than rough the homosexuals up, they were quietly scornful.

"I can understand them wanting my beautiful body," Rick had once said afterward, "but what the hell can they see in you?"

"What you talkin' about? Why I got twice as much as anything you got!" Lem had protested. "I'm Lothar, man! Don't you know the dream of every fag is to be Mandrake the Magician so he can have Lothar?"

Mandrake and Lothar—was that their relationship: the ruggedly handsome fighter, Rick Ferrar, and his subservient sidekick from out of the African veldt? Outwardly it appeared so, even to Al Lakeman at first—until he happened to overhear them talking one day and realized that Rick, not Lem, was the more passive of the two. The moment provided Al with a revealing glimpse into the close, mutually dependent union that existed between the oddly matched pair. It had even made him suspect that Rick's reluctance to fight black boxers in all but the more important bouts was not for the usual reasons—the prejudice, the myth about thicker skulls that some white fighters held to—but another manifestation of Lem's influence over him.

Al was right. Lem got a certain subtle pleasure out of watching his friend do what he might like to do were it legally permissible: beat up white men. He felt far more ambivalent when Rick fought blacks, wanting him to win but agitated by the shouts of "kill that nigger" from the racially biased crowd.

Lem's mother was disappointed when, after graduating from high school, he did not try for college. His grades were good enough to win him a scholarship, at least from a small Negro school in the South. But as Rick's reputation grew, Lem kept postponing college, secretly wanting to go but unable to separate himself from Rick at this exciting time in his life.

Not only did Rick's first bout at Boston Garden end his apprenticeship as a club fighter, raising him to main-attraction status, but it forever ended his notion of boxing as fun. Thereafter, with the addition of big-time promoters and gamblers and reporters to his following, his boxing became more of a business than a sport.

Part of Rick's contract with Al Lakeman was purchased by Walter Chatfield: a dapper, self-made man who owned many of the racetracks and boxing arenas throughout the state and who moved freely and with flair between the world of sports and Boston society. Since Rick used his beachside home in Hyannisport for a training camp that summer, he saw a lot of Chatfield during those months. And though always respectful, Rick was taciturn and uncomfortable in his presence, instinctively disliking the man though not quite certain why. Lem knew why: Chatfield was a snob and a bigot, letting them use his place to train so that he could show them off to friends, as if he were a Roman patrician and they his gladiators.

Before the summer ended, however, Lem's feelings for Chatfield encompassed fear as well as dislike—for by then Rick was having an affair with his seventeen-year-old stepdaughter, Kim. A moody, motherless, headstrong girl whose strikingly attractive face and figure were just reaching maturity, Kim missed the passing of her tomboy days when she could have fun with the men in camp without arousing their sexuality and seemed uncomfortable in the role her looks and debutante status had thrust on her. Though Lem enjoyed her vivacious behavior at the card table or on the beach and was sometimes awed by her beauty, he initially suspected she was using Rick: both sexually —the best body around—and in defiance of the social price tag her stepfather tended to place on all her men. But as their relationship continued, as he heard Rick talk more about the pleasure of her company than her body and saw the looks they sometimes shared, he was no longer certain how Kim felt. Still, their affair troubled Lem, for he could easily imagine a man with Chatfield's pride of ownership having Rick maimed or even killed should he learn of it. No matter how careful they were, it became a perpetual worry for Lem, one which he finally managed to shed only after he and Rick had embarked for Korea.

Chapter Thirteen

War, not a sense of injustice or ideas in a book, is the true breeder of revolutionaries, for only war can teach them the indispensable lesson: the trivial nature of human life. . . .
—From the notebooks of Lemuel Harper

Lem Harper fought two wars in Korea, one with the enemy and one within himself. Arriving there in the spring of 1951, at a time when the United Nations forces had finally recovered from their headlong retreat in the face of overwhelming red Chinese hordes, Lem's infantry unit was immediately thrown into the fighting for the Iron Triangle sector north of Seoul. There, among its death-infested hills, he quickly discovered that all his preconceived notions of war were wrong, that no matter how unique, how gory, no single sight or sound was as frightening as war's awesome intensity—the kind of brain-shock that kept the roar of artillery fire in his ears and the bloody images before his eyes long after the battle had ended. And just as countless other soldiers before him had learned to overcome their fear of dying by various devices, by believing they were more devout or worthy or indestructible than their fellows, so too did Lem, only in his case his hope for salvation depended less on what he was than on what he promised to become.

Weeks later, after what remained of his company had finally

been withdrawn from the southern slopes of Heartbreak Ridge and rotated to the rear, a change came over Lem. Separating himself from his fellow soldiers, even the blacks among them, he spent much of his free time thinking. Though he had now learned a great deal about the behavior of different men in battle, he realized he knew practically nothing about the North Koreans and Chinese, for while they were the current enemy, they too were "colored," and someday that status might change.

So strongly, so single-mindedly did Lem feel driven by this curiosity that in the fall of 1951, a time of stalemate in the fighting, he requested a transfer from his line outfit to a prisoner-of-war camp.

"Kojedo Island! You want a transfer to Koje!" Captain Calder, the company commander, exclaimed. "Jesus! That's one of the worst duties in Korea—for raw recruits and misfits, not for a good soldier like you, Harper. What the hell's gotten into you?"

Lem shifted uneasily under his stare but remained silent.

"C'mon, damn it!" Calder snapped. "Tell me! I'm not going to approve any request like that unless I know why. Hell, if you ask me, it's enough to get you a Section Eight. Don't tell me you suddenly turned gutless."

"It ain't got nothin' to do with guts," Lem said sullenly.

"All right, all right." Calder gestured placatingly. "I know that. But why Koje?"

"Well, I sort of been thinkin' things over . . ." Lem said haltingly, realizing that to manipulate a New Yorker like Calder without arousing his suspicion he would have to play the dumb nigger sparingly.

"Like what?" Calder prompted.

"Like what I might want to be doin' after the war. I'm from Boston, you know, and there ain't that much work for blacks. There's some good jobs to be had at the prison though. The Charlestown prison. Only if you want to get hired, it helps to have some experience."

Lem never knew whether Calder believed his story or whether the decision to transfer him had been based on doubts over his stability, but within the week he had been reassigned to the Second Logistical Command at Pusan.

Kojedo Island was twenty miles away. Barren, overcrowded, all but lawless except for the prisoners' own kangaroo courts, the cross-shaped island was not only the sight of the largest POW encampment in Korea but, to its one hundred and forty thousand inhabitants, the very personification of hell. A series of huge, makeshift compounds, thrown together out of canvas and cement blocks and surrounded by barbed wire, housed up to five thousand prisoners each. The lot of those who stood guard over them was almost as miserable. Not only were they few in number, twenty-five men per compound, but so worried over their outnumbered state that they avoided such routines as bed checks and inspection of quarters at all cost, depending on the watery isolation of the island to prevent escapes.

Lem was an exception. Assigned to Compound Seventy-six, the largest of the compounds and the one containing the captured enemy officers, he was held in some awe by its inmates because of his size and allowed to enter the compound at will. He visited almost nightly, first making the acquaintance of some of the lower-ranking officers and eventually of their leaders: Colonel Lee Hak Koo and General Pak Sang Hyen.

Lee, an early arrival at the camp and one who had probably been planted there to organize the prisoners, was a flinty-eyed man of ascetic habits. Though tolerating Lem's nightly incursions because his rigid Communist indoctrination would not let him believe that a Negro soldier, a member of an oppressed minority, could possibly be loyal to his oppressors, Lee held himself aloof from Lem, never condescending to engage in any political discussions with him beyond parroting the party line.

His superior, General Pak, however, was a more thoughtful and worldly man. One of the original group of North Koreans trained by Stalin to rule that puppet state after World War II,

Pak took a liking to Lem and spent many evenings explaining Marxist theory to him. Though Lem never revealed the underlying reason for his interest to Pak, he felt fairly certain he had guessed and that the patience his North Korean mentor showed with him derived from this tacit understanding.

From Pak he learned what he later came to regard as the Yin and Yang of revolution: those positive and negative forces which must be balanced in your favor in order to achieve success.

"On the positive side," Pak told him in his heavily accented English, "is the necessity to create myths—a mystique—as did Mao Tse-tung during the Long March. . . . The greater the leader, the more myths must surround him, for his followers must have myths, not fears, to feed on in order to die well.

"But there is an opposite side to the coin," Pak continued. "A need not only to inspire your followers but to demoralize your foe . . . In war, psychology is everything. You Americans may ridicule our almost fanatical fear of 'losing face,' failing to realize that to an Oriental it is of the greatest psychological importance."

"How come?" Lem asked. "What you so afraid of 'losing face' for, when all that gets hurt is your pride?"

"Because it is more than pride that we lose. It is the opening breach in our morale . . . Remember," Pak said in another of the aphorisms Lem faithfully recorded in his notebook, "to be maximally effective, the shedding of blood should first be preceded by the sowing of fear, so that demoralization, not defiance, follows the first drop."

Six months later, in May, 1952, the relationship between Pak and Lem abruptly came to a close. It ended the day General Francis Dodds, the commanding officer of the camp, foolishly allowed himself to be trapped and taken prisoner by Lee's men inside Compound Seventy-six. A furious General Van Fleet, the UN commander, immediately dispatched a regiment of paratroopers to Koje to break up the prisoners' fortifications and crush all resistance among them. As a further expression of his displeasure over the incident, not only were Dodds and his senior staff replaced, but most of the guards were transferred to frontline outfits.

In what seemed almost a replay of his earlier combat ordeal, Lem not only found himself back in the same vicinity of the Iron Triangle as before but sometimes fighting over the same terrain. This time, however, he was not so lucky. In one fanatical dawn attack, Lem's company's forward positions were completely overrun, and they might have been routed from their toehold atop a strategically important hill had he not almost single-handedly held the enemy off with machine-gun fire until reinforcements could be helicoptered in. For his heroism Lem received a medal and several enemy slugs in his left leg.

After emergency surgery at a mobile field unit, Lem was air evacuated to the base hospital in Japan where he stayed long enough to have a metal prosthesis inserted in his hip joint, and then was sent to Fitzsimmons Army Hospital in Denver.

Lem spent fourteen months there because of a complicating infection in the bone—an agonizing interval made even more so by his awareness that, should the infection fail to heal, the entire leg would have to be amputated at the hip and he would never walk unassisted again. It was a time of not only trial but retrial for Lem in which his belief in himself and his future, all his defenses, were disassembled—the last time Lem would ever allow himself to feel so vulnerable.

Toward the end of his lengthy convalescence, Lem spent much of his time in the hospital library, reading books Pak had recommended as well as others he had discovered for himself. With his interests ranging from history to politics to psychology, he read almost incessantly, preferring biographies—Lenin, Mao Tse-tung, Marcus Garvey— for they demanded less concentration, yet realizing that when compared to the other categories they were the least informative. More and more, Lem found himself drawn to books and articles about Black Africa, not because he felt any particular kinship with its people, but because its burgeoning quest for self-determination evoked his interest. Though Lem knew he must first return to Boston to care for his mother, hopefully to find Rick, he considered joining Jomo Kenyatta's band of insurgents in Kenya should he fail to find any peace or hope for change at home.

Between daily stints at the library, or late at night, he thought of Rick. With each passing day, each mail call, Lem grew increasingly more disturbed that he hadn't heard from him in so long. Though they had taken basic training and shipped out together, Rick had come down with hepatitis shortly after arriving in Korea and the two of them had separated. They had corresponded, however, and met periodically on R & R—the last time at Pusan when Lem was enroute to Kojedo Island.

Like Captain Calder, Rick could not understand Lem volunteering for such a post, since most of the soldiers he had known had been sent there more as a punishment than a duty.

"Why you dumb-assed nigger!" he had sneered. "What the hell do you want to go to Koje for? There ain't no women there, no recreation facilities, just prisoners! Thousands of gook prisoners. What's the matter, Lem—you turned queer all of a sudden?"

"If that were true, which it ain't," Lem said, "I wouldn't want no gooks. I'd want a beautiful hunk of man like you, Mandrake."

Rick grinned but continued to press for an answer. "Seriously, Lem, why Koje?"

"No big mystery. It may be a shithole of a place, but the fishing's good, and it's away from the fighting and I'm tired of having some white squad leader always sending me out lead man on patrol to get my ass shot at."

Rick sought a verification in his eyes, but Lem turned away— guiltily realizing that it was the first time in all their years together he had consciously lied. He had kept the truth from him, not because he was afraid Rick would ridicule or betray him, but because he was white and might not understand.

After the signing of the armistice at Panmunjom Rick too had returned to the States but, needing cash for some undisclosed reason, had put off visiting Fitzsimmons in order to arrange for a pro bout. Walt Chatfield had signed him to fight Red Bishop, a ranking middleweight, and with the date of the match six weeks off, Rick had been forced to go into training immediately.

News of the fight worried Lem: He knew how hard it would be for Rick to get back into shape after such a long layoff and that, in Bishop, Rick would be up against a crafty, durable, rock-fisted opponent.

Rick too had expressed concern over Bishop, but the purse he had been promised was a fat one and he needed the money.

"Why?" Lem had asked in the last of many telephone conversations. "Didn't you save any in Korea?"

"Yeah, but I need more."

"For what?"

"I can't talk about it now. Not over the phone. Tell you when I see you."

"You're not in some kind of trouble, are you?"

"Trouble? No, not the kind you mean. Not yet, anyway. There might be some with Chatfield later on, but I can handle it."

"Why Chatfield? The fight's clean, ain't it? You're not mixed up in some kind of fix?"

"No, nothing like that. It's just that I'm thinking of quitting afterward and—"

"And what?"

Lem heard Rick mumble a few words to someone beside him, then say, "Sorry, Lem, gotta run. But don't worry. I'll be out to see you right after the fight and tell you all about it. . . ."

The Ferrar–Bishop fight took place at Boston Garden in early January. Lem had heard it over the radio, courtesy of the Gillette Razor Blade Company. He had lain in bed, with an intravenous solution of penicillin dripping into a vein in his arm

120

and his leg immobilized in a split cast, and listened to the brutal beating Rick took for most of the fight. Though knocked
down in the third and fifth rounds, he had fought back with the
same wild, wounded-animal frenzy Lem so well remembered.
In the ninth, Rick managed to open a cut above Bishop's eye,
then zeroed in on it so that blood splattered over the ring with
each jab. Bishop's handlers worked frantically between rounds,
applying clotting agents to his cut, but they failed to stem the
bleeding and the referee stopped the fight.

Lem strained to hear the referee's decision amidst a sudden
burst of static on his radio and then, face bathed in sweat, lay
back in bed. Though glad Rick had won the fight, he was more
pleased it was over and that the vague foreboding which had
gripped him, which had made him fear that his beloved friend
might be killed in the ring, had proved empty after all.

On the clear November day when Lem was released from
Fitzsimmons, his leg as healed as it would ever be, and walked
Denver streets with the majestic, snow-peaked Front Range of
the Rockies shimmering in the distance, he was forced into one
final reflection, one last reassessment of his life. Was his drive
for respect, for revolution if necessary, really so dear that he
would allow it to deprive him of his longing for peace, the joys
of friends and family?

In answer, Lem thought back to Heartbreak Ridge, mentally
superimposing its bleak, barren landscape on Colorado's scenic
beauty. What was it their commanding general in one of his
Sunday radio sermons had told them justified such a bloodbath?
That, by keeping South Korea for the South Koreans, they were
likewise keeping America for the Americans, Colorado for the
Coloradans. But many of his black brothers had died there, too,
and he himself had been wounded, and what was left for them
to keep? Nothing! Hell, they were lucky if they got to keep any
of their pride.

Chapter Fourteen

The day Lem Harper was destined to suffer another embitter-
ment had been an uneventful one until then: a cold, drab, mid-
dle-of-the-week day, even with the spreading signs of Christmas
approaching. A monochromatic gray from dawn to dusk. Except
for his growing concern over his mother's health, most all the
days and nights he had passed since his homecoming had been
ordinary ones spent in ordinary fashion. But what Lem Harper
thought and did was hardly ordinary for one who looked like
him: a huge, shambling black man who appeared as though he
belonged on a construction crew or in a foundry, somewhere
other than where he could be found much of the time—in the
reading room of the Boston Public Library.

Having been home more than a month now, Lem had fallen
into something of a routine: spending his mornings, weather
permitting, taking long walks along the banks of the Charles
River to strengthen his leg, and his afternoons at the library.
Evenings, however, were worst and different for him. In the
early part, he would sit with his mother, telling her about his
reading and the day's events, then listening as with agonizing
slowness she would try to make her stricken vocal muscles respond intelligibly.

At nine Lem would help his mother into bed and then go
out, seeking some relief from the stale air and sense of confine-

ment of their small flat. He would walk from one end of Washington Street to the other, from the uptown theater district with its storefronts festooned with glittering Christmas decorations to the walled-in complex of bleak lights and antiquated buildings that was City Hospital.

At the outset of such a walk Lem would usually be in a somber mood, conscious only of the terrible sense of futility he felt over his once-proud mother's deterioration and the ever-present pain in his leg. But on the return, particularly after he passed the Dover Station, the dividing line between upper and lower, the fashionable section, and the slums of Washington Street, his thoughts would often escape from his present frustrations into the past, conjuring up childhood memories with each block. Here, the now-abandoned neighborhood clubhouse whose entrance had once been forbidden to him and so, in his childish imagination, had become a center for every conceivable vice. Next, the McFee house in whose cellar he and Rick had first violently met.

Where *was* Rick? The question obsessed him. If he were dead, Lem reasoned, he would have heard about it by now. As the beneficiary of Rick's GI life insurance policy as well as his own, Lem's mother surely would have been notified. Yet if Rick wasn't dead, where was he? Al Lakeman didn't know, nor did any of their mutual friends. Not even the Army knew, since all the mail they had sent to the Boston hotel he had given as his forwarding address had been returned to them bearing the stamp, PRESENT WHEREABOUTS UNKNOWN. It was Standard Post Office procedure, nothing unusual or conclusive about it. Yet once remembered, the phrase echoed hauntingly in Lem's mind. For an organization as omniscient as the United States Army not to know the whereabouts of one of their ex-members, a veteran they might want to reclaim someday, struck him as vaguely ominous.

The same walk each night, the same thoughts, the same balm of booze at the same bar—Brecht's—at the end. Though Lem knew that he was drinking heavily, more than he ever had for any sustained period before, he needed a certain level of alcohol in him along with barbituates in order to override his pain and allow him to sleep at night.

Brecht's Bar, run by a bartender named Ernie Doyle, an ex-cop who had quit the force after twenty years and after, it was alleged, he had shaken down enough pimps and panderers to afford to buy the bar from its original owner, was an after-hours' spot, almost a musicians' haunt, that required no special membership or price of admission after the legal closing hour of one A.M., only Ernie's agreement to let you in.

Lem liked this exclusiveness, its freedom from slobbering drunks, as well as the subdued, sometimes serious conversation generated by the dozen or so patrons who congregated there regularly each night. An old friend, George Robinson, a talented horn player, had first told him about the place, then helped him win Ernie's favor, and so for the past few weeks Lem had made a habit of ending his nocturnal wanderings there.

One night George had tried to do even more for Lem by bringing along a girl for him: the young vocalist who sang with his combo during their present engagement at the Savoy. Her name was Janey Towns and she was tall, tawny, and svelte. Twice married and divorced, once to a black musician, once to a white, Janey had been heading for the skids before George hired her and steered her away from drugs and the wrong kind of men. A handsome, white-haired man in his early forties, George had helped her out of kindness, not lust. Though he enjoyed looking at her undulating backside as she sang and knew she could be his for the asking, he was a family man with an attractive wife and so never did ask her. Still, Janey needed more than a father figure, he realized; she needed a man in her life, one strong enough to control her as well as daunt others—and so Lem.

While Lem found her both pretty to look at and pleasant to talk to, for reasons which he did not immediately divulge to either George or her, his interest stopped there. Thinking Lem might have a puritanical streak that disapproved of her intimacies with white men, Janey once accused him of this, not realizing it was the perpetual pain he was in that dulled his sexual drive. When he finally admitted this to her, she was surprised and at once solicitous, offering accommodations.

"You that anxious?" Lem remarked.

"I like big men. Big and black like my daddy."

"What happens if you get to likin' one too much?"

"Suppose you tell me?"

"How 'bout a trip to Africa for openers?"

"Africa! Don't tell me you're one of those back-to-Africa Negroes? Hah! What've they got there that's so special?"

Lem hesitated, then dismissed the challenge with a shrug. "Nothin'."

"Oh, c'mon, Lem. Don't put me down," she said contritely. "Tell me!"

"Well, there's Kenyatta and that Mau Mau band of his; you know—their faces painted up and drinking their victim's blood like everyone *knows* us black savages all love to do! There's also a bunch of white folks who are scared shitless over it. I'd like to see that."

"Yeah, me too. But not if I have to go all the way to Africa. Why swap one jungle for another?"

Looking for aspirin, Lem spotted the syringe and needle in Janey's medicine cabinet and was relieved to hear she had shot up only a few times before laying off. He was also relieved there was no heroin on hand, not so much for Janey's sake as his own. The throb in his hip had grown so intense following their lovemaking that he might have been tempted to shoot some himself if there had been any around.

When Lem returned home from the library the next evening, he was surprised to find their front door ajar. Hurrying inside,

125

he found his mother bright-eyed with excitement. They had had a visitor, she told him.

"White or black?"

"W . . . Wh . . . White," she said, and by the same slow process of articulation she managed to tell him he was a friend of Rick's.

"Rick!" Lem cried, feeling a resurgence of his all but abandoned hope. "When did he see Rick last, did he say?"

She shook her head.

"What was his name?"

She shook her head again.

"What did you tell him?"

In a guttural stammer, Lem's mother managed to convey that she had told him her son was studying at the library and that he should come back in a few hours.

Lem was about to lash out at her for finding out so little but held back and went into the kitchen to begin supper. He knew he would be in for a long and anxious wait before this visitor, this friend of a friend, returned.

Dan had not started out the day with the intention of looking up Lem Harper. Still harrowed by the ghostly, yet all too real and readily remembered, images of his nightmare of the other night, he had grown more guarded in his pursuit. But after having attended a lecture at Boston City Hospital that afternoon and already in the vicinity of the Harper address, he impulsively decided to drop by.

The man he sought, this friend of Rick's, had not been home, only his mother. And though Dan had not been particularly bothered by her speech infirmity or the squalor of the tenement they lived in, he felt vaguely guilt-ridden over the way he'd misrepresented himself to her and had no desire to go back. But Mrs. Harper had seemed so agitated over her son's absence, so insistent he return to meet him, that Dan had promised he would.

126

At nine thirty, after supper and a restless couple of hours spent at a movie, he again sought out the Harper residence among a row of tenement houses off Washington Street. Since most of the dwellings lacked street numbers and were of equally battered fronts, he confirmed the address with a Negro youth who stood in the doorway smoking a cigarette, though he appeared barely age ten, and then entered. The hallway was dimly lit, smelling of furnace fumes and uncollected garbage. He stepped around a hoodless baby carriage, filled with empty bottles, and began to mount the creaking stairs.

Dan's throat felt scratchy and his nose congested with the beginnings of a cold. He had swallowed a few aspirins earlier in hopes of warding off such symptoms and now his face felt flushed and he perspired heavily underneath his overcoat. As he paused on the first landing to loosen his scarf, he wished for a moment he were home—not home on Beacon Street but home in Williamstown, where he and his Uncle Woody could sit by the fire and discuss the morbid way he had reacted to medical school: the obscure anguish he felt upon entering and leaving the anatomy lab each day. What might Woody advise right now—to push on, meet this Lem Harper, or turn back? To pursue the compelling curiosity he felt toward his cadaver until he had some inkling as to why, or seek the answer through the aid of a psychiatrist? Dan had considered the latter course before, though never seriously, never without comic overtones:

"Well, Doctor," he concludes, "that's the story."

"I see," the psychiatrist says, displaying the decisive nod, the thoughtful tweak of chin whiskers, the probing look—the panoply of his profession. "Most unusual . . . Could it be you are, uh, in love with your cadaver?"

"In w . . what?"

"Love. I'm referring to the Freudian sense, of course."

"How could I—I'm cutting him to pieces?"

"Ah, but remember Wilde: 'Each man kills the thing he loves.' Perhaps you feel you've killed him?"

"No, he was already dead."

"I see." Again the nod, tweak, look. "Maybe, it's death that you love. The closeness to it."

"I doubt it."

"Yourself then? Do you love yourself?"

"Not particularly."

"But to be this disturbed you must love someone. Someone you can also hate. Otherwise there is no conflict. Think now!"

"You're right. There is someone—"

"Good, good. Who?"

"You, doctor. I love you. In the Freudian sense, of course."

A sudden loud noise, a door slam, made Dan cringe and pivot sharply. But it was only the youth he had passed earlier on the front stoop coming in. What made him so damned edgy? Because he was in a bad neighborhood? Or because this Lem Harper was a Negro? Though Dan had been friendly with blacks before—in sports, in the Army—and was unaware of harboring any prejudices toward them, he had always felt slightly intimidated in their presence, especially when they were in a group. Rather than being merely skin-deep, it almost seemed to him as if their blackness reached all the way back to their brains, bestowing a different way of thinking, of feeling, on them—an ethos which a nonblack could never hope to understand.

Still, as Dan trudged up the remaining stairs and knocked on the door, it was not so much Lem Harper's blackness that troubled him as what he might say to him. He knew the story he had concocted for Al Lakeman's benefit was flimsy and might easily be exposed. But he had no further knowledge of Rick with which to embellish it, make it sound more convincing nor, suddenly, any time.

All too soon, the door in front of him swung open and Lem, dressed in an Army-issue khaki overcoat, appeared. Dan retreated a step as the man's massive body filled the doorway, blocking out most of the inner light, then crowded him on the narrow landing. Looking up at him, Dan experienced the same dizzying sense of disproportion as if he were looking at a distorting mirror. Did the hulking figure before him really exist in the dimensions by which he perceived him or was he merely another product of his freakish imagination? A personification of his deepest fears? With his skull-shaped head and bulging eyes and a scraggly, half-grown beard covering the lower half of his face, Lem was the most imposing man he had ever seen. The most evil-looking, too, Dan thought, then saw his face transformed by a self-conscious smile and reconsidered.

"I'm Lem Harper. You the one who came around looking for me earlier?"

Dan started to reply, but his throat contracted and he merely nodded.

"What's *your* name?"

"Dan . . . Dan Lassiter," he managed to croak.

Lem's huge, fleshy hand wrapped around his in a firm, though not overpowering, handshake.

"Sorry I can't invite you in, but my mother's sleeping and I don't want to wake her. . . . She tells me you're a friend of Rick's?"

As Lem spoke, Dan became aware of how his gaze seemed to focus on him, wary and unblinking and penetrating. Beginning then and repeating whenever they talked, he felt a great need to weigh his words, as though Lem's gaze were strapped to him like the leads of a sensitive lie detector. For an instant, as he smelled the faint odor of liquor on Lem's breath and his bulk crowded him to the edge of the staircase, his fear of the man grew almost palpable. But as Dan had long ago conditioned himself to do he reacted to such a frightened state paradoxically, turning it into a rising, sometimes reckless anger.

"Yeah, I know him," he replied flatly, returning Lem's stare and signaling his impatience to move elsewhere by the way he fidgeted. "We met in the Army."

Lem reached behind him to close the door. "There's a bar I know around the corner. Okay with you if we go there?"

"Fine," Dan said, and preceded him down the stairs. Turning to look back as he held open the outside door, he noticed the stiff way Lem swung his leg out before putting it down but thought it might only be a peculiar awkwardness of his size until he reached the landing and Dan saw him limp.

As they descended the front stoop Lem suddenly lost his balance on the icy walk and groped about for support. Dan was momentarily startled as Lem clutched his shoulder and he could feel the enormous power of the man transmitted in his grip.

"Hey, I'm sorry," Lem said sheepishly. "Didn't mean to grab hold of you so hard. If I'd known it was this slippery out, I would've brought my cane. But I'm tryin' to get along without it. Canes make people nervous."

"Oh?"

"Yeah. Makes them feel that if they don't get up to give you their seat or somethin' out of the goodness of their hearts, they might get hit with it."

"How'd you hurt your leg?" Dan asked.

"Got shot in the war."

"What war?"

"Not the big war—the little one. Korea."

"Where'd you get wounded?"

"Around Kumsong. Ever hear of it?"

"I heard. I was over there, too."

"Oh yeah?" Lem said casually. "When?"

"Early on. I had the full tour—from Inchon to the Yalu and back again."

"How'd you get in so early?"

"Just bad luck. I was ROTC in college and they told me if I volunteered after my junior year they might send me to Japan. They did, too. I was over there about a month when all hell broke loose in Frozen Chosen." Dan shivered as a chill wind blew against his face.

"This is the place here," Lem said, as they approached a storefront with frosted windows and a wooden sign, BRECHT'S BAR, hanging above the entrance.

Dan followed Lem through the door.

Though warm and brightly lit, the inside of the barroom matched its drab exterior. Its wooden floor was grimy-looking and its walls, a lime-green with white molding, badly in need of repair. A collection of cardboard posters of past boxing events at Boston Garden were hung at intervals for decoration and to hide gouges in the plaster. The bar itself was short, with room for only eight stools. Behind it was a beer keg, a rust-stained tile sink, and a hanging shelf which displayed less than a dozen bottles of liquor. The one splash of color in the room was a large, unframed oil painting of a Negro jazz band whose members looked as doll-like and mechanical as mannequins in a store window. Done in bold strokes and contrasting blocks of color: shades of blue in the dress of the musicians, their instruments a bright gold, a hazy, smoky magenta for background—it was an eye-catching composition. Ernie later told him it had been painted by a prisoner on death row: a junkie and a murderer, but also a man of some sensitivity who had further impressed those who knew him by the unflinching way he faced death in the electric chair.

Asked by some brainless reporter how he felt in his final moments, he had replied: "Death? It's just another trip, man. The biggest!"

Lem preceded Dan to the bar to speak a few words to Ernie in private, then beckoned him. "This here's Dan Lassiter," he said, introducing him to Ernie and two other patrons who sat listening to the broadcast of a prizefight over the radio.

"Glad to meet ya, kid," said Ernie, a burly, balding fleshy-faced man, and wiped his hand on his apron before extending it. "Hey, good fight tonight, Lem. Kid Gavilan. Just started."

"Dan's a friend of Rick's," said Lem. "They were Army buddies."

"Yeah! How's Rick anyway?" Ernie said, sounding interested until the radio announcer's voice rose in pitch and rushed to describe the flurry of punches in the ring.

Dan followed Lem to a table away from the bar and the emanations of the radio. He took off his overcoat and tossed it over a chair, but the room still felt overheated to him. With his raw throat and stuffy nose, he felt ill as well as ill-at-ease.

"Gavilan's a good fighter," Dan said to fill the silence. "A little fancy with that bolo punch of his, but he puts on a good show. . . . Do you still follow the fights much?"

"Not like I used to," Lem said. "Before the war, I used to train Rick. Did he tell you?"

"No, but Al Lakeman did."

"Didn't Rick tell you himself?"

"No. You see, I only knew Rick for one afternoon. At Fort Ord. He was working out at the gym and we went a few rounds."

"You did? At Fort Ord?"

"Yuh. Later on, we shot some pool together and Rick told me to look him up at the Front Street Gym when I started school here."

"You goin' to school. What kind of school?"

Dan hesitated, feeling an unaccountable trepidation. He drew a breath, then said, "Medical school."

"It's all over!" Ernie yelled, and they could hear the sudden commotion of the ringside crowd over the radio. Ernie turned the set off and walked over. "Gavilan kayoed the bum in the third! Okay, Lem, I'm taking orders now. What'll you guys have?"

"Scotch and water for me," Dan said. "Make it a double. I'm catching cold and could use a stiff one."

"You want a hot toddy? That'd be the best thing for you."

"Sounds good," Dan said. "Thanks."

"Sure," said Ernie. "Hey, c'mon over to the bar. I want'a show you something."

Dan got up and followed after him, grateful to escape Lem's scrutiny.

"I got a picture of Rick pasted up back here," said Ernie, taking him behind the bar. "Cut it out of *Ring* magazine myself . . . Yeah, here. Still think he might've been middleweight

132

champ if the Army hadn't grabbed him. Might be yet—who knows—if he's still punchin'? He was plenty tough, let me tell ya. Even when I was a cop, I wouldn't try messin' with him."

Rick's picture was pasted up on the side of the beer keg, next to one of Jack Sharkey. He was posed in a crouch, coming on. Yet unlike the conventional publicity-shot smile or scowl, the expression on his face was almost a grimace: a look of irritation at having to stand still long enough for the photographer to snap his picture.

Though the face in the picture resembled the one Dan so vividly remembered, it was a younger, less marred, version and not altogether the same. One aspect was strikingly similar, however, for even in death there was no peace to be found in Rick's Ferrar's face.

Minutes later Dan returned to Lem at the table carrying his steaming drink in one hand and a bottle of whiskey topped by an inverted glass in the other. The jukebox in the corner played a scratchy version of "One O'clock Jump" and a portly Negro, carrying a guitar case, entered the bar and complained of the cold.

"Tastes good," Dan said, sipping the toddy. "Ernie tells me you're strictly a whiskey drinker."

"Yeah, whiskey," Lem said curtly. He poured some from the bottle into his glass and took a gulp. His Adam's apple rose and fell but his face remained impassive.

"So you goin' to be a doctor?" Lem said a moment later. "That's nice. I got a sister who's a nurse, only she's over in Germany with her husband. He's stationed in Landstuhl. . . . Rick know you goin' to be a doctor?"

Dan shook his head.

"How come?"

"I wasn't sure I wanted to be—then. I still had some college to finish."

"Oh yeah? And you met Rick in the Army, you say? At Fort

Ord? Let's see now—Rick got discharged around a year ago, so it must've been last November or December, right?"

"Around then," Dan said, having no idea what a safe estimate might be.

"And that's the last time you seen him? You ain't seen him since?"

The sudden change in Lem's manner perturbed Dan, made him feel increasingly edgy. Though Lem's questions seemed natural enough, there was an added bite to his tone, a certain mocking quality to the Negro dialect he turned on and off. "No," Dan said, then dared ask why.

" 'Cause I ain't seen him either."

With each made uneasy by their thoughts, they lapsed into a tense silence.

"What medical school you at?" Lem asked finally.

"State."

"Freshman?"

"Yeah. It's a tough year. Tough on your nerves. There's a lot you're expected to learn."

"Like what?"

"Basic stuff, mainly. Anatomy, biochemistry—things like that."

Again they were silent.

Dan finished his drink in a long swallow. The spreading warmth caused droplets of sweat to break out on his forehead. He was about to reach for his handkerchief when Lem said: "Let's cut out the shit, boy. Rick's dead, isn't he?"

Even hearing it said so abruptly Dan was not taken completely by surprise. But now that the words were out he felt trapped and menaced by them, witless to answer. The truth had to be told, he realized, but the truth was monstrous ineffably grim! *You murder to dissect.* Did he dare tell this mammoth, yet deceptively intelligent, black man that he, a mere medical student, had day by day taken part in the dismemberment of his friend? By what right, aside from a legal one could

134

he hope to justify such a grisly practice—let alone the rest of his involvement. What other medical student had ever sought out former friends of his cadaver? Not only was such behavior unprecedented, it was also punishable, he recognized. Yet whatever Lem might do to him could hardly be worse than what he felt right now. Steeling himself, he met Lem's implacable gaze.

Was Rick dead?

Yes, he was dead.

Beginning on the day his class was assigned their cadavers and he first set foot into the netherworld of the anatomy lab, Dan told him as much as he honestly could.

When he had finished, Lem nodded but made no immediate reply. Tight-lipped, he sheltered his half-filled glass in his hands and stared into it. When at last he did speak, his words came out haltingly. "What's left of him—of Rick? Is his face left?"

"Not much of anything is left," Dan said. "Just his back, his pelvis, his legs—all the rest has been dissected."

"Dissected? You mean, messed up? Cut to pieces?" Lem's throat muscles contracted.

"Yes."

"And did you learn much from it?" Lem asked bitingly.

"Anatomy! The three of us who worked on Rick's body learned his anatomy."

"Did using *his* body help you to learn it good? Better than the rest?"

"No," Dan said, again growing defensive. "I flunked the first exam. I let myself get rattled over working on someone like Rick and everything else about that damned anatomy lab. For a time, I even thought of dropping out of med school. But that's over. I'm doing better now."

"You are, huh? Well, you'd better! I'm tellin' you straight out, you'd better not go messin' up his body for nothin'! 'Cause there won't be that many people who'll have much to remember about a guy named Rick Ferrar. Just you and me and a girl who once loved him—that's all."

A girl, Dan thought with a stab of anguish, oddly, obscurely grateful that there had been someone to love him.

"Listen here!" Lem began abruptly, his thick lips flattening out against his teeth in a show of strained emotion. "I want to see him! I want you to figure out some way of gettin' me into that anatomy lab. I don't care how you do it—just so long as you do!"

As Lem spoke, he pushed forward in his chair, thrusting his face closer, so that Dan could see the fierce glint in his eyes. Lem's hands reached out too, gropingly, pleadingly, but did not try to touch him.

Dan winced and drew back. "You want w . . . what? No, I can't do it. Honest to God, I can't! No one, except medical school personnel, are ever allowed inside the anatomy lab. There are strict rules!"

"Don't give me no jive about rules!" Lem sneered. "You've already broken a few of them yourself. . . . Tell me, is Snider still your professor?"

The mention of Snider's name further flustered Dan. How could Lem possibly know about him? "Yes, he's still there," he answered feebly.

"He is, huh? Well, I don't suppose you told him it wasn't enough for you to mess with Rick's body, you had to go messin' in his life, too."

"No, I never did. Once I tried to get Snider to tell me Rick's name, but he refused. Advised me I'd be better off not thinking of him as a human being, just a cadaver . . . I almost wish I'd listened to him now."

"What was that you called him? . . . Oh yeah, cadaver," Lem said, repeating the word distastefully. "That's all Rick is now, ain't he? Lord! But I don't care how it eats at my gut, I still got to see him."

"Why? Why can't you just take my word he's there and not pretty to look at?"

"I've seen dead bodies before. Lots of them."

"So have I—only dead bodies aren't cadavers," Dan said

forcefully. "You know what cadavers are—dried-up meat! Believe me, they're as far from anything human-looking as you'll ever see."

"Maybe so," Lem said, suppressing a shudder. "But I still got to go see him. I can't explain why. All I can tell you is that it's important enough that I'll do whatever I have to to get you to do it. . . . Hell, I know Rick's dead and ain't nothin' going to change that. And yet, even knowin' that much, there's something I still got to do—something up here," Lem said, pointing to his head, "before he gets put into the ground."

Dan wanted to plead further, to spare Lem the sight of Rick's mutilated body as well as the danger to himself, but realized it was hopeless. "All right," he said, "I don't know how right now but tomorrow's the last full day of classes before the Christmas break and I'll try to figure out something. Give me a phone number where I can reach you in the late afternoon."

Lem nodded and poured whiskey into both their glasses. With the sudden release of tension between them, they again heard the jukebox music, though it had been playing continuously, and became aware of the presence of others. While they had talked, George Robinson and Janey Towns had come into the barroom.

"Stick around a while longer if you want," Lem said. "That white-haired fellow over there—the one talkin' to Ernie—his name's Robinson and he blows the best horn in town. Sometimes, if he's in the mood, he'll play for us."

"Okay," Dan said. Though still shaken by all that had happened, that had so escalated his involvement in the affairs of Rick Ferrar, he was reluctant to leave Lem with so many thoughts unexpressed, questions unanswered. "Look," he began boldly, "maybe my curiosity's gotten me into enough trouble already, but there's one thing I'd like to know. . . . Had you known Rick was dead before we met tonight?"

Lem shook his head. "I suspected it and hoped like hell I was wrong, but that's all."

"Then, how?"

" 'Cause I knew you were lying when you claimed you met Rick at Ord. He got his discharge on the East Coast, not the West: Fort Dix. That was one thing. But the clincher was when you told me you was a medical student at State."

"I don't understand—"

"Didn't you ever wonder how Rick's body ended up there?"

"Many times," Dan said. "He was so different from the rest of the decrepit old bodies they had in there. How did he? Did his body somehow go unclaimed? Yet even then there are laws. . . ."

"No, nothin' like that. Least, I don't think so." Lem gazed down at the tabletop for a moment, collecting his thoughts before continuing. "I can't tell you exactly, but I can guess. . . . When we were younger, before Rick made any money boxing, we had a lot of different jobs. We spent one summer workin' at some Jew cemetery out in Brookline. Lord, that job gave me the creeps, even being outdoors and all, and it didn't pay all that much. . . . Anyway, one day they held funeral services for some doctor. The rabbi said the prayers over the coffin and we buried it, only there was no body inside. Afterward, we asked one of the relatives about it, and it turns out the reason the body was missin' was 'cause he'd willed it to his medical school. That was the first time Rick and I had ever heard about anythin' like that, so we got to talkin'. Then one of the caretakers we worked with told us the medical schools were so hard up for bodies they were willin' to buy them. You know, pay somethin' in advance if you promised to let them have your corpse after you died. . . . Well, since we were hurtin' pretty bad for money at the time we decided to look into it. We asked around where to go, then showed up at Snider's office one day to find out how much he was willin' to pay." Lem grinned. "Now your Dr. Snider wasn't exactly what I'd call pissed off, but he wasn't too happy with us either—since not only was there nothin' to the rumor but he got pestered by it all the time. You know, drunks callin' him up at all hours wanting to sell their body for a few quick bucks."

Dan smiled at the mental image that Lem's word conjured up: the imperious Snider, attired in bathrobe or pajamas, trying to conclude a conversation with some wheedling drunk in the middle of the night.

"Well, Snider set us straight fast and was about to show us the door," Lem continued, "when all of a sudden he takes a closer look at Rick. Turns out, he's a fight fan and saw Rick win Golden Gloves. So we gets to talkin' about boxing and Rick turnin' pro, and next thing you know Snider offers him a job. It wasn't much, just a handyman job, but if you could stomach being around all those stiffs the pay was good, and when Rick told him he needed money to buy some new boxing gear, Snider reached into his pocket and handed him a twenty in advance."

"How long did Rick work there?" Dan asked.

"Five, six months, until his boxing career got goin' good and he quit. But he used to talk about what he'd seen up there all the time. Most of the talkin' was for my benefit, since he knew it spooked me, but Rick never seemed bothered much about death. He even said he was thinkin' of givin' them the rights to his body someday and tried to get me to do the same. I told him no thanks. That after hearin' him tell it, I wanted nothin' but a coffin and cold ground around my body, not a bunch of medical students pickin' away at it like vultures! Somethin' about that anatomy lab fascinated Rick, though, so I think he was serious about handin' his body over. Still, he never said for sure whether he did or not, so I don't really know."

"But he must've, don't you think? Otherwise, how else, after dying the way he did, could his body have ended up there? The only possible way he could've escaped a coroner's autopsy is if the cops had found a card on him saying he had willed his body to State. It *had* to be something like that or else no medical school could've got it."

"Maybe so," Lem said. "I do remember Rick making a special trip over to say good-bye to Snider before leavin' for the Army, so maybe he got talked into it then. . . . Maybe Rick figured if some medical school like State owned his body it might make him lucky. Or even if he did catch it over in Korea, they'd have to bring his body home, instead of planting it over there. . . . Anyway, that's the story—much as I knows about it— and it's why you and me are sitting here right now. There's just no figurin' how some things are going to turn out, is there?"

"No," said Dan softly. "I'm glad you told me."

Before Lem spoke again, a wistful smile passed across his lips. "Lord, there's really so much I could tell you about Rick and me. We were like brothers. From the time he was sixteen and ran away from that orphanage he was raised in, he even lived with us. Hell, talk about tough kids—there never was one tougher than him! Even guys twice his size were afraid to take him on 'cause they knew they'd damn near have to kill him 'fore he'd quit fightin'. That reckless streak of his used to bother my Ma a lot and she'd keep tellin' me it wasn't right for nobody to have that much violence and hate in him, but now I ain't so sure. I'll tell you one thing, though, I never knew Rick to be scared of nothin' or nobody. He said it was because life never showed him anything he wanted badly enough to be afraid of not gettin' or keepin'. That only when a man tried to hold on to somethin'—his looks, his money, his women—he had any reason to be afraid. You dig?"

Dan nodded, since in some small way Rick's philosophy resembled his own. "You said before that he had a girl—" he said tentatively.

Her name was Kim Chatfield, Lem told him. But before he could elaborate further, Ernie pulled down the window shades and dimmed the lights because it was now past the legal time to sell liquor. As the room darkened, drawing them together, George Robinson fit the mouthpiece to his horn and began to play the "Wang Wang Blues" in a style so melancholic, so attuned to their mood, as to make any further talk seem sacrilege.

140

Chapter Fifteen

When Dan got to the anatomy lab the next morning he was surprised to find the lids of their table unfolded and the area of the pelvis they were currently dissecting freshly moistened with water, yet no one there.

He approached Larry Parish at a nearby table. "Seen Carey or Earl around?"

"Carey was here a minute ago. Must've gone to the john. But Earl the squirrel hasn't showed yet. . . . Hey! You sick or something? You look like hell!"

"I'm okay. Just short on sleep."

"What'you been doing nights—studying or screwing?"

"What's the difference? Whichever one I am doing, I always feel like I ought to be doing the other."

"Yeah, I know the feeling."

"Say, Larry, if you're driving home tomorrow I might hitch a ride with you as far as Pittsfield. I can catch the bus from there."

"Naw, I can drive you the whole way. Welcome the company. You interested in double-dating over the holidays?"

"I'll only be home a couple of days. My Uncle Woody—he's a professor at Williams—is going to Washington for some State Department meeting and I promised I'd go with him."

"Hey, I'd almost forgot Woodrow McKinley Brock was your

uncle. I hear he was quite the operator in his day. That it was almost a tradition at Bennington for one of the political science majors to shack up with him."

"It still is, only he's more inclined toward junior faculty gals now. They're less wearing."

"Does he fix you up or do you play sharesies?"

"Jesus!" Dan said, shaking his head, "You and sex!"

"Listen," Larry protested, "after digging around in Aunt Jemima's pelvis all day, I'm lucky if I can think about it at all!"

Dan laughed and returned to his own table. After peering abstractedly at his cadaver's abdominal cavity, now gutted of viscera, he picked up a scalpel and forceps and began cleaning away fat from the forklike bifurcation of the aorta deep in the pelvis. Since he was unaccustomed to working alone, his thoughts soon centered less on what he was doing than *to whom,* making him lose heart for the dissection. Putting his instruments down, he remoistened the pelvis with the sprinkler bottle and then wandered away from the table.

He paused before a diminutive figure sitting on a shelf: a three-foot dwarf, truncated below the waist so that he was legless, yet a fascinating fellow despite his deformities. The left side of his face was intact; the right—with his eye protruding an inch, anchored loosely to its socket by leathery straps of muscles, and with his jawbone dissected to the teeth—was ghastly. He had a large hole in his gut as well, displaying a set of innards made of removable parts. Still, if one ignored such anomalies, he had rather a friendly expression when viewed from his better side and a definite twinkle to his glass eye.

Dan lingered long enough to reinsert his plaster-of-Paris intestines and otherwise tidy him up, then, excusing himself, turned to rest his elbows on the adjacent bench. Bleary-eyed, stomach-sick from the fetid smells pervading the room and the mucus-swallowing effects of his cold, he found himself seeing the anatomy lab in a strangely sharpened focus—a way he had purposely avoided for some time. Possibly because of Lem's impending visit, possibly because he felt so fatigued that his defenses were down, Dan viewed the array of bodies before him with the same sense of detachment he had experienced that first day, yet with certain differences. Unlike then, when some bizarre trick of imagination kept transposing his body in with the collection of cadavers, he was now able to regard them with a veteran's objectivity. But even so, the three-month-old process of progressive mutilation he surveyed across the lab made the scene infinitely more appalling.

He stared at the feet of the cadaver closest to him: its toes shriveled and charred like gangrenous rot; its heels a port-wine color from the lividity of stagnant blood. The corpse on the next table lay the opposite way: his head mercifully concealed in a brown paper sack but his entire left arm, from blackish, overgrown fingernails to the marble-white bone of his humerus, exposed. Shreds of stringy, brownish-yellow muscle still clung to his shoulder socket and the tendons connecting arm to fingers fanned out at the wrist like puppet strings. A metal bucket at the foot of the table was filled with flaky, parchmentlike peelings of skin.

Unlike the others in the room, one cadaver in the middle row—that of a large-sized man—lay stomach down. The hidelike skin of his back had been ripped lengthwise to demonstrate his lumbar muscles and hung down on each side in loose folds, making him look more like some monstrous, water-logged creature raised from the deep than anything remotely human. The spectacle of him sprawled out there was so hideous as to make Dan momentarily doubt its reality. Yet not only was it real, he reminded himself, but along with the clawlike hands, the forearms withered like dried-up drumsticks, the limp penises the color of overripe banana skins, just another of the unique sights to be seen in any anatomy department during its season. Only there and nowhere else.

But how could he possibly show this to Lem? No telling how a man that mammoth and moody might react? Dan knew that had he not been gradually conditioned, had he come upon a corpse as ravaged as Rick's abruptly, he could not have tolerated more than a single glimpse of it. It was a view of decomposed flesh, of the disintegration that even beyond death was the terminal human condition, which was meant to be hidden elsewhere from view in pine coffins. Like the photographs he had seen of the skeletal inmates of the Nazi concentration camps, those dead or soon to be dead, it was a spectacle so degrading and dehumanizing it might drive one mad if he were forced to gaze at it too long.

Still, despite the misgivings he felt for letting things get so far out of hand, a part of Dan remained stubbornly unrepentant. Taking a last look around at the corpses before him, he wondered who else besides himself cared a damn for any of them? What did his fellow dissectors—Earl, Larry, Roger—think? Were their dreams, their solitude, haunted too? Aside from dismembering their cadavers' bodies in order to pass the course, did they ever give them a second thought?

"Dan? . . . Dan?" Carey's concerned voice roused him. "You have such an odd look on your face. What are you thinking?"

He turned to her: pert, pleasant Carey, his only real ally in this insensitive group. "Just daydreaming. Wishing this damned course was over and I was someplace else right now."

"Oh God, so do I! I can hardly wait for Christmas vacation to start so I can get my clothes fumigated and finally scrub the stink of formaldehyde off my fingers. Pond's lotion doesn't do a damned thing for it, you know. Have your fingertips started to burn too?"

Dan nodded. "When are you taking off for Florida?"

"Tonight—the midnight train. You'll have to manage without me tomorrow, I'm happy to say."

"Too bad. Earl will be disappointed. He was saving the penis for you."

"Was he? I'm not surprised—the lewd little bastard! Now he'll just have to dissect it himself. Or you?"

"Not me!" he protested. "I'd get sick."

"Why? It's just a penis," Carey said archly.

"Maybe to you it is—you haven't got one."

"Okay, so I'm late," Earl said, joining them a few minutes later. "But wait till you hear the news: Snider rescheduled the exam for the day we get back from Christmas vacation. The very next day!"

"Oh murder!" Carey groaned. "That shoots a good holiday."

"Yeah, I'll bet the hometown boyfriend won't like that a bit," Earl taunted. "He's probably expecting you to come back in heat."

"For your information, Earl dear, only bitches go into heat. Wellesley women are merely *arousable*. But you wouldn't know, would you—since you've never dated one."

Preoccupied by the changed exam date, Dan barely heard the exchange. Though seemingly minor in comparison to his other problems, it did mean that, instead of accompanying Woody to Washington, he would either have to stay home in Williamstown or else return to Boston to study. "We sure as hell have a lot to cover for that midterm. Is the pelvis included, do you know?" he asked Earl.

"Yeah—the female pelvis, too. So I guess we'd better take a look at what they're doing to *Aunt Jemima* over there."

"About the coming exam," Snider said at the start of his afternoon lecture, and the class, like a well-trained drill team, snapped to attention. "I realize a good many of you are complaining because I've rescheduled it. But as you are about to learn, you will be held responsible for a great deal of anatomy: the entire thorax, abdomen and pelvis, at the very least, as well as one review question on the nervous system. . . . Yes, I hear the groans. But it's material you have to know. If you don't learn it now, while you still have the picture of your dissection fresh in mind, you'll have to work double hard later on to review it for your National Boards.

"Now, the reason I've changed the date is to give you as much time as you need over the vacation period to prepare yourselves. Some, of course, will require more than others. And this way you won't be so tempted to put the work off until after the holidays and find yourself with very little time left, indeed. It might mean a little less skiing or cutting down to one girl-friend, but you'll manage, and for this first semester at least you're all *married* to anatomy. So if any of you are planning to cheat, don't let *me* be the one to catch you! Are there any questions?"

"What about histology?" one student asked.

For the answer Snider beckoned to Dr. Laseur, who strode forward solemnly to the lectern where he spread several sheets of notepaper before him.

"Now copy this down," he commanded, "so I won't have to repeat myself. The histology exam will cover . . . *damned near everything!*"

"That settles it," exclaimed a loud voice in the rear. "I'm gettin' myself a divorce!"

Both Snider and Laseur laughed at the remark along with the class.

"Now then," Snider said, after resuming his place on the podium, "are there any further questions before we take up this afternoon's topic? If there are, ask them now, since I shan't be meeting with you tomorrow and the entire morning will be spent completing the dissection of the upper corpus before transsecting your cadaver. I warn you though—don't bother me with foolish questions such as, will there be anything asked on the brachial plexus or the facial muscles. I've already told you the sections that will be covered and needless queries like that will only put ideas in my head."

He waited, but there were no further questions.

"Well, with *that* out of the way, let's talk a bit about what is done with *association neurons* and *reciprocal innervation.*" Snider wrote the terms on the blackboard. "If the patient—fat, female, and forty—comes to see you complaining of a colicky pain in her right shoulder, don't be too sure it's not her gall-bladder that's the cause of her difficulty. . . ."

Thirty minutes later Snider concluded a concise but fairly informative lecture. His rare ability to explain abstruse anatomical concepts in simple, pragmatic talks like this was a feature of the man which helped compensate for his tendency to exact harsh and sometimes petty demands from his students, and the wisest of them knew it.

"Since I won't be meeting with you tomorrow—I have to give a little talk in Baltimore on my methods of teaching anatomy—let me take this opportunity to wish you all my very best, for the coming exam and for a happy holiday at home!"

With his actor's sense of timing, Snider stepped down from the podium at the first sound of hand clapping, triggering a resounding round of applause.

"One second, Dr. Snider!" James Kirby, the class president, shouted and from underneath his chair brought forth two colorfully wrapped packages, the class' joint Christmas offerings. For Snider, it was a handsome leather briefcase; for Laseur, a record album of what his wife had assured them beforehand was his favorite opera.

Dan stayed slumped in his seat while Kirby presented the gifts, too torpid to share in the festive mood. Still, there was something about the look of gratitude that shone on the anatomy professor's face that touched him. He was glad he'd chipped in to buy Snider the briefcase—and to hell with what he put on the exam!

At five that afternoon, after most of the class had gone, Dan went to Pat Walsh's office, hoping to feel him out about a means for getting back into the anatomy lab that night.

"Hi!" Pat said, spotting him in the doorway. "C'mon in and have a drink." He pointed to the bottle of Scotch the class had given him earlier.

"Thanks, I will," Dan said. "But first I have a little favor to ask you."

"If it's what I'm thinking it is, fellow, you're asking both late and in vain. Half your bunch has already been pumping me over what I might know about the midterm. The answer is 'Nothing!' Snider hasn't tipped his hand to anyone—least of all me."

"No, it's not that. . . . You might not know it, Pat, but I'm in a little trouble around here."

"How so?"

"Well, for one thing, I flunked the first exam."

"You did! Both parts?"

"Yeah, both. . . . Anyway, what I'm wondering is, well—I've been using my *Gray*'s to review a lot of anatomy lately," Dan said, knowing that to Pat *Gray's Anatomy* was like the Bible, "and I'd like a few hours in the lab tonight to go over it on the cadaver. I'm just hoping you'll be around to let me in."

"Gee, sorry, fellow. Tonight I got a dinner date with the Mrs. How 'bout tomorrow?"

Dan shook his head. "I'm catching a ride home in the early afternoon. . . . Well, never mind," he said with a gesture of futility. "Don't mean to burden you with my troubles. I'll just have to work it some other way—"

"It has to be tonight, huh?"

"Yeah. Afraid so."

"Well—okay. Go ahead then, I'll loan you my keys. Just make damned sure you don't tell anybody."

"Don't worry, I won't. You've no idea how much I appreciate this, Pat. . . ."

"Forget it. I know how rough it can get when you're worried about passing the course. I'm no great shakes when it comes to studying myself. . . . Sure, go ahead. It's the only way to learn—using the cadaver. I'll tell Paddy, the janitor, on my way out. He'll be the only one around and he won't bother you. The class gave him some booze too!"

Dan called Lem on the pay phone in a nearby drugstore, telling him curtly to come to the medical school at seven.

As the minutes passed, edging him closer toward the time of their meeting, a deep sense of foreboding so clouded Dan's mind that he could concentrate on nothing else—not the half-folded newspaper in his hand, nor the upcoming exam, nor even the greasy-looking bowl of drugstore soup barely tasted and cooling before him. And though a perverse part of him wanted Lem to suffer as he now suffered, bear the full brunt of Rick's disfigurement, his better instincts prevailed. Before leaving the drugstore, he went back to the pharmacy section and bought a twenty-foot Ace bandage with which to wrap Rick's head and face.

Chapter Sixteen

Dan returned to the medical school shortly after six. Except for lights in the lobby and library windows, the building was dark and deserted-looking. He slipped in, changed from street clothes to his white lab coat in the locker room, and then rode the elevator to the fifth floor. Anxious to get the distasteful job of bandaging Rick's head over with as quickly as possible, he was about to let himself into the anatomy lab when he first decided to make sure he was alone on the floor.

He was soon glad he had, for there were lights on in Snider's office.

Stopping so abruptly on rounding the corner that his momentum almost toppled him forward, Dan pressed his back against the wall so that he couldn't be seen from the open office door. *Snider couldn't be here!* he thought wildly. It would wreck all his plans if he were. But maybe Snider himself wasn't in there; maybe Paddy, the night janitor, was simply using the office as a cozy place to get tight.

But when Dan inched forward he saw no drunken Irish janitor. Instead, he saw Snider's bald pate bent over a writing pad on his desk, and his heart sank.

Almost as if he felt Dan's baleful stare on him, the anatomy professor suddenly looked up. Instantly jerking his head out of the doorway, Dan flattened back against the wall, frozen with fear. Had Snider spotted him? he wondered, needing all the self-control he could muster to keep from bolting for the stairs.

What the hell was Snider doing here so late? He seldom spent a whole day in the department, so why should he be here at night? For an irrational second Dan could almost believe the man's sole purpose was to frustrate him. But what to do now? Did he dare run the risk of sneaking Lem past Snider's nose into the anatomy lab? Discovery would, of course, be ruinous, but even then he might have been willing to chance it if he weren't so in the dark as to Lem's intentions.

Glum-faced, slump-shouldered, feeling not only defeated but demoralized Dan started to move away when he heard Snider's phone ring. He edged close enough to the door to hear Snider say: "No, that won't be necessary. I still have some work I ought to finish up, but I can meet you there. I'll leave right away. . . . Yes, I'm looking forward to it, too. See you in a little while, my dear."

Dan held his breath until he heard Snider hang up, then quietly sighed with relief. Things would be all right now, he thought. He backed around the corner of the corridor and waited out of sight until he heard Snider leave the floor. He looked at the luminous dial on his watch—6:30—and prayed Lem hadn't gotten it into his head to show up so early there was a chance Snider might run into him in the lobby.

"Jesus!" he exhaled, as the accumulated tensions of the past several minutes drained out of his muscles, leaving him limp. Tremulously, he inserted Pat Walsh's key in the lock of the anatomy lab door, turned it, and went in.

With the heating turned off for the night and the windows standing open to dilute the smell of freshly poured formaldehyde, it was bone-chilling in the lab. The faint light filtering in from the street was barely enough for Dan to see to thread his way between tables, but spared him the risk of turning on the overhead lights. Finally reaching the room where his cadaver lay, he paused on the threshold, feeling a sudden reluctance—the trepidation of a trespasser in a cemetery—to immerse himself in its shadowy stillness. Though he told himself the place held no surprises, that he had nothing to fear except discovery—from Paddy, from a returning Snider—the dissection room took on an almost predatory presence in the dark. Its transformation reminded Dan fleetingly of an afternoon he had spent skin diving in a deep inland lake and the change the water had undergone at twilight: less serene, less refreshing, almost ominous in its murky green opaqueness.

He snapped on the spotlight above his dissection table and broke open the lids. His first glimpse of his cadaver's pasty-gray carcass limned in the shine and shadows of the overhead cone of light made him cringe and turn away. "Damn it! Get a grip on yourself," he muttered, feeling more distress over the manner in which he'd overreacted than he did over the sight itself. He removed the Ace bandage from his pocket and wound several layers of the tan elastic around the head to hold the skull-cap in place and give it some semblance of its proper shape. Then he took several paper towels from the wall dispenser and stuffed them into the eviscerated cavities of chest and abdomen.

Before he reclosed the table lids, Dan stepped back to eye his handiwork. Had he really done more than transform a hideous-looking corpse into a ludicrous one: a mummified monster out of some late-night horror movie? That would be for Lem to decide.

With a sigh, Dan left the anatomy lab and unlocked the door to Pat Walsh's tiny cubicle of an office. He hunted in the desk for the bottle of Johnny Walker, found it, and poured himself a paper cupful. He then downed it in two gulps, grimacing at its burning passage down his gullet but feeling almost instantly better.

He poured himself another helping of the Scotch but did not immediately drink it. Instead, a sudden feeling of forlornness, of deep despair, overcame him and he shut off the desk light, sank into a chair, and sat staring into the darkness.

With almost weary resignation, he thought about Lem. He was a poised, intelligent, highly intuitive man, Dan knew, but was he completely rational? Was he possibly possessed by some strange cultish conviction: a necrophiliac, a voodoo worshiper, a disciple of some Satanic order that impelled him to make a special incantation over Rick's corpse to deliver his soul? He was, of course, none of these things, Dan thought irritably. Yet even so, even in the face of his own irrational involvement, Lem's insistence on seeing his dead friend's remains struck him as utterly macabre, utterly inexplicable.

The next instant, as an escape, he thought of sex: of a nude Nora or Carey, a soft, complaisant body that he might later take in his arms and murmur to of false love and real desire. It was a transition that no longer surprised him. The anatomy lab stimulated sexual thought. It was more than a whim; it was a necessary diversion—an affirmation that although one was awestruck and appalled by this intimacy with death, one was not yet cowed into insensibility. Still, he had come close to succumbing to such an apathetic state; he had bordered on it for weeks, he knew—as, quite possibly, so did Carey.

The last time the two of them had studied together they had drunk heavily and ended up petting in bed. They almost certainly would have gone on to intercourse as well, except that Carey was menstruating. It wasn't as frustrating as it should have been. Even though Carey had been aroused to the extent of baring her breasts, she had doubtless sensed that he was holding back, that in his present mood he was reluctant to bear the onus of being her first lover.

It had been his last and best chance with her; she had not asked to come to his apartment again. Now he felt chagrined, remorseful, desirous of making amends, but it was too late to pursue it. Too late for tonight and maybe too late in their relationship.

Too late for Nora, too, he lamented. Seducing her had been a fluke, a fortuitous matching of moods, and nothing short of a marriage proposal was likely to get her back into bed with him again. The sad truth was, he had offered too little of himself to either woman. Instead of pursuing the promise of the living, he had pursued the dead. Why? What could it possibly have to offer that enthralled him so?

It was a few minutes past seven when Dan entered the lobby to find Lem waiting outside the glass doors. "C'mon in," he said, opening the springlock and shaking his hand.

Lem was still wearing his old Army overcoat, faded on the sleeves where the sergeant stripes had been removed, the same woolen sweater and corduroy pants, but Dan hardly noticed. Instead his gaze was drawn to Lem's face—the bulging brown eyes squinting in the harsh fluorescent glare of the lobby lights, bloodshot from what Dan took to be exhaustion or perhaps alcohol.

Lem nodded and gave him a brief twitch of a smile, and then his face reverted to its usual look of grim resolution—a forbidding face for a potential enemy, Dan thought, but not so malevolent as he had once thought.

"Snider was around here a little earlier," Dan said in the elevator. "Damned near scared the shit out of me. He left only a few minutes ago."

"Yeah?" Lem raised his eyebrows. "Think he'll be back?"

"Christ, I hope not! How long you planning to be?"

Lem peered at him intensely, guardedly, for a moment. "Not long . . . All I've come for is to take one last look at Rick."

"You sure that's all you plan to do—look?"

"Yeah! What the hell else?" Lem's glower was intensified by Dan's sudden silence. Lifting his shoulder from the wall, he took a menacing step forward, only to be thrown off balance as the elevator came to a jarring halt on the floor. Lurching sideways, Lem caught the handhold to steady himself, then confronted Dan again as he held open the door. "What *do* you think?"

154

"I don't know," Dan said, "and right now I don't give a damn as long as it doesn't take too long."

"I already told you it wouldn't. What you being so touchy about?"

"What am I being *touchy* about? Je-sus! I lay my whole medical career on the line to satisfy some goddamn whim of yours and you ask me *that?*"

"It ain't no whim," Lem told him stonily. "Believe me, it ain't. And I'm sorry it puts you on the spot, but I didn't come lookin' for you, baby, you came lookin' for me. Anyway, how much are you riskin'? I thought you told me you weren't all that sold on being a doctor?"

"Well, I am now," Dan said defiantly.

"Good! Glad to hear it. Country needs all the doctors it can get. . . . Who knows," Lem said, smiling sardonically, "you might even treat me someday—that is, if you take nigger patients?"

Dan did not bother to answer. He released the elevator door, cutting off the inside light and plunging them into darkness until he found and flipped the wall switch. The corridor lit up, displaying the cross sections of human brain encased in its walls. He saw Lem gaze briefly, distastefully, at them before averting his eyes.

"Look," Dan said, pausing at the anatomy lab door, "you sure you want to go through with this? I know you've seen dead bodies before, some of them so blown to hell they must've been pretty hard to stomach. But this is a lot worse than that. What you're about to see isn't Rick's body, but pieces of it. Just pieces! Believe me, it's going to grab your gut like nothing you ever saw before."

"Maybe so," Lem conceded. "But if you can take it, so can I."

"I take it because I've got to! I have a reason!"

"So do I!"

"What, for Chrissake?"

"Never mind," Lem said warningly. "Just don't you fret

155

about it. Maybe I'll tell you later. If I decide it's any of your business."

Dan shrugged, pretending not to care whether Lem confided in him or not. He unlocked the anatomy lab door and entered, Lem close behind. Almost at once he began to shiver again, not so much from the coldness of the rooms but from some deep, debilitating chill inside him.

Lem followed almost on Dan's heels as he led him through the two intervening rooms to the table where Rick's cadaver lay. He stopped a few feet behind and to the right of Dan as he turned on the overhead spotlight and unfastened the coffinlike lids. He stood silently, trying to control his breathing, but Dan felt his presence acutely. He wondered how Lem was tolerating the reek of embalming fluid, hoping he was getting a noseful, a bellyful—anything to shorten his stay. He wanted Lem not only to be sickened by the smell but to have to admit it: to groan, curse, choke on it. But whether or not Lem sensed such a challenge, he remained silent—perhaps abnormally so, Dan conjectured, making him more fearful of what his next reaction might be. "Here," he said, unfolding the remaining lid and stepping aside, "this is what a cadaver looks like."

Lem's chest heaved and his jaw muscles contracted. Otherwise, he showed nothing. "What's all the bandages for?"

"Leave them alone!" Dan snapped. "Don't touch them."

"What if I want to see his face?"

"Jesus, don't you understand—he hasn't got a face! Unwrap those bandages and there won't be any top to his head either . . . It's Rick though—take my word for it!"

Lem stared at the bandaged, paper-stuffed corpse a moment longer, and then, with teeth clenched, lips spread wide, turned to Dan and commanded softly, "Leave me alone with him. Wait outside. I won't be long."

Dan hesitated, then quietly left. What was the difference; he had come so far. As he went through the doorway he thought

156

he heard Lem emit a low, anguished moan but did not pause to listen.

He felt a sense of relief, of deliverance, upon reaching the warmer, brighter corridor—glad to be free of Lem, of both of them, for even a few minutes. While his curiosity over Lem's behavior continued, his concern did not; the self-control Lem had displayed assured Dan he had nothing to worry about. He likewise recognized that whatever extraordinary purpose Lem's visit served, whatever the communion that might even now exist between the two of them, was not meant for his eyes or ears or understanding. Not having known Rick during his life-time, knowing him now only as his memory was reflected in others, it excluded him totally. He was nothing more than an interloper, a meddlesome intruder in their lives.

Still, if that was all, why did he now feel so remorseful, so incapable of accepting it?

But whatever quirks in his makeup were responsible for sending him so far astray would simply have to remain a mystery. He was through torturing himself with it. Tonight's ordeal had brought him to his senses. These were real people, real lives, he had been tampering with—but no more. He had finally had his fill of sleepless nights, somber moods, nameless fears. From now on, he vowed, he would devote all his energies to his studies; on the next exam he would triumph.

Suddenly a noise—the meshing and whirring of gears and creaking of strained elevator cables—startled him. Along with the sound, a sudden qualm, almost a conviction, that Snider himself was riding the elevator paralyzed him with fear. What to do? Warn Lem, run for the stairs? What? he thought, too flustered to decide.

The elevator continued to rise, then came to a clanging halt on the floor below. Listening intently, Dan thought he heard the rattle of a janitor's cleaning cart. "Jesus!" he sighed and leaned weak-kneed against the corridor wall, feeling urgently in need of a drink.

The Anatomy Lesson

He glanced at his watch. Ten minutes had passed since he'd left Lem alone in the lab. Was he all right, he wondered. Or had he fainted, gone quietly mad in there? He'd better go check, he decided reluctantly.

Chapter Seventeen

Alone now, spared the pressures of Dan's scrutiny, Lem stood with the acridity of embalming fluid burning his nose and the back of his throat, the sight of Rick's putrid flesh hypnotically holding his eyes, and suddenly felt so racked with revulsion that he had to clamp a hand over his mouth and gulp hard to keep from retching. After taking several deep breaths he felt the upheaval in his stomach begin to subside, yet no sooner did he attempt another look at Rick when a second, more violent, swell of nausea sent him hobbling toward the sinks.

Leaning over the basin, he tried to vomit, but had the dry heaves instead. He was seized by several more spasms until he found the foot pedal that squirted cold water from the tap and doused his face in the water.

Again he approached the table, averting his gaze from Rick's head and chest and on his still intact, still powerful legs. Rashly, impulsively, less out of affection than to prove to himself that he could, Lem reached out and touched Rick's thigh—only to recoil immediately from its skin-crawling coldness. "You fool nigger! Crazy psycho!" he muttered harshly. "You gone insane?" Maybe he had at that. Maybe his hate, his pain had finally driven him so? Oh, he was crazy, all right, had to be, else why had he come to this doctor-run slaughterhouse? That Dan had warned him right: It was a lot worse than he'd imagined, worse than anything he'd ever seen before.

But he had to come. It was more than a whim, more even than the desire to honor a pledge to a dead friend that had brought him here. The promise he had once made Rick had been vague, more to humor him in his drunkenness than anything else, and so carried no great sense of obligation. Yet there was no denying it: Their talk that particular evening had contained an uncanny prophecy, Lem now recognized. Although hazy as to time and place, recalling only that the conversation had taken place when Rick still worked for Snider and on a sweltering hot night while they swilled beer at some bar, Lem thought back to it now. . . .

"Oh, come on, man," he had protested to Rick. *"Stop with that jive! You ain't serious about leavin' them doctors your body and you know it!"*

Rick flexed a bicep and slapped it. "Be the best damned body they ever had! . . . Truth is, I haven't decided. If I ever do, though, you got to come visit me."

"Visit you? Shit! What would I do a dumb thing like that for?"

"To make sure they're treating me right—with respect and all. You got to do that for me, Lem, else I'll come back and haunt you. Scare your black ass good!"

Lem looked at him disdainfully. "Lord, you even crazier than I thought! What'd you take a creepy job like that for in the first place? You like being around stiffs that much, you ought to be an undertaker, not a boxer."

"It ain't that I like being around them, it's just that they don't bother me none. Way I figure it, a dead body can't hurt you— not like a live one! Besides, even if I did sign my body over to State, there ain't a chance in hell it'd ever end up there."

"Why not?"

Rick hesitated, then forced a grin. " 'Cause I don't figure to die a natural death. If I don't get knocked off in the ring, it'll be in some alley. I can feel it in my bones."

Lem

Lem frowned. It always made him uncomfortable when Rick got morbid. "Man, that's just crazy talk and you know it! What makes you even think that way?"

Rick shrugged. "I just do, that's all. Always have. . . . You want to know somethin', Lem—sometimes I look in the mirror and I don't even know who I am. Either the face I see don't look familiar or else it looks funny. . . ."

"How you mean—funny?"

"Oh Christ, I don't know. My eyes mainly. Sometimes they look so flat, so lifeless, it's like I'm already dead. That's why death doesn't scare me so much, I guess. I even dream about it."

"You dream about dyin'?" Lam asked, shifting uneasily. "How?"

"Oh, it ain't so much how I die, as being dead. Know what I mean?"

Lem shook his head.

"Well, it's a funny feelin'. You can be dreamin' along about somethin'—somethin' dangerous—when all of a sudden there's an explosion in your head—like gettin' knocked out—and after that, nothin'. Just haze . . . It's not a bad feelin'—in fact, kind of numb and peaceful—only it could be a lot better if along with it you didn't feel so, uh, sad. . . ."

"How you mean?" Lem said, listening intently now, aware that Rick was revealing a part of himself he never had before. "Sad, like how?"

"Hard to describe, exactly. Like losin' a fight, I suppose. That kind of sad. You keep wishin' you could have another crack at the guy, only you know you can't. You're still sort of numb, though, so you don't mind too much—not like droppin' a fight in real life. The sad part comes from feelin' you should've done better; that you could if only it wasn't over and you've had your last chance. . . . That's what it feels like, all right, and that's why if I ever do end up in that anatomy lab, you gotta promise you'll come visit me."

"What for?"

161

"Jesus, you're dumb! I just told you what for—that in case there's anything left to do, you can do it for me."

"Oh yeah?" Lem sneered. *"Well, how exactly am I supposed to know that? You goin' to rise up and tell me?"*

"You just come see me, that's all. You'll know."

"Oh, I knows now. You're punchy! Make about as much sense as some old wino runnin' off at the mouth."

"Oh shit! You gonna do what I ask or ain't cha?" Rick demanded, his speech growing slurred and his stare more sullen.

"Tell you what," Lem said placatingly, *"I'll do it long as you promise not to go getting yourself knocked off on purpose just to make me keep my word."*

"Oh, you won't either. I know damned well you'll chicken out first!" Rick muttered. *"Jesus! Ain't nothin' lower than a guy who'd break his promise to a dead buddy!"*

"Yeah? Well, you ain't dead yet. Just dead drunk!"

A sudden mechanical sound—an elevator door closing somewhere below him—disrupted his reverie. He ought to be getting out of here, he thought. No need to stay any longer; he'd pushed his luck far enough. No need to stay in Boston much longer either. With Rick dead, and his mother soon to die, his last ties to the past would be broken and he'd be freed of all obligations, all encumbrances. . . . Or would he?

Suppose Rick had been murdered? Suppose, hell! He *had* been murdered. Every rotting cell in Rick's body transmitted the message and every fiber in his brain received it. No believer in the occult, Lem might have been able to ignore such a morbid intuition if it were merely a hunch, a gut instinct on his part, but it was based on far more than that. The suspicion had first entered his mind the night he'd learned from Dan the cause of Rick's death and he'd spent the afternoon reading about subdural hematomas at the library.

Rick might have gotten the injury during the Red Bishop fight—the last time Lem had heard from him—but he didn't believe it. Had Rick died shortly after that it would have made

162

headlines. And even if it had taken the blood clot a week or so to kill him, Rick was well enough known around Boston for any cop to recognize him, try to tie his death to the Bishop fight. . . . No, not only had Rick been murdered, Lem bitterly surmised, but some crooked cop or morgue attendant had probably disposed of the body by slipping it in here.

Another sound—a footfall?—made Lem tense and peer searchingly into the darkness. Hearing it again, this time near the door, he turned the spotlight in that direction and thought he caught a glimpse of a shadowy figure ducking out. Turning off the light, Lem groped his way out of the lab.

Dan was waiting in the corridor by the elevator. "That you I just heard movin' around in there?" Lem asked accusingly.

Dan hesitated, then nodded.

"Then why the hell didn't you say somethin'? What you sneakin' around for?"

"I wasn't *sneakin' around.* Just wanted to make sure you were all right."

"Well, okay then . . . I'm all through, so let's get the hell out of here."

"You want a drink first? I got a bottle in the office."

"Man, I could sure use one! Especially after—you know," Lem said, nodding toward the lab doors. "Thanks . . . thanks for the rest of what you done, too. I won't be botherin' you no more after tonight."

"Forget it," Dan said. "It's over for me too. I swear it is, even though there's still so damned much I don't understand. Especially about me—what got me so sidetracked on something as crazy as this in the first place—"

"Maybe it wasn't all your fault."

"What do you mean?"

"Let's go get that drink first!"

Over a cup of Pat Walsh's Scotch—he was going to have to buy Pat a new bottle—Dan waited for Lem to speak.

"What I mean is—" he explained, "that after seeing what

163

Rick, what a cadaver really looks like, I got some understanding of the kind of hell you been through. An experience like that must do funny things to a guy's mind."

Dan nodded. "Maybe it wouldn't have been so bad if Rick hadn't been so young, so different from the rest."

"He was different, all right! That orphanage he grew up in made him that way. I never knew nobody lived like Rick did. The funny part was, he knew he was goin' to die young—he told me so—only he never figured he'd end up in here."

"Why not?"

" 'Cause he never figured on dyin' of natural causes. He always expected some hood would get to him in some alley first. He might've been right too. . . ."

"You think so?" Dan said, surprised.

"I can't be sure yet. But I aim to find out."

"How?"

"Uh-uh," Lem warned, "Rick was *my* friend, so it's my responsibility. You just stick to being a doctor. You owe Rick that for using his body the way you did, and that's *all* you owe him. Anything else, I'll take care of."

Dan replenished their drinks. "There's one more thing I can't help wondering about," he said tentatively. "This girl of Rick's, this Kim something—"

"Kim Chatfield. What about her?"

"Do you think she knows Rick's dead?"

Lem shook his head. "Probably not. I called her once, right after I got back home, only she wasn't in town . . . why you care about that?"

Dan shrugged. "I don't, I suppose . . . Still, she should be told, shouldn't she?"

"Maybe so," Lem conceded, "only not by me . . . and not until a few other things get taken care of first . . . Hell, a gorgeous gal like that is probably married to some rich dude by now."

"But what if she isn't?" Dan persisted for reasons which were not immediately apparent to him. "What if she's still hoping to hear from Rick?"

"For what—to marry him? No chance! Maybe she did love him once—enough to take some risks for him—but marriage? Not for two people different as them. Walt Chatfield never would've stood for it. No sir! Not only because he figured Rick was low class, but because he sort of had a yen for Kim himself."

"Her own *father*?"

"Stepfather! I remember the way he'd look at her sometimes, especially in a bathing suit. Wasn't exactly *fatherly*. . . . No, if Kim still feels the same about Rick, I'm sorry, but I ain't about to be the one to tell her. Could you?"

"Only that he's dead. . . . Nothing about the rest." Lem emptied his cup and stared penetratingly at him, again making Dan feel an outsider, an intruder in their lives. "Better not," he admonished. "Better end it all now. Otherwise, you might be makin' a lot more misery for yourself."

Minutes later, after tidying up inside the lab, Dan left the building with Lem. "Are you going to Ernie's place now?" he asked on the front steps. "If so, maybe I'll join you."

"No, not till later," Lem told him. "Right now I got to go home to be with my mother. But drop around to see me sometime. Let me know how school's goin'."

"You mean it?"

"Yeah, I mean it!" Lem gave him a faint, sardonic smile.

"Okay, I will."

After their handshake, Dan lingered on the steps, watching Lem's huge figure shamble away and feeling loneliness emanating from the man. Now that the long, tense night was finally over, he ought to be feeling jubilant, he mused. Instead, he felt curiously let down.

He walked along Kneeland Street, wondering if there was any point in visiting Nora at the *Post*. Then he remembered she had gone to a party at Jennings Dell's place. Having met Dell, the music and drama critic for the *Christian Science Moni-*

tor, through Nora, he had been invited to the party, too. Dan hailed a cab, intending to go, but then, envisioning the crowded living room, the intense chatter of theatrical people, the forced gaiety, he didn't feel up to it and instructed the cabbie to drive him home.

Chapter Eighteen

A wood fire blazed in the hearth of the Williamstown house, its periodic crackling tending to make Dan pause in his speech, as if punctuating his long passages. Across from him in the twin easy chair, his Uncle Woody listened raptly, stirring only to replenish their drinks or feed logs to the fire. Outside the living room window the light snow that had fallen earlier to whiten the branches of the birches and maples in the front yard swirled in a gusting wind. Beyond the grove of trees lay the ivy-covered buildings of Williams College, the quintessential small New England campus.

Dan had gotten home at dusk after a tiring four-hour drive from Boston with Larry Parish. Though he had enjoyed Larry's easy banter along the way, now lethargy had set in. As usual, when Dan was home, Woody had no female houseguests. They saw each other so seldom these days that Woody wanted to keep their visits free from distractions—for which Dan was particularly grateful. Not only would they have less than two full days to spend together but he desperately needed to talk.

Woody's greeting had been boisterous as always, but the jibes he directed at Dan's appearance surprised and disconcerted him. Despite his cold, his irregular eating and sleeping habits, he hadn't realized he looked quite so gaunt and haggard. But he did, of course, he later decided; it had taken someone who knew him as well as Woody to discern that.

Dan had been relatively subdued over dinner at the 1896 House—a large red barn converted into a popular restaurant. Old friends stopped by their table and Dan tried to be enthusiastic, but his weariness showed if they lingered too long. Sensitive as always to his moods, Woody would steer the visitors away and keep his dinner conversation light—patiently awaiting that time when the subtle pressures put upon them by their reunion would relent and his nephew would open up.

Dan did not disappoint him. Returning home around nine, he had taken a shower and then, clad in bathrobe and slippers, sipped the first of many Scotches and soda by the fire. Initially he had been content to sit and listen to more of the same kind of chitchat that had entertained him over dinner—regarding Woody more critically and reluctantly deciding that his extraordinary uncle, now in his late forties, was beginning to show his age. Though he was still trim and compact of build, Woddy's grizzly hair was rapidly receding at the temples and the pouches under his eyes seemed more prominent.

Bit by bit, they had gotten onto the subject of medical school and Dan began to talk about the troubles he'd encountered there. At first vaguely general, under Woody's sympathetic silence and occasional prodding, Dan gradually became more specific. He spoke slowly, calmly, graphically, wishing neither to shock nor to spare his uncle by his use of imagery.

Woody said less and less in return, asking a few details about Nora and Carey, but then becoming so caught up in the revelation that he did not interrupt again. When, through fatigue, Dan's voice began to falter just as he was about to describe Lem's blood-chilling visit to the anatomy lab the previous night, Woody pushed coffee in place of booze and urged him to continue.

They talked for hours, conscious of the time only when the FM station softly playing in the background signed off the air at four A.M. When Dan finally finished telling all of it, Woody stared bemusedly for a moment, trying to comprehend the magnitude, the shocking nature of such an experience, then shook his head in wonder. "Wow! that's some tale! No wonder you look so lousy. I'm damned glad you didn't crack up completely under the strain. Hell, you haven't been at school, boy, you've been at war—with yourself, with the spirits, with the ethics of medicine, with—with everything!"

"That's about it," Dan agreed disconsolately. "What do you make of it?"

Woody threw up his hands. "Damned if I know. All the time you were talking I had to keep reminding myself this was all happening to you, Dan, not someone else. It's not like you to go off the deep end. I always pictured you as being pretty cool-headed, not that you're insentive or unfeeling about people, but more on the unemotional side."

"I thought so, too. What do you think happened to me?"

"Do you believe in ghosts? The supernatural?"

Dan laughed. "No. Maybe I should after all I've been through, but I don't."

"Well, I guess we can eliminate that possibility then."

"Maybe not," Dan said. "I felt haunted, all right—if not by ghosts, then from within. I especially felt that way last night in the lab. I kept getting this feeling that, instead of any great curiosity over my cadaver, it was something much closer to home driving me; that from the very beginning it was really some special insight into myself, not Rick, I was seeking. Maybe that sounds pretty weird—Freudian—since whatever it might be is somehow tied to cutting up a cadaver, but I can't help believing it's close to the truth. At least I get a funny feeling inside me whenever I start thinking that way—as if doors were about to open in my mind, giving me a glimpse into my deep, dark subconscious. But exactly what is lurking down there God only knows. And after all I've been through, I'm not so sure I want to find out!" He grimaced. "What I would like to know, though, is why something like this should be bugging me so much now and what the hell it has to do with my cadaver?"

"Maybe not as much as you think," Woody said cautiously. "Maybe it has more to do with something else."

"What, for God's sake?"

"Your feelings about death, for example."

"What about them?"

"Look, this isn't easy to put, Dan, but people your age usually don't dwell much on the subject of death and dying. That's more for middle-aged codgers like me who still find it hard as hell to reconcile themselves to their mortality. But an ex-combat infantryman like you—you must've worried plenty about it in Korea. And then there was your mom and dad's death. Your brother Pete's, too. For someone so young, you've had more than your share. . . ."

Dan's silence prompted Woody to continue.

"Have we ever talked about it, Dan—really talked? I can't recall."

"I can't, either. What's to talk about?"

"Your feelings. Let's see, you were what—twelve—when your folks got killed? I remember how broken up Pete was; used to find him moping around the house on the verge of tears all the time. But not you. You not only kept your feelings all bottled up, you kept after Pete to shut up about his. I'd sometimes hear the two of you arguing about it at night. The one time I got to wondering how you really felt was after I threw out some of your dad's clothes and discovered you'd kept a pair of his old baseball shoes. You didn't know I knew that, did you? But I came across them one day in the attic."

"You did, huh?" Dan said with a wry smile. "Must've made you wonder what was so special about them?"

"What was?"

"Hell, I don't know. Just spotted them in the garbage can one day and didn't want them thrown away so I took them out. Since I didn't want Pete to find out—afraid he might start in again—I just hid them."

"What about Pete? I was off flying B-17's over Germany when he was killed, so I never knew how you took that."

Dan frowned. "No tears, not after the headmaster gave me the telegram, but I did some funny things. I remember coming back here to the house and just wandering around in a daze for a while. Then I did something pretty low. I called up this woman I knew from North Adams—a good-lookin', really built blonde about eight, ten years older than me—and shacked up with her. She didn't really want to come, I had to force her—had something on her—which didn't exactly make me feel too proud of myself. But she was a good lay and I laid her enough times so she got to liking it after a while and it helped get me through the worst part. After that, I just got good and mad—mad at myself for acting that way, mad at Pete for getting himself killed, mad at you for being away, mad at damned near everything. . . . You know how Pete and I were—how close we finally got to be. I used to think that because of him wanting to be a doctor so much I decided to go to medical school. But now I know that's not quite true."

"I never thought it was. What was your reason?"

Dan shrugged. "I don't know. Just wanted to, that's all. It's a lot more useful than the few other things that attracted me, like playing drums or sports announcing. I fought against it for a long time—seemed like so damned much studying—but it's actually not so bad. In fact, my marks would be a lot better right now if I hadn't gotten so screwed up with this other thing. . . . C'mon, Uncle, guardian, old friend, and buddy—so it has something to do with death. You still haven't told me what it really means."

"How the hell can I?" Woody protested. "I'm a doctor of philosophy, not psychiatry."

"Well, go ahead and philosophize then."

"Matter of fact, here's one bit I might throw at you. A quote from Nietzsche that kept running through my mind while you were talking earlier: 'Gaze not into the abyss, lest the abyss gaze into thee.' "

"You think being so preoccupied with death might be the death of me, huh?"

"Something like that."

"Okay, but how do I stop? And don't go suggesting getting laid—I've tried it!"

"How long's your anatomy course still got to run?"

"Another month or so. Till early February. There isn't much left of our cadaver now, so the rest ought to be easier to take. I wasn't around to see it—thank God—but he should've been sawed in half this morning."

"Jesus!" Woody gulped. "I won't ask how you can stand such a horror show; you've already told me that."

"Yeah, poorly. But the worst part, all the mental torture I put myself through, that's over. Last night cured me of that. From now on, I'm strictly a model, by-the-book, young medical student."

"You sure about that?" Woody challenged.

"Damned sure! Even if I am still in the dark about what caused it all, the funny business is over."

"What if it isn't?"

"Meaning what?" Dan said, frowning.

"Meaning—what if it keeps preying on your mind so you still can't settle down, be that model, young medical student?"

Dan's lips tightened as he deliberated. "In that case," he told his uncle, "I'll admit I'm really sick and either see a psychiatrist or drop out of school."

part
three

Kim

Chapter Nineteen

By the last Friday in January Dan had reason to feel contented with himself and optimistic about medical school. Momentarily freed of his obsession with Rick—now a largely excavated half-torso resembling a block of butcher's beef more than a human being—he had studied hard and attended classes regularly during this interval. Friendly with Carey in the lab and protective of her against Earl's unfair attacks, he had nonetheless made no further overtures toward her, sensing she might still be receptive but keeping pretty much to himself during his leisure hours. He did so more out of instinct than choice, subtly perceiving that, like the breather between rounds in a fight, he had been granted this hiatus to rest, to gird up for the next onslaught by a phantom opponent who might only be himself. He had seen Lem once during this time, accidentally bumping into him at the Savoy where each had gone to hear George Robinson. To Dan's relief he was friendly, but in their brief exchange Rick was never mentioned.

That Friday afternoon the results of the midterm exam were posted, and with a surge of joy Dan discovered that his class standing had leaped from the last to the second quartile. He immediately phoned Nora, whom he had not seen since New Year's, and asked her to dinner to help him celebrate. She was delighted to accept, but she also had an invitation to an after-

175

the-theater party at Jennings Dell's and reluctantly he agreed to accompany her.

Dan had mixed feelings about Dell. A short, stocky man in his late twenties, he was the son of missionary parents who had provided him with a Harvard education, a tastefully heirloomed apartment on Beacon Hill, and possibly his shy, staid disposition. At the one party of Dell's he'd already attended, Dan had stood off to the side and observed the man for a time, watching him drift from person to person—gracious, attentive, yet standoffish, never involving himself in any one conversation for long, turning and walking away whenever anyone, particularly a girl, to whom he was talking took her eyes off him to address someone else. Having heard from others that Dell seldom brought a girl to his own parties, Dan asked Nora if he was queer. She laughed and said that Dell was engaged to a lovely Chinese girl, a student at The Juilliard School in New York. But even so informed, Dan still could not decide whether the man was hetero-, homo-, or merely neuter.

Nora had to work late so Dan picked her up at the *Post* at ten thirty, took her to Dinty's for dinner, and then on to Dell's at midnight. The ranks of party-goers had thinned out by then, making it easier to navigate from the foyer to Dell's bedroom to deposit coats to the bar at the far end of his long living room.

Dan saw her first as he was bringing Nora a drink: medium-tall, straw-blond hair in a pageboy bob, large, lustrous eyes, prominent cheekbones, tan complexion, small, graceful sweep of chin—strikingly beautiful.

"She is attractive, isn't she?" Nora remarked as he continued to stare.

Dan looked sheepish. "Sorry."

Nora shrugged good-naturedly. "Oh, don't be. I've seen Kim Chatfield have that effect on men I've been out with before."

Dan felt a quiver of excitement in his gut. "Do you know her well?"

"So, so," Nora said equivocally. "I've met her here several

times and she occasionally calls me up to get a plug in my column. She does publicity for BOAC. Have you seen their latest ad?"

Dan shook his head.

"She's in it. The bored-looking blonde next to the British chap stuffing his mouth with Beef Wellington. I've had lunch with her a couple of times and she's unaffected, hard-working, and—oh, sort of lonely. Actually, I rather like her, as long as we're not at parties together. In fact, I like her enough to ignore the gossip about her."

"What kind?"

"Oh, you know. The usual dirt you'd expect a girl that rich, footloose, and beautiful to generate. That she drinks too much, has too many affairs, hates men but can't get along without their adulation. Nothing too original . . . You want to meet her?"

Dan delayed answering an instant too long. Jennings Dell was at Nora's shoulder, waiting to speak.

"Nora . . . and Dan! So good to see you," he said with his usual quick smile (was it shy or sly? Dan always wondered). ". . . By the way, Dan, when Nora said you'd be coming tonight, I got out a special treat for you. A bottle of So-chu. It's under the bar there."

"Really!" Dan was surprised that Dell had remembered the fondness he'd once expressed for it. "Haven't had a good case of So-chu heartburn for a long time."

"What's So-chu?" Nora demanded.

Dell smiled again. "It's a Korean gin made from fermented rice. Very potent."

"It's potent, all right!" Dan avowed. "Nothing could beat it for keeping your belly warm on those cold Korean nights. Nice of you to remember, Jennings."

By the time Dell drifted away, Kim was the center of a group of admiring men and Dan's chance for an introduction was gone. Nonetheless, he couldn't help stealing periodic looks in her direction. Oddly, whenever he did, she seemed to sense it and stared back at him. Or was he imagining it?

They met at last at the end of the evening. Dan was in the bedroom collecting coats from the pile when Kim walked in.

Her sudden appearance, the sense of allure and entrapment he felt now that they were alone, muddled his mind. "Hello," he finally managed to say and stood there feeling awkward, his arms laden with coats.

"Hello," she replied in a throaty voice.

Her faintly amused look, as if she were accustomed to turning men speechless, annoyed him. Boldly, he said, "Mind if I ask you a question?"

She shrugged her consent.

"Why have you been staring at me all evening?"

"Have I?"

"You have!"

"You're right." She smiled disarmingly. "I was hoping you wouldn't notice."

"But why?" he asked, intrigued.

"Because you sort of remind me of someone."

"Who?"

"Oh, you couldn't possibly know him."

"What makes you so sure?"

"Because I'm not even sure he exists. You might just be a composite of different men I've known."

"Oh? Well, I'll be damned. And here I thought I was a real person."

She laughed. "In looks, I mean. Who are you, anyhow, and what do you do?"

"Dan Lassiter, and I'm a composite."

"Rather a good-looking one, too."

"You're not bad either, except your chin's too small."

"My chin?" she said, taken aback. She reached up to feel it. "Why do you say that?"

He shrugged. "I don't know. Just slipped out. Don't you ever get tired of men telling you how beautiful you are?"

"My, you are perceptive! Or are you just trying to impress me? What *do* you do? Are you a newspaper reporter?"

"What makes you think that—being with Nora? No, I'm not."

"Then what, for God's sake?"

"Suppose I tell you over dinner tomorrow night?"

"Sorry. I'm busy. I'm free Sunday, though. But tell me now."

"I'm a med student at State. What time Sunday?"

"Oh, sevenish."

"Where?"

"My apartment. 1070 Beacon Street." She regarded him quizzically. "You do know who I am, don't you?"

Dan grinned. "Yes, I know. Nora told me."

"She won't mind, will she? I like Nora."

"No, she won't mind. We're just good friends."

"I'm glad. I've been hoping someone would introduce us. I followed you in here."

"Just because I remind you of someone who may not exist?"

"Something like that. Men do it with girls all the time." Striking a defensive pose, Kim looked as if she were about to expound further when the bedroom door opened and a tall thin man with a harried look and an air of self-importance came bustling into the room.

"Ah, Kim! I was beginning to wonder where you'd wandered off." He sounded petulant. ". . . Oh hello, I'm Graham Kincaid." Automatically he offered Dan a hand, then withdrew it as he saw his encumbered arms. The look on Dan's face flustered him. "I hope I'm not interrupting anything?"

"No, not really," Dan told him, adjusting his hold on the coats and turning to leave. "Good night, Kim. Graham. Nice meeting you."

"Yes, quite," Kincaid replied.

Returning to the living room and finding Nora in conversation with Dell, Dan put their coats down on a chair and joined them. "Want one more drink?" he asked.

"Well, maybe one," Nora said reluctantly. "But I'll be beat tomorrow." She took a closer look at Dan. "Are you all right?"

"Uh-huh. Why?"

"You look terribly flushed."

"Must be the booze. I told you So-chu is powerful stuff. Right, Jennings?"

"Right," Dell replied, looking pleased.

Chapter Twenty

Kim tossed fitfully in her bed, trying to find a cool corner of the pillow, trying not to wake up. Dry-mouthed, slightly hungover, she knew the day was Sunday and that she could sleep in. But it was already past noon, and though the window drapes were drawn the room had lightened and seemed uncomfortably warm. Kim kicked off the covers and stretched her body across the bed, half-afraid that she might find a man beside her whom she had forgotten. But while a vestige of such a fear was ever present, that hadn't happened for some time, not since she had returned from London and cut down on the gin drinking. Besides, she had been out with Graham and a group of his British compatriots the night before, and though she doubted that Graham was homosexual, not a practicing one anyway, he was simply too reserved to make improper advances. Or was he just reluctant to become amorously involved with an employee? Or, knowing her London reputation, afraid he might not be able to measure up? Or maybe he really was a fag, after all? Whatever the reason, it was just as well. Moreover, he was a stodgy boss, quite content to use her as a dressy dinner companion, a greeter of company bigwigs, but never listening to any of her suggestions to glamorize the image of the airline and help it compete more effectively with Air France, always putting her off with the claim that the average British businessman didn't

The Anatomy Lesson

go in for a lot of frills. "Blast it, Kim," he had once told her bluntly, "you're not a man. You don't know how uncomfortable it is to sit with an erection rubbing up against your trousers. That's all your sexy stewardesses achieve!"

Yet despite his occasional bursts of candor, Kim knew that both Graham and the airline work were beginning to bore her, and though it was her third job in two years she did not plan to keep it for long.

She did not care much for Sundays either, especially in the wintertime. There was not much to do in town and the extra leisure time made her restless. Even now she wished she could blot out another few hours until evening by sleeping longer. But if she did, she knew she would lie awake that night unless she took sleeping pills, and she didn't have any. Nor did she want them around. She was unpleasantly reminded of a doctor-friend in London who'd been only too willing to supply her with them, preferring her in a slightly woozy state when they made love. Kim never did understand why, unless it had something to do with his fetish for licking her skin like a puppy dog. Sunday mornings with him were a blur; she seldom emerged from her booze and barbiturate haze until midafternoon. But as a lover he had really been no harder to take than the others. Had she ever enjoyed any of them, she wondered. Or had she merely submitted out of some masochistic need to be used, even abused, sexually as she had once used a man? An abnormality born out of guilt. If Hemingway had been right that the immoral things are the ones you feel bad after doing, then she was immoral—but she was not exactly convinced about it. Certainly there had been no great slew of men in her life. She even doubted whether the eight lovers she'd had were enough nowadays to classify her as promiscuous—only her guilt feelings did that. Besides, she had stopped behaving that way months ago. She had stopped before another man, instead of merely thinking or gossiping about it, could call her a whore to her face.

Reluctantly Kim climbed out of bed, shed her nightgown, and wandered into the kitchen to start the coffee perking before her shower.

As usual, the caress of warm water on her body evoked sensual stirrings and she thought of a man: not any she had known before but this new one, this Dan Lassiter. Had he really reminded her of Rick? Or had it been a momentary illusion: his broken nose, the loose, light way he carried himself, the mood she was in? Perhaps what really attracted her to him was his being with Nora, a woman she liked and admired and wished she resembled more closely: to possess her poise and wholesomeness, her responsible job on a newspaper. Were they—had they ever been—lovers? The possibility intrigued her. Yet even if Nora had actually slept with him, there was virtually no chance she would, Kim told herself. She had no intention of breaking her three-month-old resolution for him or anyone else; the sex-free interval had been too peaceful.

The three Sunday newspapers Kim subscribed to lay on the doormat. She put the Boston *Post* on the kitchen table next to her steaming cup of coffee and started to open it to Nora's column when the headline on the sports section caught her eye: RED BISHOP LIES IN COMA. The accompanying report read that Bishop, the nation's ninth-ranked middleweight, was still unconscious after having been knocked out in Madison Square Garden Friday night. The picture that ran with the story: that of a slack-jawed fighter sprawled on his back in a boxing ring, evoked more than queasiness in Kim. She had never met the man, but until that moment she had hated Red Bishop intensely. She had hated him for the savage beating he'd once given Rick for nine interminable rounds and because his name always reminded her of the worst night of her life.

Kim put the paper aside and lit a cigarette. Strange, she mused, how things always came in bunches: her catching a glimpse of Lem walking along the street from the window of a cab Friday afternoon, seeing that medical student who reminded her of Rick at Jennings Dell's party—now the potential tragedy of Red Bishop. Ever since seeing Lem she had been tempted to call him, but had resisted. Doubtless he knew all there was to know about her and Rick and what could she possibly say? That she had simply called out of curiosity? Out of an interest that remained strong because Rick had been not only her first lover but the only one who had ever made her feel anything but anesthetized in that perverse, private part of her anatomy. Wasn't that why she had tolerated her doctor-friend for so long: because she secretly wanted the rest of her put to sleep as well? It had all been pretty sick, and ultimately sickening, Kim realized, yet that was the way she had felt. But she really didn't want to think about Rick, she told herself. She particularly didn't want to think about the night he'd fought Red Bishop; it would only depress her. But there were good memories, too. . . .

She had been barely seventeen when she first met Rick Ferrar. With a nostalgia inescapably marred by irony, she recalled how she had once chosen seventeen to be a special age for her, the awesomely exciting year of liberation when she would own her own car and could date freely without curfews or chaperones.

Men came in easy and abundant supply that year. Drawn by her wealth, her innocence, her emerging beauty, they flocked around her, eager to please and deceive. But Kim saw herself as more than a mouth to kiss, breasts to fondle, a body to rub against and hope to possess. Whenever she wore dresses instead of slacks, her thighs became a battleground between a date's insistently exploring fingers and her restraining ones. A pant's zipper parting in the dark became an especially loathesome sound for her, making her bristle with indignation when it happened on a first date, filling her with weary resignation on later ones. It wasn't that she failed to become aroused herself but that she had quickly learned there was always a relentless progression to such pleasurable activities. She knew how fast word traveled among the small coterie of summer vacationers and that, if she ever gave in, her name would gleefully be added to the list of her girlfriends who "went all the way." Thereafter, her dates would be less interested in dancing or necking, insisting on intercourse in order to gain some sort of sexual parity with the fortunate fellow who had first achieved that score. To make matters worse, the crop of young people who spent that summer on the Cape seemed far less interesting and attractive than those she remembered from previous years. Much to Kim's disillusionment, a thick coat of monotony seemed to have settled over most of the people and experiences she had looked forward to sampling with such great gusto upon reaching the special age of seventeen.

Rick's entry into her life soon changed all that, chasing the ennui and narcissistic affections from her personality and filling her with the gentle agonies of first love.

Her first glimpse of him had been from the neck-weary angle of a ringside seat to where Rick fought above her. Her stepfather had taken her and a group of her friends to Boston Garden and there, boxing in the semifinals, was a lean young fighter with an interesting face: at once proud and handsome and cruel, yet curiously immobile, seemingly detached from what was happening to him in the ring. With mounting fascination Kim watched the flat, almost unflinching, expression on his face as he took and gave blows and the sensual ripple of muscles along his sweat-glazed body. The crowd shouted his name as he punished his opponent with short, jarring body punches and she overheard her stepfather telling a sportswriter that Rick was being groomed as the next local challenger for Jake LaMotta's middleweight crown. When the bout ended and Rick's hand was raised in victory, she felt a short, stabbing envy for Al Lakeman's right to embrace him.

Hours after the fight, still tingling with a vestige of the excitement Rick had kindled in her, Kim had followed her girlfriend and their escorts on an impromptu bar-crawl through

Boston slums. Beginning at a dingy, but almost deserted, water-front saloon, the four of them had ended up at an after-hours' club in a seedy hotel on lower Washington Street. The room was crowded and roaring, filled with smoke and boisterous hard-faced men and women—clearly no place for them to be on a Saturday night, Kim realized, but too late. Trying to squeeze past a line of stags two and three deep at the bar, she felt herself being pinched and prodded. Though vaguely aware that the two college-aged boys with her provided little protection, Kim had nonetheless turned and punched out furiously at the grinning face of the man who had been pawing her—only to have the sleeve of her dress ripped off her in return. The situation might have rapidly gotten out of hand at that point had not Kim's wildly imploring eyes fallen on two familiar faces at the end of the bar: that of the young fighter she had so admired earlier in the evening and the towering Negro who, with Al Lakeman, had served in his corner.

Knowing who she was from having seen her with Chatfield, Rick had smashed his beer bottle on the bar top to get attention, and then, with Lem at his side, shoved his way through the knot of men who had suddenly gathered around Kim to leer. Though Rick's apparent chivalry puzzled those who knew him, his prowess as a brawler commanded respect. Slowly, grudgingly, the crowd around Kim parted. "C'mon, Miss Chatfield," Rick said quietly. "You and your friends—out. Make it quick."

Amidst a chorus of mumbled curses, a sea of sullen stares, Kim and her quaking friends huddled close to Rick and Lem as they were led out of the bar.

On the street, while Lem hunted for a cab, Kim tried to thank Rick, only to receive a sharp rebuke in return. "Lady, those are my friends in there," he replied coldly, "and I don't like buttin' in. Keep the hell out of places like that from now on."

"I will," she muttered, abashed and ashamed, and abruptly turned away.

186

Kim never expected to see Rick again, but in midsummer Walt Chatfield brought him out to their summer home on the Cape to train for his first main bout. Lem came, too, and with him to act as go-between, she and Rick gradually became friends. The three of them would go clam digging or to softball games together. They taught her to skip rope and play poker, and when a date came to the door they would loom up, claiming to be her bodyguards, and demand assurances of proper behavior from the startled boy.

Kim enjoyed being near him, watching the quick, graceful movements of his body as he trained or jogged along the beach and the virility he displayed in his mannerisms. And always, wherever he was, Lem was at his side, telling him what to do or else doing things for him; neither his master nor his servant. Whenever the three of them were together, it was Lem who explained things to her, put her at ease, while Rick was less demonstrative—laughing at their pranks and appearing to enjoy the things they did together, but seemingly preoccupied by other things. Always on guard, always with a certain subtle tension reflected in his eyes, he followed the slanting flight of sea gulls and the path of dogs running along the beach; at the slightest sound or movement his head would invariably swing toward the source. Rick's way of living was utterly strange and incomprehensible to her, but even this strangeness added to his appeal. Kim often longed for a time alone with him, grew a little frightened over what might actually happen during such wish-fulfillment, and then, with fear an integral part of it, wanted him even more.

Such turbulent emotion was not easy for her to endure. Not only was she sexually innocent, there was no one she trusted for advice. Her Norwegian-born mother, whom Kim had loved dearly, was dead. A woman of astonishing blond beauty but frail health, she had met Chatfield years after the death of her first husband, Kim's father, and married him not so much out of love as out of her need for security. Once realizing this, and because he was foremost a businessman, Chatfield had provided such security—and little else until her death during heart surgery when Kim was fifteen.

Walt Chatfield was the only father Kim had known, and to her he seemed a fully adequate one. A mutual pride existed between them, a wide indulgence in each other's whims, yet one which retained certain limits. Kim knew that her stepfather kept a mistress, but she never expected to be introduced to her or to welcome her in their home. For her part, Kim did whatever she pleased on a generous allowance, went out with whomever she fancied, but tried her best to keep free of scandal, promising not to marry without her stepfather's consent.

It had seemed a perfectly pleasant, perfectly satisfactory, arrangement to Kim at the time. Though she'd sensed a subtle change in her stepfather this past year—odd ways he looked at her, a growing tendency for him to wander into her bedroom while she was dressing—she passed this off as simple carelessness. That he might be eyeing her sexually was unthinkable. Besides, all her erotic musings revolved around Rick.

During late August, the weather turned uncommonly hot. Oppressed by the sweltering heat, the group in camp grew irritable and talked of finishing the month's training in an air-conditioned Boston gym. Rick was sweating off too much weight, they said. Swimming wasn't good for a boxer's muscles. He might get a bad sunburn or an infection from a mosquito bite. Listening to them grumble, Kim began to fear that Rick might leave before she ever had a chance to be alone with him.

A time finally arrived—fashioned on one of those breezeless, comfortless nights when nobody could sleep and almost the entire camp, except for her stepfather who was away, sat in the kitchen drinking beer and playing poker. After taking her second cold shower of the evening, Kim joined the others clad only in a silk robe and panties. As she bent over to catch a glimpse of the cards in Lem's hand, her robe parted at the top and she was suddenly aware of Rick's stare. For a moment she met his eyes, then looked away, sharing an expression that was more pained than embarrassed. A minute later Rick threw in his cards and rose from the table to get another beer. Gathering her courage, Kim asked him to accompany her on a walk along the beach. Without waiting for an answer, sensing her cheeks were already burning and unwilling to show her certain humiliation should he refuse, she turned and left.

Rick came up behind her as she paused at the bottom of the stairs. Taking his hand, she led him away from the shaft of light emanating from the kitchen.

"I don't want to go for a walk," she told him. "I just said that to get you alone."

"What do you want?" he asked uncertainly.

"I want you to take me to your room."

Kim felt a sudden tightening of his hand as he turned, almost dragging her in the direction of the beach. His silence tormented her. Why didn't he say something? That he wanted her too, that he didn't; that not only was she "jailbait," but as Chatfield's stepdaughter she was too dangerous to take advantage of; that having sex with her would be breaking training, would sap his strength in some mysterious way only male athletes understood. Say something—anything! She was on the verge of tears.

Not knowing what else to do, she continued to walk in silence, letting him lead her. Barefoot, they strolled along the cool strip of sand by the water's edge until they came to the large rock formation cutting off that stretch of beach.

Rick stopped and turned her to him. "Not in my room," he said in a barely audible voice.

"What did you say?"

"I said, not in my room. Too much chance of somebody spotting us there."

"Oh." Kim felt her heart thumping against her chest and a strange, uncomfortable throbbing in her pelvis. The twin sensations produced a disconcerted, almost woebegone look, prompting Rick to question her.

"Look, you sure you want to do this? I mean, you can still change your mind. Nothing's happened yet."

"I want to!" she told him in a fierce whisper. "I've wanted to ever since the night you stopped me from getting mauled in that bar."

Rick grinned. "Yeah, I remember. The way you hauled off and socked that guy. But, I dunno, Kim. You ever done it before?"

She shook her head.

"You sure you want to? Might hurt."

"I don't care!" Her voice quavered. "As long as it's you."

Rick released her hand and took her in his arms. A sweetness enveloped her as they sank to the sand. Rick quickly shed his own clothes, and as he lowered himself upon her, she moaned in pleasure. Tentatively his hands explored her body until, aware of her state of arousal, he positioned himself to enter her.

"Take me in your hand. Guide me—slowly," he commanded. "Let me know if it hurts."

Breathlessly, Kim obeyed. She felt a sudden, stabbing sensation—more a discomfort than pain—then a mounting pressure which increased as he thrust deep to spread her taut tissues, then withdrew. She felt him squirm to get more comfortable before entering her again. Now the buildup and release of pressure became more rhythmic, more predictable, until suddenly it was no longer pressure at all but an indescribable pressure-pleasure mixture, then sheer pleasure alone. Sounds intermingled in her mind—the sibilance of the surf, his periodic sighs, her moans—until they, too, merged, became one with their quickening tempo, their matching up-and-down movements which were beginning to split her mind from her body, thought from sensation; bringing her to the very threshold of convulsive pleasure, and then—strangely—arresting her on the edge. Though she kept straining, yearning, to make the plunge, she felt increasingly distracted by such discomforts as his crushing weight on her body, her aching thighs, the fullness in her bladder. She wanted him to shift his weight so that her counterthrusts could reach higher, last longer, help her regain the tempo which was so crucial to the separation, but she said nothing.

Inside her, Rick's thrusts came faster, harder. Damn, she was hurting and she wanted him to wait. But she sensed that in the throes of his own burgeoning rapture, he was losing all awareness of her. Intuitively she knew she was no different, no more special, to him at this moment than any other woman he'd had; just the provider of an opening for friction, a cushion of undulating flesh—ultimately nothing more than a receptacle for his sperm. At the height of his spasms Kim felt a quiver of such intense pleasure that she gasped. But the sensation was too brief to savor: merely a tantalizing hint of bliss that had somehow eluded her. Next time, she hoped. Maybe she would achieve the separation next time. But as Rick withdrew, as he sprawled lengthwise across her body and she smelled the stale beer-odor on his breath, Kim could not help acknowledging deep pangs of disappointment. In those crucial moments, her body had betrayed her. Or had it been the workings of her conscience: the realization that Rick had used her in the same way she had intended using him? An ironic turnabout. Or perhaps she had expected too much from her first experience. Now that she was more knowledgeable about sex, she would be more relaxed, more aware of the need to speak out. But would someone like Rick listen? He'd better, she thought resolutely, or she would find herself another man.

Rick did listen. Whether he was amused or offended by her display of boldness in speaking out, the next time they made love he was not only more patient, more aware of her degree of arousal, but agreed—possibly for the first time, Kim suspected, as she saw him fumble distastefully with the condom— to provide the contraception.

In mid-September, with her stepfather in California and his

Boston apartment available to them, they made love there nightly for an entire week. By then, with the intensity of her orgasms increasing, Kim grew obsessed with sex, isolating herself from her friends and impatiently waiting for the hours to pass until Rick appeared each evening. Despite her repeated urgings to sleep over at the apartment, Rick never would; not even on their last night together. Nor would he say why, aside from the feeble claim that he slept better alone. At the time Kim had speculated he was afraid that her stepfather might return unexpectedly or, more remotely, that Rick had another girl he was going to from her—only later learning about his sweat-drenching nightmares.

The following week Kim left Boston for Poughkeepsie and her freshman year at Vassar. She and Rick met only twice more after that: once when he was on furlough in New York before leaving for Korea and the night he fought Red Bishop.

At five o'clock Walt Chatfield phoned from Logan Airport, having just returned from a London business trip.

"How was your flight?" she asked.

"Bumpy."

"Did BOAC treat you all right?"

"Oh, fine. . . . Say, Kim, if you're free I wonder if you'd care to join me and a few friends for dinner tonight?"

"No, sorry," Kim replied coolly. "I've already got a date. . . . Where's Lydia?" Very efficient, very British, Lydia was an angular woman in her early thirties, her stepfather's current secretary and mistress.

"Oh, she stayed over a few extra days to visit her sick mother. Should be back the end of the week. Who's your date and how firm is it?"

"Very firm. His name's Dan Lassiter and he's a medical student."

"What school—Harvard?"

"Only met him the other night, so I haven't asked him yet. If it's not Harvard, though, I'll be sure and let you know."

"Aw, Kim—just asking. After all, it *is* the best medical school."

"I'm sure it is," she remarked dryly, "and I'd be properly appreciative if I were his patient, not his date."

"What kind of guy is he?"

"Oh, tall. Good-looking in a rather rugged way. Broken nose. In fact, when I first saw him from a distance he sort of reminded me of Rick Ferrar."

"Rick! No kidding?"

"Heard anything about Rick lately?" she asked. "I'm curious to know what's become of him."

"Not a word. I asked Al Lakeman about him recently, but nobody's heard a thing. Speaking of Rick—did you read the news about Red Bishop? I just saw it in the paper."

"Yes, I did. Too bad. I hope he'll be all right."

"So do I! I had him booked to fight Pender in the Garden this April. . . . Well, call you for lunch during the week. Have fun on your date."

"You, too," she said, hanging up the phone with a faint sense of relief, realizing she was no longer as fond of Walt Chatfield as she had once been. Not since that horrible night a year ago. Had it really happened? Sometimes it seemed unbelievable. Of course they'd both been pretty drunk, and on top of the booze she'd taken pain-killers and sedatives. But whether Walt had pulled open her robe to shame or seduce her, harsh, unforgivable things had been said—about her morality and her mother's, about Rick—and things would never again be the same between them. Wasn't the mere fact that her own stepfather could have acted that way toward her one of the reasons for her low self-esteem? But Kim hadn't let herself dwell on the implications of that night for some time and she didn't want to do so now.

She put a Brahms' symphony on the phonograph, then stretched out on the couch in the growing darkness of the living room.

The last of her file of memories concerning Rick had been compiled on the night he fought Red Bishop; the last and the worst and the most oft-remembered, especially in those dismal, disheartening moments immediately after sex—after hoping, trying, failing to come—when she wished the man above or below or behind her would simply vanish like some dream image, sparing her the need to feign enjoyment while her tense, tired, body felt soiled with sweat and sperm. Frustrated and ashamed, she would then think back to the night Rick fought Red Bishop and its bitter denouement in this apartment.

Kim had come to realize that the making of that night had begun long before she ever heard of Red Bishop. Possibly, as she now believed, it had begun while Rick was still in Korea. She had written him there, not long letters nor as often as he might have wanted, but at least monthly and he had written back. Like the man himself, Rick's letters were terse and unemotional, sketchy about the things that had happened to him and how he felt about them. But after Lem was wounded and after the last savage burst of combat before the ceasefire, the tone and content of his letters changed. In a remarkable one, Rick had confessed much about his miserable upbringing in an orphanage, his morose, almost impersonalized outlook on life, his recurring dreams of death. But he'd finally seen enough of death and dying, he wrote; his once-morbid fascination with it was over. Though his dreams of dying persisted, he now saw them for what they were—not a subconscious yearning for extinction but mere nightmares. Having survived two years of combat, he wanted not only to live, but to live as other men— without grudges or violence, in peace. It was quite a revealing letter coming from Rick, and it had moved Kim deeply. But she was still in college then, still essentially immature, and though an earlier affair with an English instructor was over, she was at present deeply involved with an older, more stimulating man, an established novelist. Thus she failed to read into Rick's letter all that had been implied. When she thought of marriage these days it was with her novelist friend, not Rick. Though it seemed deplorably snobbish and insensitive to her now, she had never considered that Rick might have marriage in mind. But he had—all during those arduous years in Korea—and he told her so, blurted it out between split and swollen lips after the Bishop fight. His proposal took her completely by surprise, so much so that she hadn't been able to conceal it, and the look of incredulity on her face infuriated him.

Though more than a year had passed since that night, Kim still possessed almost total recall of what followed. Rick's face, already badly bruised from the Bishop fight, turned even uglier as he seized her arms. For a moment as he shook her, bent her back over the arm of a chair, made her confess her two other lovers, Kim feared he might have gone completely insane. He had complained earlier that his head hurt and she had given him aspirin, but what she saw reflected in his eyes now was neither pain nor rage but the gleam of madness. Then, the verbal abuse began. "Whore!" he had rasped at her, "Whore! Whore! Whore!" until the ugly epithet reverberated in her brain.

As Rick's anger-convulsed look grew more pronounced, as her bent spine felt as though it were about to snap, Kim became so hysterical with fright that, when it came, Rick's slap was almost therapeutic. Initially a fist, opening only at the last moment, Rick's hand exploded across her face with bone-crunching force, knocking her across the arm of the chair and tumbling her to the floor. Rolling on her side, Kim lay with her head bent, her legs drawn up in a fetal-like position. Sobbing uncontrollably as she felt the warm, sticky gush of blood from her broken nose spilling onto her fingers, she'd awaited his next move—his kick, his arms lifting her up to slap again, his hard, nude, knowing body. *Oh God, how could it be possible?* How could she still want him after this, she asked herself incredulously. But she did. It was sick, shameful, she thought—she was as insane as he—but she no longer cared. In the pain-blinding aftermath of his blow, she had gone through some sort of identity crisis, a self-revealing moment of astonishing clarity in which she saw herself as weak, vain, despicable—and desperately sought absolution. Rick's brutal blow had been fair retribution for the sins of selfishness and insensitivity she had shown him, but now she needed pity, forgiveness, love. And so she lay waiting, sobbing. . . .

Scene's end, memory's end, but playing on so vividly in her mind that Kim again experienced the same sense of forlornness —the zipper in the dark, the gagging hair in her mouth—that she had felt upon hearing Rick slam her apartment door behind him. Then, gradually, the intruding sound of music, the unmistakable theme of Brahms' Third Symphony, yet out of place, not belonging. . . .

Opening her eyes, Kim emerged from reverie with a shudder, aware that the long afternoon was finally over and the sky filled with the purplish haze of night. She moved to the window. Peering down at Beacon Street, people strolling by, cars stopped before the light, she suddenly identified with the fear of a small girl left alone in the house while her parents were away.

Moving to the mirror, Kim inspected her face, the skillful repair job that the London plastic surgeon—a former lover— had done on her broken nose. If only she'd let it go at that, not gotten involved in such a degrading affair, she might have been far better off, she lamented. But his hands had been so gentle, so graceful that she had wanted them on her body as well. And he was glad to accommodate: a rich American girl, a suitable subject to sedate and seduce and practice his little fetishes on. Was she cursed? Was she like some sort of sexual Flying Dutchman, destined to drift from man to man, never establishing a satisfactory relationship with any of them? If so, then Rick was to blame. No, correction—her guilty conscience was to blame; Rick, and what she was afraid might have happened to him as a result, bore only a portion of that responsibility.

She glanced at the clock on the mantel. It was past six, time she started getting dressed. But her mood had soured and she was no longer as enthusiastic about going out with Dan Lassiter. Where would they go on a Sunday night? What would they have in common?

A movie, she thought. That would kill most of the evening and she would be safest there, spared from being bored or pawed, and hopefully—if his resemblance to Rick proved illusory—spared from her memories.

Chapter Twenty-one

As Dan rang the doorbell to Kim's second-floor apartment he felt a sudden sense of foreboding. Was his obsession with Rick to begin all over again? Hadn't Lem warned him to stay away? Doubtless he would have been attracted to someone as beautiful as Kim no matter who she was, but would he have been this attracted? Still he couldn't help being curious as to what she was really like—why two people as seemingly different as Kim Chatfield and Rick Ferrar had fallen in love. But beyond this, if what drew him to her was the bizarre temptation to share a part of Rick's life with him, then Dan knew he was indeed heading for a recurrence of previous trouble.

Now, as he waited, Dan began to feel even more was amiss: Either Kim had forgotten their date or, since he had neglected to call to confirm it, she assumed he had, and no one would be home. He was about to press the bell again when the inside lock clicked and the door opened. He was even more relieved to see Kim standing there in a knee-length, gold-brocaded dressing gown.

"Hi. C'mon in," she said. "I'm almost ready. Just putting the finishing touches on my face."

Dan stepped inside the door, then turned to stare. Unlike the serene, self-assured woman of the other night, Kim now appeared slightly harassed. And despite the benefit of fresh mascara, her blue-green eyes looked weary.

As Dan removed his coat and followed her into the living room, the clock on the mantel chimed the hour. "Seven on the nose!" Kim remarked, giving him a mischievous look. "You do believe in being punctual, don't you? A psychiatrist I know might make something of that. Claims his men patients reveal a lot about themselves by the way they keep their appointments."

"Oh? How?"

"Well, if they always come early that suggests they're premature ejaculators. If they're late, impotent. And if they're always on time," she said, fixing him with an intimidating stare, "they're compulsive. So happens he's French, my psychiatrist friend, and, as you can guess, highly sex-oriented. Even so, he might have something. . . . Are you compulsive?"

"About what?" Dan asked. "Not about neatness, anyway; you ought to see the mess I left my apartment in. Besides, your friend seems to have covered all the bases. What do normal men do?"

"Doubt if he knows. Normal Frenchmen don't go to psychiatrists—not for sex problems, anyhow."

"What do they do?"

"Blame it on the woman, I imagine. Wouldn't you?"

This time Dan laughed. "Hey, aren't you being a little rough on me? So far I've been accused of being compulsive, smug about sex, and God knows what else—and I've only been here a few minutes. What gives?"

Kim smiled at his aggrieved look. "I guess I'm just in a bitchy mood—no fault of yours—and a damned poor hostess. Forgive me. The bar is right behind you, Dan. Fix yourself a drink while I get dressed."

He had reserved a table at The Charles, a small, intimate restaurant that featured fix-it-yourself salads and homemade pastries. Kim had emerged from her bedroom in a flattering black sheath dress and far better mood, and as Dan drove her red Pontiac convertible he looked forward to a pleasant evening. His first hint of trouble came on entering The Charles where a long line of people waited for tables. Even though it was now several minutes past their reservation time, the headwaiter informed them there would still be a short delay, suggesting they wait to be called at the bar.

That turned out to be even worse luck. As Dan led her down the crowded bar, a female voice suddenly shrieked: "Kim! Kim Chatfield!" The raucous greeting was immediately followed by a wildly waving hand belonging to a tall, large-boned, thin-faced girl wearing gaudy harlequin glasses.

"Why Kim, you gorgeous creature!" she shrilled as they approached her. "Imagine bumping into you here!"

"Not so loud, Vicky dear," Kim replied coolly, "or people might think you cultivated that ear-splitting voice peddling fish. Let me introduce you to the handsome doctor I'm with. Dan Lassiter meet Vicky Flood. Vicky and I were once roommates in college—that is, until I found out she was keeping a detailed diary of all my comings and goings."

"Nice to meet you, Vicky," Dan said uncertainly. "I'd like to read that diary."

"So would a lot of other people!" Kim interjected. "But even if Vicky could write well enough to get it published—which she can't—it'd still be banned in Boston. Right, Vicky dear?"

"Oh, don't mind her, Dan," Vicky said, undaunted. "She's just being bitchy. Can't help it, poor thing. Been badly reared. Her stepfather is some kind of gambler. Are you really a doctor?"

Dan shook his head. "Just a freshman med student."

"Well, you don't look at all like the other medical students I've known. Not at all," Vicky confided, openly admiring. "Phil!" she cried, turning to her escort and tugging so hard at his sleeve he almost slipped off the barstool. "You've heard me talk about Kim Chatfield. Well, here she is in all her wicked beauty. . . . And Dan something-or-other."

"Philip Whitcomb," he said, twisting around to shake hands. "How are you two enjoying yourselves?"

In a crowded bar? Dan thought, nettled. "Oh, fine! Great!" he exclaimed. Then, leaning toward Whitcomb, he spoke confidentially. "But if you won't mind a little friendly adivce, I wouldn't sit where you are too long if I were you."

"Oh? Why's that?"

"House policy is that as long as the headwaiter knows you're buying drinks, he'll keep you waiting forever for a table."

"Do you really think so?" Whitcomb looked worriedly at his watch as they moved on.

"This has been the damnedest day for running across people I didn't want to run across!" Kim grumbled, after the waiter had finally seated them. Warned off by her sullen look, Dan did not question her. Now that the two of them were alone he hoped they might recapture some of their earlier good humor, but Kim continued to seethe over the unwelcome encounter.

"She really did keep a diary, you know," she told him over another round of drinks. "I accidentally came across it one day and it was vicious! Full of dirt. Not only about me but other girls in the dorm. Anyway, once I found out about it, and what the jealous little bitch really thought of me, I moved out."

"I don't blame you," Dan told her.

"But that isn't the reason I despise Vicky so much," Kim continued bitterly. "Later on she did something far worse—at least I'm pretty sure she did. We had a third roommate that year, a shy, sweet farm girl from Elmira named Sue Jensen. I was almost sure Sue liked me better than Vicky and when I moved out she'd want to come with me, but she didn't."

"Why not?"

Kim frowned. "I wish I really knew. My hunch is that with all the snooping Vicky did, she might've had something on Sue and was blackmailing her into staying. At least I wouldn't put it past her. Sue was such a shy, dependent person; she hardly ever went out with boys. And even though I don't think there was any lesbian stuff going on between them, there was something almost sick about the way Sue let Vicky lord it over her all the time. Anyhow, they roomed together the rest of that year and would have done so the next, only Sue committed suicide that summer. . . . Did you ever have a close friend of yours commit suicide, Dan?"

Dan almost said no and then remembered Lloyd Tompkins. Jesus, he hadn't thought of Lloyd in years! But the two of them had been friends all through grammar school until, at the age of ten, Lloyd had killed himself. The strange—the almost haunting—part was that a few days before, while they were walking home together, Lloyd had suddenly said to him, "Are you afraid to die? I'm not."

"How come?" Dan had asked.

" 'Cause I had a baby sister who died, and God never would've let her if there was anything bad about it."

Since Lloyd was in the habit of making weird statements like that, Dan had not paid too much attention, certainly not enough to tell his parents about it. But three days later they found Lloyd hanged to death in the cellar of his home.

"What are you thinking?" Kim finally asked, as the silence between them grew prolonged.

"About death," Dan replied, deciding not to tell her about Lloyd. "I saw a lot of it in Korea."

"Did you ever kill anyone?"

"I don't know, but I sure as hell tried."

"Did that bother you?"

"Not much. Maybe it should've, but I was so sure I'd end up getting killed myself that it didn't."

"What made you so sure?"

He shrugged. "Maybe so if it happened, it wouldn't come as too big a surprise."

"But it didn't. Did that come as a surprise?"

Dan slowly nodded. "Made me wonder if there might be something more than chance to who lived and who died."

"Do you really think there is?"

"Don't know. But I do think there might be more than one kind of death."

"How do you mean?"

Dan hesitated. Preoccupied though he had been over this subject, it was the last one he wanted to talk about.

"Tell me," Kim prompted. "How many kinds of death do you think there are?"

"At least two. One you're prepared for and one you're not."

"But I don't understand. How are you prepared?"

"Your body tells you. After all, millions of cells die each day, even brain cells, and they must be capable of telling you something. Give off some sort of warning signal. In other words, that form of death—slow, planned, maybe even welcome—comes from within. The other kind, though, gives no warning at all but strikes out of the blue. That's the form of death I hate so much, the one I'd like to be able to thwart someday if I ever become a doctor."

"But can you?" Kim said, intrigued. "How can you hope to thwart something that's inevitable? Death always wins, doesn't it?"

"Sure. But even for death there might be a time beyond which victory loses much of its satisfaction. Like when I was a kid and kept getting beat up by this bully on my street. Years later, when I was boxing in college, I finally got back at him. Really gave it to him good. But by then I was a so much better fighter than he that it didn't mean much. Maybe it's the same with death. Who knows?"

Kim gazed at him appraisingly. "You sound as though you thought about it a great deal."

"Maybe too much," Dan said wryly.

"Why? You haven't been ill, have you?"

"No, but I deal with it everyday in the anatomy lab. Not dying itself—the end product."

Kim looked puzzled for a moment. "Oh, you mean your cadaver. There's rather a chilling mental image associated with that word, isn't there? Chilling task, no doubt. I've heard talk about it from other med students I've dated. Does it really disturb you that much to work on them?"

"It did at first, only let's not talk about it. All these morbid subjects. Let's talk about something more pleasant?"

"All right," Kim agreed. "But I'm not altogether sorry. Otherwise, I might never have seen this serious side of you. I like people who aren't afraid to admit they feel things deeply, even something as universally frightening as death. Makes me feel that if I wanted to tell them something I thought important, I'd be less likely to get a blank stare or a smart-ass remark in return."

There was such a long queue in front of the movie theater where they had planned to go that they chose the British melodrama playing up the street instead, returning to Kim's apartment around eleven. Whether merely a carry-over from the dull movie they had seen, or for some other reason, she had grown so subdued that when she invited Dan in for a nightcap he understood the gesture was made out of politeness and did not plan to outstay his welcome.

Soon after entering the apartment, Kim excused herself and left Dan to fix the drinks. "Turn on the TV, will you?" she called from the doorway of her bedroom. "I want to catch the weather forecast. No one dares work for BOAC without knowing the weather."

Dan poured drinks—a stiff Scotch for himself—while the eleven o'clock news was concluding, then sat on the couch opposite the TV set to listen to the weather. He had to wait through a muddle of meteorological maps and jargon before the weatherman came up with the forecast: cold, windy, intermittent snow flurries. Not wanting the TV to distract them, Dan was about to turn it off when the weather gave way to sports and something so eerie and unexpected happened that he slumped back, stunned. For an instant, as he tried to surmount the shocks of incredulity set off in his brain, Dan felt as if he were seeing a ghost, and in a sense he was—not ectoplasmic but celluloid.

Over an unseen voice reporting the latest medical bulletin on Red Bishop, the picture on the TV screen showed two boxers savagely pummeling each other in mid-ring. Dan gawked at the image of Rick as he had once gawked at his first sight of battle dead in Korea. In an astonishingly clear closeup, he saw Rick's eyes glaze over, his jaw go slack, his weary shoulders slump so that he was barely able to keep his guard up, as Bishop backed him into a corner and clubbed him with three successive hooks to the head. Then, just as it seemed certain Rick was going to go down he suddenly shook his head, not so much to clear it, Dan sensed, as to deny his near-helpless condition, and drove his right hand into Bishop's temple, knocking him off balance. But the surprising blow stalled Bishop's relentless attack only momentarily, and he was soon back with a fresh flurry of punches. Not only seeing but vicariously feeling the brutal beating Rick was taking, Dan sat with a fixed grimace on his face, hearing the off-camera commentary of the sports reporter only vaguely:

". . . Who among Boston's boxing fans can ever forget the Ferrar–Bishop fight? One of the most action-packed bouts ever held in the Garden. . . . But boxing is a cruel, unpredictable sport. Now both men are finished with the ring: Rick Ferrar, unheard from in months, probably retired; Red Bishop in a coma. . . . Fight fans, remembering the ring deaths of so many boxers in recent years, hope it will not happen again. But I for one have already seen enough tragedy come out if it. The time is long overdue when we should either demand that boxing be made safer or else eliminate it entirely from the sports scene. What do you think? . . . In basketball tonight, the Celtics 98, the New York Knicks 95. . . ."

Although the face of the sportscaster, a crew-cut, square-jawed, older man, had superseded the ring action on the screen, Dan's brain refused to relinquish the afterimage of a live Rick.

How long had the film clip lasted—thirty, forty seconds? It didn't matter. Like his first view of Rick's body in the anatomy lab, the accompanying surge of emotion had been so electrifying as to indelibly imprint the image in his memory circuits.

A sniffling intake of breath, a muffled sob, suddenly made Dan aware of Kim's presence behind him. Twisting around, he glanced up at her, immediately realizing from her grief-stricken look, her brimming eyes, that she too had seen the boxing sequence. He sprang to his feet, took a faltering step toward her, then paused. He was dry-eyed, Dan knew, but what else might his face reveal. Whatever it was, Kim regarded him with a bewildered look.

"Oh, Dan!" she suddenly wailed and came into his arms. "I can't take any more of this. I've paid and paid, but it won't go away, that awful feeling. It never leaves."

Much as her lament aroused his curiosity, Dan did not question her. *Later,* he thought. Right now he felt an overwhelming tenderness, a sense of shared loss, shared futility—the way he had once felt after grasping the full meaning of Pete's death. It was almost as if, instead of being his cadaver, Rick had been a brother. Hers, too. There was a kinship binding them all together.

Dan raised her chin and kissed her lightly on the lips and eyes, tasting the saltiness of her tears. If he felt any twinges of desire at all, they were low-key. More than that, he wanted to comfort her. But when Kim returned his kiss open-mouthed, he realized her needs were more urgently passionate. He kissed her long and ardently, then drew her down beside him on the couch. Gently he caressed her breasts, first through the rustling fabric of her dress, then within her low neckline.

Slowly easing her down on the cushions, he pressed his fingers into the hollow of her knee. Beneath him, Kim lay limp. With each advance of his hand, she tensed slightly, then relaxed. A low sound began in her throat as Dan kneaded the soft flesh of her thigh. But, as his fingers slipped deftly beneath her nylon panties, she suddenly drew back.

"No, stop!" she whispered harshly. "I do want you. Oh, God, I do! But not here. We can't!"

"Why not?" Dan muttered in confusion.

"We can't, that's all. Please don't make me explain. I'll come to your place—okay?"

Bewildered, Dan removed his arms from her and she sat up to straighten her clothing. Then, aware of his perplexed look, she said, "Oh, Dan, I'm sorry to leave you—us—hanging like this. But I promise I'll make it up to you. Give me your address and I'll be there in a half hour."

Dan's doubting look prompted her to reassure him further. "Don't you see," she said pleadingly, "this way I can stay all night. Please, Dan, trust me. . . ."

"Okay," he said finally and rose from the couch. Looking down at Kim, at her flushed face and imploring eyes, he realized his conquest was virtually assured; it was unthinkable that she would disappoint him in his present state of arousal. He would have her in bed, for the night, possibly longer.

As Dan went to the hall closet for his coat, he heard Kim repeat his address to herself.

Chapter Twenty-two

Dan found his basement apartment even messier than he remembered it. Hurriedly he hung up clothes, changed sheets, stacked books, washed dishes, until he had restored some semblance of order to the drab one-room dwelling. Then he stood by the front window, anxiously watching the street for Kim's red convertible. At last he saw it pull up to the curb, and a minute later she was at his door, dressed in the tailored suit she would wear to work tomorrow.

"God, a Murphy bed!" she exclaimed after their kiss. "Haven't seen one in years. Is it safe?"

"Sure. The hinges are so old it falls down sometimes but never up. . . . Want a drink?"

"No, thanks. All I want is a bathroom and a couple of hangers for my clothes."

She didn't stay in the bathroom long. When she emerged, wearing his cotton robe, Dan was already in bed. For a moment Kim stared down at his shadowy face and muscular torso, then, shedding the robe, posed briefly in the shaft of light coming from the bathroom before joining him in bed.

"Are you nervous?" Kim asked after feeling him tremble.

"Nervous? No, are you?"

"Not yet. Feels too good so far."

"When *do* you get nervous?"

"Later on," she said. "If I try too hard to come."

"Then don't try too hard."

"I didn't used to; I didn't have any trouble coming either."

"But now you do?"

"Now I do. Or did. I haven't let a man make love to me for a long time now."

"It bothers you that much?"

"Of course, it does. Wouldn't it you? Why else have sex?"

"You know what Lord Chesterfield once said about it?" he remarked lightly, afraid this introspective talk might lessen her chance for enjoyment.

"No, tell me," Kim said, sounding dubious.

"That the price is exorbitant, the pleasure fleeting, and the position ridiculous!"

"That's what Lord Chesterfield said?"

"That's what he said. What do you think?"

"I think he sounds like an English fag. . . . Even if the pleasure is fleeting, it's better than none. Besides, the reason my not being able to come bothers me so much is because it makes me feel abnormal. Oh, not sexually abnormal—I've read *Kinsey* and know a lot of women are frigid—but neurotic. Even sad, in a way. . . ."

"In what way?" Dan asked.

"Exploited, guilt-ridden. Sorry I didn't stay a virgin longer. I don't know—"

"Even now? With me?"

"I don't know how I'll feel with you. How can I? We haven't done anything yet!"

Dan did not reply. Feeling him begin to draw away from her, Kim sighed and said, "Me and my big mouth! Now I've really put the screws to you, haven't I?"

"You do talk a lot," Dan told her softly, "but I'll try to manage."

And he did. After some gradually mounting foreplay, he performed at length; maintaining the same steady thrusts and withdrawals so tirelessly that the tight snarl of conflicting emotions within Kim began to unravel—not totally, not enough to make the separation complete, but sufficient to allow her to relax and enjoy periodic shivers of pleasure. For a moment, upon hearing his breathing quicken, she considered faking an orgasm, but decided against it. Dan was man enough to deserve her honesty, and she liked him well enough by now not to regret spending the night with him.

While Kim was in the bathroom, Dan smoked a cigarette, watching the orange glow of burning tobacco light up the tips of his fingers and marveling over the extraordinary sequence of events that had led to their lovemaking. Despite his earlier resolve not to allow himself to become this involved with her, it had all happened so fast, within minutes of the time they had returned to Kim's apartment from the movies. And what seemed equally extraordinary to him was that once again, as had occurred at Dell's party, it was Rick who had brought them together. A brief, bizarre reminder of him, a television apparition, had caused Kim to overcome her antipathy toward sex, made her eager to go to bed with him.

And though grateful for this ghostly intercession, Dan was deeply troubled by it as well. Now that he knew how strong Rick's hold on Kim was, now that the two of them had become lovers, he realized he could no longer tell her Rick was dead. The time for that—if indeed there had ever been a time—was past. He could conceive no possible way to broach the subject without being forced to reveal his special source of information—and this he was unwilling to do. Could he possibly tell a girl he'd just made love to, a girl like Kim who despite the superficial dazzle of her beauty seemed curiously vulnerable, that he had spent the past five months dissecting her ex-lover? The mere thought was enough to make him cringe.

When Kim came out of the bathroom, wearing the tops to the pair of flannel pajamas she'd found and bringing him the bottoms, they kissed and talked until Kim drifted off to sleep.

Dan tried to follow, but his brain remained stubbornly active. In between brief periods of dozing, he lay huddled on his side of the bed, afraid of waking Kim by tossing and turning, and ruminated over the odd and ever-expanding web of circumstances that interwove his life with Rick's. But this was not his only source of misgivings; he also had some solely about himself. Even while engaged in the act of love, Dan had experienced a certain sense of detachment. It was not fear of failure, of impotency that brought it on; it was habitual with him. Having first been made aware of the vagaries of beautiful women by Marge Downing, he had always striven to bring Marge to the helpless state of orgasm first so as to achieve a signal sense of superiority over her. He had practiced with Marge until it became a sort of sublimation, a deliberate cooling of ardor, that had improved his sexual performance. But it had always discomfited Dan, made him realize what a cold and calculating person he was. Although not so much tonight; not so much with Kim. Whatever qualms he had felt while making love to her had been minimal. He seemed to be undergoing some kind of personality change, one in which his innate self-reserve was being shed like petals from a pod. And despite the potential perils of such a transformation, he welcomed it. In making him more fallible, it also made him feel more human. When had he ever stopped feeling that way? After Pete's death? When he was sixteen? Even though he now possessed the mind and body of a man, deep inside he still clung to many of the fierce hatreds and passions of a sixteen-year-old. Strange he had never realized that before, Dan mused, as he lay listening to the wind whistle through cracks in the window casing and Kim's deep breathing, and wished his brooding thoughts would abate and let him sleep.

Outside the basement window a light snow began to fall over the greater Boston area and many other events came to pass with the night. There was a knifing in a North End pizzeria that would make the headlines of the early morning edition of the *Daily Record;* an automobile accident in Cambridge that involved six persons, killing a woman in her mid-thirties. At four A.M. on lower Washington Street, Ernie Doyle closed his bar and walked with Lem to the nearby police precinct to talk to the desk sergeant, an old friend of Ernie's who had once shared the same beat with him. The three of them talked at length, and when his shift ended, the sergeant went with them to examine certain police records at the city morgue.

Chapter Twenty-three

Kim woke in the first gray light of dawn. Shivering, she thought, *God, it's cold in here!* and slipped out of bed to search in Dan's closet for something warm to wear. Failing to find a heavy robe, she donned a black wool sweater which made her skin itch and hung to her knees but stopped her teeth from chattering so that she could brush them. From the bathroom she went into the kitchen, noticing the microscope and the box of slides on the table and Dan's meager supply of cooking utensils. But at least the breadbox and refrigerator were well stocked. Pushing up the sweater sleeves, she began to fix breakfast.

The sound and smell of bacon sizzling woke Dan and he got up to investigate.

"Good morning." He smiled at the sight of a busy-fingered Kim in high heels and his oversized sweater.

"Hi," she said. "Is it always so bloody cold in here in the morning? I tried turning the radiator in the bathroom every which way but still couldn't get any heat. Doesn't it work?"

Dan looked at his watch. It was a few minutes before seven, the hour the janitor usually fired the furnace. "It works. Whenever that penny-pinching landlady of mine wants it to. You should hear the pipes start knocking any minute now. My God, it's barely dawn! How come you're up so early?"

"Because I was cold and hungry and have to be at work by

nine and wanted to spend some time with you first. Don't just stand there freezing to death. Get some clothes on. Breakfast's almost ready."

Twenty minutes later, with the apartment warm, his stomach full, and Kim sharing the special intimacy of the breakfast table with him, Dan felt the best he had in months.

"Interesting place you have here," Kim remarked, looking at the anatomical charts on the wall and the Marilyn Monroe calendar over the sink. "A little, uh, clinical, maybe—but interesting."

"Like to share it with me again tonight?"

"Why, Dan," she said coyly, "you're not suggesting we shack up, are you? For the icebox you live in, you need a thick bed comforter, not a girl."

"You were pretty comforting. Cook good, too. I know the place looks pretty tacky compared with yours—but how about it?"

"I can't tonight. My cousin Carol's coming in from Wellesley. She drives in once a week to see her fiancé, a B.U. law student, and usually stays over at my place. So I'd better be there. But ask me again soon."

"I will," Dan promised, "real soon."

Snuffing out the butt of her cigarette, Kim plucked the glass slide from the platform of Dan's microscope and held it up to the light so that the violet stain of the imbedded tissue shone through. "What is it?"

"A slice of liver," Dan told her.

"Liver! I took a quick peek at it earlier and tried to figure it out, but I never thought of liver. Doesn't look like it."

"It does under the microscope. Wonder what you'd look like under there?"

"I bet you do. But I'm not sure I'd want anyone looking at me that close."

"Why not?"

"Because he might find out there's not much there. Like try-ing to look at a snowflake—no depth, no staying power."

Dan slowly shook his head. "You're full of the damnedest insecurities. Do you honestly believe that?"

"Well, if what you're thinking is that a good-looking girl like me has no business feeling that way, then you're wrong. You got a good taste of how bitchy I can be last night—and how changeable. I'm giving you fair warning on that right now."

"Okay, I'm warned," said Dan. "But I'm still willing to take my chances. I'd like to see you as much as possible."

"That's sweet of you. But would you still feel that way if I told you last night was something of a fluke, that I'm not usu-ally that responsive to a man or that nice to him afterward? In fact, whenever I've gone to bed with a guy in the past, it's usu-ally ended the relationship. That might make me sound hard, cynical, even a bit immoral—and maybe I am. Not that I've had a whole slew of affairs. I haven't. Only a few really, but for all the wrong reasons and they made me feel shabby afterward."

"Is that how you feel now—shabby?"

"You know it isn't!" Kim reached out to squeeze his hand. "If it was, I wouldn't be telling you all this. . . . Still, I was sort of a pushover for you, wasn't I? You know—screwing on the first date. Were you surprised?"

"Very much," Dan admitted, knowing better than to elab-orate on such a question.

"Well, this may surprise you, too," Kim went on. "I didn't want you all that much. Not only had I sworn off sex—so much so that I haven't let a man do more than kiss me good night for months—but you really didn't arouse me that way. Not at first, anyway. Oh, you aroused me later on all right, but that simply wasn't why I wanted to spend the night with you."

"Why did you?"

Kim hesitated. "No better reason, I guess, than I didn't want to spend it alone. Don't ask why. I'm not ready to tell you. Later, maybe, but not now. Just take my word that things had ganged up on me so badly yesterday I thought I'd have to borrow some sleeping pills from a neighbor to get any sleep. I don't like doing that anymore—not since the night a prowler broke into my apartment."

"Sweet Jesus!" Dan exclaimed. "What happened?"

"Oh, he didn't rape me or anything," Kim said with a faint smile. "In fact, I was so drugged with sleeping pills I didn't even know he was there until he banged down the lid of my portable hi-fi trying to lift it. Even then I only caught a bare glimpse of him climbing out the living room window. But it was enough to give me a good case of the jitters."

"I don't blame you," Dan said. "I'm just damned glad nothing worse happened."

"So am I! But as long as we're on the subject, there's one more mystery to clear up." Kim paused to sip her coffee.

"Why you insisted on coming to my place last night?"

Kim sighed. "You *are* perceptive! I'm soon going to be an open book to you."

"Why did you?" Dan prompted.

"Because I think my apartment's being watched."

"Watched? By whom?"

"Either by men who work for my stepfather or private detectives. I'm not entirely sure they're still there, but I have a strong hunch they are. He hired them without asking me, right after he heard about the prowler. Once I found out, I told him I didn't want them around—that they'd only upset the other tenants—and he promised to call them off. But all he did, I think, was hire new ones. I suppose I should be grateful for his concern, but I'm not. In fact, it irks the hell out of me, since I figure he's doing it not so much for my protection as to keep tabs on me."

"Oh?"

"Oh! You see, my stepfather and I have what you might call a *strained* relationship. He doesn't quite approve of my way of

216

living or some of the men who've been in my life, and there's a lot I don't approve about him. But I won't go into that now. I'll let you decide for yourself what you think when you meet him."

Dan frowned. "Why must I meet him?"

"Because he already knows I'm dating you—I told him yesterday on the phone—and because I know he'll approve of you."

"What makes you so sure?"

"Because I know him. What a status seeker Walt really is. And doctors have so much status these days it even rubs off on medical students. Too bad you couldn't have gotten into Harvard," she said, mimicking her stepfather's patronizing voice, "but State's a good school, too. At least it's in Boston."

"Oh great!" Dan groaned. "When does the grand inquisition take place?"

"Haven't arranged that yet, but I can tell you where. At the Harvard Club for lunch. Always at the Harvard Club first. . . . You'll come, won't you? I promise I'll make it up to you."

"How?"

"You already know that."

"Then, when?"

"On the weekend. . . . Walt's not that hard to take, really. He's worldly and intelligent and knows absolutely everybody in town, from Cardinal Cushing to Rocky Marciano. And he can get you all sorts of free tickets to sporting events. In fact, you two might hit it off great."

"And if we do—you willing to throw Friday night into that package, too?"

"Maybe," Kim said teasingly. "I was thinking about spending it with you anyway. At least, for dinner."

While Kim washed dishes, Dan sorted through his histology slides, putting some in the slotted box that he would take to class along with his microscope. Kim watched him as she worked but remained silent until they were having a last cup of coffee.

"There's really so much I still don't know about you," she

217

said pensively. "You're a great listener, but you don't talk much about yourself. You're like someone else I once knew in that respect. In fact, it's another thing you and Rick have in common."

Rick's name triggered a sharp twinge of discomfort in Dan. Logically, he knew he should ask—Who's Rick?—but he didn't. Instead, he said, "What do you want to know?"

"Well, you've barely mentioned a word so far about medical school. Compared to the other med students I've dated, you're an absolute sphinx. I still don't know if you like it or hate it or what."

"Tell me about those *other* medical students first," he said, feigning jealousy. "All Harvard men, I presume?"

"Not quite—one Harvard, one B.U. But both talked my ear off."

"About what?"

"Oh, how hard they had to study and how seldom they had time to date, so I ought to be extra nice to them. And if that didn't work, they'd turn morbid on me. Try to impress me with the grisly details of the latest autopsy or operation they'd seen. . . . But that comes later in med school, doesn't it?"

"Yes. The first year we don't watch autopsies. Or see patients. Not lives ones, anyway."

"What do you do?"

"Mainly work in the anatomy lab."

"The anatomy lab?" Kim repeated uncertainly. "Where they keep the cadavers? What's it like in there?"

Dan lit a cigarette he did not really want to allow him time to think. "What's it like? Gruesome, ghoulish, generally unpleasant. But mainly smelly. That embalming fluid stench really clings—to your fingers, your clothing, everything! That's why you see that can of Ajax cleanser and those bars of Lava soap in my bathroom. But you get used to it in time, along with everything else. Even the cadavers. You try not to think too much about what you're doing to them, only what you can learn that might someday help others."

"Is that where you have to go now—the anatomy lab?"

Reluctantly Dan nodded and the awareness of where he was going and to whom shadowed the rest of his conversation.

Chapter Twenty-four

Dan rode with Kim as far as the BOAC offices on Arlington Street, then walked the few remaining blocks to the medical school. Though he entered the anatomy lab precisely at nine, he was not surprised to find that most of his classmates had preceded him. With final exams less than two weeks away, they were busy reviewing the anatomy of the pelvis while simultaneously trying to complete the dissection of the legs.

None appeared busier nor more anxious than Earl. With time growing short and his ambition to excel ever greater, he and Dan exchanged sharp words several times that morning over the way things should be done. Arguing the lack of benefit to be derived from a meticulous, time-consuming dissection of the superficial nerves of the thigh, Dan finally succeeded in persuading an initially undecided Carey to his point of view.

"Jesus, you two don't want to learn anatomy! You just want to futz around!" Earl snarled in disgust and stalked off in the direction of the library.

"Don't let that creep bother you, Dan," Larry Parish commented from the adjacent table.

Dan went over to him. "I'm trying like hell not to, but this constant bickering is really getting on my nerves. Christ, I wish he'd loosen up!"

"Hah! The only part of Earl that ever loosens up is his bowels! . . . How was your date last night? Did you go to The Charles like I suggested?"

Dan nodded. Not knowing Boston's better restaurants that well, he had phoned Larry to ask his advice on where to take Kim to dinner. But he had remained uncommunicative as to her identity. "Nice place," he said tersely.

"Never mind that," Larry said, "tell me about the girl. You sure I don't know her?"

"Quite sure, lover."

"Then why the big mystery? Christ, it's not Snider's wiggly-assed secretary, is it?"

"Now you're being lewd, pal."

Larry laughed. "All right, you have my almost sincere apology. . . . Hey, buddy, why don't you ask her to the med school dance? You know—the *prom*," he added derisively. "We could double-date."

Dan shrugged noncommitally. "When is it?"

"Day after the finals. Should be a good time to cut loose. Or cut your throat! Think about it. Might be fun."

Dan did think about it—about proms, about weekends together, about long car trips into the snow-covered Berkshires with Kim for skiing. Thoughts of her filled him with such warmth and excitement that he found it increasingly hard to concentrate on his studies.

By Thursday evening, with their weekend together so close, Dan's attempt to study met with an unyielding resistance. Tempering his once steadfast desire to learn the most anatomy he possibly could, he now considered much of it useless information; like the Latin verb conjugations he had once struggled to memorize, more traditional than practical. Unless one meant to be a surgeon, which Dan didn't, he would likely forget all the minutiae concerning bones, muscles, and lymphatics in quick order. The essential aspects of anatomy would doubtless be reviewed in the clinical years, at a time when they would make considerably more sense.

Yet much as Dan tried to rationalize his futile attempts to study, none of his arguments left him satisfied for long. Far more worrisome was the fear that he might be backsliding; that after a successful month-long spurt, his determination to succeed, or even survive, in medical school was once again on the wane.

His habit was to call Kim between ten and eleven P.M. from the upstairs pay phone. But giving up even a token attempt to study by nine that night, he telephoned her then.

"Hi," he said when she answered. "Name's Dan."

"Dan who?"

"Hard to say. I'm a composite."

"Oh, that Dan! How come you're calling so early?"

"Can't study."

"Not on account of me, I hope."

"Not entirely. I'm not exactly sure what's wrong, but I can spend hours reading over the same chapter and still not remember one damn thing. Maybe I'm pressing too hard, although it sure as hell doesn't seem hard compared with what the rest of the class is doing."

"Or pretend that they're doing," Kim pointed out.

"You think they're just faking, huh? Well, if so, they've sure got me fooled. Wait till you meet some of those guys socially. They could be dancing to 'Stardust' and still thinking over the bones on a skeleton. Half of them never go out with a girl anyway, which gives them plenty of time to study. Well, at least they don't have to worry about passing the course."

"You'll pass, too," Kim assured him. "Your trouble right now might just be that you're trying to overdo. Like what happens to a boxer if he overtrains: He grows stale. His only hope then is to break away from the routine for a while to unwind."

"Want to help me do that tonight?" Dan asked hopefully. "It'd be great to see you, even for only an hour or so."

"Of course. Just tell me when. I'll throw on some clothes and pick you up."

"I'm ready now. Just honk when you get here. We'll go someplace for a drink."

"Let's just go for a long ride first," Kim suggested. "It's not too cold out and that might relax you even more."

Dan would have given much to have averted the tense encounter that ended the evening. It might have been averted, too, had he been thinking more clearly. But he had been so glad to see Kim, so content to ride with her along glittering Storrow Drive, that when they passed The Savoy on their way back, he suggested stopping in for a drink.

The billboard outside the entrance read: ALL THIS MONTH— THE GEORGE ROBINSON COMBO.

"George's a friend of mine," Dan told Kim at the door.

"Oh, really? I've heard how good he is. How'd you meet?"

"At an after-hours bar on Washington Street. He and some of his buddies go there to jam. You'll like him. He's not only a great horn player but a great guy."

The crimson glow of lanterns hanging from the ceiling on the rust-colored wallpaper made the interior of The Savoy almost as dimly amber as a photographer's darkroom. As they entered, George Robinson was spotlighted on the bandstand, carrying the lead in a frantic Dixieland rendition of "Limehouse Blues." At the finish of his solo, he smiled at Dan and waved his horn toward a cluster of dark, seemingly empty tables at the far end of the room. Dan skirted the bandstand to see what George was pointing at and was startled to discover Lem sitting in the shadows. A moment later, as Dan led Kim over to him, Lem rose slowly, clumsily to his feet.

"Lem! Is it really you?" Kim suddenly cried out. "Dear Lem." She rose on her toes to kiss his cheek. "It seems so long ago since we saw each other."

"It *was*. A hell of a long time ago!" Lem replied, conscious of the way Kim was staring through him into the past; conscious too of the grim, almost plaintive look on Dan's face as he gazed briefly at him, then away. "Hey, how you doin', Doc?" Lem asked him.

"Oh, fine," Dan said hoarsely. "Good to see you again."

Kim's eyes darted suspiciously from one to the other. "I didn't know you two knew each other. How come?"

Lem grinned. "Oh, Doc and I run into each other all the time. Either here or at a joint called Brecht's."

"That's the bar I was telling you about," Dan said hastily, "where I met George. He introduced us."

"Hmm," Kim mutered, looking somewhat mollified, if not completely convinced. "I find it damned odd that you two know each other, though."

"Well, since we do, let's all have a drink." Lem pulled a chair out for Kim and signaled for the waitress.

"How long have you been back in town?" Kim asked him.

"A couple of months. 'Fore that, I spent more than a year in a Denver hospital. Took that long for them Army docs to patch me together."

"Yes, I know. Rick told me."

No sooner had she spoken Rick's name when Dan saw her frown, as if she had not intended to mention him at all—at least not before Lem did.

As Dan turned to order drinks from the waitress hovering at his shoulder, he heard Kim casually ask the inevitable question.

"Tell me, how *is* Rick these days? I haven't seen him for over a year."

Lem glanced at Dan, trying to catch his eye, but Dan's stare held fast to the table. Then he shrugged and said: "Rick? I wish to hell I could tell you."

"Why can't you?" Kim sounded incredulous. "Surely you, of all people, must know!"

Lem shook his head. "I ain't heard from him in a long time either. No calls, no postcards, nothin'!"

Kim frowned again. "Rick certainly has a funny way of treating his friends. The war must have really changed him."

"Yeah. Changed all of us," Lem said wryly. "Some better, some worse."

Kim sipped the cognac the waitress had brought her, then said to Lem reproachfully, "Why haven't you called me? Let me know you were back home? . . . One summer," she said, turning to Dan, "Lem was like an older brother to me. He and his friend Rick spent a month out at our place on the Cape and we did all sorts of crazy things together. Remember, Lem, how you and I used to drive that old station wagon along the beach at night to cool off? Or sit out on those big boulders by the water's edge and talk?"

Lem grinned. "Yeah, I remember. Them were good times, all right. Maybe the last good times I had."

"What are you doing these days?" Kim asked.

"Got a sick mother to take care of right now. After that"—he shrugged—"maybe I'll travel a little, get some more schooling, I don't know. . . . But never mind that. Tell me about you and the doc. How long you two known each other anyway?"

"Oh, about a week. We met at a party. . . . Actually he didn't pay too much attention to me, so I had to chase after him. Right, Dan?" Kim gazed at him fondly.

"At a party?" Lem shook his head in wonder. "Small world, ain't it?"

"Yeah," Dan said, relieved that Lem now knew he hadn't purposely sought Kim out, but still discomfited by the searching side-glances Lem periodically sent his way. He was glad when George and Janey Towns joined them for a drink between band sets and then afterward, when the surrounding tables had filled up with a late-night crowd and the music from the bandstand had grown so deafening that they lapsed into intermittent small talk. Before leaving, however, Kim made Lem promise to call her at home so that they might talk over old times and arrange for the three of them to get together again.

When Lem rose to shake hands with Dan, they exchanged hard looks.

"That's a good woman you got here, Doc. Take good care of her."

"I intend to," Dan said. "Maybe I'll drop by Ernie's to see you some night soon."

"Yeah, do that. Few things it wouldn't hurt for you and me to talk over."

Out in the street, Dan helped Kim into the car before climbing into the driver's seat. "What's the best way to get to your place from here?"

"I don't want to go home. I want to spend the night at your place," Kim told him, looking straight ahead.

Dan stared at her, feeling a twinge of uncertainty that detracted from his anticipatory pleasure. Did Kim really want him, or was she using him as a surrogate to blunt a resurgent memory of Rick?

"It's all right, isn't it?" she asked after a moment. "You do want me to, don't you?"

"Of course, I do," he answered hastily while reaching for her hand.

"Then say so! Don't leave me dangling like that."

"Sorry, I guess I was thinking about something else."

"Like what?"

"Like how much food I got in the fridge. I usually go grocery shopping on Fridays."

"Is that all! What interests you most—me or food?"

"Right now, you. But come seven o'clock tomorrow morning that may change."

"Well, don't tell anyone, but there's an all-night market off Kenmore Square where you can relieve your anxieties. . . . Damn you!" Kim cried in mock exasperation. "Boston's chock-full of exciting bachelors who'd give almost anything to get me in bed with them and all you think about is your stomach! Were you ever starved as a child?"

Dan grinned. "Not that I recall. I guess I just have different appetites for different times. As my Uncle Woody once told me —don't ever take a woman to any place without a kitchen, if you can possibly help it. Sex may be great but ain't nothing beats home cooking!"

Their lovemaking that night was not only intense but, now that a certain familiarity existed between them, even more satisfying than before. This time, however, Kim did not drift off to sleep so soon afterward. As Dan had half-expected after their encounter with Lem, she was ready to talk about Rick. Wasn't this what he'd wanted all along? he asked himself. Then why did he feel such a sense of uneasiness?

Propped up beside him in the Murphy bed, still feeling the sweaty afterglow of sexual consummation, Kim talked candidly and for the most part calmly, betraying her inner state of tension only by the unsteady way she held her cigarette.

Dan listened with fascination, with occasional pangs of jealousy, as she told him about the time Rick had rescued her from a near-assault at the Hotel Roosevelt and their earliest times together. But when Kim began to describe the wild, almost maniacal rage that had seized Rick during their last night together, he stopped listening so intently. Though he tried to look attentive, his mind kept flashing back to that morning in the anatomy lab when his dissecting team had ripped off Rick's skullcap and discovered the ugly blood clot pressing into his brain. If, as he strongly suspected, Rick had received the injury in the Bishop fight, then Dan knew he might well have been suffering its effects all the time he was with Kim. Instead of her rejection of him, it might have been the pain and derangement caused by the hematoma that had made Rick so irrational. And there was no way, none whatsoever, he could possibly tell Kim this. In a kind of agony, Dan ground out his cigarette and lay back in the shadowy darkness of the bed to hide his anguish from her.

". . . Anyway," she concluded a moment later, "he gave me a fine going-away present, the brutal bastard—a broken nose!

Oh, it doesn't show; I got it straightened a few months later in London. But I still bear a scar, a mental one. . . . You see, Dan, there's still so much I don't understand. Even though Rick and I were lovers, I never let him think I wanted us to be anything more than that. Oh, maybe at first—I was so young and impressionable then that I sort of equated sex with love. But not later on. Certainly in none of the letters I wrote him in the Army."

Kim snuffed out the butt of her cigarette and reached for another. But even after lighting it, she remained silent, reflective.

Dan forced himself to ask: "Did you ever tell him about the other men in your life?"

"No, why should I? I'm sure Rick must've had plenty of other women those three years we were apart; he was bound to. So what right did he have to lash out at me? I wasn't his wife. I wasn't a slut either. Maybe I did deserve a dressing-down for not being more honest with him, but I didn't deserve being called a whore or slapped around like one!" Her eyes blazed with resentment. "Oh, how that *infuriates* me! It's something I've got to have out with Rick when I see him again. I may be a female, but I can be just as tough and ruthless as he is—it's the chief lesson he's taught me. Even though nobody—not even his great buddy, Lem—has seen him in over a year, Rick's bound to turn up one day and, when he does, I intend to see him. If he won't meet me on his own, I'll have my stepfather make him. I don't give a damn what it takes, I'll manage it somehow!"

"See what talking about him does to me, Dan?" she said after a deep, calming breath. "How it turns me cold: the frigid bitch I am with most men. Maybe it's not all Rick's fault; maybe I'm just using him as the scapegoat for the guilt feelings I have over all my affairs. But once I get to thinking about the way he hurt and degraded me, it all spills out and I can't help feeling bitter. Sometimes for days!"

"Even now?" he asked. "Is that the way you feel right now?"

Kim looked thoughtful and then shook her head. "No. Maybe talking about it helps. And I certainly don't feel the least bit guilty about letting you make love to me. How could I? It felt too good. In fact, I feel pretty damn feminine right now. Enough to want to do all sorts of nice things for you."

"Like what, for instance?"

"Oh, cook for you, decorate this dingy apartment for you, and this!" she said, putting out her cigarette and turning toward him.

Chapter Twenty-five

The weekend Dan and Kim spent together was a splurge of lovemaking, of fancy dining out, of intimate talks and tender looks—interrupted only briefly by drinks at the Ritz-Carleton with Walter Chatfield on Saturday night. Kim's stepfather was returning to London on business and had insisted that they meet him.

At his specific request, since he claimed to be on a tight schedule, they arrived at the hotel by seven, only to be kept waiting twenty minutes. Finally, Chatfield came bustling through the revolving door, issuing orders to the doorman for a limousine to stand by to transport him to the airport and the bellhop to take his luggage before giving Kim a kiss on the cheek, Dan a firm handshake, and both an apology.

Dan appraised him in a glance. A short, trim man in his early fifties, Chatfield had thinning gray hair, a round ruddy face with slightly upturned nose and a winning smile. But for all his air of affluence and sophistication, his wily blue eyes and bluff manner served to remind Dan more of a Pat O'Brien-type reporter or a politician than an international sports entrepreneur.

Chatfield's smile diminished slightly when Kim took Dan's arm, not his, to enter the bar off the lobby, but broadened again once they were seated and fawned over by the bar personnel.

Chatfield was obviously a man who not only relished special attention in public places but made sure he got it by rewarding it handsomely. Nonetheless, Kim had been right—Dan and he did hit it off, especially after Chatfield found out that Woodrow Brock was an uncle.

"Hell, I know Woody!" he exclaimed. "Known him for years. Ever since we boxed in the same college tournaments—he for Williams and me for Harvard. I was a senior then, so a couple of years older, and, of course, featherweight not welterweight, but we both ended up regional winners that year. After that I hung up the gloves, but Woody—hell he kept right on going until he won the national title the next year. He almost made the Olympics, didn't he?"

"Almost," Dan confirmed.

"What happened?"

"Eye injury. His doctor made him quit after that. Afraid he might get a detached retina."

Chatfield clucked sympathetically. "Too bad. He was quite a boxer in his day. Terrific moves. Terrific savvy. Really a joy to watch. . . . But, hell, he hasn't done so bad after quitting the ring either. What was the title of his latest book?"

"*The Presidential Infusion*. About the changes that take place in men like Teddy Roosevelt or Truman once they assume the Presidency."

"Oh, yes, I've been meaning to read that, and now I will. Pick up a copy the first chance I get."

"So will I," Kim said. "Dan and I are driving up to Williamstown next weekend so I can meet Woody and I want to get the book autographed."

"Next weekend, huh?" Chatfield mused. "Sure wish I was going with you—love to see Woody again—but I'll probably still be in London."

"Oh?" Kim said. "Why so long?"

Chatfield smiled secretively. "Oh, I just might spring a little surprise on you."

She look dubious. "What kind of surprise?"

"Never mind. Not ready to say. But nothing for *you* to worry about, Kim. If I do decide to go ahead with it, I'll call you, since you might want to join me over there. Hasn't that boss of yours, Kincaid, been after you to make a trip back to the home office with him?"

Kim nodded. "He's really been on my back about it, but I keep putting him off. Graham never listens to any ideas except his own, and they're all out of J. B. Priestley. You know—show the roast beef, the brandy, and the proper respect for the sensibilities of the upper crust, and that's all it takes to get the average Englishman to fly BOAC. . . . Besides, he wants to leave next Friday, which would mess up the ski weekend Dan and I had planned."

"Well, London *is* pretty grim and gray this time of year," Chatfield said, "so I can't say I blame you. But I hope Kincaid sees it that way. What if he insists?"

"Then let him—for all the good it will do him!" Kim said disdainfully.

"Well, I'd hate to see you get fired," Chatfield cautioned. "If worse came to worse, couldn't you and Dan put your plans off a week?"

Kim glanced at Dan. "Not very well. Dan has final exams next Friday, and after studying like mad he really needs a break. Besides, we've made plans with Woody to drive up to Stowe together. . . . If Graham really wants me with him, let him postpone his meeting."

Chatfield shrugged resignedly. "You never did show much tolerance for the pressures us poor businessmen are under. But if that little surprise I'm contemplating comes off, I'd sure like to have you over there. So be sure and let me know if anything comes up to change your plans."

"I will," Kim promised. "But don't count on it."

Chatfield sighed. "As you've probably noticed by now," he said to Dan, "Kim is one girl who knows her own mind. Isn't that right, daughter?"

"That's right, Walt. I don't like too many demands made on me. I don't care all that much for surprises either—remember?"

Chatfield squirmed slightly at her pointed stare. "Yes, I remember," he said, quickly concealing his embarrassment with a smile. ". . . See the kind of guff I have to take, Dan? But I can certainly understand your wanting Kim around to help you cut loose after your exams. I know from doctor-friends what a wicked grind medical school can be."

"It is," Dan said. "Especially the first year."

"You're at State?"

Dan nodded.

"Well, I happen to know several of your professors. Don Childress, your chief of surgery, and I are particularly close friends. Have been for years, ever since he took out my appendix. If I can ever put in a good word for you, just let me know."

The bar manager interrupted at that moment, tapping Chatfield gently on the shoulder to show him the time. "Thanks, Palmer," he said and rose to have a few words in private with him.

"Well, got to go, I'm afraid," Chatfield said, returning to the table. "But it's certainly been a pleasure meeting you, Dan."

"Same here," Dan said, rising to shake hands.

"Just to show my appreciation to you and Kim for meeting me on such short notice," Chatfield told him, "I've instructed Palmer that I'd like you to be my guests for dinner here tonight. You don't mind, do you?"

"No, of course not," said Dan.

"Good!" Chatfield beamed, patting him on the arm, then bending to kiss Kim on the cheek. "I'll call you in a few days, honey. Let you know if my little surprise works out."

"All right, Walt," she replied tonelessly. "Have a nice flight."

Hat and coat in hand, Chatfield waved to them from the door, then walked briskly out of the bar.

"Well," Kim sighed, "I'm glad that's over! I'm also glad you two got on so well. Better than he and I."

"I noticed."

"Curious?"

"Only to the extent that you want to tell me."

Kim smiled wanly. "Tactful of you."

"No, selfish. I just don't want you to get going on anything unpleasant. I want you in a good mood for dinner."

"And after dinner?"

"Especially after dinner!"

"How wise and worldly you are, my dear Dan. And how horny! I don't give a damn if Graham does fire me. It would take more than that for me to miss out on another weekend with you."

Chapter Twenty-six

With the onrushing events of Friday's final exams less than five days away, Dan reluctantly agreed not to see Kim during the interval and to devote every free moment to catching up on the bookwork he'd postponed over the weekend. But without her bright, warming presence, his apartment seemed even bleaker and colder than usual in the morning, and despite the frantic activity of his classmates the hours spent at school dragged. The worst moments came in early evening—from the time he returned home to an empty apartment and opened a can of soup or hash for supper until he forced himself to sit down at his desk to study.

When he phoned Kim on Monday night, her cousin Carol had been there and their conversation was brief. Kim told him that she and Graham were flying to New York in the morning to meet with their advertising agency and that she would be back the next day. But when Dan called her apartment late Wednesday night no one answered, and the repeated, almost mournful-sounding buzz of the telephone left him with a vague sense of unease, making it more difficult for him to concentrate on his reading the rest of the evening.

On Thursday Dan returned home from school in early afternoon and went through suppertime and seven solid hours of studying in determined style until, at ten o'clock, he decided to take a short break to call Kim. He climbed the stairs to the pay-phone in the front foyer, only to find it already in use. Sinking to the top step, he waited impatiently for the girl on the phone to finish, but listening to her cooing and giggling in a way that presaged no early end decided it would probably save time to use the phone booth in the cocktail lounge on the corner.

The cool night breeze blowing against his face provided a refreshing change from the stale, smoke-filled air of his apart-ment, and as Dan strolled along, he felt considerably more op-timistic over his prospects on the exam. Even though he had reviewed barely a fifth of the subject matter he could expect to be tested on, at least that much was now behind him. The rest would soon follow, he told himself confidently, during the all-night session he planned.

This time, reaching Kim on the third ring, Dan's spirits were raised only briefly by the reassuring sound of her voice.

"Dan!" she exclaimed, "I'm certainly glad you called! Where have you been? I must've phoned you at least a dozen times since afternoon and either the line's been busy or else that bitchy landlady of yours kept telling me you weren't home. Even at nine thirty, she insisted you weren't. Got rather nasty about it, too. Where the hell have you been?"

"Been? Home, that's where!" Dan fumed. "I haven't budged from my desk for hours! And that Dago bitch of a landlady knew it, too, because I passed her on my way in. She was just too damned lazy to drag her ass down the stairs to call me." About to go on complaining, he broke off suddenly, almost in-stinctively. "Anyway, sorry you couldn't reach me. Really gripes the hell out of me!"

"Oh, never mind. It's all right now that I finally got you. I really would've hated going away without letting you know first.

"Going away?" Dan repeated. "Going where?"

"London. I'm catching a flight out tonight. In just a few hours."

236

"You . . . are?" Dan muttered in a voice thick with disappointment. "Is, uh, Graham going with you?"

"No, he's flying over on the weekend. I'm going with my cousin Carol. For a chaperone." She laughed. "That should make you feel a little better."

"Not much." His mouth felt so dry he could barely speak.

"Oh, poor Dan! I feel like an absolute bitch springing this cold on you. And I'm just as disappointed over missing out on our weekend in Williamstown as you. But I simply have to go. . . ."

"All right, so you have to," Dan said, his voice hardening. "For God's sake, why?"

"Well, for one thing, Walt's getting married on Sunday. That was his little surprise. With Lydia's mother so sick, he's finally decided to make an honest woman of her after all these years and I promised I'd fly over for it. Then, there's the meeting Graham's been after me to attend—the company's annual planning conference. He's finally begun to listen to some of my ideas, and he promised that if I came to London with him I could present them to the company bigwigs myself. I've got an entire campaign planned! So you see, much as I hate to disappoint you and much as I'll miss you, I really do have to go." She paused to give him a chance to reply, but he didn't. "Dan— are you still there?"

"I'm here," he said wearily. "How long will you be gone?"

"Two weeks. Three at the most. It'll pass quickly. And I really do have to go, you understand."

"So you keep saying. Now suppose you tell me the *real* reason. From all you told me before, I didn't think either your stepfather's feelings or your job were that important to you. Sorry, baby, but I'm just not buying it."

"Damn you!" she wailed. "Damn that infallible intuition of yours! I thought I was being so convincing and yet you ask that. . . . Why do you have to be so perceptive where I'm concerned?"

She fell silent for a moment. When she spoke again, her voice no longer contained the same brisk, self-assured tone, sounding less like the public Kim than the girl he had known during so many unguarded moments. "Look, Dan, you know what I was like when we met: how down I was on men. I just never expected to meet you—someone who could make me feel so warm and feminine and, well, loving. But it's all happened so fast my head's in a spin. And relationships like ours never stay the same. Maybe once in a while they grow into something deeper and more permanent, but most times they generate so much heat they just run out of gas. And you can get yourself pretty badly burned in the process. I don't want that to happen to us. Honest to God, I don't. . . . What I'm really trying to tell you, Dan, is that I need time. Time away from you."

"Maybe so," Dan conceded grudgingly. "But why does it have to be right now? Why can't you leave for London after the weekend? Do you have any idea how much this shakes me up? And with a big exam coming up tomorrow. . . ."

"Don't you think I know that!" Kim implored. "But I got very little sleep last night thinking it all out and it's really what I feel I ought to do."

"Then do it. . . . Well, if that's all—" he said, suddenly weary beyond the need or desire to discuss it further.

"Wait!" Kim said quickly. "There's another reason—a far more important one—why I feel I have to get away. Only I don't want to discuss it—not even with you. I just found out about it yesterday and it's upset me something fierce. I just need time—time alone—to reconcile myself to it. . . ."

"But my God, Kim!" he pleaded. "Can't you tell me more than that! If it's something you don't want to talk about on the phone I'll come over to your place."

"No! I don't want you to!" she said emphatically.

"Why not?"

"Because it doesn't concern you. Honest. Nothing you could possibly say or do would make the slightest difference in the

238

way I feel. It's just something I have to get over in my own way. Maybe when I get back—maybe then—I'll tell you about it. I couldn't now, not without coming apart at the seams."

"Jesus, Kim—you haven't driven some poor guy to suicide, have you?"

"Suicide!" she gasped. "God, no! Why would you ask that?"

"From the way you sound, it must be something at least that drastic."

"Dan, don't!" she pleaded. "Just believe me when I say I don't want to talk about it and don't press me anymore. Please, Dan . . . I only wish—oh, damn, damn—" she said, choking back a sob. "Look, I've got to hang up now before I start bawling good. . . . Luck on your exam. . . ."

"Yeah, thanks," Dan muttered to himself after the line went dead. "I'm really going to need it now."

Chapter Twenty-seven

The following Monday was Cleanup Day in the anatomy lab: a time when each group of students was expected to gather together the remains of their cadaver in a four-foot-long pine box for burial at a later date and scrub down their table with disinfectant.

Cleanup Day was an ancient tradition at State, antedating even Snider's tenure as professor, and symbolic as well as practical. Now that the last toes and tendons and muscles had been hacked to bits, the ordeal of cadaver dissection, the probationary rite of freshman medical students, was finally over. For many in the class, it would be the last time they ever set foot inside the anatomy laboratory of State or any other medical school. In the weeks and months ahead, their recollection of this experience would burrow ever deeper in their minds, growing dimmer in detail and clarity, until by the end of their freshman year all but a few isolated instances would be forgotten. The memory of that harrowing half-year would then lie buried in their subconscious—perhaps to emerge briefly at the sight and smell of subsequent freshman medical students or as their own deaths drew near, but never in casual conversations with friends or even fellow physicians.

Again, as he had in every task undertaken throughout the semester, Earl took the lead in the cleanup operation, fetching the necessary disinfectant and deodorizing solutions from the fifth-floor storeroom and arbitrarily deciding, like some whole-sale butcher, which scraps of flesh were worthy of burial and which were to be discarded in the refuse bucket.

It took an hour of steady work to make the gray metal surface of the dissection table glistening-clean and pick the perforations that connected it to the trough of embalming fluid beneath clean of debris.

"Well, that does it!" Earl said triumphantly. "Old Snider shouldn't be able to find any fault with this job. Not that I give a damn. I won't be seeing much of him anymore!"

"You won't huh?" Dan challenged. "I thought you signed up for his course in the history of medicine?"

"Yeah, I did," Earl admitted sheepishly. "For the same rea-son as everyone else—to get on his good side. But the final exam was a lot easier than I expected and now that I'm pretty sure I passed I've had enough of the great god Snider. . . . Well," he said, finally, packing his dissection kit into his oversized black bag, "I don't suppose I'll be seeing much of you two either."

Surprised by the wistful note in Earl's voice, Carey and Dan exchanged glances. "Oh, maybe not so much," she said, "but we'll certainly be seeing enough of each other around the school."

"Yeah, sure," Earl agreed, "only we'll never have to go through anything like this again. Thank God. Even though we were lucky in working with the best cadaver in the class, I'm sure glad it's over. Aren't you?"

"You know it!" Carey told him.

Bag in hand, Earl took a last reflective look around. "Well, guess I'll go up to biochemistry lab and check out my equip-ment. See you, Car. You too, Dan. . . ."

"Yeah," said Dan absently, not unmoved by Earl's surprising display of sensitivity but struck more than ever by the difference in their attitudes. *The best cadaver in the class.* Was that all

Rick Ferrar had represented to him? It seemed so callous, so heartless, to pass Rick off that way, but maybe Earl's way of thinking had been wiser.

"Well, what do you know," Carey said a moment later, "that was a switch: little Earl turning sentimental on us. Maybe there's hope for the boy yet. But I think I understand what made him act that way. Much as I've looked forward to this day, I feel kind of funny myself. Hard to realize I'll never have to spend another horrible morning in here. I almost have guilt feelings about it, don't you?"

"I might," Dan said, "if I were all that confident I passed the finals."

"Oh, but you must've!" Carey protested. "It wasn't that tough an exam."

"No, I suppose not—not if you were well enough prepared for it."

"Weren't you?" she asked pointedly.

"I did my share of studying, if that's what you mean. But it takes more than that to pass a big exam. You've also got to be in the right frame of mind. I wasn't, I guess."

"Why not?"

"Oh, a long story," he said, dismissing it with a shrug.

"You used to be willing to tell me long stories—remember?" she reproached him.

"Yeah, so I did." Taking in Carey's pretty, placid face, he thought how uncomplicated she was compared to the mystery that was Kim. "Probably get around to telling you this one someday. Right now, I'll buy you a cup of coffee if you promise to stop pouting."

"Oh, all right," Carey said reluctantly. "But I still think you're worrying unnecessarily over that exam. I'd bet anything you passed it."

Dan arched an eyebrow. "Anything?"

"Well, *almost* anything. Depends on what you have in mind?"

"The same thing I had in mind the last time you were at my place. We still have a little unfinished business, you know?"

Carey began to blush. "No, I don't know! Tell me about it?"

"All in due time. But what if I lose that bet—do I lose out with you, too?"

"Maybe you already have?"

"Hometown boyfriend?"

"I *do* have one."

"Lucky guy," he conceded grudgingly.

"Not really. Happens to be a seminary student."

"So what? He hasn't taken his vows of chastity yet, has he?"

"No, *he* hasn't. But maybe I have. Now that anatomy's over I don't feel the same way about it."

"How do you feel?"

"Oh, calmer. Less curious. Maybe even a little calculating. If you want to know any more, you'll simply have to tell me what got you so unstuck before that exam."

"Might surprise the hell out of you."

"Why? Do I know the girl?"

"What makes you so sure it was a girl? Men do get upset about other things, you know?"

"Like what?"

"Like this place," Dan said, looking one last time around the lab. "Now, let's get coffee."

A week later, while in biochemistry lab, Dan was approached by one of Snider's poker-faced research assistants who told him that the professor of anatomy requested his presence in his office.

Snider was sorting through a stack of blue examination booklets on his desk when Dan entered. "Sit down, Lassiter," he said. "Relax. Have a smoke if you want one. There's a pack on the desk. What I have to say to you will be brief—but, I'm afraid, unpleasant. To get right to the point: Your performance on the anatomy portion of the finals was unacceptable—to pass the exam or the course. Yours isn't the only one, mind you, nor is it the worst. There are a few others I've decided to flunk too. But it's bad company to be in, Lassiter."

With no visible change of expression, Dan said, "I realize that." He had guessed the moment he was summoned to Snider's office what the probable outcome would be and had reconciled himself to it.

"All right, then," Snider continued. "Before I say more, let me ask if you have any explanation to offer for such a poor performance?"

"A reason or two, maybe," Dan replied. "But no excuse."

"Go on. Tell me about them."

Dan shrugged. "Not much to tell. I've had some personal problems lately, and trying to cope with them got me pretty far behind in my studies. So I foolishly tried to catch up at the last minute—you know, cram all night—only that didn't work out so well. I felt so damned dragged out the next morning I couldn't think straight."

"And if you can't think straight, you can't write straight?"

Dan nodded. "It may not be very original, but that's pretty much the whole story."

"These problems in your personal life," Snider began tentatively, "care to tell me about them?"

Dan stared at him for a moment and slowly shook his head. "No, I don't think so. They're not very original either. . . . Besides, I'm pretty sure they're over by now."

"Let's hope so," Snider replied, concluding from Dan's expression that he had said all on the subject he meant to. "There's also the matter of your poor attendance in the lab. Even though it started picking up toward the end, you still missed a number of sessions—ten in all—in November and December. Frankly, Lassiter, I consider that an even more grievous mark against you than your failure on the exam. As I've told your class time and again—the dissection's the thing! The few topics I've discussed in my lectures are quite inconsequential in comparison and can be dug out of any of the standard textbooks. The lab work simply can't be made up."

"I know," Dan said ruefuly. "I have a damned good idea what I missed by not being there every day."

"Exactly! In fact, were you just any student I'd make such absences a much more serious issue; claim it showed a real lack of interest on your part. But in your case I'm a little reluctant to do so—especially in the light of our previous talk. I do feel some obligation to ask, however, if some of the misgivings you had over cadaver dissection then might not have contributed to your present difficulty."

Dan smiled wanly. "Maybe I should push that, since it seems to score points with you. But it simply wouldn't be true. I didn't lie to you: The dissection did bother me. It bothered the hell out of me for months—even to the point of giving me nightmares. But it let up after a while. Particularly after the Christmas break when there wasn't that much humanly recognizable about him. So you see, much as I might like to get myself off the hook on that basis, I can't. It wouldn't be true."

"Perhaps not," said Snider, "and even though I suspect there's more to your feelings about the matter than you're willing to let on, I deeply appreciate your honesty. . . . Tell me frankly, Lassiter, did you find the amount of work we expected of you too overwhelming? Or that we whipped you along too fast?"

"It was hard as hell keeping up, if that's what you mean. I'd be a fool to deny it. But I suppose you just have to learn it. You can't very well be a doctor—a good one anyway—without it."

"And you want to be one of those, I take it. Not good enough, mind you, but *good* in the best sense of the word. Am I correct in assuming that's what you aspire to, Lassiter?"

"Either that or take up some other profession."

"Well, that much you can decide for yourself between now and the time of the makeup exam in a few weeks. We haven't set an exact date for it as yet, but I'll let you know the moment we do. I must warn you, though, if you fail it, I seriously doubt if the dean will allow you to continue in school."

"I won't!" Dan said resolutely. "I really know more anatomy than I showed the last time, and I've no intention of failing any more exams."

"That's the spirit!" Snider smiled encouragingly, then redirected his attention to the stack of exam booklets on his desk.

But as Dan started to rise, Snider suddenly waved him back down. "No, wait! Stay a few minutes more. There's still one or two things I'd like to get across to you. . . . You know, Lassiter, it's been my unpleasant duty to fail one, sometimes two, freshmen each year. It's not invariable you understand; last year and four years ago there weren't any failures. But that's how it usually averages out. And I'm far from secure in my judgment. Some of the boys I've seen dropped from State I feel certain would have gone on to make fine physicians had they been better prepared, either academically or emotionally, to cope with the rigors of that first year. But others! Look, let me tell you some of my pet peeves about medical students. Too damned many of them think once they get their med school acceptance letter the big battle of life is over and it's all downhill from then on; that no matter what temporary obstacles teachers like me raise in their paths, they are now members of an elite and highly profitable profession. Well, maybe so, but we aren't a business school—not yet. We happen to be training future physicians to be something more than money-makers. A young doctor must not only be familiar with his tools but also with the disease process he's treating. And for that the diagnosis is paramount. I have scant respect for the kind of practitioner who treats a patient's symptoms piecemeal, without ever considering him as a whole person, one who harbors a disease either of the mind or of the body and capable of affecting both. And in order for you to make a correct diagnosis you must apply certain basic principles. If your patient complains of right upper quadrant abdominal pain, you must consider the structures put there by nature which might possibly give rise to such discomfort. Perhaps it's a gallstone or a peptic ulcer; the pathology might lie

246

in the kidney or ascending colon. Whatever the case, it's your working knowledge of anatomy that's of primary use to you, and for that reason we make amply sure you know it.

"Another thing, I take it in large measure as a personal failure whenever a freshman student is dropped. After all, I've had the first crack at him and it's my job to keep him enlightened. I doubt that many of you realize the substantial financial loss, among other things, that the school suffers when a student fails. As things stand now, your tuition covers only a small fraction of what it costs to educate you and when a freshman is dropped not only is his spot in the class wasted, but a gap is left throughout the remaining three years. We thus lose training not one future doctor, but two! Regardless of where the fault may lie—whether in his personality or mine—the loss is something we have to seriously contend with. For that reason, and because I have faith in you, I hope for both our sakes that you'll redeem yourself by doing brilliantly on the makeup exam.

"You will, of course, only if you want to, and that's something I can't decide for you. Nor will I give you the benefit of the doubt if your performance is borderline. You know, when a young doctor finally gets out in practice, he soon learns there are certain patients he can cure and certain ones he can't. But there is no such thing as a *batting average* in medicine. Here, a percentage point is measured in human life—and even *one* life lost over a long span of years is an excessive price to pay for a moment's negligence. Believe me, no doctor who practices medicine today—whether he does so for the money or out of pure altruism—lacks the conscience to suffer the truth if he's not giving his best to his patients. Doesn't matter how big his bank balance or how excessively his patients praise him—he knows!"

Snider paused as if gathering breath to go on, but then smiled and shrugged. "Well, that's enough preaching for one day. You probably have a biochemistry experiment cooking upstairs and I've held you long enough. Mind you, though, that's not all that could be said. So if you're ever disposed to listen to more of my rather verbose convictions I'd be only too glad to welcome you here again. I sometimes think far too few of my former students ever give a moment's thought as to why men like me forsake the niceties of clinical medicine and are content to teach. But there are times when it helps immeasurably to be able to look beyond the limits of the classroom and the laboratory and be reminded that my efforts are being passed on to the public by my former students.

"Don't forget that, Lassiter. I might be reading more into these visits than is warranted, but I still have a feeling you and I have a lot more to talk about. So don't be any stranger around here for the next three years—'cause if you are and if we ever cross paths when you're out in practice, you'll get the coldest stare you ever saw outside of a dead mackerel!"

Chapter Twenty-eight

Dan might have been deeply disconsolate when he left Snider's office that wintry gray Monday afternoon to slosh home in a mixture of drizzle and melting snow. But instead of brooding over the consequences of his flunking the final and the extra burden this placed on his struggle to survive in medical school, he concentrated more on the insights Snider had imparted to him. These same insights were to forge the anchor which held Dan to his desk during the dreary days ahead when his brain felt awash in a torrent of medical minutiae. Not only was there anatomy to review, but he had to make some effort to keep pace with the prodigious reading assignments in his new courses in biochemistry and physiology. Still, he persevered, setting up an ambitious study schedule for himself, one that required a minimum of six hours of reading each night, and adhering to it rigorously for the next week and a half.

But then, like some recurrent malady for which he had developed no adequate defense, it all came apart on him again.

It started on the Sunday before the week of the makeup exam when skimming through the inside pages of the Boston *Post,* he suddenly spotted a picture of Walter Chatfield with his new wife and stepdaughter arriving at Logan Airport. The jarring discovery that Kim had been back in Boston for at least two days now sent a tight, tingling constriction across his forehead.

In the three weeks she had been away, he'd gotten one letter and two postcards from her. In each, Kim had claimed she missed him and would call him immediately upon her return. But maybe she *had* tried to call—unsuccessfully? Although he'd had harsh words with his landlady over the last time Kim failed to reach him by phone, even threatening to move out if it ever happened again, it seemed entirely possible that the bitch was up to her old tricks.

After dialing Kim's number he waited anxiously through several rings before a strange voice—Kim's cousin Carol—answered. A long pause ensued after he asked to speak to Kim. Following some muffled conversation between Carol and whoever else was there with her (and Dan strongly suspected it was Kim herself), he was told she wasn't at home. Asked if he would like to leave a message, Dan ignored the question. He informed Carol he would call again and, on hearing her hang up, slammed down the receiver.

The momentary surge of fist-clenching fury that had overcome him presently simmered into a slow burn which goaded him mercilessly for the next hour. Had Kim really been in the apartment or hadn't she? Was he right or wrong, intuitive or paranoid? He had to know; with his make-up exam now only three days away, he couldn't afford to keep on brooding about her. Yet what else could he do? Did he dare barge into her apartment and have it out with her? It was rash action, he realized; not only could a showdown like that ruin everything, but it would be completely out of character for him.

Minutes later, while he was riding the subway, staring back at his reflection in the car window, Dan's misgivings deepened. Even disregarding the complications that might arise over her cousin Carol, possibly even her stepfather, being in the apartment with her, he instinctively felt he was trying to resolve a delicate situation in the worst possible way. But he had to know why Kim was avoiding him.

The walk from Kenmore Square to 1070 Beacon Street turned

out to be a windy affair. With the preludes of a March rain-storm swirling dust in his path, Dan was soon forced to stop in the shelter of a doorway to remove a cinder from his eye. Despite several swipes at it, the particle of dust or else the residual irritation continued to make his lid blink spasmodically and his eyes water. Finally he gave up, ignoring the gritty discomfort as best he could, and went on to Kim's apartment building.

Soon after ringing her doorbell, Dan heard footsteps approaching and fervently hoped it would be Kim herself who came to the door.

A short, attractive brunette peered out of a crack in the door. "Yes?"

Trying to keep his disappointment out of his voice, he said, "I'm Dan Lassiter. I'd like to see Kim if she's home by now."

"You must be the friend who called earlier," the girl said, opening the door fully to reveal herself in a terrycloth robe and bare feet. "Gee, I'm sorry but she hasn't come home yet."

"Do you expect her back soon?"

"Oh, I'd imagine so."

"In that case, would you mind if I came in and waited? I have to see her about something pretty urgent."

"Oh, you can't very well do that," she protested. "I was about to bathe and I'm hardly dressed to receive visitors.

"I'm harmless enough," he assured her. "Really, I am. I'm sure Kim would vouch for that." Trying but failing to keep his irritated eye from watering, Dan rubbed at it with a knuckle.

The girl smiled at his persistence. Then, leaning forward to peer openly at him with the myopic stare of someone caught without her glasses, she asked, "Are you sure you're all right?"

"Just got something caught in my eye, that's all. Look, I don't mean to make a nuisance of myself, but I'd consider it a real favor if you'd let me wait for her while you take your bath. I could read a magazine or something." He took a tentative step forward.

251

"No . . . really," she insisted, backing away from him but keeping a firm grip on the doorknob. "It's not that I don't trust you, but if you know Kim well at all you know how unpredictable she is. There have been times when I've known her to just drive around town by herself for hours."

"Her car's in the parking lot," Dan said flatly.

"Then maybe she went to the movie at the Kenmore? . . . Come to think of it, I do remember her mentioning something about wanting to see the Fellini film there."

A look of barely concealed contempt passed across Dan's face, then he feigned enlightenment. "I'll bet that's where she is, all right—or wishes she was."

His sarcasm made the girl frown. "Look," she said irritably, "if you'll give me your phone number, I'll promise I'll tell Kim to get in touch with you the moment she comes in."

"She knows my number. She's called it often enough."

"Fine! I'll be sure to have her phone you then."

"Thanks a lot," Dan mumbled. Then, with his eye stinging and his head throbbing, he was unable to tolerate this humiliating charade any longer. "Matter of fact, Carol, you can tell her right after you close the door—since I'm pretty damned sure she's in there. Forgive me for saying so, but you're really no great shakes as an actress. Kim's better. She can make a trusting soul like me believe damned near anything when she puts her mind to it. Tell her that, too, why don't you?"

"Well, pardon me! It *wasn't* nice meeting you." Carol sniffed as she swung the door shut.

Still seething with anger and frustration, Dan returned to his apartment. Of all possible outcomes for his rash venture, Kim's refusal to see him at all seemed the least definitive and, because of this, the hardest to endure. By some Herculean force of will, he managed to open his anatomy text and study late into the night. But between paragraphs and pages, bathroom and coffee breaks, he continued to dwell so on the galling encounter that when he gave up in exhaustion at two in the morning he knew he'd retained barely a tenth of what he'd read.

At school the following morning he found a note from Dr. Snider in his mailbox confirming Wednesday as the day for the makeup examination. But even then he could not shake thoughts of Kim from his mind and realized he was in serious straits.

At noon he left the school and walked to the BOAC office on Arlington Street. Again he was frustrated. Not only wasn't Kim on the premises, but according to Kincaid's secretary, she no longer worked there, having been transferred to their London office. Dan tried to find out something more about the move, but that was all the secretary was able to tell him, suggesting he come back later and query Kincaid himself for details.

At one o'clock Dan plodded back to school to hear a lecture by Dr. Thomas Coleman, head of the physiology department. No wonder, he reflected, that Coleman—a tall, stooped, almost whispery-voiced man in his early sixties—found it necessary to take attendance at such sessions; otherwise none of the students would bother to show up for his boring and relatively uninformative talks. Growing more and more fidgety as Coleman continued to drone into the afternoon, Dan decided to cut the laboratory exercise that was scheduled to follow and go home to study.

No sooner had he opened the door to his apartment than Kim was everywhere: in the kitchen in his long sweater cooking breakfast; in the bathroom combing her hair in that special, sway-backed, legs straddled way of hers; in the bunched-up sheet and blanket on the bed.

There was no use studying now, he realized, feeling the dregs of a familiar anxiety beginning to swirl in his brain and sink him into deep despair.

Kim had been forbidden fruit for him, he mused. If their meeting had been predetermined at all, it was for only one reason: not to fall in love with her but to tell her about Rick.

253

And now that he had failed to fulfill such a behest, he was paying the penalty.

Removing his shoes, he lay on the bed, hands clasped behind his head. If Kim had been just another girl, *his* girl, he might have been able to forget her. But he had never been able to think of her as his girl—she had always been Rick's as well. Despite the full exercise of logic, he could never quite separate his feelings for her from his obsession with Rick from his determination to survive in medical school. The three were inextricably interwoven in his mind. Thus he might as well face it—there would be no studying, no passing the makeup exam, no career in medicine—and reconcile himself to it now. Since Kim had proven to be his downfall, only by seeing her, confessing his deceit to her, could he possibly hope to remove the cloud of guilt that hung so heavily over him. . . . Or was it sheer madness to think that way? He had simply been jilted. So why let an overactive imagination carry him away? All this nonsense about cadavers and curses—he had been skirting the slippery edge of madness long enough. What was it Karl von Clausewitz, the military strategist, had written: "If defeat is inevitable, lose at the least possible price." It was high time he came to his senses, he reflected as an overwhelming lassitude spread through him. Sleep, he thought. All he really needed to restore his sanity was a few hours sleep.

A knock on the door woke him in early evening. The girl who lived in the apartment above told him there was a phone call. Wild intuition filled him with the belief that it was Kim as he hurried up the stairs in his stocking feet. However, taking the phone in hand, he was more surprised than disappointed to recognize Lem Harper's voice.

They spoke briefly and Dan agreed to meet him.

Chapter Twenty-nine

They met in the downstairs reading room of the Copley Square library. The medical textbook Lem had open on the table aroused Dan's curiosity, but he did not comment on it. After Lem had returned the book to the librarian's desk the two of them went to a cafeteria off the square for coffee.

The morose mood that Dan was in only deepened as they walked in silence. On leaving the library, he had asked Lem what this meeting was all about, but Lem had put him off. Now, as they sat at an isolated table in the sparsely filled cafeteria, he asked again with mounting irritation. He sensed from Lem's taciturn manner that he had nothing good to tell him and so wanted to hear what it was, get it over with as quickly as possible.

"Well?" he prompted. "I've got more important things to do than sit around here all night."

"Like what?" Lem asked.

"Like study for a big exam. Get to the point, Goddamn it."

"I want you to stay away from Kim."

Dan glared. "You do, do you? Why? Did she call you?"

"We spoke."

"Well, I'll be a sad son of a bitch!" Dan said with rising indignation. "She got you to be her messenger boy! What're you supposed to do—try a little persuasion and if that doesn't work some arm twisting? . . . Well, screw that! Just tell Kim I won't be bothering her anymore. I've finally had a bellyful. . . . One of the reasons I haven't gotten around to seeing you or anyone else for weeks is 'cause I've been studying my ass off. It isn't that I'm so conscientious either. I don't have any choice!"

"How come?"

Dan laughed harshly. " 'Cause I flunked my final exams. I thought I'd finally gotten myself straightened out in medical school, only it turns out I was a damn sight premature. And I'll tell you something worse: I flunked that exam not 'cause I didn't know my stuff—I did—but because I let myself get so screwed up over Kim's going away. And that makes me even a bigger damn fool than you might've thought. Only no more! I've got a makeup exam to take day after tomorrow, and if I flunk that, it means I'm washed up in the doctor business. But don't worry—I'm going to pass it. Nothing you or Kim or anyone else can do is going to stop me now. Just tell her I got the message and won't be bothering her anymore—okay?"

Lem shrugged indifferently. "I'll tell her anythin' you want, Doc—only that ain't the reason I want you to keep away from her place."

"What is it then?"

" 'Cause it ain't safe."

"What the hell do you mean, it ain't safe?"

"It ain't for you. You show your head around there and you might just get it busted."

"Oh shit! That's absurd." Dan almost laughed, but Lem's sudden scowl stopped him. "You've got to be kidding?"

"Well, I ain't! You just cool down, lover-boy, and listen. Kim's place is being watched."

"I know that! It has been for weeks—ever since she had a prowler. . . . So what?"

"So, if I got this figured right, one of the people they're watchin' for is you. You show up around there and you could get stomped on pretty hard."

"Why? Just because I've been screwing Kim?"

"Those guys don't care what you been doin' to her—only why? That's the part that concerns them."

Dan's face creased in confusion. "What the hell business is it of theirs?"

" 'Cause Chatfield's plenty worried about it, too. All of a sudden he's worried about a whole lot of things, including you. Only you ain't his main worry—I am!"

"Look, will you stop talking in riddles, for Chrissake."

Lem smiled sardonically. "Yeah, now that I finally got your attention. For openers, Kim knows now that Rick's dead."

Dan winced. "So she finally knows. Somehow or other I didn't think you'd tell her. . . . You were the one, weren't you?"

Lem shook his head.

"Who then?"

"Al Lakeman. I ain't exactly sure who Al heard it from 'cept he was some sports reporter. And Kim found out when Al called her to pass the news on to Chatfield in London."

Jerry Kerson! Dan decided. Jerry had promised to keep it quiet. But, of course, that had been months ago and he'd probably forgotten.

"Anyway," Lem went on, "Kim called me right after Lakeman called her to find out how much I knew. But I played dumb. Made out like it came as a complete surprise. Since she was leavin' for London the next day she got me to promise to find out all I could and let her know when she got back."

"What else did she say?"

"Man, she was cryin' so hard over that phone I couldn't catch half of the words she said. Mainly that Rick and her'd had some kind of fallin' out. She wouldn't talk about it, but it sounded pretty bad. . . . You know?"

"Yeah," Dan said grimly. "I do know. Rick asked her to marry him and got turned down."

"Marry her?" Lem scowled. "So that was it—that's why he needed the purse from the Bishop fight so bad. What else did she tell you?"

"What else?" Dan gave him a mocking smile. "That Rick's

proposal surprised the hell out of her, and when she said no, he went sort of berserk. Hauled off and belted her so hard it broke her nose. They hadn't seen each other for years and she still doesn't know what she might've said or done to turn him so wild. That's what makes her feel so damned resentful."

"Did she tell Chatfield what Rick done?"

"She didn't say. But he must've wondered who broke her nose."

"Yeah, he must've," Lem acknowledged with a sneer. "Well, that explains it. . . ."

"Explains what?"

"Why he had Rick killed."

"Why—what!" Dan drew back from the table. "Rick was . . . killed?" he whispered. "But that's impossible!"

"Oh yeah?" mocked Lem. "What's so impossible?"

Dan's voice faltered as he tried to overcome his sense of horror and disbelief. "But I thought—I always figured—that the subdural Rick must've got in the Red Bishop fight was what killed him."

"Yeah, well, maybe Bishop did give him one, but it wasn't the one what killed him. He got that a night later in some alley."

"But how do you know?"

Lem glanced over his shoulder with instinctive caution. "How? 'Cause I've done enough checkin' these past few weeks to know the whole stinkin' story. . . . I knew from the start Rick's body never would've been handed over to a medical school so soon after the Bishop fight without some kind of coroner investigation. Without it even makin' the newspapers. So with the help of a cop friend of Ernie Doyle's, I got a look at the morgue sheet they made out on him. And I got hold of the morgue attendant who was on duty that night—guy called Cawley. Oh, I got ahold of him, all right." Lem's eyes narrowed menacingly. "Right around the neck. I guess I should've strangled the little bastard while I had the chance." He flexed his

258

huge hands in front of him. "One good squeeze would've done it. But he told me what I wanted to know and there's goin' to be enough killin' 'fore all this is over and so I didn't."

"What'd he tell you?"

"That Rick's body was dragged in around four, five, in the morning by two guys, one a cheap hood named D'Mato and the other an ex-pug, Turan Demeril. Turk, they call him. A fat, mean bastard, built something like Tony Galento. Used to be a pretty fair heavyweight like him, too, only now he works for Chatfield. . . .That's right," he said accusingly, "*works* for him."

After a sip of tepid coffee, Lem went on. "Anyway, what probably happened was findin' out about Rick slippin' it to Kim must've made Chatfield's blood boil. Got him so riled that he ordered Turk to round up some boys and go after him. Maybe he told them to kill him, maybe not, but whether Rick fought back too hard or whether those dumb bastards didn't know when to quit—that's what they did."

"But even if Rick was killed accidentally, why bring his body to the morgue?" Dan pointed out. "Why not just dump it someplace?"

"Ordinarily they would've. The way I figure it, they were probably gettin' ready to do just that when in goin' through his wallet they came across that card Snider once gave Rick—you know, the one sayin' he'd donated his body—and realized what a perfect way it was of gettin' rid of him without anybody ever findin' out. You dig so far?"

Dan nodded. "But how'd they get the morgue to release his body to State without more of an investigation?"

"How? I'll tell you how," Lem said disdainfully. "By slipping that creep, Cawley, a few hundred bucks to falsify the records. Boston happened to be in a helluva cold spell around then and they got him to put down that Rick had been found frozen to death. Maybe he was. Maybe those bastards froze him in some lake first before bringing him in."

Dan suppressed a shudder. "Do you think Chatfield knew all this? At the time, I mean?"

"Maybe not at the time—but he does now. I made sure of it. I told him."

"You? How?"

"By sending him a letter telling him I knew what he'd done and that I was goin' to kill him for it."

Dan paled. "You mean you actually would?"

"Kill him?" Lem repeated. "Why not? Hell, I done enough of that in Korea to know how easy it is. But whether I ever get around to killin' Chatfield or not, I want that no-good son of a bitch to sweat. I want him to have to look twice every time some big nigger comes near him in a crowd or whenever he's out alone in the dark. . . . Far as Turk and D'Mato are concerned, though, I am goin' to take care of them. Killin' them won't be hard at all—no harder than the gooks I shot in Korea—since they're killers themselves. I'm even goin' to get some pleasure out of it."

"Maybe you will," Dan allowed, "only why risk it? Why not tell the police all you know and let them handle it?"

"The police! Oh yeah." Lem's eyes glittered. "I almost forgot 'bout them. 'Course before I report it to the cops, couple of things got to get taken care of. You goin' to help me glue Rick's body together so that we got a corpse to show them? Or maybe I could just bring his brain down in a jar! Oh shit, Doc—you know better'n that! Even if I could make Cawley spill his guts to them, that still wouldn't be proof anybody murdered him. Like you said, Rick could've got that hematoma in the Bishop fight. Except for you and me and the guys that killed him, who's to say different? . . ." As Lem paused, a wistful look came over his face. "Truth is, Doc, I wish the police could handle it. Once my Ma dies, which won't be too long now—she's back in the hospital again—there's more important things I want to do with my life. But Rick was like a brother, and I got to do this one last thing for him. I just got to, understand?"

260

Dan nodded solemnly.

"But you—your only job is becoming a doctor, so stay out of it. That's why I'm tellin' you to keep away from Kim."

"So you said, only I still don't understand why?"

Lem sighed deeply. "Jesus, man, I don't know where your mind is—maybe still in them medical books—but you just ain't thinkin' too clearly. So let me spell it out for you. Now that Chatfield knows Rick wasn't just beat up but killed, he must've got Turk to spill the whole story—right? That being the case, he not only knows how Rick was murdered but how they got rid of his body. Now if I were Chatfield I'd kind of worry about the coincidence of you, being a medical student at State and all, goin' out with his stepdaughter. In fact, I'd worry about that a helluva lot—enough so I'd want to have a little talk with you. Now you dig?"

Dan shut his eyes for a moment, trying to comprehend the enormity of all Lem had told him, but the same sense of blurred reality persisted. Despite the harsh cafeteria lights glaring off the white tableclothes, it all seemed so dreamlike, as if he were more a detached observer than a participant in this incredible affair. But not only was he actually sitting with this huge black man, finally a friend, who planned to kill two, possibly three people, he himself was now in some danger. That he was seemed only fitting—since were it not for him Lem might never have learned how Rick died or even that he was dead at all. Much as this convoluted awareness had the power to bedevil Dan, he did not dwell on it. In a swift and sudden departure, his thoughts were not of Rick or Lem or himself. "Does Kim know?"

"Not from me, she don't."

"How much do you think she does know?"

"As much as Chatfield's got the guts to tell her—which is nothin'! Besides, she's just about out of it. From what she told me on the phone, she'll be headin' back to London to live any day now."

"What else did she tell you?"

"About what—you?"

Dan nodded.

"Not much. Only that she's really sorry 'bout the way she's treated you and hopes you'll understand."

"Understand what?" he demanded.

Again Lem shrugged his massive shoulders. "Beats me. Maybe that after what happened between her and Rick she's had it with men for a while."

"No! That's the way she felt before. There's got to be more to it this time. The last time we talked, just before she left for London, she sounded so upset about something I actually thought some poor bastard might've committed suicide over her. But it must've been learning about Rick's death that made her act that way. I want to know why?"

Lem glanced at his watch. "Look, Doc, I got to get to the hospital and you got studyin' to do. I already told you the important things. How much longer you want to sit around talkin' about this?"

"As long as it takes for me to get a few things settled in my mind!" Dan snapped. "Like why learning about Rick's death almost drove Kim out of her mind?"

Lem fidgeted. "Hell, how should I know? Maybe she still loved him?"

And hearing that, Dan's stoicism, his last line of defense was breached, and like the first faint muscle twitches of an epileptic heralding the electrical storm in his brain, he could feel his self-control giving way. As if to head it off, words poured forth. "Oh sure"—he sneered—"she loved him, all right. Loved getting her nose broken, too. Or just maybe what she wanted was revenge. She kept talking about how she was going to have a showdown with Rick someday. Find out why he'd treated her so brutally. Only now she can't. Now that he's dead she'll never know. But we know, don't we? It was the hematoma that made him act that way. Maybe the first bleed wasn't enough to kill him—not until another good knock on the head by one of Chatfield's goons started him bleeding again—but you should've seen the size of that clot. It covered the whole damn top of his skull! Rick must've been feeling the pain, the pressure of it all the time he was with her. That's what you were trying to look up in that medical book earlier, wasn't it? How long it takes a subrural to kill. It's not like an epidural, the other kind of hematoma boxers get that kills quick. A subdural takes longer—hours, even days. But it's my guess you already knew that. You just don't give a damn about Kim's feelings, do you? You want her to suffer because you hold her partially responsible for what happened to Rick."

Lem shook his head in wonder. "Man, that Kim must be some woman! She not only gets Rick killed, she's got you so crazy you about to flunk out of medical school. Hell, I don't even know what you're accusing me of, Doc? What you want me to do?"

"Tell her how Rick died. Say you found out from the police, an autopsy report—anything—just so long as she knows Rick was out of his mind the last time he saw her. Tell her face-to-face, so she'll believe you!"

Lem regarded him with a mixture of disbelief and disdain. "Face-to-face, huh? That *all* you want? Hell, I'm not even livin' at home anymore. I'm hiding out. You know what would happen if I showed my head around there?"

"Then call her. Have her meet you someplace."

"Her and who else?" Lem's derisive stare relented after a moment. "Look, maybe there's some truth to what you say. Maybe I don't give a damn about Kim no more. Oh, I don't necessarily hate her—Rick knew the risk he was takin' messin' with her—but her feelings just ain't that important to me. So what if Rick slapped her around a little. Lots of broads get slapped around. She'll get over it. I just can't see why I should stick my neck out on her account. For what?"

"For Rick's sake!" Dan pleaded. " 'Cause he'd have wanted you to do!"

"Oh yeah? How you know that? You finally so whacked out by this whole thing you hearin' Rick talk to you now?"

"No, but he haunts me same as you. Only instead of wanting to kill some guys, I want to stop a girl from feeling so tormented she's ruining her life. For Chrissake, tell her, Lem! Never mind whether you blame her in part for Rick's death or not, tell her!"

"Hell, if you feel that strongly about it, tell her yourself!"

"I would—only how can I? She won't see me, won't even speak to me on the phone. And if I told her that much, I'd have to tell her the rest: from the time Rick became my cadaver to the time this whole insane business with him began. And I can't. Honest to Christ I can't! Tell her, Lem! I'm begging you!"

Lem hesitated then shrugged resignedly. "All right. Shit, if it means that much to you, I will. Only not until a few more important things get taken care of first."

"No, now!" Dan almost shouted. "She might be gone later. You've got to do it now!"

As Lem shook his head, Dan again felt seized by a sense of impending loss of control. But instead of being another fore-runner to the storm this was the storm itself. As had happened before in combat, all caution, all restraint, fled, leaving him at a psychic standstill, a suspension of feeling that transformed him from a creature of logic and self-preservation to one of im-pulse and instinct and fury.

"You gonna tell her now or not?" he asked one last time.

"Not me," Lem said.

"Then Goddamn it!" Dan cried, slamming his fist on the table, "I'll do it myself!"

Abruptly pushing his chair back, he rose, raging. Lem tried to grab him as he passed, but Dan brushed his hand off and stalked out of the cafeteria.

He didn't know how he would get into Kim's apartment, but he'd find a way.

Chapter Thirty

"Dan!" Kim cried, as she saw him standing in her doorway. She had been expecting Jennings Dell. It was Jennings who had just phoned to tell her he was in the neighborhood and insisted on dropping by for a moment to say good-bye. Now, as she noticed the drawn look on Dan's face, she felt not only abashed at the way she had been avoiding him but also afraid.

"I've been meaning to call you," she said feebly.

"Have you?"

"Yes. Carol told me you came by yesterday and I meant to get in touch with you." As she spoke, she backed away from Dan's steady advance until they were in the living room.

"Sit down!" he said brusquely. "I want to talk to you."

Kim stared at him. The corners of his eyes were so creased that he appeared almost permanently squinting—a look she had never seen before. "All right," she said, trying to stay calm. "Do you want a drink? You look as if you could use one."

"No, I don't want a drink. I don't want anything from you. I'm here to give you something."

Suddenly he lunged, gripping her by the shoulders and pushing her down on the couch, then dropped down beside her. She wore the same gold-brocaded robe he had seen her wear once before. She was a beautiful woman, he thought. Even with fear and anxiety furrowing her face, she was still the most beautiful woman he had ever known. And she had almost been his, might have been if he hadn't tried to prevent her from ever missing or loving Rick by keeping the truth from her. The remorseful thought temporarily weakened his resolve and his face sagged.

Worried, Kim asked, "Are you sure you're all right?"

"I'm all right," he muttered, grimacing in contemplation of what he was about to reveal. ". . . Remember you once asked me what the anatomy lab was like and I told you? I told you how it looked and smelled and how I felt about working in there. One feature, though, I wouldn't tell you about—the most important of all—the cadavers themselves. Most of the bodies they get for us to work on are old and decrepit, really ugly looking even before you start cuting them open. But not all. Every once in a while the school manages to get hold of the body of a young person. Mine was like that, young and handsome. A real prize physical specimen. In fact, he was so well preserved, so vital looking, that when I first saw him lying on a table in there I almost thought he was alive. And he was, at least for me. I kept him that way."

As Dan doggedly went on talking in this morbid vein, Kim's eyes gradually widened, until when it became apparent to her whom he was describing, when he finally mentioned Rick's name, she gasped and drew back in horror. "Rick was *your* cadaver? All this time, all the time you were with me, he was. . . . Oh my God! Oh, how could you?" She stared at him with revulsion. "You must be insane!"

"Maybe I was," he acknowledged. "Insane, obsessed—what does it matter what it's called? But I don't feel any of those things now. I almost wish I did—otherwise I might not be feeling what I do so strongly."

"I don't care what you feel! Just get out of here! Leave!"

Dan blinked at her shrill command but made no effort to heed it. "Kim, please. I don't feel driven any longer. Oh, I tried to shake off my involvement—after I met Lem, after the dissection was about over and there wasn't much left of him. And I

266

almost did. Then I accidentally met you. Or was it an accident? And it started up all over again."

"But why?" Kim wailed.

"Why? Because all of a sudden I started seeing myself as you first did. A kind of composite of Rick and me. I even thought I might be able to ease the pain of his memory for you. But then I made a mistake. I began to care deeply about you. Maybe I would have anyway, if we'd met under different circumstances —but we met because of Rick. Even when we were in bed together your thoughts were mainly of him, weren't they?"

"No! Only that first time," Kim answered without hesitation. "Afterward, they were always of you. But why tell me all this now? To torment me? To get back at me for the way I treated you?"

"No! To stop your torment, and mine, because of what I knew and didn't dare tell you. You see, Kim, Rick died of a huge blood clot on the brain—what we call a subdural hematoma—that he got during the Red Bishop fight. I know! I saw that big, ugly glob of congealed blood myself when we—my dissection group—opened his skull. That's what killed him, all right. It had to, the way it was pressing into his brain."

Kim stared back, uncomprehending.

"Don't you understand what I'm trying to tell you?" Dan persisted. "That because of that blood clot Rick wasn't able to think straight the last time you saw him. He was sick, in excruciating pain, maybe even dying all the time he was with you. It wasn't your refusal to marry him or your affairs with other men that made him treat you so savagely—he was out of his mind!"

Kim covered her quivering face with her hands. "Oh God," she moaned. "If only I'd known! Oh God, forgive me. Please forgive me!" Twisting around, she buried her face in an arm of the couch and burst into tears.

Dan grimaced as he watched her. At last, he'd done it; he'd finally told her, he mused. And even though he had envisioned worse results—Kim in uncontrollable hysterics—he experienced no great satisfaction. Instead, a kind of sadness overcame him, along with the same sense of exhaustion and relief he had felt in Korea when the shelling and shooting of another battle finally ceased.

But the sense of redress, of honor fulfilled and debts paid, proved only temporary. As Kim's sobs continued, he vaguely realized something more than sorrow, more even than the gruesome picture of Rick's slow dismemberment in an anatomy lab, must be involved. Gently he touched her shoulder and, when she did not move away, took her into his arms.

"Oh Dan, I'm so selfish," she finally said. "I know how terribly hard it must've been for you to tell me all this. Especially after the shabby way I've been avoiding you! Dan, I'm sorry," she said, caressing his face. "But I knew that if I saw you again, I'd have to tell you all this and . . . and. . . ."

"No! Never mind all that. It's all over now."

"But you did it for me? You did it to console me. If you only knew the absolute hell I've been through over Rick—not so much for what he did to me but because of what I was afraid I might've done to him."

"What do you mean? . . . What did you do to him?"

"Just hold me, Dan, until I stop shaking so, then maybe I can tell you."

Gradually her trembling ceased and she lifted her head from his shoulder. "You see," she began, and immediately faltered. ". . . It's such a horrible memory I'm not sure I can tell it to you without going all to pieces again. Maybe a good strong drink might help."

Dan poured half a tumbler of Courvoisier for her. He then sat beside her on the couch, holding her free hand and waiting for her to compose herself.

"You see," she said at last, "after Rick left me that night I was not only terribly upset but in terrible pain with my nose. So I gulped a handful of sleeping pills, and when they didn't calm me, I started guzzling gin—enough to put me into a drunken stupor. Then all of a sudden the door opened and my stepfather came in. He was pretty drunk himself—happy-drunk from winning a bundle on the Bishop fight—until he took one look at me and demanded to know what'd happened.

"I wouldn't tell him at first, afraid of what he might do to Rick. But he kept insisting, kept really pressing me, and finally I thought, the hell with it. Why should I protect a brutal bastard like Rick? Let him have some of his own medicine. So I told Walt it was Rick. But then I made a big mistake." She squeezed Dan's hand painfully. "I went too far. Walt got the idea that Rick hit me because I wouldn't let him make love to me. That he was trying to rape me. But like a fool I said, no. That Rick and I had been lovers a long time—my first one. That was a terrible mistake all right because once I told him that Walt turned pale and started looking at me awfully funny. 'You let a punk, a nothing, like Ferrar be the first one!' he yelled at me. And when I wouldn't say anything, just kept crying, he grabbed me and started shaking me. My head was splitting and I begged him to stop, but he kept shaking and berating me in some kind of jealous rage—like I was his wife or something. Then. . . ." Kim suddenly faltered. "Oh Dan, I don't know if I can tell you this—then he threw me on the couch and climbed on top of me. I was so drunk and dazed by then I couldn't offer any resistance. Not at first, anyway. But then he pulled my robe open and started pawing me—all the time cursing me and my mother, claiming we were both such whores that this was all we were good for. . . . Maybe it was what he said about mother, because all of a sudden I started punching and scratching and pushing him off. Then I grabbed that heavy ballerina statue on the table over there and threatened to brain him with it if he didn't get out of here."

"Did he?"

"Not right away, but I guess it made him realize what he'd tried to do to me, his own stepdaughter. Once that sunk in, he apologized all over the place. Tried to pretend that he'd never meant to rape me—only to shame me into realizing how I had cheapened myself by having an affair with someone like Rick. All teary-eyed, he told me how my mother had had an affair with a boxer once—a Frenchman—and how much it had hurt and humiliated him. But when I wouldn't listen, when I blamed him and how coldly he'd always treated mother for what she'd done, he left in a huff. He made sure he got the last word in though, and it really chilled me. 'Don't worry about Ferrar,' he told me just before going out the door. 'There's only one way to teach a punk like that his place and I know how!' "

"Do you think he did anything?" Dan asked innocently.

She shrugged. "Walt knew enough not to come near me until I'd had a chance to cool off. I asked him later on though, and he denied it. Claimed Rick had skipped town right after the Bishop fight and, knowing Walt was out to get him, had stayed clear of Boston. And that's what I believed until Al Lakeman told me three weeks ago that Rick was dead. I think I'd suspected it all along but wouldn't face up to it—too afraid I was the cause. Then, when Lakeman said Rick was not only dead but had been dead since last winter, the nightmare really began for me. I was absolutely convinced Walt had had him murdered because of what he'd done to me. That he'd arranged it through those underworld thugs he occasionally deals with. That's why I was so upset the last time we talked on the phone—why I had to leave for London in such a hurry. I had to find out the truth. And I knew the only hope I had of getting it out of Walt was face-to-face."

"What did he say?"

"He denied even knowing Rick was dead. But something about the way he looked when he said it made me feel that either he was lying or he knew much more about it than he was letting on. But he didn't actually have Rick killed, did he, Dan?"

"No," he said, after taking a few painful moments to digest

270

her story. "The blood clot on Rick's brain was at least several hours old. Which meant he must've got it in the Bishop fight, since he was found dead the next day."

"Where was he found?"

"That I don't know. Possibly in his hotel room, possibly collapsed on the street."

"And you're absolutely sure that he died of that blood clot and nothing else? You swear you're not holding back anything?"

Dan hesitated a split second, then shook his head. "I'm sure the blood clot was bad enough to kill him, that's all."

"But how did his body end up at State?"

"When Rick was younger, he worked for Snider in the anatomy lab. He must've willed it to them."

Please don't ask any more, he silently pleaded—*why there was no coroner's investigation, nothing in the newspapers*—and was profoundly grateful when she didn't.

"Oh, Dan, how awful your knowing all this and not being able to tell me! But you did. Even after the awful runaround I gave you."

"I didn't do it just for you, Kim. I did it for myself, too. Otherwise, I couldn't have slept, studied, even thought straight. It was the only thing I could ever do for Rick to repay him."

"Repay him?"

"For the use of his body—and the destruction of it."

"You say that as if it haunted you. Did it?"

"In a way, I suppose."

"In what way?" she asked softly. "How could an otherwise levelheaded person like you get involved in something so macabre?"

Dan smiled ruefully. "I've asked myself that same question a thousand times and I haven't a clue. If I believed in ghosts— which I don't—I'd say I was possessed. But whatever possessed me was no ghost. It was up here." He touched his head.

"Does Lem know about this?"

Dan hesitated. "Yes, he's known for some time."

271

"Then why didn't he tell me?"

"Because I was supposed to tell you. I agreed to. But I couldn't—not after meeting you, getting to care about you so much. I doubt I ever would've told you if I hadn't felt my knowledge about Rick's death might make some of your torments and doubts easier to bear."

"Oh, it has, Dan," she told him, moving into his arms. "It has! I did try to love you, you know. But with this hanging over me, I felt too guilt stricken, too much like a jinx. I don't feel that way anymore. I *do* have to go back to London for a day or two, to give up the apartment I've leased and talk BOAC into giving me my old job back. But as soon as that's taken care of, I'll hurry back."

"When do you leave?"

"Tomorrow morning. Nine A.M. But at least we have tonight to spend together."

"No, I'm afraid not. I've got a lot of studying to do." He explained why.

Kim looked dismayed for a moment, then brightened. "All right, so tonight's out. But at least let me stop by your place on my way to the airport in the morning and say good-bye properly."

Before Dan could reply, the phone rang and Kim answered.

"Oh, hi, Walt," she said cheerfully. "Yes, I'm all packed, except for a few odds and ends. Tell Lydia I found that book she wanted. . . . No, I'd rather not right now. Dan's here. . . . That's right, Dan Lassiter. . . . What? Of course, I'm all right. Why shouldn't I be?" She looked perplexed. "But that's ridiculous. . . . No, I just told you—just Dan. Why should Lem be here? What's this all about, anyway? . . . Well, if it's nothing, why do you sound so upset? . . . All right, I'll ask him, but he was just leaving. He's got studying to do . . . I said I'd ask him! Where are you now? . . . But it'll take you almost an hour to get here. . . . All right, Walt, I will!" she said impatiently. "But it just doesn't make any sense. Good-bye!"

Kim hung up the phone with difficulty, as if it took special concentration for her to fit the receiver in its cradle. Even then she did not move away from her place by the phone but sat staring morosely at the marble top of the antique escritoire it rested on. At last she turned to Dan with a aggrieved, accusing look.

He stared back at her, feeling an aching hollowness in the pit of his stomach. Though Kim had not spoken a word, he knew what was troubling her. He had always known somehow there could be no happy endings to horror tales.

Rising from the chair, she began to pace restlessly between the couch and the mantle. Finally, she stopped before him and said bitterly, "Well, nice try. You almost had me believing it. But now I want the truth. Rick *was* murdered, wasn't he?"

Dan's throat contracted. "What makes you think that?"

"Because Walt is terrified of your being here. Terrified of you. And he wouldn't be unless he was afraid of something you know. Something you might tell me. That's it, isn't it, Dan? *So tell me!*"

Dan rose wearily from the couch to stand before her. "No," he said, "nobody murdered Rick. He was already dying when your stepfather's goons jumped him. The most they might've done was speed up the process a little."

"But don't you see," she argued, "they still had orders to maim or even kill him, orders from Walt. And I'm responsible for that. Blood clot or no blood clot, I'm still responsible for the beating Rick took. Except for me, Walt never would've sent those killers after him."

"No, that's true. And if I hadn't drawn a certain cadaver six months ago or met you at a party or came here tonight hoping to console you, you never would've known that for sure either. . . . Things don't always work out the way you'd like them to, do they, Kim?"

She nodded dully.

"But you didn't kill Rick by telling your stepfather about

him any more than I did by cutting him up. He was already doomed. Nothing could have saved him. Nothing!"

Tears welled up again in Kim's eyes and Dan reached for her, but she pushed him away. "No, don't!" she whispered harshly. "Don't touch me." She backed a few steps away from him until she came in contact with the desk, then leaned against it. Gradually the anguished look on her face was replaced by a more reflective one. "Well," she said, "looks like I'll be moving to London, after all. Be sheer torture to stay here—after all the things you've given me to think about. . . . But you did try. I mean—you *did* try to make me feel better. You deserve something—some reward—for that." She smiled provocatively. "C'mon, Dan, what do you say?"

"Say to what?"

"To what!" Her laugh was coarse, mirthless. "To a little quickie? Walt won't be here for another hour, so how 'bout a quick one—a little going-away present from me to you. After all, you've earned it."

"Kim—stop!"

"Stop, hell! Don't you understand? I want you."

Dan shook his head. Kim's sudden mood-shift, the gleam of naked lust in her eyes, the agitated movements of her hands over her body, bewildered him. "No, I don't understand."

Kim unzipped her robe, revealing her black bra and panties. "Now, do you understand?" she taunted. "Now, do you remember what a great piece of ass I was for you?"

Dan stared at her, feeling no desire, only confusion and dismay. This was a Kim he had never seen before, did not know how to cope with.

Angrily, she pulled her bra down and, cupping her bare breasts in her hands, commanded, "Take them! I'm giving them to you. Hurt them; make me feel some pain."

She took his hands and pressed them against her breasts. Suddenly he could stand the pitiful spectacle of her standing half-naked before him no longer. He grabbed and held her so tightly

274

that she gasped. For an instant, she clung to him, sensing the tenderness he felt, but only for an instant. Then she cried out, "No! that's not what I want. I want to be hurt!"

Still gripping her elbows, Dan pushed her back so he could see her face. "Why?" he asked, first in dismay, then in anger. "For Chrissake why?"

"Oh God, don't you know any female psychology at all? There are plenty of men in this building. Screw me or I'll get one of them—all of them—to do it! You don't believe me? Well, I'll show you. . . . Let go of me!"

Writhing and twisting, she fought to free herself from his grip. "Let go, damn you!" she shrieked, as his fingers dug into the flesh of her arms to keep her fists and nails from his face. Finally, as her struggling grew more violent, Dan realized that unless he did something to curb her hysterical state she would hurt both of them. Withdrawing one arm while pinning her with the other, he was about to slap her across the face when, as if she sensed more than saw what he intended, Kim's struggles abruptly ceased, her eyes opened wide, and she cried out: "No, Rick!"

Dropping his arm, Dan released her and stepped back, feeling sick and dazed. Without his support Kim staggered and almost fell, but steadied herself in time. Gradually, her breathing slowed and a look of sad sanity came into her eyes. Fleetingly, she glanced down at her bare breasts but made no move to cover them.

Almost as an afterthought, she asked, "What should I tell Walt when he comes?"

"Tell him nothing," Dan said. "Tell him I just dropped by to say good-bye. Don't worry, there's no possible way the police could prove Rick was murdered now, so he's safe."

She looked at him with dawning comprehension. "All right, so he's safe. Lucky him. . . . But what about us?"

"Us?" He sighed. "There never was any us. There was you and me and Rick. . . . No matter how many times I told myself

I loved you, there was always this barrier between us. There was always Rick."

Kim nodded. "I know. But does he always have to be there?"

"Maybe not. . . . We'll just have to wait and see."

"Yes," she said wistfully. "That's the way it is with most people who think they're in love—they just have to wait and see. I'm willing if you are. . . . And if not, I'll just have to find another composite—this one of you."

Dan smiled wanly, feeling a stabbing compassion for her utter vulnerability. But he also realized this was all he could feel for her, at least for now. Only time could help unknot the tangle of hurt and guilt and self-hatred that existed within her.

Turning slowly, he took one last look at the crystal chandelier, the antique French furniture, the real Utrillo hanging above the mantle: one last reconnoiter of what had been a luxurious but losing battlefield. Then he kissed her lightly on the lips, grabbed his overcoat off the armchair, and left.

Dan felt a sense of freedom, if not finality, as the door to Kim's apartment shut behind him and he began to descend the stairs. Now that the long dreaded denouement was over, he felt benumbed and inexpressibly weary. But he felt a small measure of satisfaction as well. With his conscience clear, he could almost imagine the exorcism of Rick's ghost; the once sharp image of that unsmiling fighter's face beginning to blur in his memory. At long last, his obsession with Rick Ferrar was over.

But it was not over. Dan made that discovery at the foot of the stairs. As he opened the heavy outer door, he stepped back to let a man come in from the street. Suddenly he heard the man say, "Hey, buddy. Got a light?"

Dan turned and regarded the tall, broad-shouldered, swarthy man warily, until seeing the natty Chesterfield coat he wore and the unlit cigar protruding from his mouth, he relaxed slightly. He reached into a pocket and handed him a book of matches. As he lit his cigar, the man said, "Hey, don't I know you from someplace? You're Dan something, ain't ya?"

276

Dan smiled and nodded slowly, then without warning brought up his right hand to hit the man harder than he had ever hit anyone before. The blow landed high on his left cheek, too high for a knockout, but with enough impact to send the man staggering back against the door, buckling at the knees. Dan sucked his knuckle, certain he had cracked it, and then, finding this familiar outlet for all the fury and frustration bottled up inside him, was about to step forward to hit the man again, beat him senseless, when he suddenly sensed a movement behind him. He half-turned, far enough to catch a fleeting glimpse of a bearlike man with an oversized head, lantern jaw, and the grayest complexion he had ever seen on a living human being. He heard the gray-faced man grunt like an animal as he brought the blackjack in his hand crashing down. Dan felt an excruciating pain in back of his right ear and sank to his knees. As his brain rocked from one side of his skull to the other, it registered one last thought, one final moment of lucidity: These were the same men who had killed Rick.

Dazed and blinded, he felt himself being lifted and dragged, faintly heard one man tell the other to bring the car around front, but the words were like distant echoes in some deep chasm of his mind.

Dimly he perceived the gray-faced man bending over him. The man grabbed him roughly by the arms and hauled him to his feet. Then he spun Dan around, caught him under the armpits and frog-marched him through the door, knees jabbing him painfully in the back with each step.

Out in the street, the icy-cold wind blowing against his face revived Dan enough so that the same thought that had dimly crossed his mind before recurred: These were the men who had killed Rick and now meant to kill him. Though he still lay limp in the clutches of the gray-faced man as he propelled Dan across the sidewalk and dumped him across the vibrating hood of an automobile while he opened the front door, Dan was thinking more clearly now.

"Is he still out?" he heard the driver of the car ask.

"Yeah, like a light, Joe," the hulking, gray-faced man assured him and shoved Dan into the front seat of the car.

He fell heavily against the driver's shoulder and was pushed away. As his partner climbed in, Joe gunned the engine and Dan made his move. The heel of his right hand shot out, stiff-arming the gray-faced man in the side of the head and almost pushing him out of the car door. Then, with all his strength, he jammed his left foot down on top of the driver's, pressing the gas pedal to the floor and sending the car lurching forward into the stream of moving traffic. There was a loud screech of brakes, then a jarring crunch of collapsing metal as the auto-mobile behind them slammed into their left rear fender, spin-ning their car sideways so that it slewed horizontally across the road. The force of the collision threw Dan's head forward, bang-ing it against the dashboard. In a suspended, panic-filled instant he heard a bedlam of squealing brakes and tooting horns, then a second crash, as another car struck them head on. The second impact hurtled Dan backward and a third collision, on the driver's side, catapulted his free-floating body clear out of the car. He struck the pavement with stunning force and in a reflex action kept rolling until he came to rest against the raised edge of the curb.

Slowly, painfully, he opened his eyes to the dim shadows of people huddled around him. He kept blinking until his hazy vision began to clear and he could focus on the faces of two elderly people, a man and a woman, peering down at him with frightened looks. He tried to prop himself up on one elbow but hadn't the strength. In a croaking voice, the old man asked, "Are you all right, son?"

Dan nodded. "Just help me up, will you?"

The old man shook his head. "You might be hurt bad. Better just lay there until the ambulance comes."

Dan tried to think, to appraise his situation, but with his head pounding severely he couldn't seem to connect thoughts.

Instead, he acted on instinct, sensing he was still in some danger and there was something more he had to do.

"No," he said as the old man took off his coat to cover him. "Help me up."

"But the doctor—" the old man protested.

"I *am* a doctor," Dan lied. "I must help—"

Still frightened, the man and woman each took an arm and lifted him. Dan's head spun dizzily at first, but after a moment his vertigo subsided and he found he could stand with their help.

Blearily, he looked into the street: at the dented or twisted bodies of four or five cars jammed in the middle of the road; at white steam hissing from cracked radiator blocks; at the glittering shards of glass from broken headlights and taillights strewn over the pavement; at how, like monsters with one eye gouged out, like metal Cyclops, the remaining headlight of some cars shone weakly. Sounds also assaulted his ears: the cries and moans of injured people, the ceaseless blare of a short-circuited car horn, the periodic screech of brakes as the lineup of stalled cars extended into the distance; finally, the fast-approaching wail of sirens. Gently extricating himself from the arms of the elderly couple, he took a faltering step forward, turned to mutter his thanks, and then, without further explanation, staggered away.

He walked slowly, unsteadily, weaving from side to side, but the chill wind helped numb the terrible throbbing in his head and gradually his stride grew stronger.

He knew one thing: He had to get away from the police, from the gray-faced man, from 1070 Beacon Street. He was in danger there, although he wasn't at all sure what kind of danger or why. He remembered being in a car crash and that people were injured, but he couldn't recall whose car he'd been in or where they were headed or what he'd been doing in this end of town when he should've been home studying. He *must* study, he told himself. He couldn't let Snider, Pete, himself, down.

The Anatomy Lesson

At the corner of Beacon and Kenmore, Dan paused to look around. The neon signs of the square seemed dazzlingly bright and the trolley tracks glittered like streaks of silver. Fascinated, he watched the traffic light change from red to yellow to green. Liking the soothing green best, he stood staring at it until he became aware of people moving around him on the sidewalk like eddies in a stream.

Hearing a continuous low-pitched roar start up, he looked around for its source. Coal pouring down a chute? A cheering crowd at Fenway Park? But there was no coal truck in sight and the floodlights of Fenway were dark. Gradually he realized the roaring noise must be inside his head: There was blood in his ear. He knew that blood in the inner ear could produce such sounds from his boxing days. He remembered Archie Moore telling him that. Woody had introduced them, and Archie had told him to protect his ears always. Archie Moore—he'd liked Archie and was sorry that he was dead. But Archie wasn't dead. Rick was dead. . . .

Dan suddenly stopped walking and tried to sort out his thoughts. A young girl coming toward him slowed to stare, then hurried along. Self-consciously, he reached up to smooth his hair and felt the sticky moistness behind his right ear. The palm of his hand was bloody when he removed it. Puzzled, he moved over to a storefront window to study his shadowy reflection. A pretty blond girl in a swimsuit poster smiled at him from behind the window, smiled provocatively, the way Kim smiled.

The sudden reminder of Kim supplied the last link needed to restore his memory. It began to whir and play again. What if he hadn't gone to see her, hadn't told her about Rick—oh God, if only he hadn't known. But he had known and he had almost succeeded in convincing her that she wasn't responsible for Rick's death. Then, like the wail of a banshee, had come Chatfield's phone call and he'd succeeded in nothing.

What in hell had ever gotten him started on all this? Dan demanded of himself. Why hadn't it been enough for him to follow the routine, the directions in the dissection manual that outlined each nerve and vessel in his cadaver's body? But he didn't know why. For reasons which still remained totally obscure, he had charted his own course—wanted to learn not just the anatomy of his cadaver but the very essence of the man that cadaver had been. And his dogged pursuit of the elusive traces and echoes that remained of Rick Ferrar had brought no peace, only added woe, to all concerned. For Lem, a murderous mission; for Kim, an affirmation of her guilt; for himself, a compelling reason to doubt his sanity.

Plunging deeper into despair, Dan followed a bleak instinct that led him into the bowels of Washington Street, a slum littered with yesterday's newspapers, yesterday's lost dreams.

He plodded aimlessly on, past the bars closing by public edict at one A.M. and sweeping their patrons into the streets, past the cabdrivers keeping their car engines idling for heat, past the drunks leaning against car fenders or huddled in doorways. And though Dan was now accustomed to seeing the blowsy, prematurely aged faces of the women-drunks, their shabby clothing and silly grins, he had never hardened to them nor failed to respond politely to their gibberish or requests for handouts. But tonight their faces seemed especially pitiful—as if his sensitivities had somehow been amplified to make tangible the pain of unrelenting despair. Here, not on a Korean battlefield, was hell. Or at least limbo. And he truly felt for these wretched souls; for the first time he stopped trying to cushion his own deep hurt with a layer of steely stoicism and reacted toward them as a humane person—as the future physician he now knew he would never be—should react.

Chapter Thirty-one

By the time Dan reached the bottom of Washington Street the neon bar signs were dark, the cabs gone, and the sidewalks almost deserted. A young patrolman reported in to his precinct from the call box on the corner. An ambulance bounced along the uneven pavement, skidded on the steel vein of trolley tracks, and sped on. A mongrel scavenged in the spill from the garbage cans in front of the Hotel Roosevelt.

At last, Dan reached a familiar landmark, a railroad bridge, and beyond it the darkened front of Brecht's Bar. He knocked and waited for Ernie to recognize him through the peephole in the door, then was let in.

"Good Jesus!" Ernie exclaimed after seeing him in the light. "What the hell happened to you?"

"Auto accident."

"Here, let me take a look at that."

He winced as Ernie fingered the bruise on his forehead and separated strands of blood-matted hair.

Dan brushed his hand away. "No, don't. I'm all right. All I need is a drink."

"Well, okay," Ernie said dubiously. "But if you ask me, you ought to have a doctor take a look at that."

"Maybe later . . . Lem been in?"

"Not yet. Probably still at the hospital."

"This late?"

"Yeah, his mother's on the critical list—which means he can stay as long as he wants. She's just about had it, I hear. But he ought to be in 'fore long."

Dan nodded and started to follow Ernie to the bar when a sudden twinge of pain caused him to stumble.

"Easy now," said Ernie and helped him to a chair. "Hey, you sure you're all right? How much bleeding did you do from that scalp wound?"

"Not much . . . Why?"

"Because you're white as a sheet. What say you skip that drink and let me drive you over to City Hospital?"

"No!" Dan said adamantly. "I'd rather have the drink. Then I'm going to wait around for Lem. Maybe after I see him, I'll go over."

"Okay," Ernie said, realizing from the determined look on Dan's face that it was futile to argue further. "But you just sit here and take it easy, huh?"

Dan nodded. Leaning over the table, he rested his head in his arms until the pain hammering at his temples eased, and then looked around. There were two other people at the bar: a lanky Negro who played bass viol in George's combo and Janey Towns.

Janey brought a double Scotch over to him. "Here, Dan, this ought to cure what ails you," she said cheerfully, before pausing to take a closer look at him. "Baby, you look in tough shape! Ernie's right; you better get over to the hospital and let them docs check you over."

"No!" Dan started to shake his head, then winced with the pain of it. "Got to see Lem first."

"But you're still bleeding! Look at this." She dabbed at his left temple with her handkerchief and showed him the dime-sized spot of blood on it.

"Oh, hell," Dan muttered, "That's not even enough to interest a mosquito."

"Maybe not. But that cut of yours *could* get infected. . . . I just live around the corner. If you ain't goin' to see a doc, at least come over to my place and let me put some iodine and a bandage on it."

Dan hesitated. "I don't want to miss Lem."

"You won't! Lem knows where I live, and if we're not back, Ernie can send him over."

Dan pondered the offer. "Okay," he said. "Thanks."

"Well, good!" Janey sighed. "Glad you got that much sense. Drink up and then we'll go over."

Dan took two long swallows of the Scotch, then rested the glass on the table. When Janey returned from telling Ernie where they were going, he looked up and grinned. "You're a damned good-looking girl, Janey. Sure you trust me over at your place?"

"In the shape you're in!" she mocked. "I could knock you over with a feather. Besides, I didn't know you crossed that line."

"What line?"

"C'mon now, don't kid me, honey. You know what I'm talkin' about. 'Cause if you don't, Lem'll be only too happy to explain it to you. He's a racial purist, that man! No mixing of black and white for Lem 'cept on a piano. Know where he's goin' once his ma dies? To Africa, that's where."

"Africa! Why there?"

"To join Kenyatta. He got a lot of hate in him, that man. Too much, if you ask me. Otherwise, I could really go for him. . . . Fact is, the way he feels about whites, I'm kind of surprised you and him are friendly."

"We have—had—a mutual friend. He's dead now."

"Yeah? Well, now you got another one—me. And I ain't dead. Might not do you no good now, but remember it sometimes when you're feelin' lonely."

The bar was stuffy, and as they talked, Janey had undone the top buttons of her blouse and Dan was aware of her cleavage. His thoughts flashed back to Kim's bare breasts and he mentally compared them to what Janey's might be. Was that what it always came down to for him: thoughts of sex to dispel thoughts of death. It was almost a conditioned response by now. But if life was mostly illusionary, if the only true affirmations were to kill or to fuck, then so be it. If he was reading her right, Janey seemed willing enough. But was he? Was he up to it with his head throbbing the way it did? "You got any aspirin at your place?" he asked.

"Yeah. Something stronger, too. . . . Oh, not dope," she said, noting the guarded look on his face. "Codeine. I need it for menstrual cramps."

As Dan rose from the table, he heard Ernie unlock the front door and swiveled his neck in that direction. But the sudden motion triggered such a sharp pain in his head that he staggered sideways giddily and might have fallen had not Janey reached for him. He clung to her for a moment, inhaling the faint fragrance of perfume on her neck and unconsciously pressing his groin against hers. He slowly withdrew his arms to steady himself on the table.

"I'm okay now. Let's go to your place," he muttered and was about to turn toward the door when a huge hand closed on his shoulder, spun him around, and shoved him down in the chair.

"Man, you look great! Just great!" Lem Harper observed coldly.

Dan waited for his dizzy spell to subside, then looked up blearily at the massive black body towering above him. His gaze moved slowly upward to encompass the thick chest, the skull-shaped head, the ever-brooding eyes that regarded him now with a mixture of curiosity and contempt.

Though he had always stood a little in awe of Lem, a fit of reckless indignation swept over Dan. "Hallelujah!" he cried. "Everybody shout hallelujah for the new black Messiah! The great Emperor Jones!"

Lem's face contorted in anger. "You're drunk!"

"Yeah—a little," Dan admitted. "I also got me one hell of a headache, front and back."

"From what?"

"From what? Well, let's see. . . . This one"—he bent his neck forward and pointed to the egg-sized lump behind his right ear— "came from a blackjack. And the one you see on my forehead, from an auto accident. . . . Oh shit, why don't you sit down! You look too damned imposing looming over me like that and it hurts my head to look up." He watched with bitter amusement as the glint of anger in Lem's eyes was gradually replaced by one of concern.

"All right, I'm sitting. Now what's it all about, Doc? What happened?"

"Nothing that should surprise you."

"Cut the smart-ass talk and tell me!" Lem snapped.

Dan told him.

Lem listened intently as Dan spoke, but except for asking him to repeat his description of the two men who had waylaid him, he said nothing. Once Dan had finished, he called to Janey to bring him another drink, then went to the bar to get Ernie to make some phone calls. When Lem finally returned to the table, he gestured Janey away and spoke in a low, conciliatory tone of voice.

"You did me a helluva big favor tonight, Doc. But I guess you knew who them two guys were when you took them on, didn't you?"

Dan nodded.

"Anyway," Lem went on, "from what Ernie could find out, D'Mato was the only one killed in the crack-up. Got his chest caved in."

"How about the other one?"

"That ain't so good. All Turk got was a sprained wrist. They taped it at City Hospital around an hour ago and then let him go. Which means he's still on the loose."

"Well, I'm sorry to hear that," Dan said, "but I'm damned glad nobody else got killed." He started to get up.

"Where you goin' now?" Lem asked.

"Over to Janey's. She's going to bandage me up."

"You sure that's all she's goin' to do for you?"

The look of disbelief on Dan's face swiftly changed to one of anger. "No, she's also going to help me get my rocks off. I always get horny after killing someone. For Chrissake, what's the matter with you!"

Lem sighed. "You and me—we just never seem to have a friendly conversation. He broke into a grin. "But you're all right. Yeah, you're really all right! If I ever need me a white friend again I'm goin' to think about you. . . . Now c'mon."

"Where?"

"Over to City Hospital to get that cut taken care of. Then home to rest so tomorrow you can start studying for that big exam. I'm goin' with you."

"You're what?"

"I said, I'm goin' with you."

"What the hell for? To make sure I don't end up at Janey's? Jesus, she was right about you. You are a racial fanatic! Well, forget it. I'll go over to City Hospital with you, but then I'm going home—alone!"

"Uh-uh. You ain't goin' no place alone. Not tonight, you ain't."

"Why the hell not! What makes you think I need a nurse-maid? What are you afraid of anyhow?"

"Not here," Lem suddenly cautioned. "People are listening. Let's go outside. . . . C'mon," he coaxed as Dan looked reluctant. "We goin' to City Hospital anyway."

Dan said good-bye to Ernie and Janey and followed him out.

"Now listen," Lem said after moving into a doorway out of the wind, "with Turk still on the loose, you ain't safe. So I'm givin' you a choice. I already got Ernie's gun in my pocket. Either I go home with you or else I go huntin' him. Make sure Turk gets it 'fore he gives it to you. You decide how you want it. Which way I go from here's up to you."

Dan stared at Lem, realizing the huge black man was serious, but wondering if his protectiveness might not have another motive. "All right, come on. There's been enough killing for one night. But if that's not your only reason for coming, you're wasting your time. Because I've no intention of studying for that exam. Or taking it. Or staying in medical school. It might've taken me a hell of a long time to realize it, but I don't belong there."

"Why the hell not?"

" 'Cause I'm too damned unstable, that's why. . . . Both you and Kim accused me of being a little crazy tonight, and you're right. Hell, I know damned well you are! Nobody in his right mind would've done what I've done. Certainly, no medical student. Don't you understand? I'm too unbalanced to be a doctor!"

"Now hold on," Lem protested. "Just take it easy. Don't forget, you've been through a lot tonight."

"I know what I've been through. It took tonight to finally convince me. Look, Lem, I know what I'm doing—what I'm giving up. The funny part is, I really do want to be a doctor, now more than ever. But I know that can never be. Not the way I think. Not the way I went off the deep end over Rick. I just can't."

"Why? 'Cause you felt somethin' for a dead man that maybe you shouldn't of? Felt too much? Well, if that makes you crazy, then I guess I am, too—'cause I feel lots of things about people— my own people—that maybe I shouldn't. I don't know how much that talky bitch, Janey, told you, but you must have a pretty good idea by now what I plan to do with my life. Hell, you got it easy compared to me. I ain't goin' to devote the rest of my life to fightin' disease, I'm goin' to take on the whole God-damn white race—all the bigots among them anyway! Sounds kind of crazy, don't it? But just feelin' that way don't make *me* crazy. Maybe the best part of life is feelin'—feelin' for anything —even things you know you can't do nothin' about? No, Doc, you ain't unstable. Just different is all. . . . And I'm goin' to tell you one thing you ain't goin' to like: You might figure you've paid your debt to Rick by tellin' Kim about him, but you haven't! You still owe him more. It ain't like owing a guy money or a favor you can return. What you owe Rick for is something special—knowledge. And the only way you can repay someone for that is by using it. I know! You'd be surprised how much knowledge I got stored away in this nigger head of mine. It's why I'm goin' to Africa, so I can use some of it. And that's what you got to do, too. Nothin' but you becoming a doctor can justify what you done to Rick's body. Nothing else could!"

Dan sighed wearily. How many times had he given himself that same argument? More than anything else, it had kept him in medical school this long. And how many more times would he keep hearing it if he didn't agree once and for all to accept its burden?

"Okay, Lem," he said resignedly. "Where do we go now?"

"First to the hospital and, if they say it's okay, to your place so you can get some sleep."

"Sleep!" exclaimed Dan, reaching into the last intact reserve in his mind for a shred of humor. "How the hell you expect me to get any sleep when I've got a Goddamn Mau Mau for a roommate!"

Chapter Thirty-two

The day was a beginning and an ending. It was the second week in April and the end of a hard winter. The last snows had fallen and melted away under the warm afternoon sun. Islands of grass sprouted and spread so that a fragile green fuzz covered the lawns of city parks. The air was scented with the smell of moss and budding flowers, and flocks of birds soared high over Boston rooftops. From the morning spent at the medical school to the late afternoon at a cemetery outside Boston, the day was substantial and fast-moving. By the time it was over, many things had come full circle for Daniel Lassiter. When the scraps and bones of what had been Rick Ferrar were finally buried, much more was laid to rest. Not only had Dan's obsession with him ended but its mystery was revealed. A hidden door in his psyche had opened and down that dark passage he finally came face to face with his long repressed feelings toward death. The confrontation surprised and shocked him, but it also liberated him, leaving him with a sense of inner peace he had not known since he was twelve.

At nine that morning, as Dan waited with his classmates outside the sixth-floor lecture hall for Dr. Coleman's arrival, Snider's shapely young secretary walked down the corridor in studied ignorance of the murmurs and wolf-whistles that followed her and handed Dan an envelope.

290

"Love letter?" Larry Parish taunted.

"It's from Snider, I guess."

"Well, open it!"

"Later. C'mon, let's grab some seats inside."

"No, go on. Open it now. I want to know if you passed."

Dan tore the envelope open, scanned the note with a single glance, then stuffed it in his pocket. Though he appeared shaken for a moment he managed a weak smile. "I passed."

Larry slapped him heartily on the back. "Great! I knew you would. Things just wouldn't be the same around here without you. I never *did* know who had the more active sex life, 'cause you'd never talk about yours. But you know what they say about still waters. . . . Hey, I got some extra dough, so why don't we do some celebrating tonight?"

Dan looked dubious. "I don't know. I was planning to go to the burial they're giving the cadavers this afternoon and I don't know how I'll feel after that."

"That thing today? I thought it was supposed to be sometime next week."

"No, it's today. I'm sure of it," Dan told him. "You going?"

"I ought to, but I can't. My old man's in town for the medical meeting at the Statler and I promised to meet him for a drink. . . . Say, are you really going? I've had enough of cadavers."

"Me, too. But I promised myself I would."

"I'll bet you'll be one of the few who does go. Too nice a day for a funeral. . . . Well, call me around seven thirty if you feel like going out."

"Okay, I will."

"And if you don't, I want to hear all about Reverend Snider's little sermon tomorrow. Matter of fact, it wouldn't surprise me if he tried to raise a few of them from the dead. Hate to miss that. Probably convert to him on the spot, wouldn't you?"

"I already have."

The Anatomy Lesson

"Hey, I almost forgot—you've been pro-Snider all the way. But would you still be if he'd flunked you?"

"He had reason enough to. . . . Well, here comes Coleman sleepwalking along. . . . See you later."

Coleman's lecture was on gut secretions, a subject that interested Dan, but hard as he tried to concentrate on it, his thoughts kept returning to Snider's note. Taking it out of his pocket, he unfolded it and read it again.

DEAR MR. LASSITER:

This is to inform you that your final grade in anatomy will be seventy-six percent.

Although such a percentage is adequate to allow you to pass the course, I feel it pertinent to remind you that it is hardly a grade of distinction or even up to the average, and this fact, I hope, should be of some concern to you.

Sincerely,
NATHAN SNIDER, M.D.
Professor of Anatomy

Okay, so it wasn't a grade of distinction or even up to the average, Dan thought. After all he'd been through, who cared? But he did care. During the next hour Snider's words of admonition, because they were meant and because he took them so personally, nagged Dan to the extent that he barely heard Coleman's voice or thought of anything else. He knew they demanded, or at least deserved, a reply. But except for confessing the truth, which was out of the question, what could he possibly tell Snider? How could he possibly hope to make amends for the twenty-four percent of anatomy he had failed to learn? Maybe if they talked, Snider might suggest something? But did he really have the guts to face the man again? Twice before he had given him an apology and a promise and, though meaning both at the time, had subsequently done little to prove himself sincere. And though recognizing that his underlying motive

292

for wanting to see Snider might be self-reproach, an obscure need for atonement, and that the likely outcome would be a stiff rebuke, he was nonetheless determined to follow it through.

He would plan to see him tomorrow or, at least, during the week. . . . But at ten o'clock, when the class took a brief recess before physiology lab, he thought: *Why not right now?*

When Dan entered his inner office, Snider was at his desk reading a newspaper. Hesitantly, he asked, "Can you spare me a few moments, sir?"

Snider regarded him with a faint, forbearing smile. "Well, I'm expecting a visitor, but I have time until he comes. What's on your mind?"

"It's about your note, sir."

"Yes, I imagined it would be. Actually, Lassiter, there's little more to say. I expected much more of you. But now that the exam is over and you have your final grade I can only reiterate my disappointment in your performance. Did you expect me to feel differently."

"No sir, I didn't."

"Then what's the purpose of discussing it further? If anything, I tended to be a little lenient in your grade. However, if you'd like to verify the corrections I've made in your exam booklet for yourself, why I'd—"

"No! It's nothing like that. The truth is, I'm surprised you passed me at all and right now that's what bothers me. Maybe I feel I don't deserve to pass—that knowing only seventy-six percent of anatomy, of any medical subject, just doesn't give me the security I'll need to consider myself worthy of a patient's trust and care. You see, Dr. Snider, I remember what you once said about there being no such thing as a 'batting average' in medicine. I happen to believe it. In fact, I believe it so strongly that I can't accept the grade you've given me. You don't think it's much good and neither do I."

"It's always flattering to be quoted, I suppose," Snider said skeptically, "but what's the point?"

"The point is, I want a favor. A way—any way at all—for me to learn the twenty-four percent of anatomy I failed to learn during the semester."

Snider leaned forward in his chair. "Are you *sure* that's what you want? Not that I like doubting you, Lassiter, but I recall hearing this same kind of talk from you before. How can I be sure you're any more sincere now than you were then?"

Dan returned his gaze steadily. "You can't! You can only ask yourself what the hell I'm doing in here if I'm not sincere? You've already passed me in the course, so I don't have any worries there. And I wouldn't dare show my head in your office if my only motive was to get you to up my grade. So what does that leave?"

"Go on."

"It leaves a guy who has already screwed-up twice but is still interested in learning anatomy. I realize it's a little late for that —that the best opportunities went with the dissection. But there must be some way to do it."

"There is," Snider said after a pause. "You know, Lassiter, after correcting your exam the other day, I made it my business to find out a little more about you. Frankly speaking, Dr. Southwell felt your attitude, as reflected by your attendance in the lab, was simply not up to par. Had it been his decision I doubt he would have passed you. The rest of my assistants—with the sole exception of Pat Walsh who seems to think you have something to recommend you—agree that you've been lackadaisical, showing little interest in either the demonstrations or the dissection. And now this! I simply don't know what to make of you. Are you as big a mystery to yourself?"

"I was," Dan admitted, "but not anymore. You see, it's taken me a hell of a long time to find out that I really want to be a doctor. I didn't think I had it in me."

"Why not?"

"Well, for one thing, I didn't want to for the usual reasons: the prestige, the independence, the desire to help people. Not even for the money. I didn't know what my real motive was, but

I do now. At least, I have a pretty good idea. If it weren't so involved and complicated, I'd try to explain. But now that I'm sure being a doctor is what I *do* want, I've got to be a really good one. I've got to know all I can—one hundred percent of everything, if possible, which includes anatomy. In other words, for me it has to be all or nothing. Can you understand that, sir?"

"No, not entirely. But I intend to try. I not only intend to understand you better, but to help you in every way I can. . . . Now then, in addition to being on the GI Bill, what are your finances like?"

"They're okay. I was left a small trust fund by my parents."

Snider smiled. "I'm not prying, you understand. I simply want to make sure you have no problem meeting your medical tuition. One further question—have you made any plans for the summer?"

"Nothing definite. An old Army buddy wanted me to come down and stay with him in Acapulco and I thought about doing that, if nothing better turned up."

"Well, in that case, how would you feel about forgoing not just a part but all of your summer vacation in order to learn some anatomy? Answer me honestly now. . . ."

"I'd be indebted to you."

"All right, then, hear me out. . . . It's my practice to hire one or two freshman students to work for me each summer doing careful dissections of certain parts of the human body—what's referred to as prosections. Mind you, the work is time-consuming and meticulous. On a hot summer's day, you might greatly prefer to be swimming at the beach in Acapulco than digging through a formalin-soaked pelvis. Another drawback is that the departmental budget only allows me to pay each student two hundred and fifty dollars for the whole summer—little more than twenty dollars per week. So all told, the proposition I have to offer you is pretty unrewarding from either a fun or financial point of view. . . ."

Snider paused to light a cigarette. "In fact," he continued, "over the past few summers, I've been unable to interest enough students in it to meet our needs, so the work has either been done by members of the department or not at all. It's simply not the sort of job that appeals to young medical students, or any-one else, for that matter—with the possible exception of a few anatomists or surgeons. I tell you this so as not to mislead you in any way. But I also tell you that it would provide an excellent opportunity for you to review each anatomical region of the body through good, clean, dissection—and if that's what you want, then I'll be happy to take you on. . . . However, there's no need to give me your answer now. Think it over. Perhaps later on, you'll change your mind in favor of Acapulco. . . ."

"But I won't," Dan said determinedly. "If you'll permit me, Dr. Snider, I'd like to take you up on your offer right now."

"Splendid, Lassiter. Splendid! You're hereby hired to start in mid-June. That will give you a week or so to spend at home first."

"That's fine. Anything more I ought to know about the job?"

Snider nodded. "Just one thing. Since your only purpose for taking it is to learn some anatomy, then by God you're going to learn some! I'm putting you on warning as of right now that whenever our paths cross in the lab this summer I'm going to have a dozen questions to spring on you. Miss one—just one, mind you—and I'll ride you off to Mexico on a rail!"

Interrupting their laughter, Snider's secretary opened the door to inform him his visitor had arrived.

Dan rose from his chair. "Thank you for giving me this chance, Dr. Snider. I'll look forward to a hectic summer."

"Thank you, Lassiter," Snider replied, "for just as much."

The look on the anatomy professor's face was reflective, un-certain, as they shook hands. Then he said, "I never told you this, but I knew your cadaver personally. He once worked for me here in the department. . . ."

Dan almost said, *I know,* almost suggested that Snider be more careful in the future about the cadavers he got from the police morgue, but he held back. Instead, with his hand on the doorknob, he said quietly, "I'm sure we'll have a lot to talk about this summer, Dr. Snider. So thanks again."

While waiting for his visitor to enter, Nathan Snider stood in front of his office window watching a group of white-clad medical students cross the street below and pondering the probable future of Daniel Lassiter:

No, he won't make one of the great ones; he hasn't the right stuff in him for that—the egotism, the scientific detachment, the impatience for further knowledge, the frustration that comes from being just average. But what's equally important, Snider confirmed, *he'll be one of the* honest ones—*and I'll be proud of him yet!*

At five that afternoon, Dan attended a unique burial. He rode out to the Pinewood public cemetery outside of Medford in Roger Hickman's car along with another student who'd worked in Roger's group. Ahead of them, in lieu of a hearse, Pat drove a rented truck that carried twenty-seven rough pine boxes, the remains of that year's collection of cadavers.

Roger drove carefully, following Pat's lead. Behind him in this curious cortege were two cars, Dr. Snider and Dr. Southwell in one, and three medical students in the other. As he drove, Roger puffed on his pipe, the student beside him in the front seat studied his biochemistry notes, and Dan gazed out the open window as a light breeze blew across his face and tousled his hair.

He wished Lem were here to help him bid Rick a final good-bye, knowing he would have wanted to be. But Lem was gone. His mother had died the day of Dan's makeup exam and he had phoned that evening to tell him the news. Lem had remained in Boston only long enough for her funeral and to collect the insurance money bequeathed him, then left for Africa.

Though Dan had not seen him since the time they had spent

together at his apartment, Lem had left a note for him with Ernie.

DEAR DOC,

Sorry I couldn't stick around long enough to say good-bye in person, but it wasn't safe. Don't worry about Turk—he's been taken care of. Don't worry about me either, just about being a good doctor. I don't know how long I'll be away, or where I'll go from Kenya, but I promise we'll see each other again. Good luck and thanks for everything.

LEM

Dan had shown the note to Ernie who confirmed that Turk was dead, but how or by whose hands he refused to say. From the sly look on Ernie's face, Dan wondered if he might not have had a hand in it. The burly, granite-faced man was capable of almost anything, he suspected, and Lem had been his friend. Whatever the case, it was skillfully done, since Turk's death never made the newspapers. The whimsical notion occurred to Dan that, using the same route of disposal, Turk's body might end up next fall in one of the anatomy labs of Boston's four medical schools. Ernie chuckled at the possibility, but would neither confirm nor deny it.

"Nice day, huh?" Roger remarked offhandedly, suddenly aware that no one had spoken for several miles. "Wonder how much farther it is to the cemetery?"

Next to him, Sam Enders reported, "We're in Medford now, Rog, so it can't be too far. . . . See—Pat just turned up that road. I think the public cemetery is only another mile or so."

"What worries me," Roger told them, "is that not more than a handful of our class will be showing up. I hope that doesn't get Snider sore."

"What if it does!" Sam sneered. "The reason I'm going hasn't a damned thing to do with Snider's feelings."

"Why are you?" asked Dan.

"I dunno. The cadaver's sake, I guess. I did learn a lot of anatomy from him. How about you, Dan? After all, your group had the best body in the whole class."

"I know," Dan said.

"I thought ours was pretty good, too," Roger claimed defensively. "We sure could've had it worse: I mean—with a cadaver like Aunt Jemima! But, you know, the thought of him being buried makes me feel kind of funny. I almost hate to watch it."

"Why?" Dan asked.

Roger shrugged. "Oh, I don't know. He looked like a nice old guy—at least the first day he did. But after that I don't think I thought of him more than once or twice as a real person. I suppose that's why seeing him buried is going to make me feel kind of sad. Like I neglected him or something."

"You didn't neglect him, Rog," Sam pointed out. "You just whittled him down a little so he'd fit into that pine box. Jesus, you'd think the school would buy better coffins to bury them in than those crates, wouldn't you? Anybody know if their names will be on their graves?"

"No," Dan answered. "According to Pat Walsh, just their numbers. But he told me you could buy a small stone or a terracotta marker with their name on it if you wanted to."

"You going to?" Sam asked.

"Yes, I am."

"Well, then I guess we will, too. Okay with you, Rog?"

"Sure!" said Roger. "It's the least we can do—if it doesn't cost too much."

The Pinewood public cemetery comprised several acres of pine trees and what was now pale-green grass surrounded by a high, hatched wire fence. A private cemetery across the road with ornate, marble tombstones, American flags and more than a dozen mausoleums made its many rows of small wooden crosses or book-sized terracotta markers appear shabby in comparison.

The Anatomy Lesson

Following Snider's lead, the small group moved to a plot of ground beyond sight of the main road where a sign nailed into a large oak proclaimed it as: PROPERTY OF MASSACHUSETTS STATE MEDICAL COLLEGE. Here, twenty-seven graves had already been dug in the spring sod. Beside each, a two-by-three-foot white cross lay on the ground. A cemetery caretaker and two young assistants helped Pat Walsh unload the boxes from the truck and lower each into its own excavation. A grove of pine trees shaded the area, and with the sun no longer on his face, Dan suddenly felt the afternoon grow cold. He listened to leaves rustling in the wind and the chirping of birds until the last coffin was in place and Snider called them together.

Hands in his pockets, head slightly bowed, Dan stood in the midst of the small gathering and listened attentively as Snider read a long passage from the Old Testament with simple and touching dignity. Then the anatomy professor introduced the minister from the local community and stepped back to let him read the Committal Prayer. The Reverend Lewis was a frail elderly man with a blotched and wizened face. Yet his eyes were bright as a bird's and as he recited the Scripture from memory, they shone with a strange intensity—making Dan wonder if somewhere in his mind's eye this doddering old man might be picturing some fellow clergyman saying the same prayer over his body in the not too distant future. He began:

"In life we are in the presence of death, then to whom may we seek for succor but Thee, Oh Lord. . . ."

As Dan listened to the familiar words he had heard so often from Army chaplains in Korea, his thoughts drifted back to other times, other burials. At age twelve, at the sudden demise of his parents, the concept of death had been completely baffling, a mystery beyond his comprehension. Willing to believe, as had his dead friend, Lloyd Tompkins, that death was the will of God and that God in his benevolence meant it as a reward, as a way of drawing those whom He loved closer to Him, Dan had been comforted, had even been able to reconcile himself somewhat to their loss. For who was he, and how important were his needs when compared with God's?

"For Thou art life and life everlasting. For as much as it hath pleased Almighty God to take out of this world the souls of these, our departed brothers, we therefore commit their bodies to the ground. . . ."

But with the loss of his brother Pete, Dan's feelings toward death had undergone a drastic change. He now knew that most of the anger and sense of futility he'd felt then was based on guilt; on the belief that Pete had been the better son, the better brother; that it should have been he, not Pete, who was killed. He had even harbored the irrational belief that by not being the firstborn, the one old enough to be drafted, he had somehow contributed to Pete's death. Worst of all, when compared to his good and gentle brother, he himself was so selfish, so basically hostile and unfeeling toward others, as to be almost unworthy to live—and he had tried to prove it with Marge Downing.

"Earth to earth, ashes to ashes, dust to dust. Looking at Him who doeth all things right. . . ."

But Korea had changed him again. There, death was so casual and commonplace that he came to realize its true nature: that it was neither the will of God nor the reluctant retriever of select souls, but senseless, random slaughter. To death, a man's worth, his uniqueness as an individual, meant nothing. It took its toll of them as indiscriminately as a man crushing a horde of ants under his boot. The deaths of several of his buddies not only forced such a realization upon Dan but forced him to try to counteract it by the formation of two convictions. The first, temporary but invaluable to his peace of mind, was a tenuous faith in his invincibility: the belief that even for such a monstrous force as death, a certain few were immune and exempt from its plaguelike devastation. He had no clear notion as to why he should be one of the fortunate few, but in the midst of each firefight, as his sense of aliveness was enhanced by his ability to shoot and kill others, he felt its protective shield. And afterward, surveying the dead and wounded around him, he was filled with a perverse sense of power and elation. It was, of course, a necessary aberration, an imaginary device to preserve his sanity. But many other combat soliders, in different words, in different ways, proclaimed a similar invincibility, and many of those were soon dead. So there was no such talisman, no such immunity, Dan reluctantly concluded. There was only random chance to guard him aginst the indiscriminate ravages of death.

"Looking at Him who doeth all things right, for He who is the judge of the whole earth will do right, at whose coming He will change these vile bodies of ours and fashion them unto the likeness of His own glorious self, to whom be glory and honor forevermore. Amen. . . .

"Our Father, who art in heaven. . . ."

But the other conviction that Dan had formed about death in Korea was not abandoned; it grew steadily stronger until it dwarfed all of his other ambitions and led him into medicine. That belief was in the dual nature of death, one good and compassionate, one ruthless and evil; one from within and a necessity, one from without and a curse. He had learned in physiology that each cell carried a structure inside it called a lysosome—a suicide sac, really, containing within its membrane all the enzymes required to digest and destroy the cell—and yet still an integral part of that cell: its necessary end. So, too, the death that came from within: a slow and recognizable and ultimately merciful ending for tortured minds and tired bodies, for a piece of machinery that, however marvelously constructed, had finally broken down.

Not so its maliciously marauding brother who struck without warning, without care. Dan felt so powerful a revulsion for this form of death that he was to make it his personal enemy, one he bore an unremitting grudge for having robbed him of his parents, his brother, and countless wartime friends.

Nonetheless, no matter how strongly he recognized such feelings within him, they did little to elucidate what lay at the core of his obsession with his cadaver. He would probably have to seek psychiatric help to find that out, he thought gloomily, and even then he might never know.

The reading of the Lord's Prayer ended the simple services and the Reverend Lewis retired from the gravesite. Snider shook each student's hand and thanked him for coming. Then the group broke up and headed for the parked cars.

Dan started to leave with them, only to be seized by an eerie and compelling conviction that something more was to be revealed to him in this place. Though mistrustful of the instinct, he told a puzzled Roger to go on without him, that he would take a trolley back to Boston.

Feeling awkward at remaining behind, Dan put himself to use. He helped the caretaker cross-check and plant the crosses beside each grave and, once coming upon the one with Rick's name and number penciled on it, held it and stared at it with such fierce emotion that were it not for the wind blowing against his face and drying the hint of tears he might have wept openly.

The caretaker noticed the mournful look on his face and asked: "Was this guy a friend of yours?"

Dan started to speak but, realizing the futility of explanation, merely nodded.

"I thought you was one of them medical students," the caretaker said, "but I guess not. Not if this guy was a friend of yours. How'd he die?"

"Head injury," Dan told him.

"Huh! And he left his body to a medical school. Nice of him. Not many do that, and even if more did, those med students wouldn't appreciate it. You can tell that from how few of them ever bother to show up here. Must've been a nice guy, your friend."

"Yeah," Dan said and was relieved when the caretaker nodded and went on with his work. Then, for a long, timeless moment, he felt lost and alone in this dusk-darkened place, this world of the dead, but without self-pity—since for all he knew the dead too might be lonely.

Impulsively, he picked up a shovel. "Mind if I throw a little dirt on him?"

"Naw, go ahead," the caretaker said. "Least you can do for a friend."

And what a strange friendship they'd had, Dan mused, as his first shovelful of dirt splattered over Rick's pine coffin. Then, suddenly he knew; with that one symbolic gesture some concealing layer within his psyche seemed to crumble and he knew. He had not been possessed by Rick, by his restless, roaming spirit. The very opposite was true! It was *he,* not Rick, who had tried to do the possessing: to take over his life and be its keeper, its preserver; to prevent the ultimate extinction, the one death wrought not in its victim's body but in the memory of others. He would not allow it. His every effort had been devoted to keeping Rick alive, not only in his own mind but in that of his friends. Everything he had attempted, everything he had done, had been toward that aim, no matter what the consequences, no matter even if in some transcendental way it had been against Rick's own wishes.

Dan suddenly recalled the nightmare he'd had in which Rick, in the guise of a savage and sadistic boxer, had tried to mutilate him. He remembered the words Rick had spoken in the dream. "Keep away from me," he'd snarled at Dan as they clinched. "Stay away, hear, or I'll kill you!" That was the true meaning of the dream. His guilt was not because of Rick's dismemberment, but because of his subconscious wish to possess and manipulate his life. And he had done it. All of them—Lem, Kim, Walt Chatfield—had felt his manipulations. . . . But why? What deep, destructive impulses within him had ever made him conceive and carry out such an irrational desire? Because all his life he had felt so cheated by death that just once, one time, he had wanted to rob it of one of its victims? . . . Because being too young and afraid of dying himself, he had not been able to do this with the one person that he'd wanted to the most, his brother Pete, and so had chosen Rick as a surrogate—mistaking the intimacy forced upon them by the anatomy lab for a more personal one.

The anatomy lab, of course, had contributed mightily to his aberration. Everything about it—the gloom, the stench, the charnal house horrors—had contributed. But what had influenced him most, he realized, was the insensitivity shown by his fellow students. How dared they feel so indifferent to the horrible handiwork of death when he himself felt so strongly!

Maybe if Rick hadn't been his cadaver, maybe if he'd had an Aunt Jemima or a Goldcoast Charlie to work on, it might never have happened. But there was so much about Rick to identify with—his youth, his profession, his unyielding toughness—it had made the transference that much easier. Not only had he tried to take over his girl, his friend Lem, but he had carried matters so far, Dan marveled, that he had almost died like him!

Then again, there was another, a more subtle aspect, that had made the anatomy lab so conducive to his delusionary state of mind. If death meant disorder and dissolution, then anatomy was its antithesis.

There was a structure, an order—an anatomy—to all living things, from mind to body, from thoughts to emotions, from youth to old age. Even beyond its reinforcement of his feelings toward death, his experience in the lab had filled him with a certain reverence for the incredible intricacy of the human body—not so much religious in nature as the awe he might feel on beholding any great work of art. It had also instilled in him an ardent desire to master, to preserve the workings of this marvelous structure, as any mature physician would do.

So it wasn't so strange that his obsession had begun and been nurtured by an anatomy lab, after all, for even more than a hospital or a battlefield, it was a meeting ground between life and death. Nor did he fear that in returning to the lab, to new cadavers, he might fall victim to another obsession. Now that he finally understood its derivation, he felt he was safe from it. He actually looked forward to spending the summer in the lab and learning the additional vital knowledge it would impart. His obsession with Rick Ferrar was over, but his obsessive battle against death was only beginning and he needed to arm himself with all the knowledge there was.

Dan sighed deeply as if an unbelievably heavy burden had suddenly been lifted from his shoulders. Picking up the shovel again, he continued to rain clods of dirt on the coffin of Rick Ferrar until it was completely covered and the excavation filled.

Author's Note

The portrayal of the first year of medical school, particularly the anatomy course, in this novel is an accurate one—as it existed twenty years ago. Happily much of it no longer applies. Most medical schools have now abandoned the "sink or swim" practice of starting off freshmen in the gross anatomy lab, thereby sparing them the harsh realization that their inability to stomach it automatically bars them from a career in medicine. Furthermore, faced with a dire shortage of cadavers—the result of the dwindling number of unclaimed bodies throughout the nation—all medical schools depend heavily on bodies being willed to them by an *informed public* and maintain a strict display of decorum in the anatomy lab. In my view and that of most physicians who have benefited so enormously from the experience of cadaver dissection, medical education in this country would suffer a marked loss of quality without a continuing supply of such bodies. If instead of rotting underground, my own body can make one final contribution to medical progress by joining the ranks of the "working dead," then I feel deeply obligated to offer it. If this novel can persuade any reader to do the same, its writing will have been worth every effort.

M. G.